THE FLAME
& THE MOTH

VOLUME TWO ETHEREA

October 2016

OTHER TITLES BY
VIVIAN MAYNE

Ghosts of the Talisman
Volume 1 - Etherea

The Flame and the Moth
Volume 2 - Etherea

THE FLAME & THE MOTH

VOLUME TWO ETHEREA

VIVIAN MAYNE

Published by
Koru Designs

The Flame and The Moth by Vivian Mayne
Volume 2 - Etherea

Paperback

Second edition

ISBN 978-0-9930049-0-2

The moral right of the author has been asserted.
This is a work of fiction. Names, characters,
organisations, places, events and incidents are either
products of the author's imagination or are used
fictitiously. No part of this book may be reproduced,
or stored in a retrieval system, or transmitted in
any form or by any means, electronic, mechanical,
photocopying, recording, or otherwise, without express
written permission of the publisher. The book author
retains sole copyright to her contributions to this book.

Published by
Koru Designs, Cornwall, UK
korudesignsuk@gmail.com

Cover image by Coka

Illustrations and cover design by Fiona Routledge

CONTENTS

*N.B. When speech is displayed in an italic typeface,
a telepathic conversation is taking place.*

CONTENTS cont.

For KSR

*I will love you for as long as
there are stars above you*

An old Cherokee told his grandson:

'My son, there is a battle between
two wolves inside us all.
One is Evil. It is anger, jealousy, greed,
resentment, inferiority, lies and ego.
The other is Good. It is joy,
peace, love, hope, humility,
kindness, empathy, and truth.'

The boy thought about it, and asked,
'Grandfather, which wolf wins?'

The old man quietly replied,
'The one you feed.'

Author unknown

1

ᕕᕗ

in the air tonight

March 1997, New York

It wasn't the first time Finn Milton had astral planed through New York City but it would prove to be his last. During the final hours before dawn, his spirit soared at high speed through the vibrant neon stretches making up the city grid. He flew down the Hudson River in the direction of the harbour, passing the Manhattan financial district, the Woolworth building and Ellis Island. An oasis of light illuminated the modern architecture, with hints of purples and reds offsetting the incandescent yellows of the street lamps.

Gliding up the Hudson, he skimmed past silver skyscrapers including the lofty rectangular trade centres. The view was regimented, organised and perfectly aligned. He perched on top of the Empire State building with a wide grin on his face, before speeding toward the urban reprieve of Central Park.

As a child, he was addicted to the escapism found within graphic novels. Flying through the metropolis of New York had been on his wish list for some time. Only recently he rediscovered how to master the exhilarating skill and within a relatively short space of time, it became his favourite adrenaline-fuelled pastime.

Without fail, once a week he would fly around the city without another soul being aware—or so he imagined. He never expected to encounter anyone like him so far from his home in England. But each time he visited Central Park, he caught the attention of a handful of seasoned astral-planers. The group were old friends and liked to hang out in the park on the weekends.

Finn was considering heading back when he sensed them. One of his abilities was heightened hearing. He could hear their thoughts. Curiosity got the better of him so he decided to expose himself by projecting his spirit, making it more visible and defined.

A glowing white version of his true physical-self emerged.

He was a tall, slim man of thirty years with short hair laced with white streaks, dressed in jeans and a long-sleeved T-shirt.

A moment later a perfectly formed thought entered his mind: *You should take more care to whom you reveal yourself, Finn Milton.*

The spirits emerged from the darkness, their white forms growing more illuminated by the second.

Finn counted six of them. They were all older than him by at least twenty years. A stocky dark skinned man with a thick moustache and curly hair was staring at him.

He knew immediately that this had been the one who had addressed him.

Finn: *Who are you?*

1st planer: *My name is Desmond. So tell me, what's a limey like you doing so far from home?*

Finn smiled at his derogatory comment. The stranger had a broad New York dialect and hailed originally from Jamaica. The other five male spirits watched on silently, allowing Desmond to communicate.

Finn: *I'm working in New York but I've never seen any planers like you in the city.*

Desmond: *We like to be cool about our existence. You must have a code like ours back home. There aren't too many of us left these days. We won't reveal ourselves to just anyone, Finn. You should know that.*

2nd planer: *It's him.* The spirit was of a tall large man in his seventies.

Desmond: *How can you be so certain, Dennis?*

Dennis: *I recognise him. It's him. We don't see many people with hair like that.*

Desmond: *My friend Dennis has visions. He thinks he's had one about you.*

Finn: *Really?*

Desmond: *He wants to show you. His visions tend to be about the future, so it's possible this one hasn't happened yet.*

Dennis: *I can see your soul light. The omen must be true but I never expected it would be you. We've been watching you for some time and hoping we would get the chance to talk to you.*

Dennis stared at him as though he was expecting to find an answer to some long forgotten question.

Finn: *What omen?*

Dennis: *Don't you know anything about the omen? Surely you must have heard about it? Your soul light is telling but you're so ordinary and young. I was expecting the Flame to be more attuned to his senses. You, it seems, are completely ignorant of who you are. Touch my arm and I'll show you, although I can't guarantee you'll like it.*

Finn was more than curious, barely grasping at what he was saying yet willingly glided towards him. Lifting his ghostlike hand, he touched the spirit and immediately processed all his thoughts and memories. He closed his eyes, fully trusting him. Like an unspoken truth, he inherently knew they posed him no danger because they felt the same way about him.

After a few seconds of total darkness, the shape of an old building came into view and Finn knew where he was. It was a place he could never forget. The house belonged to the Connelly family. The Parsonage was their family home, located in his hometown of St Ives in Cornwall. He had a few memories of the old house and none of them were good. It was pitch dark and he was in the garden. A semi-dressed *man was lying on the grass, close to the house. A moment later he watched a spirit fly into the man's body and then he began to wake.*

Before the man had the chance to open his eyes, a human stranger was crouching over him. His hands were clasped firmly around his neck. Colourful soul light was beginning to slowly drain from his mouth and sucked into the other man who was tall with short patchy dark hair. His flaky grey skin was darkened with black veins. His determination was clear ... he wanted to kill him.

Finn watched as the attacker moved away from the weakened man and began to glow with colour. Above, an army of white ghostly-cloaked beings appeared, each one holding a long spear. They were illuminating the garden. Propelled by the stolen power, the antagonist tore into the night sky in the direction of the army. The spiritual soldiers were decimated by a seamless flow of energy released from his hands. He was glowing with an eerie bright light, his veins coursing with power, as each one of the soldiers disappeared.

On the grass, a woman was crying, kneeling beside the limp body. Finn suddenly recognised her but was confused to why she was there. A broken spirit left the man's body in an awkward jerky movement before disappearing forever into the night. Looking closer, he realised in horror that he was looking at his own dead body, which was half naked and badly scarred across the torso. His eyes were sunken and his mouth was sagged half open. In the space above the garden a new battle had commenced. It was so bright it looked like daylight, only it was the middle of the night.

Finn opened his eyes and stared at Dennis in shock: *What the hell was that? Did I die?*

Dennis: *It is entirely possible that you are fated to give your power to a monster who will annihilate the spirit world. This can never be allowed to happen. From the moment he meets you, he will know who you are and more importantly, he will know your potential. He will crave your soul light like an addictive drug. If he takes it all, it will kill you. At the same time it could kill him. You must find a way to defend yourself. I will block your mind, for you must protect your soul. There are dark times ahead and I fear for your life.*

Dennis touched him and relayed a thought. Immediately Finn was able to shield them all from reading his mind. It had been a long time since he had been able to block his mind and it brought him instant relief.

Finn: *Thank you for sharing this. I've had little control over my telepathy of late. What were those ghosts?*

Dennis: *You have all the answers, Finn, but your mind has been tampered with. You have forgotten the events of last year. You are the only mortal to have visited Etherea and been allowed to leave. It's there in your mind, every last detail, for I could read you easily before. You must learn to unlock these memories in order to learn the truth.*

Finn: *What are the Sentries and where is Etherea?*

Dennis: *Sentries are spiritual soldiers from Etherea, an afterlife for our kind—mortals with ancient mystical abilities. Sentries have been watching the Earth for thousands of years, stopping evil in its tracks. If this mortal steals your soul light, he'll be able to destroy Sentries. If this travesty comes to pass, darkness will fall over the world and humankind will slowly perish. Our world will never recover. It would lay everything open for the return of Arris, which will spell the end of everything 'light'.*

Finn: *Who is Arris?*

Dennis: *That, my friend, can wait for another time. Arris is not your concern, he is trapped a long way from here. You must concentrate on the matter at hand. I see only possible visions of the future and this one is worrying. Even if you stop this man from reading your mind, he will use other methods of persuasion. We are ordinary compared to you. Your power is infinite, Finn. The Sentries allow you to carry soul light because your spirit is pure. In the wrong hands, this power can cause carnage and suffering. My guess is the Moth, as we call him, is a charmer. He can plant commands in your mind and control you. The only true way to stop him is to block your mind. Whatever he blackmails you with, whoever it is, even if it's someone close to you, you must block your mind to him. This will be the hardest test of all, because if you're not strong enough, he will kill you and then there will be no one strong enough to stop him.*

Finn: *But this is only a possible future or one that may never happen.*

Desmond: *There is a greater chance it will. You saw it yourself. You fail to stop him and you die. Dennis is seldom wrong and I've known him all my life.*

3rd planer: *There is a chance, Dennis, show him.*

Dennis: *No, Alan, he won't comprehend, again the future can change.*

Alan: *You must tell him about his mother.*

Dennis: *It could alter the outcome too much. I don't know if she survives, that part was unclear.*

Finn stared at them, unable to hear their exchange. Dawn was starting to break and he was beginning to feel intensely tired.

Dennis: *Good luck, Finn. We will pray for your soul when you leave this week.*

Finn: *This week? But I'm staying longer than that.*

Dennis: *You'll be flying home on Thursday, I assure you.*

Finn: *How can you know this?*

Dennis: *I can see you, Finn, for I have the gift of sight. You have visions also but you haven't leant how to process them yet. In time you will, for your mother had this gift also. The Moth is already making his first move and you must be ready for him or this will all be for nothing. In a few days he will arrive in St Ives. When the time comes, you will be like an irresistible flame so you must be ready to fight. Use your powers wisely and keep our future safe. It's always a pleasure to meet someone who has the ability to make a difference. Your unique gift has the potential to save countless lives. Goodbye, Finn.*

Finn laughed suddenly at how ridiculous his prophetic words sounded but not one of them was smiling back at him and they had all heard Dennis.

The spirits vanished one by one.

Slowly he rose into the sky feeling somewhat defeated. He flew cautiously towards lower Manhattan over the tall skyscrapers and alighted to the balcony of a small glass-fronted apartment, perched twenty floors above the sidewalk.

His mood turned sombre when he thought about the vision.

Floating through the closed glass balcony door into the dark interior, his spirit wound its way into the bedroom where his pregnant fiancée Ellie Morgan was sleeping next to his body. He watched her for a moment, smiling at her extended belly. He kissed her forehead and dropped inside his body. Immediately his spirit began fusing itself back into its physical resting place.

Due to its nature, he could only astral plane when there was a long clear window of time after in which to recover. He opened his eyes, took a deep breath and tried to digest the revelation from Dennis. Seconds later he fell into a dreamless sleep which lasted fourteen hours.

2

~

back to haunt

a few days later, Cornwall

Michael Connelly approached the wooden front door of the Parsonage with his two grown up sons, exhausted from a long journey from Dublin. It had been months since there had been any news from his cousin Logan. No one was answering the phone so he decided the only course of action was to travel to Cornwall to find out what was going on.

He was standing on the cracked granite doorstep of an old crumbling building, crawling with thick cobwebs and riddled with constant inaudible whisperings. It was seeping with dark secrets, neglect and rumoured hauntings.

Its long history was fraught with death and misfortune. In 1900, the other branch of the Connelly family settled in Cornwall. Michael's ancestor Liam and his wife relocated to St Ives because he had romantic ideals and his wife had a passion for painting landscapes. Liam accepted the role of local pastor and the Parsonage became their home.

Their only daughter Shannon raised her grandson Logan when her daughter died following his birth. After Shannon's death, the Parsonage was bequeathed to Logan.

Michael turned the handle and pushed the unlocked door. There was no sign of life from the dank and creepy house.

'Cillian, check out the garden. Jarlath, come with me.' He stepped into the cold dark hall. 'Hello? Is anyone here? This godforsaken place reeks worse than it did before.'

Cillian Connelly was twenty-nine years old, tall and athletic, with straight black hair brushing his shoulders. His long nose was bent and his eyes were steely grey like his father's.

He forced his way into the long abandoned garden bursting with brambles and gorse. Something felt out of the ordinary when he approached an aging olive tree. Beyond it lay a patch of dead cabbage plants, withered and rotting. He kicked one and it fell to pieces. The ground was hard from the previous night's frost but there was far more to the grounds than met the eye. Aside from its unnatural chill, there remained a presence of something sinister.

'Dad wants you inside.' His brother approached, snapping him from his thoughts.

Jarlath was shorter than his brother and younger by two years. His hair was fair and short, his expression vacant. Where Cillian had a sharp academic mind, practical Jarlath was a skilled carpenter. From the outside, it was plain to see they were related but their personalities were poles apart.

'Is anyone here?' Cillian asked.

'The house is empty. I don't think anyone's been here for some time.'

'Another wasted trip, no doubt.' Cillian approached the back door, biting his lip.

Logan and his twin offspring Branna and Jared had often visited them in Ireland. Cillian had been drawn to Jared because they were so alike. He mistrusted Branna because he couldn't read her mind. Taking advantage of any opportunity, he would steal away with Jared and they would be missing for hours often exploring the ancient burial grounds across the river.

'Dad, what's going on?' Cillian asked.

'There's no one here. It's not like Logan to vanish without a trace. It makes no sense.'

'What about the curse? If their talisman was destroyed then they would've been exposed.' Cillian said. 'Logan rattled on about it every time we saw him. He was paranoid. Maybe something happened to it.'

'When I was here last August I helped him to hide that talisman. He was terrified of losing it so we went to great lengths to find somewhere safe, travelling hundreds of miles in the process. We went to Wales for Gods sake. Logan committed many horrific crimes over the years and he was right to be paranoid. The talisman was their shield from *Etherea* but there was no way Milton could've found it. There must be some other explanation.'

'This house is disgusting.' Cillian stroked his finger through a thick layer of dust on the surface of the table. 'What do you know about Milton?'

'He's from around here and was born with supernatural abilities like complex telepathy and telekinesis.'

'How come he has these powers? Is he like us?' Jarlath asked.

'There are families around here, like ours back home, who possess ancient mystical abilities. I once heard a legend about a Sentry from *Etherea* who fell in love with a mortal woman. She went on to bear his child, the first human born with this mutated DNA code, but no one knows if it's true or not. It could have something to do with aliens for all I know. Maybe we'll never know the reason why we are this way.'

'What was Milton's curse?' Cillian was growing impatient and started tapping his foot.

'He was forced to fall in love with a mystic girl. From the moment they met as children, they were locked together by it. Fate brought them together once every ten years but only for two weeks. She would forget him and he literally became invisible to her. Only during that fortnight could they be together and only during that time could she remember him. The last time Milton was here, the couple were back together because their time had come around again. If he successfully broke the curse then it can only mean one thing and I shudder to think it if that's the case.'

'Maybe he's here, Dad.' Jarlath said.

He planted a firm hand on his youngest son's shoulder. 'Then we'll find him. His father and cousin live here too. We can walk into town. I'm not leaving until I know the truth.'

'Even if it's something you don't want to hear?' Cillian asked.

'I have to know one way or the other. Logan was a good friend.'

Michael closed the front door. The key was sitting in the lock as though the house had been abandoned. They walked on to town without saying a word and stopped for lunch in a Cornish inn. Cillian flicked through the local phone book while they waited for their meals to be served. 'I have the doctor's address, it's not far from here.'

'That will be our first stop,' Michael said. 'Bastian Pengelly isn't half as gifted as his cousin, he will be a pushover.'

Cillian was not one for relationships but for some strange reason, he couldn't take his eyes off her. Sitting at the bar, two women were having a drink and one of them was checking him out. She was tiny with blonde spiky hair. Her light pink lips were half-smiling. She was attractive in a quirky way. Not his usual type, but he sensed she had supernatural abilities. This made her different. A small smile passed his lips as he headed for the bathroom.

His so-called entanglements were short and always on his terms. He chose a single independent life and had little patience. No one was going to tell him what to do. Besides his dark and brooding good looks, he was able to cast spells and manipulate people. His powers extended to reading minds and altering their perception. His telepathy was top drawer and he owned an unnatural pride in his dominance over others. It was always about control.

When he returned to the bar it was empty save for his father and brother who had started eating. The women had left. Grudgingly, he threw himself into the chair next to his brother and picked at his lunch.

'Bastian Pengelly must know where Milton is,' Michael said. 'If Branna's around, I want to talk to her too.'

'How old is Milton?' Jarlath asked.

'Thirty but he's powerful and I'll need your help, Cillian, when the time comes. I witnessed Jared's abilities but Milton's stronger. Let's hope the doctor is useful. I don't like people who waste my time.'

At around four o'clock, Dr Bastian Pengelly arrived home from a long hospital shift. He unlocked the front door of his fisherman's cottage and went inside. Dropping his medical bag on the kitchen table, he turned on the kettle to make a cup of tea. Loosening his tie, he idly checked the post. There was a note from his wife, Caron. She had taken their daughter Cara to Truro and wouldn't be home for a few hours.

Opening the back door, he stepped into his courtyard garden. Last summer, a party in his back garden had been instrumental for his cousin Finn to reunite with his long lost soul-mate Ellie. The memory filled his mind and made him smile. Finn would be home soon, meaning plenty of motorbike trips. They were close and had been in regular contact since his departure to America.

There was a knocking at the front door. He walked back into the kitchen and slowly crossed the lounge. He ran a hand through his blond curly hair. The second knock was much louder. Instinct told him to ignore it but a third more urgent hammering followed. He was an inch away from the handle when he decided to open it.

When the door swung open, Cillian pushed it back hard, knocking Bastian off his feet. Wasting no time Cillian yanked him up by the shirt and deposited him on his knees beside the fireplace. The front door slammed shut and Michael followed his son inside.

'Hello, Bastian.' Michael said with a wily smile. 'Did you think I would forget you?'

The previous August, Bastian had been summoned to remove Finn from the Parsonage after Michael, Logan and Jared had beaten him up. It had been one of the scariest experiences of the young doctor's life.

'What do you want? You can't just barge into someone's house.'

'We can do whatever we want,' he replied, looking around. 'Cillian, check if we're alone. It's much better that way, don't you think?'

Michael picked up a framed family photograph, which made Bastian cringe. 'There shouldn't be any complications with your family absent and you have a very attractive young family, especially your pretty daughter.'

'Leave them out of it, you bastard.' Bastian snapped.

Cillian approached the back door and stepped into the garden. The small courtyard had old grape vines hanging from a back wall and the entrance to a garage. Having looked around thoroughly, he went back inside.

'My son has a special ability he would like to share with you. Ah, Cillian, talk of the devil.'

'It's just us.' Cillian's grey eyes bored into Bastian's face like a drill. 'Nice couple of bikes in the shed, at least you have some taste.'

'We need information, Bastian.' Michael said. 'You know why we're here. Where's my family?'

'I don't know.'

Cillian twisted his shirt collar making it harder to breathe. 'Come on, Bastian, you have a choice and this doesn't have to hurt.'

'I swear, I don't know where they are.' Beads of sweat were rising on Bastian's forehead and his heart was beating faster.

'Finn Milton. Where is he?' Michael asked. 'You're close to your cousin, you can tell us.'

'I'm not going to tell you anything. Finn's done nothing wrong.'

Cillian smiled on reading his mind. Fear was consuming the doctor. His father nodded his approval and the young Irishman knelt level with his face, lifting his hand to his forehead.

'Shall I find the truth, Father?'

'Be my guest,' he replied.

'No, please don't.' Bastian blurted.

'It will be my pleasure.'

Cillian closed his eyes holding his open palm firmly against Bastian's forehead, keeping him still. A slow-building grinding sensation started, followed by a heavy persistent pressure then all of Bastian's memories were opened and played out. Blood began to trickle from his nose and onto his top lip. His body convulsed for several seconds before Cillian removed his hand. Unconscious, Bastian toppled to the floor with his eyes wide open and completely white.

'Honestly, Cillian, do you have to be so violent?'

'He could be brain damaged but I don't care, Father. That was so quick, I'm getting better at this.'

'What did you see?'

On processing the doctor's memories, the facts suddenly hit him. Michael had been so optimistic about finding Logan *alive*, the idea had grown into full-blown arrogance. The straight truth would incense his father intolerably so Cillian paused to formulate how to best explain it. 'Milton took the talisman to *Etherea* and came back to this world—which is unheard of.'

'And how did he manage to do that?'

'I don't know how he came back but he astral planed to *Etherea* wearing the talisman on his wrist. The Sentries' destroyed it. When the curse and Shannon's blood cloak were broken, Jared's soul was taken by the Sentries. He tried to stop Milton but failed. He's gone, Father. Jared's dead.'

'But how did Milton learn about the talisman?'

Michael was shaking. 'Logan and I hid it miles away.'

'Branna swapped the bracelets before you left. The one you hid was a fake she had fashioned. She fooled you both, the stupid witch. She was working with Milton all along and no one knew. They became friends but in doing so, she betrayed her own kin.'

'How could she? It beggars belief, betraying her family.' Michael said. 'Did you see anything about Logan?'

'I couldn't find anything, I'm afraid. Milton survived but he isn't here, not in St Ives anyway.'

'Where is he?'

'He's in New York, which is unfortunate for the doctor who has paid for his absence with brain damage.'

Michael raised his hand to his brow. 'We'd better get out of here. What now?'

'We take out Milton's father,' Cillian said. 'Jarlath's staking out his house. We can force Finn to return if we put his family in hospital. Sometimes brute force is the only way.'

'He's going to pay. With the cloak lifted, Logan would have been at the Sentries' mercy. He was right to be concerned about that talisman. I never took it seriously but Milton has got a lot to answer for. He must be made to suffer. I'm going to kill him for what he's done to my family.'

'Get in line, Father. I'm going to relish ending his life. He is not getting away with murdering Jared.'

The sky turned dark grey as they walked along Wharf Road and past the Lifeboat station. It was a cold and stormy March day not unlike the weather they were missing back home. The waves were lashing relentlessly against the Lambeth Walk. Passing the Arts Society, they entered The Warren, a narrow lane lined both sides with old fishermen's cottages. Jarlath was waiting for them beside a low brick wall, beyond which lay the harbour. A wall of water splashed over and hit Jarlath squarely on the head. Soaked through, he pointed at the house directly opposite and Cillian climbed the steep granite steps wearing a smile.

Cillian promptly kicked in the blue stable door and the wood splintered away from the frame. With his father behind him, he walked straight into September Cottage.

Half an hour later, Cillian wandered off alone to explore the town and appease his mood. All they had to do was wait for the consequences of their actions to begin. Jarlath and Michael returned to the Parsonage to get changed into some dry clothes. The rain was lashing down in sheets. He found shelter in the doorway of a hair salon and absent-mindedly, looked through the glass door.

Inside, the young woman who had caught his attention earlier in the pub was cutting hair. She was chatting away like a tiny bird with a big smile on her face.

He closed his eyes and concentrated on accessing her mind. Her expression melted and her mouth dropped open when he tried and their eyes locked. He threw her an intense stare. It was making her uncomfortable and he was smiling.

'Joo, are you alright?' Her colleague asked. She was distracted holding a pair of sharp scissors, all the while staring at the dark stranger. Her face was blank and then she shook her head. The moment passed.

Cillian decided to head off and watch her from a clear distance. He would wait for the right moment to engage and sure enough, a little while later she left work. It was late afternoon when he followed her to the home of Bastian Pengelly and became acutely more interested in her identity.

The front door of the cottage was wide open and she went inside without knocking. The next minute, an ambulance arrived with its sirens blaring and its lights flashing. Two paramedics hurried inside with a stretcher. A blonde-haired woman left in the ambulance with a child, leaving the other woman behind.

Cillian stood unnoticed as the drama unfolded and when she began to walk in the direction of the harbour, he wasn't far behind her. She entered The Warren and stopped at the bottom of the steps to September Cottage. She climbed the steps and disappeared inside. Professor Milton would be found straight away. Cillian had left the middle-aged man sprawled unconscious on the kitchen floor, covered in bruises and scorch marks. His clothes were burnt and torn to pieces. One of his legs was twisted and broken. Before long another ambulance arrived to take the injured party away.

Cillian watched the woman depart looking more anxious than before. He focused on reading her mind to learn what she was thinking. In her mind he could see a house with two cars parked outside. One was an old red Mini, the other was covered up with a tarpaulin. Jarlath had already given him the address of Finn Milton's home. Checking the location on his folded street map, he sprinted ahead with a small smile of victory on his face.

By the time she arrived at the house, Cillian was leaning against Finn's covered Porsche. He owned an intense dark look and sensed recognition in her eyes.

'Can I help you with something?' She asked.

She was trying to read his mind with telepathy but it was blocked shut. Only someone with supernatural abilities was able to accomplish such an act but his telepathy was much stronger than hers.

His stern gaze was making her feel uncomfortable so he decided to pile on some sensitivity. 'I'm sorry. I saw you walking up the street and I had to meet you. I hope you don't mind. I'm not from around here and I sensed a kindred spirit in you.'

'You gave me a fright,' she said, searching for her door key in her bag.

'Sometimes it's the only way to make an impression. You're a very attractive woman.'

'Who are you?' A small smile crossed her mouth.

He didn't answer straight away but could sense her relaxing.

'I'm Cillian Connelly.' Boldly he stepped closer and began stroking her short spiky hair. 'You're Joo, or do you prefer Juliet?'

'Stop doing that,' she said almost incoherently.

'Why? Don't you like it?'

He was reading her mind and whispering in a tone barely audible: *Aperi mihi animum. Et oblitus es, Juliet Williams. Ut recorderis, et mandata mea tantum, Cillian Connelly.*

Cillian took her in his arms and kissed her. She resisted to start with but he knew she wanted him to do it again. The confusion in her mind was lessening when he kissed her again. He had focused a silent obedience charm on her. It was his favourite and most effective spell, having perfected it over the years. He was confident and knew she couldn't break free of it. It was already too late.

It was impossible to fight the invisible force invading her mind. She pressed her hands against his chest but couldn't push him away. He had planted a complex spell in her mind. When it unfolded, he stepped back to inspect his work with abnormal pride. 'You'll do whatever I tell you to do, Juliet.'

It had only taken a few seconds but she had totally forgotten who she was. The charm had worked. 'Do you need anything before we go? You won't be coming back here in a hurry. You're all mine now.' He knew what she desired more than anything. She had been single for a long time and yearned for some male attention. 'No final requests? I didn't think so. Come on, Juliet. Time to go. I'll take good care of you now.'

Lifting her handbag from her shoulder he tossed it into a bin along with her phone. Before leading her away he snuck her door keys into his pocket then clutched her tiny hand tight until it hurt. In time she would be missed and that was the rub—she shared the house with the one person he was looking for. With his cousin and father lying in intensive care, battling to stay alive and his house mate missing, it was only a matter of time before Finn Milton would fall effortlessly into his nasty little trap.

3

~~

news

It had been a few days since the visit to Central Park but Finn couldn't stop thinking about Dennis and the ominous vision. For the moment, he hadn't shared it with anyone.

Unable to sleep he had risen ridiculously early and decided to work outside on the balcony. After proof reading the script on his laptop for over an hour, something felt wrong. Something he couldn't shake. He could feel it in his bones. The early morning urban atmosphere was oppressive for March.

He pushed his laptop aside and stared at the skyline from his chair on the outer balcony. Enormous, glass fronted buildings provided a continuous and monotonous view from the apartment. Cities had never been on his list of favourite places. New York was constantly noisy and cold with no fresh air to fill his lungs. The huge steel structures were crammed with millions of people and he longed for the green countryside and fresh air of home.

Sliding the glass door, he went inside and entered the bedroom where she was sleeping. The blinds were closed creating patterns across the tiled floor. He sat on the edge of the bed, finding the ends of her long curls and teasing them gently through his fingers. It was so quiet he could hear her breathing. He could hardly contain his feelings for her. He loved her with all the fabric of his soul.

They had arrived in New York the previous October. His friend and employer, Brett Pieterson, had given them the sole use of his comfortable Manhattan home. The prime purpose of the visit was for Finn to compose a complex screenplay for a new movie, which

Brett would be producing. The project was almost complete. An experienced playwright, the opportunity marked new territory for Finn professionally.

For the time being, he was looking forward to going home to Cornwall with Ellie for the birth of their first child. Starting a family was by far the most important milestone in his life.

She opened her eyes and he gave her a welcome kiss. 'Good morning, Sweetheart. How are you feeling?'

'Better, I finally managed to get some sleep.' She said, propping herself up.

'You need to rest more. Bastian told you this would happen. I have some good news. Brett called last night while you were sleeping. We can finally make plans to go home.'

'Not before time, I want to have the baby at home.'

'And you will, I promise.' He stroked the gold and opal ring on her finger. It had belonged to his late paternal grandmother, Emma Milton. She had given it to him when he had been a teenager before she died. He remembered her fondly because she had been a big influence in his early years.

Before setting off to America, they walked to a special place near Lands End called Nanjizal where he proposed. Her acceptance left him feeling ecstatic. Building a new life together had given him real purpose, even though his memory remained elusive.

While living in New York, he had grown more confident with his abilities. After a supernatural event the previous August, the couple both suffered extreme amnesia. In time, Ellie remembered everything but he hadn't fared so well. His version of the past was a maelstrom of fragmented memories, some of which gave him regular nightmares.

The phone was ringing in the lounge and he groaned, not wanting to get up off the bed. 'I'm going to ignore it. I don't want to talk to anyone, it's too early.'

'It could be important, Finn.'

The phone continued to ring when he entered the lounge. Using telekinesis, the receiver flew into his hand. 'Hello? Finn Milton speaking.'

'Finn, is that really you?' The female voice sounded tense.

'Caron?'

'Oh my God, Finn, it's your dad and Bastian. I don't know where to start.'

He walked out on the balcony and gripped the railing hard, acute tension starting to erupt inside him. 'What happened?'

'They're in hospital. They were attacked.'

'What?' He couldn't believe it. 'Why?'

'I don't know.'

'How are they?'

'They're both in intensive care.' She explained. 'I'm not sure which one is worse.'

'Oh hell. When did this happen?'

'A few hours ago, I was out with Cara when someone broke into the house and left Bastian unconscious in the lounge. He's in a coma, Finn. And that's not all... Joo went to your dad's place and found him badly beaten up. They're both at Treliske. When are you coming back, Finn? I'm scared.'

'We need to arrange some flights to London. You don't know if the Irish Connellys are in town, do you?'

'It's been months since all that happened,' she said. 'It can't be them, surely.'

'Have you seen Branna?'

'Not recently, why?'

'It's not important. I'll get home as soon as I can. Give Cara a hug from me and I'll call you when we land.'

'Thanks Finn, you and Ellie have a safe journey. It'll be so good to see you.'

A feeling of dread filled his soul, one he could hardly contain. It was Thursday morning.

Dennis had told him they would leave on Thursday. He wondered what else Dennis would be right about as he looked at the meagre collection of belongings they had accrued since arriving. Their first home together was always going to be temporary but how many of his actions in the future had already been written? Suddenly it meant nothing to him. All he could think about was getting to the airport. His father and Bastian were in terrible danger. He thought about contacting Branna because she might be able to heal them. He rang her number but frustratingly there was no response.

Ellie was getting dressed. The pregnancy was making her glow. His eyes fell on her as she padded in front of the wardrobe. Her reflection was caught in the long mirror, her hair flowing down her back. It was a moment's distraction. His eyes were paler than usual and were watering when he slowly approached her.

'Finn, what's the matter?'

'Dad and Bastian are in hospital. Someone broke in and attacked them. They're in pretty bad shape. We have to leave as soon as possible. I'll arrange some flights and start packing. We only need to take a few things with us. We can't be here, Darling. I'll ask Brett's PA, Lisa, to get everything else shipped home. I must get hold of Branna.'

'I can't believe it. Are they going to be okay?' She asked.

He didn't know how to answer her question and left the room with his head bent low. Anger was seeping from his pores and his hands were glowing with tiny white sparks.

His life had changed radically the previous year when a dark curse had been lifted from his soul. Prior to this, his life had been a living hell for over twenty years.

Born on the same day in 1966, he met Ellie Morgan for the first time on their tenth birthday but their fate was controlled by a witch's curse. It forced them to love one another. After two weeks, she forgot him but not in the normal sense. In her mind and soul, he disappeared as though he had never existed. He lived with the pain for ten years before she was able to see him again—but for only fourteen days could she see him before it reverted back.

Twenty years later, he discovered his life had been caught up in an act of ice-cold revenge. Not only had he been cursed to love Ellie, but cursed to lose her. The emotional heartbreak was destroying him. Before the intervention of an unexpected ally, he had no idea if he could stop the grievous cycle of events.

Having survived a perilous journey to the *Etherea* underworld, the curse was finally broken but his memory was damaged. Finn and Ellie shared the same strange amnesia when they both woke up to a world without their curse. For three weeks they failed to remember their feelings until they touched outside Bastian's home and rekindled their love.

Their relationship grew strong as time passed and they accepted a temporary posting in New York. Living exclusively in a new city where they knew only a handful of people meant their time was their own. During that time spent inside their precious little bubble, nothing had touched them. But what was waiting back home scared him more than anything he could imagine. His dad and Bastian meant the world to him. He poured himself a whisky and drank it down in one.

'I thought you were going to stop drinking during the day,' she said.

'I need a drink and I need to get hold of Branna. Her mobile number must be in my old address book in the flat in London. I can't get a reply on her usual number. She must have changed it or moved house or something. I won't be able to contact her until we get to London. I hope there's enough time.'

He found it impossible to sleep on the flight; his mind was imagining all manner of scenarios. Ellie drifted off after half an hour. He eyed her with envy, wishing he could fall asleep easily and she was sleeping a lot lately. His mind wandered to his abilities.

He was aware of the telepathy and telekinesis, but the memory of accessing them fully had eluded him for some time. Apparently he was capable of immense power, due to something called soul light residing within him, but the notion only filled him with fear. He had to switch off the anxiety or exhaustion would be a close companion when they landed in England.

The vibrating burr of the plane made him drift off into an unwelcome vision.

He was walking along Burrow Road where his cousin lived in St Ives. The sky was clouding over and he could smell the sea. A storm was brewing and he could feel the cold breeze on his face.

It felt good to be home. The detail was vivid.

He found himself outside Bastian's house but the front door was wide open. Stepping into the sitting room, Bastian was on his knees. An unfamiliar dark haired man was raising a hand to his forehead.

Michael Connelly was staring at his cousin with an expression of deadly intent. The other man began to forcibly mind lock with his cousin, which lasted only seconds but seemed to go on for much longer. He released his hand and Bastian fell unconscious to the floor.

Finn felt powerless, all the while being unable to do anything when they left him for dead. Bastian was still. Blood was pouring from his nose and his eyes were completely white. Finn began to panic and shouted for help but no one could hear him. There was no sign of anyone who could physically help him.

'Finn. Hey Finn, wake up.' Ellie was prodding him.

He woke up disorientated after the dream, finding himself belted into a plane seat.

'Are you alright? You were shouting in your sleep.'

'Was I?' The dream was clear in his mind. His heart was pounding. Michael's face was staring at him in precise detail.

'You had a bad dream,' she said. 'You've been having a lot of them lately.'

'It was Bastian. I know what happened to him and it's worse than we first thought. The Connellys *are* back in St Ives.'

'How can you be so sure?'

'It was a vision,' he said. 'We can't go home, it isn't safe. We must stay with Rose until we know more.'

'I'm scared,' she said.

'I know it doesn't help, but I am too. It was so real. If Bastian was forced to mind-lock, he could be brain damaged. It explains the coma Caron was describing. Maybe we shouldn't be talking.'

He began to commune telepathically with her. The last thing he wanted to do was draw attention in a packed plane with a weird conversation.

Finn: *I wish I could control my abilities. It's so frustrating knowing it's there but I can't access it properly.*

Ellie: *I didn't know it bothered you so much.*

Finn: *I'm only thinking of self-defense. I must look up some of Bastian's friends. He said something about them having abilities and I would like to meet them. I don't think I can do this on my own.*

Ellie: *Do you know Joe and Serina Praed?*

Finn: *Joe Praed? I went to school with him before we moved to London.*

Ellie: *They're both gifted.*

Finn: *How do you know them?*

Ellie: *Serina and I are friends. I'm sure they'd help. After all, your quest did bring about the demise of the Connellys. A lot of people are grateful for what you did. They hurt a lot of people. You're a local hero among the gifted. Besides you're right, you are going to need their help.*

Finn: *How do you know all of this, Ellie? Local hero? What tosh. We haven't even been there.*

Ellie: *I talk to Joo on the phone. Just because you never use the phone doesn't mean I don't.*

Finn: *I do use the phone. Why didn't you tell me?*

Ellie: *I didn't think you'd believe me, Honey.*

Finn: *I could do with a night-cap.*

'Do you want me to get it?' She asked.

'It might help me sleep.' He said, yawning. 'I'll go.'

'Stay here, I need to stretch my legs.'

She stepped into the aisle. He watched her and thought how radiant she looked. After everything they had been through, the one thing that still rang true was his unconditional love for her. Only as she turned could he see the perfectly formed mound below her thin cotton shirt. He could hear both their heartbeats in unison and it made him feel content for a brief moment.

On arriving at Heathrow airport, he hired a comfortable saloon car. He tried calling Caron to let her know they were back in London but without any joy.

'No answer?' She asked.

'She must be at the hospital. Right, let's get to Camden. I must find Branna's number and then get my head down for a couple of hours. We can't drive to Cornwall like this, I'm too tired and you're too pregnant.'

The baby kicked and she gasped. 'Boy, you're active today.'

He felt her belly and another kick. 'He's going to be strong.'

'As long as he takes after me, I'm not too worried.'

'What are you saying?'

'I want him to be normal,' she replied.

'Honey, we are a long way from normal. We probably always will be. You have to accept it, this is who we are. We are both gifted and our child is going to be special no matter what.' He lent over and kissed her, holding her close. 'I love you.'

He was more than concerned about his father and Bastian but satisfied that Ellie was healthy and not suffering from any physical stress. It would be early the next morning before they would arrive in Cornwall. It was all he could think about as he hit the M25 motorway and drove towards London and his old bachelor flat in Camden Town.

~

Michael poured a large whisky from Logan's drinks cabinet. The day before, Cillian had returned to the Parsonage with a young woman in tow, which hadn't gone down too well.

'Why have you brought her here?' He growled. 'Are you planning on taking her home with us? She isn't a puppy, Cillian. You can't expect us to take on this responsibility while you're out all the time. I don't want anything drawing attention to us. Sometimes I wonder if it would've been easier if I'd made this trip on my own. You need to consult me when you make these decisions.'

'She happens to share the same house as Milton and is best friends with his fiancée.' Cillian said. 'With Juliet missing, it's bound to spike his attention. I thought you'd be thrilled about it. We can only turn the screws tighter.'

'Did anyone see you lead her away?'

'I'm not stupid, it was dead quiet. You should trust me. I know exactly what I'm doing. I always do.'

His father looked unconvinced. 'Keep her locked in Branna's room. I don't want anyone finding her here, is that clear? It looks like we may be here longer than I thought. You'd better get used to this place for a while even though it pains me to even suggest it.'

'You needn't doubt my abilities.' He said. 'Juliet is putty in my hands.'

'Son, if this works, then it's nothing short of genius. If it doesn't then you will dispose of her, make no mistake about it.'

'It won't come to that. Milton must be on his way to Cornwall by now.'

'I want to kill him.' Michael said, clenching his fists. 'We need to watch their house. Have you tracked down Branna, yet?'

'No, the club's closed but if she's around, we have time to find her now. She can't be far. Someone must have seen her.'

Cillian entered the kitchen. Sitting obediently at the table, Joo was wearing a catatonic expression. 'Come with me, Juliet, and I'll show you to your room. Don't look so surprised. I'm not going to hurt you, not yet anyway.'

She followed him obediently to Branna's old bedroom where he closed the door behind them. The bare room only boasted an unmade bed, a pine wardrobe and a small wooden bench. Notable to Cillian, the room was the only one in the whole house that had been cleared of all its belongings.

'What do you remember?' He held her hand and kissed each one of her fingers.

'I only remember you,' she replied, sitting on the side of the bed.

'This is how it should be, my dear. I need to buy you some new clothes. Your taste is crass but nothing I can't improve upon.'

'Where am I?'

'For now you are somewhere safe. We have to wait for someone important to show up and then I'm taking you home. You're going to love it in Ireland, Juliet.'

Finn first encountered Branna Connelly when he was sixteen years old. Years later she became a crucial ally in his search for the truth about his curse. Over the course of a few weeks, they became good friends, but most important of all, was her incredible ability to heal. He couldn't help but admire her. She had been born with mixed supernatural abilities and offered to help him cope with his mind-blowing abilities when he lost his memory. She would help Bastian and his father to recover if only he could find her mobile number and ask her. As soon as they arrived at his old bachelor flat in Camden, he began rummaging through the mess on his writing desk in the small sitting room.

'Branna can heal them. I must find that address book. She gave me a mobile number last year, which she swore she'd never change even though it was for a very old phone. Her home number isn't working. It must be here somewhere. I really should try and be more organised.'

The surface of his wide desk was cluttered with numerous notebooks, files, loose papers, pens, an empty whisky glass and an ashtray. The shelves above were overflowing with awards, papers, books, plays and reference volumes. Eventually he uncovered an old tatty address book, which only he could have found. Thumbing through it, he tapped the page with her phone number and began to dial the numbers.

'Hello?' A soft Irish accent spoke.

'Branna? It's Finn.'

'Finn? I thought you were in New York,' she said. 'How are things with you?'

'We're on our way to Cornwall in a couple of hours. I hate to ask but I need you to do something and I can't tell you how important it is to me.'

'Of course, tell me what it is,' she responded.

He explained, as best he could, the events that had happened concerning his father and cousin. Placing the handset down he looked at Ellie. Her oil paintings of windswept land and seascapes occupied most of the wall space. She was looking at them curiously. They had barely visited the flat since the previous year. He had been living either in Cornwall or New York. The London chapter of his life was over as far as he was concerned. He had pretty much abandoned everything in a chaotic mess. Organising what he was going to do with the flat would have to wait for another time.

'Is she going to help them?' She asked.

'Yes, we're lucky to have her as a friend. I think I can sleep now, at least for a few hours before we leave. Will you be okay?'

'I'll be fine. I might order some food in. Do you want something for later?' She asked.

'That sounds great.'

He fell asleep as soon as he landed on the bed, lying face down on the duvet. He was out for the count.

Slowly she pulled off his black jacket. He never stirred as she undressed him further and slipped off his boots.

She moved back into the sitting room and approached the table. Her hand fell on a small leather bound journal poking out from beneath a file. An elastic band was the only thing keeping the pages together. Torn in places, with many scribbles and doodles, his handwriting was hard to decipher.

She idly flicked through it with one hand on her extended belly. The loose photos were familiar and she smiled.

Turning to the start of the journal she found a date and a message written in faded ink:

December 25th 1976. Happy Christmas Finn, love Dad

Turning to the last entry, written the previous July, she began to read.

July 18 1996

Note to self: Fix the leak in the bathroom. Finn, you must stop drinking whisky. Drink more water.

If you ever find yourself reading this Ellie, I want you to know I did tell myself this on many occasions. I'm not proud of myself. Well not much. I do drink too much but I fantasise

*about you knowing about me, it's all I have. I can't shake it.
You are with me all the time. Every day I wake up you are there
in my mind and I'm left desperate and wanting. I have to keep
moving, it's the hardest thing of all but I make myself even on
the worst days.*

*If I can get through each day, I know it will bring me
closer to holding you again. I miss you so much I cannot stop
thinking about you. There is this constant longing in me. It
hurts so much. You are my only reason for living but it makes
no sense to me. Oh, why do I love you so much?*

She closed the notebook and hastily pulled the elastic around
it, lifting some papers over it to conceal it. He had written it while
he had been cursed. The journal had all the missing years in when
she had been absent from his life. With the curse destroyed, he was
changed man to the one in the journal. She ventured through the
tiny bespoke kitchen and stepped onto the roof garden.

It sparked a memory with Finn on a hot summer afternoon,
making love on the decking—making a baby. She couldn't help but
smile and ordered some take-away sitting on a wicker chair with the
cordless phone. The dry climbing plants had withered considerably.
The sunlight was fading behind the tall buildings and she decided
to call a few people since she had the place all to herself.

After several failed attempts to reach her best friend Joo Williams,
she called her aunt in Cornwall, the closest person she had in the
world to a mother. When her real mother died when she was a
child, her aunt stepped in to raise her as her own.

'Hello Rose, it's me.'

'Ellie, are you alright?' Rose was painting in her artist's studio at
Eternia Cottage, Penberth. 'Caron told me you were on your way
back. It's been truly awful here with what's happened to the boys.'

'We're stopping here in London for a few hours because Finn
needs some sleep, then we're setting off for Cornwall. Is there

any news? Finn just spoke to Branna and she's going to try and help them.'

'Thank God, they really need her, especially Bastian.' Rose responded. 'He's in a coma and Caron is beside herself. It's dreadful. Milton's conscious but not in brilliant shape physically. We have no idea how it happened or why.'

'Finn wants us to stay with you in Penberth for a few days.'

'Of course, you can use your old room. I'll never change it. It will always be your space, Ellie. You never have to ask.'

'Thanks, Rose. Finn believes the Irish Connellys are back. He thinks they were attacked to make him come home.'

'This is doing you no good. There were no witnesses and it might have nothing to do with them. I agree it's odd for both of them to be mugged in the same day but it can happen.'

'Bastian mind-locked with one of them,' Ellie said. 'That's why he's in a coma.'

'How do you know that?'

'Finn had a vision.'

'These visions,' Rose said. 'Milton has them too but more often than not they don't mean anything. They're like dreams. Finn's mother had them too. Sometimes visions are merely amplified fears. All I want is for you to get here safely, Sweetheart. I've been so worried about you being so far away. I'm so relieved you're coming home. The baby must be huge by now.'

'He kicks all the time. I had no idea it would be like this. It's exhausting. Men have it so easy. It feels like I'm double my normal size.'

'Put your feet up and I'll see you in the morning.' Rose said with a smile. 'The key's in the usual place in case I'm asleep when you get here. The bed will be made up.'

'Thanks, it's appreciated. I can't wait to see you, it feels like we've been away forever.'

Finn didn't recognise where he was. The sky was darkened with no stars or moon visible. His ghostly spirit offered the only light in the inky void. The temperature was freezing cold. Fear began to dominate him along with the unease of being stuck in the dark. Recollections flooded back of a time when he was trapped in the 'in-between' – the empty void between the mortal world and the next. He was finding it increasingly difficult to comprehend what was happening.

A single form emerged from the darkness to be totally defined. Although completely white, the spirit was dressed in a long hooded cloak and carried a spear in one hand. As the Sentry approached, one more appeared then another and another. Suddenly he was surrounded by identical beings all looking at him. The silence was deafening. He couldn't read their minds. They began to stare into his mind, rampaging through his thoughts and memories as though it was a library waiting to be trashed. Then it stopped.

One of the Sentries spoke into his mind: You will become one of us, Finn Milton and sooner than you think. This is not over for you, not by a long shot. You must stop the charmer or he will destroy your soul. You cannot fight alone this time. You must not be the victim. We can only help you if you discover their cloak. There must be a talisman. Do not delay.

Finn had been asleep for four hours when he opened his eyes. He could still see the hollowed eyes of the Sentry with no visible features. What was spoken to him sounded important. The feeling of intimidation remained with him until Ellie appeared in the doorway. His confused expression did little to disguise the fact he had experienced another nightmare. Either that or a Sentry had actually visited him in his sleep with a dire warning. His whole body felt cold and he shivered. Dark shadows hung under his eyes, which were watering involuntarily.

'Are you alright, Darling?' She asked.

He rubbed his eyes and brought his arms around her, kissing her. He calmed himself further and smiled.

'You smell nice.'

'Always the one to change the subject, Finn.'

'It was another crazy dream, ghosts this time. Some of them make no sense to me. So, what have you been doing?'

'I ordered some food,' she said. 'Now you're back in the land of the living, my back's aching like crazy. Can you give me a rub please?'

He raised the duvet and she lay on the bed, lifting up her top. She sank into a marvellous state of delirium while he worked his fingers across her slim back.

'How does that feel?'

'So good,' she said, turning over. 'You should've let me drive. We would've been almost there by now.'

'You're far too pregnant to be driving, Miss Morgan. We ought to do something about that.' He lent back onto his elbow, letting his fingers run over the warm skin of her round pregnant belly.

'About what?'

'Your name.'

'What's wrong with my name?'

'I want to marry you before the boy comes.'

'You're mad, Finn. I'll look like a whale in the wedding photos. We're only going to do this once and I want to look my best on our big day—after the baby comes.'

'You are beautiful, Ellie, no matter what you say.'

'I'm pregnant and huge.'

He read her mind. 'Who did you speak to earlier?'

'I called Rose and your dad is awake,' she replied.

'That's good news. What about Bastian?'

'No change, I'm afraid,' she said. 'He's on life support.'

'Hopefully Branna can change that. I need to see my father. Come on, it's time we hit the road.'

Thirty minutes later, they were driving along Great Portland Street in the rented Audi. It was pouring down with rain on the way to the M4 motorway and the South West of England. One thing he could always rely on in England was the weather. There was always weather. It would be hours before they'd reach Penberth in such treacherous conditions.

'I'm certain Michael's in St Ives.'

'You're paranoid,' she said. 'You don't know for sure. Rose said these visions aren't always real. It could be your fears playing tricks on you.'

'None of it feels right. You and the baby mean far too much to me and generally my paranoia's spot on, Honey.'

'I tried phoning Joo and I can't get hold of her. She isn't answering the phone at home or her mobile. It's not like her to disappear and I'm worried about her.'

'When did you last speak to her?'

'Three days ago,' she replied.

'I'm sure she's okay, she's a big girl.'

'Maybe, I don't know. Do you want to listen to some music?'

'Yeah, Solid Air by John Martyn would be good right now,' he said. 'It might calm me down.'

After much rummaging in her travel bag, she found the elusive CD and slipped it into the player. The roads blended into one as they drove further west listening to the soundtrack and ethereal sounds of John Martyn. The rain lashed relentlessly against the car for hours until they crossed the River Tamar and entered the county of Cornwall. Within a minute the rain shrunk to a light drizzle before stopping altogether. She smirked at him and squeezed his left hand resting on the gear stick.

Ellie: *It feels so good to be back. It makes you appreciate it more when you go away. They're going to be all right, you do know that, don't you Finn? They'll pull through this.*

Finn: *I only hope Branna makes it there in time, Sweetheart.*

4

~~

truth

A tall woman with long black hair, dressed in jeans and a long leather coat, tapped on the door of a cottage in Burrow Road. After several locks were unbolted, the door slowly edged open. A puffy-faced blonde haired woman greeted the visitor, her expression drained of emotion.

'Hello Caron, I came as soon as I could.'

'Branna.' Caron said. 'What are you doing here?'

'Mummy, who is it?' A young girl's voice carried through from the sitting room.

'Finn told me to come here urgently.' Branna explained plainly. 'I can help Bastian and Milton. Where are they?'

'In hospital.' Caron's tone was defensive. There were dark shadows under her eyes. 'So you've spoken to Finn? That's more than I have.'

'He's on his way to Cornwall,' she said with an air of complete calm. 'Did Bastian ever tell you about my healing ability? I'm quite capable.'

A small smile flickered on Caron's face and her aggressive tone appeared to melt.

'You'd better come in. I'm sorry but this whole business has made me extremely nervous. I don't like the idea of a Connelly in my home. Branna, this is my daughter. Cara, meet Branna Connelly.'

'Actually, I'm no longer a Connelly. I'm a Smith now.'

'When did you and Murray get married?' Caron asked.

'We had a quick service two weeks ago at the registry office. It was nothing fancy. Murray and I wanted to keep it quiet.'

'I had no idea,' Caron said.

'No one did,' she replied.

The young girl studied the strange dark woman with long black hair and found herself gasping. 'You're a powerful raven.'

'I suppose I am and it appears you have abilities as well, Cara. You are quite fascinating for such a small person.'

'Now is not the time for comparing your abilities,' Caron said with a degree of tension in her voice. 'They're in Treliske in Truro. When are you free to go?'

'Right now,' Branna said. 'I don't think we should delay.'

'Thank you. I'm sorry but I had no idea you would be so kind.'

She tried to lift her spirits. 'People can change, Caron. I would've come sooner, had I known about it.'

'You *can* change into a raven.' Cara said on the way to the hospital from the back seat of the car. 'And you can heal.'

'Yes,' Branna said.

'You're telepathic,' the girl added in awe.

'Cara, can you please stop with this chatter! You're far too young to be thinking like this.' Caron snapped.

Bastian's wife had no abilities whatsoever and was alarmed by the strange new developments in her daughter. She had inherited abilities from her father and her telepathy was mature for her age amongst other emerging gifts.

Cara: *Mummy hates that I can do things. Daddy's cool about it though.*

Branna: *What can you do?*

Cara: *I can move things and read minds.*

Branna: *That's very clever. Can you read my mind?*

Cara: *Only if I concentrate very hard. Yes, I can. Oh, you are very powerful.*

Branna: *I will have to watch you, Cara. I don't meet many people who can do that. It makes you very special. You remind me of your Uncle Finn.*

Cara: *Are you going to fix my dad? I miss him so much, I hope he's going to be alright.*

Branna: *I hope so.*

Cara smiled to herself: *That's very clever.*

Caron drove on towards Truro and parked close to the hospital. Branna walked ahead through the corridors casting spells so that they wouldn't be stopped by anyone working on the night shift. Soon they were standing quietly outside the single room where Bastian lay in a coma. He was hooked up to a life support machine, which was keeping him alive.

'Watch out for anyone, I won't be long. I hope.' Branna opened the heavy door, which slowly closed behind her. Caron and Cara watched through the glass as she approached the bed, pulled up a chair and turned on the side lamp.

Branna: *Right Bastian, let's see where you've gone to.*

She closed her eyes and rested her fingers on his forehead and focused inwards. At first there was nothing. He was breathing with the help of the machine but there was severe and aggressive damage to his brain tissue. She began healing without applying too much pressure. Next she searched for his conscious mind and talked to him using telepathy. She held his hand and gave it a squeeze.

Branna: *Bastian, can you hear me? I can pull you out of this but you need to give me something. Bastian, where are you?*

The near fatal damage to his brain had been healed but he was non-responsive. She glanced at Caron and shook her head discouragingly. The next moment his fingers tightened around hers. His eyes were opening then he was choking from the tube in his throat. Panic set in with the disorientation.

'Hey, take it easy, Bastian,' she said. 'Try not to breathe through your mouth.' She reached for the tube. 'Relax and I'll remove it. Your muscles will be slow to react, let me work on them before you sit up. Be patient and you'll be fine. Trust me, you've been through quite an ordeal.'

Caron and Cara entered the room when Branna skilfully withdrew the tube. He began to cough erratically. Caron rushed to his side, overjoyed at seeing her husband alive.

'Oh Darling, I thought we'd lost you,' she said with tears falling down her cheeks. Cara jumped on the bed, resting her head against his chest and hugging her father.

'What happened to me?' He asked.

'You've been in a coma,' Caron said.

'A coma?'

'How do you feel?' Branna asked.

'I've got a damn fine headache.' He sighed. 'Branna, what are you doing here?'

She touched his forehead and eased the pain. 'Finn told me to find you and it was a good job he did. He was right, you were in a very bad way.'

'Finn's home? Everything's gone mad,' Bastian said.

'He's on his way,' Branna said.

Bastian began removing the needles in his arm. His strength was returning. 'I wasn't expecting him home until next month.'

'Now I need to fix your uncle, Professor Milton.'

'What's wrong with Finlay?' He was taking his clothes from Caron and getting dressed.

'He's in another ward,' Branna replied. 'He had a similar visit to yours, only he got the bejabbers beaten out of him.'

'Oh no,' he said. 'They did this to make Finn come home.'

'Who did this to you?' Branna asked. 'Can you remember anything?'

'Michael Connelly and his son broke into the house but I can't remember his name.'

'Cillian,' Branna said with a modicum of distaste. 'He's a very dangerous man. You were lucky he didn't kill you.'

'I don't feel right discharging myself but I don't fancy staying here either. Are you sure you don't want a job?' He smiled.

'That's not going to happen, Bastian.' Branna replied. 'I would rather be anonymous. You know how this works. I would be locked up in a lab. We don't tell a soul what we have witnessed here.'

'The staff are going to want to know what happened to me,' he said. 'You don't just wake up from a trauma like that!'

'I'm sure you can come up with some feasible explanation, you're a doctor,' she said plainly. 'Now let's find the professor and get the hell out of here before someone does notice us and calls the police.'

Branna went ahead casting more spells. The wards were barely lit as they passed through the hospital.

When they entered the men's ward, Professor Finlay Milton was fast asleep. Bastian found him and Branna pulled a curtain around the bed to disguise what they were doing from the rest of the ward. Milton was waking up, in traction and covered in plaster, to find Branna offering him a warm smile.

'I thought I was dreaming when I saw you,' Professor Milton said to her.

'I wish it was under happier circumstances, Uncle, but it never is.' Bastian remarked. 'Now let's check you out.'

'I heard all about your coma, Bastian. I can see you've been fixed up,' he said. 'How are you feeling now?'

'It isn't something I would like to dwell on, Finlay. I owe Branna my life. Now let's get you sorted.' He picked up a chart from the end of the bed and began to explain his injuries to Branna.

'Shoulder bone.' She suggested, looking back at Bastian.

'I'm going to remove the plaster uncle, can you handle a bit of pain?' Bastian asked quietly as he sourced some medical tools.

'Do what you have to do, I really don't care. I'm not going anywhere like this,' Milton replied soberly.

Bastian began to cut away the plaster, before dropping it into a bin liner. Branna healed the newly exposed tissue and knitted the broken bones back together, regenerating the damage at a cellular level until it was almost minimal. Half an hour later the worst of his injuries were repaired and Milton began to flex his limbs again. He was able to move his legs, one of which had been badly broken.

No one had checked on the ward the whole time. Branna was exhausted. She had never healed so many wounds at once.

'That's you done for now,' she said.

'You're a dream, Branna,' he said. 'Thank you. You're an absolute miracle woman. I like your healing ability very much.'

'No problem,' she said with a smile. 'You should be able to walk but you'll have bruises for a while.'

'Are you taking me home?'

'That's the plan.' Bastian located a wheelchair and helped him to his feet. 'Unless you want to stay here and explain how you miraculously recovered?'

'I don't think so,' Milton replied.

'Time to go.' She opened the curtain. 'Let me go ahead and clear the way. I don't think anyone else was awake in here. The last thing we need are witnesses.'

By the time they reached the car park no one had stopped them.

'My father taught me that little trick.' Branna said. 'He used to call it being invisible although the thought of him now just leaves a bad taste in my mouth.'

'It's strange I need to be thanking *him* for something,' Bastian added, climbing into the back of the car with his daughter and Branna.

'Where's Finn?' Milton strapped himself into the front passenger seat. 'I expected him to be with you.'

'He's on his way,' Caron replied starting up the car. 'Finn and Ellie flew into Heathrow a few hours ago.'

'He needs to know what he's up against, he can't even block his mind,' Bastian said. 'He's forgotten so much.'

'I can help with that,' Branna said. 'Maybe tomorrow, if he's up to it.'

'Thanks for your help,' Milton said. 'It feels so good being able to move again.'

'I wanted to help you,' she said. 'It was the least I could do. I will always be in debt to your family for my freedom and the life I am able to live now that my family have gone. You have no idea what it means to me.'

༡

After the long drive through the dark the Audi arrived in Penberth. Finn crept up the stairs with Ellie to her old attic room trying desperately not to wake up Rose. It didn't take long to fall asleep on the soft double bed. He woke in the early hours with Ellie curled up beside him in a fetal position. The room reminded him of all the other times he had been there and it gave him goose bumps.

'It feels good having you here, Mr Milton,' she sighed.

'There are far too many ghosts and broken memories in this room,' he said wistfully. 'I can remember dancing with you to *LA Woman* right here when we were ten years old. That was so long ago. Do you remember?'

'Of course I do,' she replied.

'I can remember it like it was yesterday. I was so infatuated with you, I could hardly sleep. It defined me for so long.'

'It's alright to have memories Finn, *just* don't let them define you.'

'You are *my forever girl*. I love you so much. It's *all* I've ever known.'

༡

Branna opened her eyes and could hear her husband Murray snoring beside her. Climbing out of bed stealthily, she pulled on her cotton kimono wrap and stepped downstairs. Her long black hair fell down her back. Barefoot she walked on the stone tiles in the tiny back garden.

It was a clear night and the sky was covered in stars.

The air was cold and bracing.

There was a presence of another soul.

'Who's there?'

Ghost: *Branna.*

The ghostly outline of a beautiful young woman formed before her eyes. She looked about twenty years old and was strangely familiar. Her white wispy hair was swaying.

Branna: *Who are you?*

Ghost: *I'm Duana.*

Branna: *My grandmother, Duana? I thought you were in Etherea.*

Duana: *It's complicated but I am unwelcome in Etherea. My crazy mother made a cloak for James. It must be found and destroyed by a Sentry. It was bound to a necklace.*

Branna: *James Connelly? I don't know who he is.*

Duana: *The cloak still protects his chosen bloodline and they must be stopped. One of them is worse than your father.*

Branna: *His bloodline?*

Duana: *They are already here. I can see so much of myself in you. We are not supposed to communicate with the living. Even in this state there are rules, even if we are banished to live above.*

Branna: *I often wondered what happened to you.*

Duana: *You do not need to be burdened by my plight, it happened a long time ago. I have been watching over you since you were born. Make haste, Branna.*

Branna: *But where is the talisman? And who is James Connelly?*

The ghost disappeared, leaving her with little to go on aside from the name of a relative she had never heard of. She went inside and sat on the edge of the bed, looking at Murray. Her husband was a kind and honest man but he knew nothing about her powerful and dark family. She had been purposelessly hiding the truth from him.

As far as Murray was concerned, her brother and father had relocated to a small hamlet in Ireland called Meath. It was a deception on her part to protect him. Their dead bodies were lying in the soft brown earth at the end of the Parsonage garden. Murray would need to know everything. With that concept running around in her head and the existence of another talisman, it was proving difficult to get back to sleep.

～

Rose Tremaen was in her kitchen when Finn and Ellie emerged early the next morning. She was emotional and hugged them both profusely. 'Thank God you're both home. It's so good to see you.'

'It's lovely to see you too,' Ellie said.

'Has there been any change with Bastian and Dad?' He asked. 'I would've stopped at the hospital but it was too early.'

'Caron just called,' Rose said with a smile. 'Bastian woke up during the night.'

'That's brilliant news.' He remarked.

'He's home and in better shape than he was yesterday,' she added.

'He's home? What about Dad?'

'Branna fixed him up as well,' she replied. 'He's back, safe and sound in The Warren.'

'That's the best news I could've hoped for. Rose, would it be alright if we stay here for a few days?'

'Finn, you don't know anything yet.' Ellie interjected.

'I'm just playing safe,' he said. 'We don't know what we're up against yet.'

'You can stay here for as long as you want,' Rose said. 'It's always been Ellie's home and you're practically married.'

'Thanks.' He was pleased their accommodation had been arranged so quickly and gave Ellie a hug. 'I must go out and see Dad.'

'He will be pleased to see you,' Rose said. 'He was in a great deal of pain even though he refuses to admit it. You know what he's like.'

'I can't wait to see him.' He felt a growing sense of relief and owed Branna a huge favour.

Branna was pushing the scrabbled eggs around the plate with her fork. Murray was studying her keenly.

'Something's bothering you this morning, I can tell,' he said in a soft Cornish accent. 'You're not usually this quiet.'

Her mind was brimming with the prospect of her Irish relatives staying up the road in her old home. The memory of Duana's ghost was fixed clearly in her mind. The visit of the elusive spirit hadn't scared her in the slightest but the mere suggestion of her father's cousin Michael being around had caused her great concern.

Michael had always kept close ties with her father. They had been tight like brothers. She experienced an uncomfortable truth with him from an early age. The way he looked at her made her stomach turn. He would be looking for Jared and Logan. Only they were dead. His path would eventually lead him to her door and more importantly, her husband, who knew nothing about him or their rather unconventional lives.

She had never been able to live an ordinary life even though she had tried to. The stain of her family's terror would always haunt her. Murray needed to hear the details and she would have to explain her abilities. She was uncertain if he would accept it or even stay with her. Either way she was left with little choice but to tell him the truth.

'You've been quiet since we woke up,' he said. 'What is it?'

'There are things that have happened in my life. Things that I didn't want to tell you. Things I would rather forget.'

'It's fine, Branna, I do know a bit about your family. You don't have to tell me if you don't want to.'

'You need to know everything because it affects us now more than ever.' She laid down her fork.

'What are you talking about?'

'A few hours ago I was visited by a ghost.'

'A what?' He spat out a mouthful of warm tea. 'Have you gone completely mad?'

'No, but you're going to have to trust me.'

'Of course I trust you but there's no way that ghosts exist, Branna.'

'There is this other world that exists and it is one you have no concept of. What I'm about to tell you is for your protection. Believe me, ignorance is no longer acceptable. You need to know everything, even if it seems ridiculous at first, starting with this.'

Standing in the open plan lounge, she gradually transformed. Her body shrank without warning. Within seconds her skin and clothes had merged into a solid black colour. Her whole body adopted a texture of feathers as she shrunk smaller and smaller. Finally she resembled a complete and very large black raven. The bird blinked and stared at Murray whose eyes almost popped out of his skull. The bird flexed its wings and hopped onto the sofa. Branna had disappeared and turned into a living, breathing raven.

'Branna, is this some kind of a practical joke?' He was in total shock at the revelation. 'What the hell is this?'

Moments later she effortlessly turned back, standing up to her true height, and fully dressed again as though nothing had happened. She sat down and his mouth sagged open.

'Please tell me that didn't happen!' He was shaking his head. 'This isn't possible. How can anyone do that?'

'I've been able to transform into a raven since I was six years old. I'm telepathic and can heal by touch with a great deal of concentration. We belong to a tiny community who have inherited abilities from their kin. My family, we *were* all gifted.'

'Were? You mean there are more people like you? I need a whisky.' Murray moved to the drinks cabinet and poured a large measure into a crystal glass. He downed it in one and then poured another. 'I can't believe what you've just shown me. People can't do that sort of thing. Period.'

'They *can* Murray and my father and brother are both dead.'

'Dead? Oh heavens Branna, why didn't you tell me about this? It's not exactly unimportant.'

'I hoped I would never have to, but something serious has happened. There are people who need me, people I care about and I have to help them and you need to know because you're my husband.'

'What does this involve exactly?'

She wasn't sure how he was going to handle hearing anymore but it made more sense to carry on. 'I'll tell you everything but is this overloading you?'

'I always knew you were special but I genuinely had no idea how special. I guess you can fly too?'

'As a raven I can.'

He gently held her hands and kissed them.

'I married a raven. I need time to think about this, it came at me sort of left field. These people, are they in some kind of trouble?'

'I think so,' she said. 'Do you remember when you made me that copy of a gold bracelet?'

'How could I forget? It was the start of our relationship.'

'The original bracelet was possessed by a demon,' she said. 'It was tied to a curse, my kind refer to as a talisman. All the stories you've ever heard about witches, ghosts and magic, well, most of them are true. My great-grandmother was a witch. She cast a curse which was locked to that bracelet and it had to be destroyed.'

'So there *was* a story attached to it. It sounds absolutely crazy.'

'None of this is common knowledge. The majority of people have no idea about this and it must stay that way. You must never repeat any of it.'

'Are there many people like you?'

'There used to be,' she said. 'My family did some terrible things. They killed a lot of them and when their talisman was destroyed it exposed them and they were banished. You see, the talisman doesn't only hold curses. It can hide people's crimes from a spiritual underworld.'

'A what?'

'We live among ghostly Sentries who watch out for dark magic crimes. These crimes cannot be detected if the perpetrators have talismans. An enchanted talisman could conceal them supernaturally. These Sentries come from an underworld or spiritual haven called *Etherea*. When we die, gifted mortal souls go there to exist in the afterlife. I have never seen it but I know it's real.'

'So there is more than one heaven?'

'Kind of but it's complicated.'

'So why are you telling me this now?'

'Some of my Irish relatives are investigating my father's disappearance. My father's cousin Michael is here with his sons, Cillian and Jarlath. My brother and my father never had official deaths. Before the curse was broken I had a run in with my father, which ended badly. I stabbed him and he bled to death. I'm not proud of what I did but I stand by it. This happened before we got together. To hide the truth I buried his body in the garden. Honestly Murray, Logan was an evil man. He threatened to kill friends of mine and he never joked about anything. I had to stop him or there would've been even more carnage. I have never killed anyone before.'

'Branna, why didn't you tell me at the time?'

'I wanted to but I chose to protect you. You're innocent in all of this. Logan would've killed you had he known you were even slightly interested in me. I know how this sounds. How can anyone possibly have a father like that? But he was mad and controlled every aspect of my life. I didn't want to kill him, believe me. Logan was hell bent, driven by an iron will and fuelled by constant paranoia.'

'What happened to your brother?'

'A Sentry took his soul due to his rather extensive history of crime; all committed using his powerful abilities. My father trained him relentlessly from an early age. He was my twin but Jared was as dangerous as Logan and constantly trying to impress him. He died in Penberth and his body was delivered to the Parsonage where I buried him next to my father. No one knows about this other than a few people I trust with my life. I want to put it all behind me.'

'How come you were not punished by the Sentries for killing Logan?' He asked.

'I was expecting the consequences but one of them allowed me to live. I didn't abuse my gifts by killing Logan with a knife. They're only interested if something untoward happens, where someone is hurt or killed by misuse of magic.'

'So what happens now?'

'According to the ghost, Michael has a talisman which would make him and his children invisible to Sentries. They can commit crimes using their abilities and not be seen or stopped. It makes them very dangerous. If he learns of how Logan died, he'll come for me and make me pay for it. The talisman must be destroyed so that we'll have a fighting chance of stopping them when the time comes. This is what the ghost was warning me about. My friend Finn will need my help to find the talisman because it affects him as much as me.'

'Who's Finn?' He asked.

'Finn Milton was cursed by my great-grandmother Shannon before he was born. It was a curse of the heart. It all started for him when he was ten years old. Years before, his great-grandmother Jessica married Shannon's eligible lover and it broke her heart. Shannon composed an act of cold revenge by crafting an enchanted talisman out of an antique bracelet. She attached two spells to it.

One was for Jessica's first-born great-grandchild who turned out to be Finn and the other to protect her kin's crimes from *Etherea*.

'Last year, a Sentry explained the curse to me. I never knew the full horror of what my family had done until I helped Finn to discover the truth and as a result, we became friends. This ultimately led to him astral planing with the talisman to *Etherea* where the spirits destroyed it. Astral planing is another one of Finn's abilities. With the curse destroyed my family lost the cloak they were hiding behind. It brought about the sudden demise of my brother. He committed so many evil crimes, it was inevitable but Michael *will* blame Finn for Jared's death because Finn destroyed the talisman.'

'I've never heard of Finn Milton,' he said. 'He isn't from around here.'

'Finn's father is Professor Finlay Milton. He's spent most of his life in London but he was born in St Ives. He's a writer.'

'That's hectic,' he said. 'I know Professor Milton but I never knew he had a son. I never even knew he was married.'

'Finn's a tortured soul because of my family. They were despicable towards him and his family. The curse killed his mother in childbirth and Logan killed her father shortly after. At the same time, Shannon struck Jessica down and left her in a vegetative state.'

'You *like* Finn a lot. I don't have anything to worry about, do I? This is someone I've never met and he means a lot to you, I can tell.'

She laughed it off swiftly. 'Of course not, Finn was taken a long time ago. He's never been available.'

'I'm only checking there won't be any issues with him in future,' he said, half-smiling. 'You *are* my wife.'

'Finn and Ellie are having a baby soon. She must be close to giving birth.'

'Who's Ellie?'

'Ellie Morgan is engaged to Finn. They have always been kind of together. She was cursed as well but it affected them differently.'

'The artist Ellie Morgan? Pregnant? What else are you going to shock me with today?'

'Why?'

'She's one strange spinster, always has been, very talented though,' he said. 'I thought she was a virgin.'

'I can assure you that she hasn't been one of those for a very long time. With Ellie cursed as well, it had a profound effect on their personalities. They had such a terrible time. I helped them when no one else could. I've made few friends in this town, but these are real people I care about.'

'Wow, this has been enlightening to say the least,' he said. 'It's a good job we don't have ghosts around here all the time or curses for that matter. I had no idea. I don't think I can take any more revelations. Is that all?'

'For now. I wasn't sure how I was going to explain it to you. It's not normal breakfast conversation, is it?'

'Come over here and give me a kiss. I love the fact you help other people, it's one of the things I love the most about you. Just do me a favour and warn me before you decide to change into a bird. It might be a little freaky for a while.'

5

~~

home

Finn had only been away from St Ives for a few months but it felt good to be walking to the old cottage where his father lived in The Warren. He had spent the first ten years of his life in September Cottage. It held special memories for him because it represented a peaceful happy time before the curse. Everything about St Ives was familiar as though he had never been away. He climbed the granite steps to the blue stable door, which opened before he had the chance to knock. Always impressed by his father's precognitive skills, he immediately gave him a long hug.

'I can't believe you went to such lengths to get me home, Dad. You only had to ask,' he said with a warm grin. Seeing his father upright and out of plaster was such a relief. Aside from a few bruises, a fortnight of stubble and a graze on his forehead, his father looked remarkably well.

'It's good to see you too, Finn. Thank you for sending Branna to help, she was truly amazing.'

'It was the least I could do. Ellie stayed behind in Penberth with Rose. It's safer there and they have loads to talk about. It's not long before the baby comes and I want her to be miles away from this when it kicks off.'

'How *is* Ellie really bearing up?'

'She's very tired and worried about me.'

Milton looked at him. *So am I, Finn. We need to mind-lock. I have something to show you.*

Finn: *What is it?*

Milton: *You're not safe and neither is Ellie. One of my gifts is being able to share my memories with others. I want to show you one, here take my hand.*

Finn couldn't remember ever receiving a mental image from his father before, never mind a full-blown memory. His father had always kept his abilities hidden but it seemed he had started to open up. He thought of the astral planer Dennis and how similar the connection was. Closing his eyes, he felt a tugging when his father's soul pulled him in.

He could see the interior of September Cottage.

All was quiet bar the light sound of chinking metal. His father was engineering a motorcycle part on the kitchen table when there was a knock at the front door. Except it was hardly a knock. The door was blown inwards and two men marched in. He recognised one of them straight away, Michael Connelly.

'What do you want?' His father asked the stranger.

'Information about your son,' Michael replied.

'Who are you?'

'I'm Michael Connelly and this is my eldest son, Cillian. Where's Logan? It would be better if you tell me now. I figured you'd know something since your blasted son had so much to do with them. I know he killed Jared.'

'Finn didn't kill him,' he replied.

'But he knew what would happen if the talisman was destroyed,' Cillian added. 'It's the same thing.'

'You're nuts,' he said. 'Jared killed people. It was a regular pastime of his. He was completely off his rocker. You have no right to demand anything of me.'

'Not good enough, I'm afraid,' Michael said. 'I want Finn to come home and confront me with the truth.'

'That is not going to happen,' he grunted.

'I have no argument with you, Professor Milton,' Michael said. 'Only your son who has a lot to answer for.'

'You'll have to get past me first,' he said. 'I'll never tell you where he is.'

'Maybe when he hears how close to death you are, he'll come running,' Michael said. 'You could simply pick up the phone and ask him. It's far more civilized than violence.'

Cillian reminded Finn of Jared. There was no colour in his eyes and he possessed the same dark hair.

Finn could sense the rising energy in his father's hands. Cillian extended his hand but Milton pushed him through the air towards the far wall using telekinesis before he had a chance to act.

He crashed into a bookcase and many books toppled with him to the floor. He cut the side of his face against the wooden shelves and his cheek was bleeding.

He looked incensed and stared at Michael. For a moment nothing happened then Cillian fired the first bolt of energy from his hand.

It struck the side of Milton's head and he toppled over. Michael proceeded to kick him in the chest. Milton could no longer fight them off. The wound in his skull had weakened him.

Next he was waking up in a hospital bed dressed in a great deal of plaster and high on morphine.

Finn stared at his father with horror. He recognised Cillian from the vision on the plane. The stranger had attacked Bastian. The undiluted violence made him feel sick to the stomach.

'They hurt you to get to me, I guessed as much. It's all I've been able to think about since Caron called me yesterday. Michael blames me for their disappearance because I destroyed that damn talisman.'

'They're looking for answers but I haven't seen Logan Connelly for months. It was something Branna said. She would never be living with Murray if he was still around.'

'She ran into a Sentry when I came back from *Etherea* last year and he let her off,' he sighed. 'She was worried they were going to take her soul.'

'What are you talking about?'

He rolled his eyes. 'Oh, me and my big mouth. I shouldn't have said anything. You can read me or I could tell you.'

'Finn, listen to me,' his father said with a frown. 'I don't actively read your mind for my own personal satisfaction. You can tell me the truth. That might be a start.'

He studied his father. His eyebrows were knitted together, and he was losing his patience.

'Branna killed him before I travelled to *Etherea*.'

'Seriously?' Milton lit his pipe and settled back into the sofa. 'She killed her own father?'

'She stabbed him in the heart and buried him in the garden. He was planning on killing Ellie and me, so she took evasive action. Since she didn't use her abilities to kill him, by *Etherea* standards, they weren't interested in punishing her.'

'That woman has some cast iron balls,' Milton said. 'At least that solves one mystery—there's one less Connelly to worry about. I like Branna even more now.'

'Agreed but it's the others that concern me. I can't believe they put Bastian in a coma.'

'I was in such a state at the time, I didn't realise Bastian was brain damaged. We're lucky to have Branna to fall back on when we get beaten half to death. Are you back here for good?'

'Hopefully,' he half-smiled. 'We always wanted to have the baby in Cornwall. I've asked one of Brett's assistants to sort out our stuff and send it on. As soon as Ellie's up to it, we're going to get married.'

'You deserve to be happy.'

'I don't remember what it was like, the day to day stuff. I get odd flashes but it doesn't add up to anything tangible. Getting back to the matter at hand, I think the Connellys have another talisman. How else could they get away with attacking you? It makes sense considering they're still alive.'

'I don't want you getting involved in this. You're might not be so lucky this time.'

'What was the name of that Sentry from *Etherea*? The one who helped us.'

'You can't go looking for them. If these people have cloaks, the Sentries can't help you. They can't even see their crimes. Branna's related to them, maybe you should speak to her. She'll know what their weaknesses are.'

'I will but I need to catch up with Bastian first. I can't believe I almost lost both of you and I wasn't even here.'

~

Bastian was resting on the sofa and looking a lot brighter than he expected. It was remarkable he had survived. 'You gave me such a fright,' he embraced him. 'I thought I was going to lose you when I first heard about it.'

'It makes an unpleasant change it being me,' Bastian replied.

'It was too close for comfort. Thank goodness Branna was here to fix your head. Dad's going to be okay too. He showed me the memory of what happened. The Connellys are out for my blood again.'

'What are you going to do about it?'

'I don't know yet.' He was pacing the room.

'You can't do it alone. I have friends who can help you. Many of them have abilities. Here's Joe Praed's number. He's very handy in a fight and one of my best friends.'

'Thanks,' he sighed. 'I'm just relieved you're okay.'

'Me too. I'm officially on sick leave for two weeks. My boss wasn't too impressed when I discharged myself last night so I'm here to help if you need me.'

'You need to take it easy, Bast. Ellie hasn't spoken to Joo since we got back. Has Caron seen her?'

'I don't think so. Not since the attack,' Bastian replied.

'It's weird, I hope she's okay. It's not like her to vanish off the side of the Earth.'

'Joo *can* take care of herself,' Bastian said.

'Yeah, like *you* can.'

'Finn, I was unprepared for what happened. They broke their way in and knew exactly what they were doing.'

'That's because they were looking for me,' he added.

'They were looking for Logan and Jared, only I don't think they're going to find them anytime soon,' Bastian said.

'Either way, if you see Joo can you let me know?'

'Of course I will, Finn. She can't be far.'

'Can you remember the name of that Sentry who helped us last year?'

'Why do you want to know?' Bastian asked.

'Because I can't remember his name.'

'Really? You never stop, do you?'

'Please Bast, it would really help me out.'

'He was called Guilar, not that it makes any difference, you shouldn't go anywhere near *Etherea*. It's dangerous. Seriously Finn, don't do anything stupid—at least not without me.'

Later at Penberth, he walked with Ellie along the lane to the slip and they sat on the rocks. The emerald sea crashed against the rocks. The daffodils were giving the green valley a yellow glow. For March it was a warm sunny afternoon.

They had the place to themselves. He had little to say but could feel her mood growing tense.

'Something's the matter.' She said. 'What is it, Finn?'

'I'm thinking of contacting a Sentry.'

'What? Have you gone completely mad?'

'I believe the Connellys have a cloak,' he said. 'Maybe they can help me find it.'

'When are you thinking of going?'

'Later tonight.'

'You're mad,' she said. 'Nothing new there I suppose.'

He frowned. 'I'm not as mad as I used to be.'

'I guess that curse had a lot to do with it.'

'And *you*, of course,' he retorted.

'Me? What did I do?'

He didn't want to say she had repeatedly broken his heart and with all the pent up emotion rushing through him it had come close. Although he didn't blame her for what had happened he could remember the damage. 'Nothing, forget it. I'm sorry. It's not you… it's me. I'm all over the place at the moment.'

'I don't want you taking any silly risks, that's all.'

He wished they could escape and be far away. Being alone with her would have to suffice. It felt like an impossible dream, one that he couldn't wake up from. The worst part was 'not knowing' what might happen when he finally confronted the Connellys and whether it would play out like the vision he had witnessed in Central Park from a planer called Dennis.

When it grew dark, he projected his spirit, flying at ridiculous speeds across Mounts Bay from Penberth. Before long he could see the Lizard lighthouse on the tip of the peninsula. Even in the dark the *Lion's Den* exposed its dark gaping mouth, carved out of the grassy cliff top. The sea was churning like a cauldron below and the sky was covered with stars.

He recalled the ghostly Sentry from Bastian's memories for he had none of his own. In his nightmares were fragments of Sentries but nothing fully defined.

As he was beginning to lose hope he felt a change in the air. Two large Sentry guards floated from the cave and made their forms ghostly visible. They wore large white billowing cloaks and carried long spears. The Sentries looked identical although neither of them seemed to have a face. He knew immediately that they could taste his fear.

Sentry #1: *What business do you have loitering here, human?*

The first Sentry, who was named Qarii, poked a long finger at his spirit making it disperse and come back together. It was cautionary but the altercation unhinged him mainly because the Sentries were so large. He would have to find some inner confidence, something he was struggling with.

Finn: *I need to commune with a Sentry called Guilar.*

Sentry #2, Flacus: *Are you out of your mind mortal? What makes you think you're entitled to anything? You have a life up here. Etherea is our domain.*

Finn: *This is important.*

Qarii: *You need to go to Etherea.*

Finn: *No. I can't do that. Absolutely not.*

Flacus: *Why?*

Finn: *Because I've been to Etherea and I don't want to go back. If you could give Guilar a message, I'll leave and never come back.*

Flacus: *Who are you to make demands of this nature? No one leaves Etherea, only the Sentries. Who are you?*

Qarii: *Flacus, this is Finn Milton, the one filled with soul light. Last year he broke into Etherea uninvited with a powerful talisman. Don't you remember?*

Flacus: *The Finn Milton? Surely not – you were the subject of discussion for months. Of course, I understand why you would not want to go to Etherea. You would have to be crazy to do that for they would not let you leave a second time. You are taking a huge risk coming here. It would be too easy to take your soul. I can sense how vulnerable you are. I can sense your fear, young mortal, and it is appetising.*

He couldn't believe he had been the subject of spiritual gossip. The Sentry laughed again, a deep resonating sound. It rippled through his soul before they liberally read his mind. Feeling desperate, he regretted not listening to his father's advice, which it seemed, was always right.

Finn: *Can you please ask Guilar to speak to me?*

Qarii: *I doubt that he would.*

Finn: *Why?*

Flacus: *We are not allowed to assist or commune with mortals.*

Finn: *There are cloaked people with a talisman committing terrible crimes in St Ives. This is a matter of life and death.*

Flacus: *Gifted death? We like those ones. Your reputation is impressive, Milton, I can see it for myself. Your mother certainly had a hand in your fate. Part of her soul is inside you and you have no idea.*

Finn: *What are you talking about? I'm nothing special. What does my mother's soul have to do with any of this?*

Flacus: *Everything. You have no concept of who you are or what you are capable of. You are quite a paradox.*

Finn: *Who I am? I'm just trying to stay alive.*

Flacus: *You have many possibilities at your disposal and the sad fact is that you will never realise your potential, not in this current life form. You spend your time wasting your abilities when you should stop and listen to what is being said to you.*

Finn: *But these people are innocent. What is wrong with you people? You have so many powers but you don't use them.*

Flacus: *That's rich coming from you.*

Finn: *I don't use them because I hate violence. I never asked for these powers.*

Qarii: *Yet you have them. They are not there for violence alone. It was no accident that you were born with abilities. Why do you think there are so few of you? You are a freak of nature, Finn Milton, a remnant from the old world that should have disappeared years ago. You are able to pass on your abilities to your children just like your mother and father did with you. One day you will be a Sentry. You will bring your powers with you when you die. You will use them – all of them – and you will be honoured by the many.*

Finn: *That's reassuring. I get to be a super guardian in the afterlife – like I get a say in it.*

Qarii: *It is an honour to be a Sentry and a position not awarded lightly. One day you will become one of us. Do not underestimate our code for it is already written.*

Finn: *Really? I wouldn't be so sure about that. I don't see any honour in your kind of justice.*

Flacus: *It is time for you to leave this place. There is no point to this conversation anymore. You have little respect for our code. That much is clear.*

Finn: *Talk to Guilar, please.*

Qarii: *If you agree to never come back, I will inform him of this interaction but he is not allowed to interfere. Next time I will not be so forgiving, I will take your soul below. Leave now before I change my mind and snatch you, for you are beginning to piss me off.*

Finn didn't need to be told twice and never once looked back once he took flight. The feeling was mutual. He could hardly believe the strange altercation with the Sentries and had no idea if his visit had made a difference.

Flying out to sea, he pushed on until he found the harbour at Penberth. Darting up the lane to the side of Eternia Cottage he flew in through the wall of the attic. Seconds later he sank into his waiting body lying next to Ellie. Shivers ran throughout his body as it adjusted to his spirit returning. Closing his eyes he fell into a deep sleep, completely spent.

In the hour before dawn, Branna flew as a raven the short distance to the Parsonage. There was a black saloon car parked outside beside her father's old abandoned land rover in the drive. She circled the house and stooped low at the back, settling on the roof. One of the windows on the first floor was ajar. It opened into her old bedroom.

She hadn't been back to the Parsonage since moving out the previous year. At the end of the garden, her twin brother Jared was buried next to her father Logan. Only a few close people knew about their resting place and the truth concerning their deaths.

At the time, she grabbed the few things that mattered and set up in the living space above her shop in town.

Two weeks later, she moved into a converted pottery just off Fore Street, with her boyfriend, Murray Smith.

Within six months they married. At no time had she intended on returning to the Parsonage.

Branna hopped onto the window ledge and edged closer to get a better view. Being a large bird made it awkward to manoeuvre in such a small space. Voices emanated from inside and Cillian was talking. 'How are you feeling?'

'Better but I don't know what happened to me last night,' Joo said. 'I was confused about where I was.'

'Don't worry.' He was stroking her hair. 'Everything's going to work out because we're leaving for Ireland soon.'

'Where does your family live?'

'Near Dublin in a place called Meath. My family have lived there for many generations. Now I'm going out for a jog but I'll be back. Please don't leave the room. My brother can be irrational and it would be safer if you stay put. I wouldn't want him to hurt you when I can do that myself.'

'If that's what you want,' Joo said.

'Of course it is, good girl. I can see you have a brain. Obedience is something you must understand.'

~

Once the door closed behind him, Branna jumped through the window and hopped onto the bedroom floor. The short slim woman was sitting on her old bed, staring at the closed door as though fixed in a trance. Her blonde hair was brushed straight and she was dressed in pink silk pyjamas.

When she noticed the raven she cried out.

Branna: *Don't scream, Joo. Stay calm. Please.*

'What are you? How can I hear your thoughts?'

Branna: *I'm Branna, you know me. What are you doing here?*

'What *am* I doing here? What are *you* doing here? I'm with Cillian and he's taking me to Ireland. I don't know anyone called Branna.'

She swiftly transformed herself into a woman. 'Joo, you have to get out of this house.'

'How can you do that? How do you know my name?'

'Change from being a bird? I've always been able to do it. Cillian's put a spell on you. I can sense it.'

'You're talking nonsense.' Joo's voice had a hard edge to it. Her personality had changed. 'You're jealous. You'd better leave now or I'll scream.'

'What? Why would you do that?'

'Because I don't know you and you shouldn't be here,' Joo said resolutely. 'You're trespassing.'

Branna stepped forward and touched her forehead but Joo bolted away. There hadn't been time to work on the spell shrouding her mind. 'Don't touch me. Cillian!' She shouted. 'Cillian! Come quickly!'

Branna sprinted to the window, changing into a raven as she picked up her feet. She jumped on the sill as the door opened. Catching the angry look on her cousin's face, she took flight immediately. He sped to the window only to see her fly away from the house.

'Branna,' he sighed. 'I knew you were still alive.'

Joo was sitting on the floor, shaking.

'Are you alright? What did she do?' He asked.

'She tried to touch me.'

'It's a good job she didn't. I must get this window nailed shut. She won't get in again. You need to stay here for your own safety. I'll protect you until the end.'

'Thank you, I don't know what I would do without you.'

'I ought to be thanking *you*. You're making such a difference and you have absolutely no idea.' He flashed his teeth at her in a kind of smile and opened the door. 'It'll be over soon, I promise.'

⁓

The light drifted through the round bedroom window and across his face. Finn began to wake and felt his hand around her belly. She arched her back into his chest and lay spooning him silently in his arms.

'Morning, my dear.' He stroked her hair as she rested her face on his shoulder. 'I love you.'

'I love you too, Sweetheart, but our baby's getting far too big.'

He could hear the baby's heart beat. 'He's amazing. I can sense he's gifted.'

'I know,' she said. 'I can too.'

'I'm going to raid the kitchen and make you something special to eat.'

Half an hour later, he had prepared a full English breakfast but she was picking at her food with little appetite.

'Joo's not answering her phone. I can't get hold of her.'

'Maybe she's gone to Sussex to visit her aunt,' he suggested.

'I'm not so sure. She hasn't been at work for the last few days and she was roistered in. No one has seen her.'

'There has to be some rational explanation. Maybe she's finally found herself a man.'

'I don't know, Finn, it's not like her,' she said. 'Rose has gone into Penzance to meet up with some old friends, we have the place to ourselves. Did you have any luck with the Sentries last night? I didn't hear you come back.'

'I met two Sentries and they had a terrible attitude,' he said. 'You don't want to hear half of it.'

'Did you find Guilar?'

'No but perhaps they'll pass a message onto him. You'd think they'd be impressed if someone told them about a new talisman but they told me to never come back.'

'That's not such a bad thing,' she said. 'They're not supposed to talk to us, remember?'

'What time are Serina and Joe arriving?'

'Around eleven.'

'I need more coffee,' he said 'What are they like?'

'Serina's an architect and Joe's an interior designer. They've been together for years. She doesn't take any prisoners so you need to brush up on your wit, she tells it like it is. They both have strong connections with the Connellys. Logan killed Serina's grandparents and Jared killed Joe's mother. There are too many people affected by that family. They're more than happy to lend a hand and there are others too like Jerry and Simon Nancarrow.'

'A real *posse*. It sounds rather impressive.' He was trying not to sound sarcastic but it came out much to his disdain.

She rolled her eyes at him. 'They *hated* the Connellys and know what happened last year. Bastian has taken great pleasure in spreading your good word.'

'I can't believe him sometimes. I don't want to be some kind of hero. I'll have a word with him next time I see him.'

'He's so proud of you. You can't blame him.'

'I wanted to break the curse so we could be together,' he said. 'I didn't want anyone to die. It's nothing to be proud of. I find it embarrassing and to be honest, I don't want the attention.'

After a couple of hours spent reading a book in the garden, he headed into the kitchen. She was basking in the last rays of sunshine before the forecast storm set in. The flowerbeds were full of yellow daffodils, hyacinths and purple crocuses.

He said. 'These people like to be on time.'

'I never heard that. How did you?'

He opened the front door smirking at his sonic skills to find Serina and Joe Praed waiting on the doorstep.

'Hello.' He said, allowing the smirk to fade.

'Finn, isn't it?' Joe immediately extended his hand and embraced him as though he had known him for years. 'It's so good to finally meet you. I've heard so much about you from Bastian. This is a fantastic house by the way.' Joe was the same age as Finn with a few grey whiskers. Tall and athletic with soft brown hair, he had kind pale blue eyes and a crooked smile.

'It belongs to Ellie's Aunt Rose,' he replied, surprised when Serina gave him the same over-familiar greeting. 'It's been in her family for generations.'

The guests walked inside and he closed the door behind them, shaking his head at their strange familiarity. Serina had short fair hair, bright blue eyes and a short slim figure. Both wore jeans, sweaters and boots.

Serina: *Bit skinny, I was expecting him to be bigger, Joe. He doesn't look that powerful. Wild hair though, I like it.*

His white streak was testament to the shock he acquired coming back to life the previous summer. He was immediately taken off guard. 'Everything's on the inside, I can assure you.'

'Oh, that explains a lot.' She said. 'Where's your missus? I can't wait to see her.' Catching sight of a smiling Ellie, she gave her a big hug. 'Ellie, you look so huge. You're not having twins, are you?'

'Only one and it's a boy. You know, don't you?' Joe said, raising his eyebrows and picking up the presence of the baby.

Finn was feeling a bit uneasy. It was odd being among new people with similar abilities. 'I knew it was a boy at two weeks.'

Serina smiled. 'That was clever.'

'I was told, but I *could* sense it.'

'Finn, you don't have to worry about what you say to us. We're all friends here,' Joe said peaceably.

'We've known about you for years. Bastian's a close friend. If we had known last year, we could've helped you.' Serina spoke softly and seemed distracted. 'Bastian's okay? Oh, Branna healed him *and* your dad? That's fantastic news. What a relief. We were so worried about them when we heard.'

'Are you reading my mind?' He asked.

'I'm sorry but it was necessary,' she replied.

'Necessary? Rude more like,' he added. 'How can you do that when I'm blocking you? Your telepathy must be top drawer.'

'I *am* talented in the mind department,' she explained. 'You've lost your memory but not your abilities. It's all there. Your gift of energy is unusual to say the least.'

'What does that mean?' He was suddenly perturbed.

She rested a hand on his wrist. He didn't move it although he thought about it.

Serina: *I mean you no harm. You don't need to be afraid of any of us. You've misplaced your confidence but it's still there.*

'Dad said there are others – like you – with abilities,' he said, trying to shift the attention.

'Jerry and Simon Nancarrow are good friends of ours,' Joe said. 'They want to help too. Bastian told us about the other Connellys and they sound dangerous.'

'They beat up my dad and mind-locked with Bastian to get to me,' he admitted. 'They mean business.'

Ellie suddenly found it hard to breathe. 'I can't believe you never told me.'

'I'm sorry, Darling.' He hurried to her side. 'I didn't want you to worry.'

'Ellie, he's not on his own this time,' Joe assured her. 'If they want Finn then they'll have us to deal with as well.'

Ellie squeezed his hand. 'This is never going to end, is it?'

'It will, I give you my word,' Finn said. 'I'm going to sort it out.'

'How? Look at what they've done already. Who knows where we would be without Branna?' She began to cry. 'What if you really get hurt this time? What am I going to do without you?'

'Do you want to lie down?' Serina suggested, sensing her stress levels rising.

She brought a protective arm around her and Ellie nodded before they disappeared upstairs.

'You can't keep anything from her,' Joe said. 'I thought you knew about intimacy between telepaths.'

'She hasn't read me for a while, not since I learnt how to block in New York.'

'You and Ellie are both telepathic,' Joe said. 'There are times when you can't block someone even if you're the best blocker in the world.'

'This is a right mess and now I've upset her.'

'Serina can help you with your abilities. Her brother Tom is gifted too.'

'There are so many of you, maybe if I'd been living here things would've been different.'

'You're here now and there are plenty of people who will gladly help for what you did for them,' Joe said.

'So I keep hearing. It sounds like I've become notorious. I don't want to hear about it to be honest. I'm no hero, Joe.'

'Whether you like it or not, you are considered heroic by many people. You haven't been living here for the past twenty years to know what it was like. You changed everything and made our lives safe again.'

'I never wanted any attention or these powers,' Finn said.

'I know you hate being the centre of things but you're stuck with your abilities. Get over it. Embrace it. So, do you have any beer?'

He fancied something stronger and lifted a bottle of single malt out of the cupboard and grabbed two small glasses. 'This will hit the spot better, Rose won't mind.'

'Good man. What happens now?' Joe asked.

'Dad showed me the memory of his attack. One of them was Michael, Logan Connelly's cousin from Ireland. I met him last year when they beat me up. They're all crazy and have this unnatural appetite for violence. What worries me the most is that Joo is messed up in this somehow. It's not like her to disappear without a word and I promised Ellie I'd find her.'

'We can have a look around today if you want,' Joe suggested, sipping the whisky.

'It sounds like a plan. I have to check the house and catch up with Branna anyway, I was planning on going into town later.'

He knew they had something in common, something the Connellys had stolen from both of them. The only difference was that Joe had known his mother before her untimely death. Thinking he needed to fully trust him, Finn decided to open up.

'Growing up in London I didn't know anyone with abilities apart from my father who never told me anything. I deliberately didn't make any friends but Bastian was always there for me. He was the only person I could really talk to. I've never had the confidence to share my true self with normal people. No one would understand and it would sound completely alien to them.'

'You also weren't yourself for a long time,' Joe added.

'How much did Bastian tell you?'

'After you went to New York, he got us together in case there was ever any more trouble. He knew you wouldn't approve and he wasn't wrong, was he? No bother, he told me not to listen to you too much. He said to not take 'no' for an answer.'

Finn frowned. 'He can be so cocky and has a foghorn for a mouth.'

'He said you're different now,' Joe smiled. 'With the curse gone, you're a new man so everything's bound to be weird.'

'I get confused but I can always forgive Bastian. It's all jumbled up at times. Ellie told me you lost family to the Connellys.'

'We *all* did,' Joe sighed. 'You made St Ives safe again for a while. It was something we all wanted to do.'

'What are your abilities?' He asked.

'I have heightened senses and brilliant eye sight. I can run fast, astral plane at will and have telepathy. My telekinesis is quite basic. Serina has abilities similar to yours, although it stopped developing years ago. It looks like yours hasn't.'

'What does that mean?'

'I don't know. All I know is what *we* can do. It's different for every family. I can put people to sleep by using my mind. It comes in handy late at night in the pub when some of the older folk get too much.'

'You don't?' He smiled.

'Only once, but don't tell Serina, she'd kill me. Have you thought about planing to the Parsonage?'

'No,' he replied.

'From what I hear they don't plane themselves. You could always do it from our barn, they would never know where your body is. I'll come with you.'

'I don't want to go there,' he insisted.

'How about later when it gets dark?'

'You're not going to give up, are you?'

'You never know, we might even find out what they're up to,' Joe said.

'I must check with Ellie first.'

'I'm sure she'll be alright,' Joe said. 'Have you decided on a name for the boy?'

'The baby's name? We both like Sam. Samuel is a good name, after my grandfather.'

'We can drink to that,' Joe poured another whisky and they toasted the baby's name. 'To Sam Milton.'

'Thanks Joe.' He resigned himself to accepting his help.

'What for?'

'I don't know,' he said. 'You surprised me, I never expected to meet people like you.'

'Don't think for one minute you're moving here and intending on living the life of a hermit, like your old man. That isn't going to happen, far from it. You're completely outnumbered. We'll be dragging you out on a weekly basis. We're all different and great company as you'll learn in time.'

Bastian had always surrounded himself with a tight bunch of friends. He had never stopped to wonder if they were gifted: Joe, Jerry, Simon and Serina's brother Tom. He had brushed shoulders with them all down the years on odd occasions but failed to remember any of them well.

Joe added, 'Bastian said you weren't shy of a tipple and he was right. I think you'll fit in with us.'

Serina came back and joined them at the table.

'Is she alright?' Finn asked.

'She's asleep,' she said. 'You need to keep her stress levels to a minimum. Ellie's got a lot on her plate with the baby and none of this is helping.'

'I'm not handling this very well,' he said.

'She was shocked by your confession but she's fine,' she said. 'So, what did I miss boys?'

He glanced at Joe and found him smiling. He explained about going to St Ives and planing to the Parsonage from their barn later on.

'I'll stay with Ellie until Rose gets back from Penzance if you want. Why don't you head off? It gets dark early,' she suggested. 'I'll explain everything to Ellie when she wakes up.'

'Let's take your car, Finn,' Joe said. 'Did you know Joo was missing?'

'No, I didn't,' Serina replied.

'We haven't been able to reach her. I hope she's not mixed up in this,' Finn said. 'It feels like it's happening again. Every time I come back it's the same story.' The phone began to ring and the receiver instantly flew across the room into his waiting hand. 'Hello?'

'Finn? It's Branna.'

'How are things with you?' He asked.

'As strange as ever. Finn, are you coming to St Ives today? I need to see you urgently.'

'I'm about to leave Penberth.'

'How quickly can you get to my place? I don't want to tell you anything over the phone.'

'I'll be with you in less than an hour.'

'Great, I wish it was good news, see you soon, bye Finn.' Branna rang off leaving him feeling a little subdued by her message.

'So it's settled. Come on, let's go,' Joe said brightly. 'I'll leave you the car, Darling.'

'Let's hope you find some answers,' Serina said.

Finn started up the Audi and turned it around by the time Joe closed the door to the cottage.

'Everything alright?' Joe asked as they set off.

'Yeah, I really hope we find Joo,' he said. 'I couldn't care less about the Connellys. I'm not looking forward to what Branna has to say. It didn't sound too good.'

'Joo means a lot to you, doesn't she?' Joe asked.

'She's like a sister to me, although I probably wouldn't say it to her face. There have been times when we've been there for each other and she means the world to Ellie. They've been best friends since they were kids. She means a lot to both of us.'

6

impression

Finn parked the rental car in front of a large converted barn, detached in its own grounds. Originally part of an old farm, it was surrounded by a meadow garden framed with pine trees and bursting with wild flowers and grasses.

'This is our place,' Joe said. 'What do you think?'

'It's brilliant.' Finn replied.

He had never stepped inside a barn conversion before and was impressed by the rich and thorough use of seasoned oak everywhere. The main room had a ceiling of curved and knotted exposed roof beams. The aroma was intoxicating. A small fitted modern kitchen hardly used up any space on one side. A dining area led to a round sunken lounge flanked by a custom-made glass conservatory. It was roomy and designed for comfort.

'Serina made all the plans. She's an amazing architect. We bought the land a few years ago when the barn was derelict. It was in a right state, but we managed to do most of the work ourselves. I'm a dab hand with wood and handled the interior. We only moved in a few weeks ago.'

'Where did you live before?'

'When Mum died, we sold the cottage in The Digey and moved to Carbis Bay for a while. Serina and I have been together since we were teenagers. We always wanted to move back but never thought it would actually happen. It was the Connelly turf for so long, it's hard to believe they're not here anymore. You can actually go out at night without the fear of running into one of them.'

'Logan and Jared are gone,' he said, 'but I'm not so sure about the others.'

'How did Logan die?'

'Branna killed him.'

'No way,' Joe was enraptured. 'There's more to that bird than meets the eye.'

'You have no idea. Branna stopped Logan from coming after us,' he explained. 'We owe her our lives. I hate to think what would've happened otherwise. It could've turned out differently. We ought to go as she's expecting me and it sounded important.'

'Another little warrior woman, I can't wait to meet her. You must show me the kitchen you demolished with Jared Connelly. I've heard all about it.'

Joe seemed to know everything. Finn shrugged his shoulders, buttoned up his jacket and pulled on a black beanie hat. 'I didn't have time to fix it up before we left last October. It's in a right state.' They began the walk down the hill into town.

'When are you and Ellie getting hitched?'

'When she's ready,' he replied. 'She wants to wait until the baby comes.'

'But you'd rather do it sooner,' Joe said.

'I would do it tomorrow if she'd agree.'

'After we've sorted out this mess and kicked these fools out of town, we can pitch in and organize something amazing at short notice.'

He smiled. 'Thanks Joe, it's the mess I'm not looking forward to. I can't really focus on a wedding. That's a plan we've put on ice for the moment.'

'Since the people of St Ives have had a taste of what it's like to live without the Connellys, they're not going to accept any more of them moving in,' Joe said. 'I can promise you that.'

'Let's hope there aren't too many of them.'

'Indeed,' Joe added.

They approached the old pottery near Ayr Lane and Finn tapped on the front door. A moment later Branna opened it and embraced him immediately.

Falling over one shoulder, her black hair was tied back in a long loose plait. Dressed casually in a long black skirt and white shirt, she wore nothing on her feet. There was a new gold band on her left hand and a thick gold bracelet on her right.

'Come in,' she said softly to both of them. 'It's great to see you, Finn. I trust you had a productive time of it in New York.'

'Yes I did thanks, the best part was being with Ellie. Branna, meet Joe Praed. He's one of Bastian's friends and wants to help us. You can trust him.'

'Nice to meet you, Joe,' she said, reading his mind. 'Another ace planer. That might come in handy.'

Joe shook her hand. 'Branna.'

She went ahead and made a pot of tea and they alighted to the lounge, sitting on a large leather sofa around a coffee table carved and polished from a sliced trunk of an oak tree.

'Let me cut to the chase,' she said. 'Michael's looking for Logan and Jared. He's at the Parsonage with his two sons Cillian and Jarlath.'

'He's looking for me too,' he added. 'So, he hasn't tracked *you* down yet?'

'No but I changed my name to Smith when Murray and I wed last month. We also moved house so it might be proving difficult to find me.'

'I had no idea you got married, you're such a dark horse, Branna. You seem very happy,' Finn said.

'We are.' She stroked the gold wedding band. 'I never thought anything like this would happen to me.'

'Branna Smith,' Joe half-smiled but she was wearing a sober expression. 'Bit of a lame name compared to Connelly. Then again, you're not like the others, I can sense that much.'

'I know how unpopular my family were but right now we have work to do,' Branna retorted. 'I had a visit from the ghost of my late grandmother Duana. She told me Michael's kin have a talisman. It was forged for James Connelly, a distant relative but I've never heard of him.'

'How come Duana's not in *Etherea*?' Joe asked. 'She must have been gifted. I thought all gifted souls go there when they die.'

'She committed suicide which disqualifies any association with *Etherea*,' she replied. 'Duana died shortly after my father was born. Sadly, I don't know much about her but I do know that their talisman is a necklace.'

Finn said. 'You're right, I had a vision about it. I guess that's another talisman we need to find then.'

'How long have you been having these visions?' She asked.

'They started in September. Most of them make little sense, but lately they've been extremely vivid.'

'You could do with having a vision about James so we can find out where he fits into the equation,' she said. 'The last thing I want to do is go to Ireland on a research trip.'

'Yeah, you're right, if only I could choose my visions,' he replied with a wry smile. 'How well do you know your cousins?'

'Not very, they were always closer to Jared than me, but Cillian's the one to worry about. He can be unpredictable and has mind control abilities.'

'What kind of mind control?' He was curious and wondered if Cillian was the charmer Dennis referred to in New York. The vision was uttermost in his mind.

'Something happened to you when you were away.' She said intuitively. 'How are you doing that? You've never been able to block me like that before.'

He smiled. 'I met some planers in New York and one of them fixed my telepathy.'

Joe said. 'Serina can read you though.'

'Serina has the ability to read anyone. I haven't even told Ellie about it because I didn't know what to make of it.'

'What happened when you met these planers?' She asked.

'I used to plane around the city once a week, as you would if you lived there. Before we left, I met some spirits in Central Park. There was one called Dennis who can see the future. He recognised me from a vision and he showed it to me. It was mental and I'm still finding it hard to believe.'

'That planer altered your telepathy,' she said.

'He warned me about a charmer who would try and steal my soul light and wield it as a weapon. If this Moth, as he called him, is successful it could be the end of the spiritual world, for everyone.'

'What happened to you after he took all your soul light?' Branna was wearing a concerned expression.

He was always economical with the truth and glanced into her eyes. Nothing got past her. 'I died and Cillian was flanked by loads of Sentries. He killed them all using my soul light. I don't know what happened after that because the vision stopped.'

'This is pretty serious stuff,' Joe said. 'Were you planning on keeping this to yourself? Bastian was right about you. It's no wonder you get into trouble, Finn. Why haven't you mentioned this before?'

'It's been a lot to take in after everything else that's happened to us,' Finn replied. 'It was a vision. It might not happen. It could be fake for all I know.'

Branna sat on the sofa and appeared to be thinking. 'It doesn't sound fake to me.'

'What do you reckon?' Joe asked her.

'Cillian's a charmer,' she said. 'A very astute one.'

'Then we have to keep him away from Finn.' Joe said.

'That might not be so easy,' she said. 'He's looking for him.'

'He hurt my dad and Bastian to get me to come home. Dennis said the Moth would know about my abilities as soon as he met me. He described me as a Flame, something the Moth couldn't resist however hard he tried.'

Branna added, 'Cillian is impulsive, sadistic and self-obsessed.'

'He sounds like great fun, a bit like the rest of his family, present company excluded of course.' Finn responded. 'Joe and I are planning on visiting the Parsonage. We're going to astral plane and see what we can find.'

'You should be very careful,' she said. 'There's more, I'm afraid. That's why I wanted you to come round. I flew over there earlier. I thought I might be able to find the talisman but I was wrong. I should've told you this first really.'

'What is it?' He asked.

'Your friend Joo Williams is being held hostage at the Parsonage. Cillian has her all charmed up like a kipper in my old bedroom. She didn't even recognise me. It was weird, like she was someone else.'

'No way,' he blurted. 'I'm going around there right now to sort this out. I knew something wasn't right. Ellie's been worried sick about her.'

'You can't face Cillian yet,' she said.

'Give me one good reason why, Branna.' Finn was growing angry, his fingers sparking.

'Because he will charm you into submission. First we find the talisman, then we confront them. Without it, we have no chance of beating them. Surely you haven't forgotten what happened last time? Especially if you think he might be after your soul light. You are a sitting duck, Finn.'

He knew she was right. At least they knew where Joo was and that she was in remote danger for the time being.

'How is she?' He wondered how long she had been held captive.

'Totally brain washed,' she replied. 'I don't think Cillian would hurt her but at best, he's unpredictable. The upside is that his charms are incredibly simple to break. If you can get close enough, you only need to plant an older memory in her mind, then she will turn back to normal.'

'Well, you learn something new every day,' Joe said.

'You wouldn't believe how incapacitated you're under a charm, Joe,' she said. 'Most people have no idea how easy they are to break. For now we need to concentrate on finding their talisman. I fear without it we will struggle to beat them at all.'

'I figured they had a talisman so I went to the Lizard portal to ask for help but the Sentries didn't want to know.'

'Sentries cannot detect talismans or cloaks,' she said. 'I can understand their reluctance to even believe you. I'm going to try and contact Duana to see if she can help any further. Trouble is, it's not easy summoning a ghost, especially one that doesn't want to be found. I wish I knew more about James.'

'We need to figure out what to do next,' Finn said.

'You must wait. Whatever happens you must not allow Cillian to read your mind.' She attempted to read his mind and he winced suddenly at the attempted mental intrusion. 'That's impressive, I can't read you.'

'You're so demanding.'

Joe said. 'You should meet my wife, Serina. You two have a lot in common, in the mind department.'

'I look forward to it,' she said. 'Cillian's powerful and the one to watch out for. Michael's a coward although he can wield some form of telekinesis. Jarlath's into martial arts, the last I heard. Either way, they're all dangerous.'

'So there are three of them. Nothing major to worry about.'

Branna rolled her eyes at his naivety and sarcasm. 'I wish that was true, Finn.'

'It sounds too familiar to me,' Joe said, thinking about the demise of his own family. The memory was buried deep in his mind and Joe recoiled when she found it. Her twin brother Jared had murdered his mother when Joe's father had a foul disagreement with him. It was so like her brother to take quiet vengeance and attack the weaker party.

'Joe, I'm sorry about your mother,' she said. 'Jared is gone and no longer a threat to anyone. It disgusts me how my family destroyed lives with their thirst for power.'

'I figured that Finn wouldn't be friends with you if it had been any different,' Joe said, heading for the door. 'I think we should go, Finn, we have a few more things to do today and it's getting late.'

'We need the talisman before anyone else gets hurt,' she said. 'If we destroy the talisman, *Etherea* will take care of them and it'll be over.'

'I need to look up some old friends.' Joe said and they exchanged phone numbers. 'It won't take long to round them up. I'll be in touch if you want to join us. I hope you decide to. It was nice to meet you, Branna. I believe as a whole we have a better chance of defeating them.'

Finn gave Branna a hug and they made their leave. Outside it was beginning to rain and he zipped up his jacket. 'At least we know where Joo is. I need to check on our house next. This is turning out to be a disaster in the making, Mr Praed. Fancy walking up another hill?'

'Lead the way, Mr Milton,' Joe said. 'I can't say visiting Branna was much fun. Your life is crazy, I can't wait to see the state of your kitchen.'

'I'm definitely going to help you out with that kitchen. On the way back to mine, I need to drop off an invoice to a client. I won't be long.' Joe said after they walked away from the house. 'He lives on Barnoon Hill.'

'I'll wait for you outside,' Finn said. "I need a cigarette.'

The sky was growing dark and plump with rain clouds. He looked at the boats below in the harbour, bobbing about in the water. Lights were coming on all along Wharf Road as dusk blended into the night. Two minutes passed and a tall dark haired man approached. He was sure he had seen him somewhere before but the man's mind was blocked to reading him.

'Can you show me the way to Porthgwidden beach?' The request came in a soft and persuasive Irish accent. He closed the space between them like a predator and uttered some words in Latin which were barely distinguishable: *Et dicetis ad me plane aperta et animum. Tu ergo audieritis vocem meam, Finn Milton.*

Finn hadn't sensed the enchantment or heard the spell. It had been too slight of hand. A numb feeling crept over his senses and he could no longer block his mind. The man reminded him of Jared Connelly even though he was taller. He found himself answering him. 'The beach?'

'I'm sure you can show me, you've got plenty of time. I would like to see the Island. It's a shame the weather's on the turn, I was hoping to take some photographs.'

He nodded and began walking down the hill towards Fore Street and the Wharf, with the other man close behind, completely forgetting that he was waiting for Joe. It was like being trapped in a dream state without being able to question the logic of it. His feet were moving as though they were being controlled by something else.

'I'm Cillian but I figured you would know that already, Mr Milton.'

'It's Finn.'

'It's a pleasure to finally meet you, Finn. I've been waiting for you. I hope you had a safe trip back from New York without any unforeseen incidents.'

'Cillian.' He could hardly believe how easily he had been overthrown and already it was too late. His thoughts were sluggish as though they were trapped in thick mud.

'It's incredibly easy to block someone when you're prepared but I prefer to play dirty and slip in through the back door, if you like. This is the only way to handle someone like you. In my position, I'm sure you'd agree with me, Finn.'

He was dazed as a strange new feeling overpowered him. He was unable to question why he was walking away with this stranger. It reminded him of a spell that Branna had cast on him at Godrevy beach when they had been teenagers.

He was unfamiliar with persuasion charms but it wasn't a stretch to master if you knew how to bend your mind. Branna was convinced he could learn but he refused to. Right at that moment, he was incensed at discarding a skill that had instantly nullified his powerful senses.

'What do you want from me, Connelly?'

'Deep down, you know, don't you? Struggling with it, are you? I underestimated you Milton, you have a very interesting mind and I have full control over it. You're very good friends with my cousin Branna. That does interest me. I would very much like to find her. We have a lot of catching up to do.'

'What?'

'This little charm doesn't last for long but it doesn't need to. We need to go somewhere quiet where I can probe your mind while it's locked open.'

'Oh, great.' He was kicking himself for being so unguarded.

'Don't try and resist or it will hurt more than anything you can imagine. You have no idea how much hassle this has caused me. I never wanted to come to Cornwall.'

He could feel the sensation of wet sand crunching under his trainers. They were on Porthgwidden beach and it was pouring with rain. He could feel the wetness on his skin through his sodden clothes. In the distance lightning began to fork over the sea and thunder rumbled. Godrevy Lighthouse appeared shrouded in mist and illuminated when more lightning flared.

The beach was deserted. He could not believe how clever and sly Cillian was. It was dark and there would be no witnesses. 'Stop here! Get down on your knees.'

He fell willingly to his knees and the wet sand seeped through the denim of his jeans. He could feel Cillian dropping two fingers on his forehead. Rain trickled down his face. The coarse grinding sensation in his mind began to intensify when he started to probe him. A trickle of blood fell onto his lip from his nose to be washed away by the rain.

Cillian mind-locked completely and Finn convulsed with no control over anything.

The events of the previous year became clear to the mind reader but the *Etherea* visit had been wiped entirely from his memory. There was the recent visit to the portal where he had asked the Sentries for help but to no avail. A conversation with Branna earlier sparked his interest. She had killed Logan and buried his body in the garden of the Parsonage. Finn could sense him flicking through his memories like he was using a library microfiche.

At first there was a flicker and then it grew into something more. Finn could not conceal the bright soul light existing within his spirit, brimming with soft iridescent colours. He sensed a change in tactic as Cillian began to extract the soul light like a vampire. There was a sharp pain rising in his chest until he grew weaker and lost consciousness.

Although he couldn't see him, Joe was standing a few feet away silently focusing a stream of mental energy. Cillian toppled, landing on the sand with his eyes wide open.

Hastily Joe grabbed Finn's body and threw it over his shoulder with his head lolling down. Blood was running down his face and his eyes were half open. Rain was pelting down in sheets as Joe hurried across the beach towards relative safety.

'Let's get you out of here, mate.' He trudged through the wet sand. 'It's a good job you're not heavy, Milton. It seems I can't leave you on your own either.'

When he reached the car park, Joe was greeted by a loud cawing noise. A huge black bird landed on the tarmac in front of them. She transformed into a striking woman, fully dressed in jeans, jacket, and leather boots. Her long black hair was loose about her shoulders.

Joe couldn't believe it. 'Branna? What the hell are you doing here?'

'I can't explain it,' she said. 'I had a feeling about Finn being in danger so I went out for a flight.'

'There's a strange guy on the beach, he was mind probing him,' Joe explained. 'One minute Finn was waiting for me in town and the next he was gone. I managed to track him here. Luckily, I made them both go to sleep.'

'That's a good trick,' she said. 'I see Cillian didn't waste any time probing him. Finn's unconscious.'

Cillian's body was lying on the beach, several hundred metres away. She withdrew a handkerchief to wipe the blood from Finn's face. Swiftly she touched his forehead and closed her eyes. There was severe tissue damage to his brain, which she healed quickly. He began to regain consciousness, acquiring a splitting headache into the bargain. Their clothes were soaking wet and Finn was shivering.

'Are you okay, Buddy?' Joe was surprised he had woken up so quickly.

'I don't know what happened.' He rubbed his eyes.

'Cillian charmed you,' she said.

'He was stealing my soul light,' he said on remembering. 'It's started. Everything Dennis showed me is going to happen. Cillian knows you killed Logan. I couldn't stop him.'

'It was only a matter of time before he learnt the truth.' She said. 'Don't blame yourself. You need to talk to your father about soul light. I knew it would come up at some point and it's too important now.'

'Why?'

'Because it's time you understood what it means.'

'How do you know all this stuff? Why am I always the last to know?'

'I can see you're annoyed but it isn't my place to explain it to you, Finn. It's your family's inherited power, not mine.'

'Are you talking about that glow you have?' Joe asked.

He rolled his eyes and stood up shakily. 'I've always had it. I don't know what it is but your cousin certainly does and he wants it for himself.' He tried to walk but was unsteady and stumbled. His eyesight was fuzzy and he felt light-headed.

'You could do with sleeping that off,' she suggested. 'He put Bastian in hospital with that trick.'

'I think you're right,' he said. 'I don't feel so good.'

'Why don't we head over to your dad's place?' Joe suggested. 'You can rest there for a bit and it might give you a chance to talk to him about soul light.'

'Yeah.' he said, 'I think you're right. Thanks for your help, both of you. I do appreciate it. I'll keep you in the loop from now on, I promise.'

Branna added. 'Be patient and we'll sort this together. The sooner we get that talisman the better chance we have of bringing Joo home safely.'

Finn was absolutely exhausted when he arrived at September Cottage. Joe left him at the door and headed back to the barn. His father heard him come in but didn't rise from his desk. He was soaked to the skin and his shirt was stained with blood. He headed straight for the downstairs bathroom. His headache was thumping so he took some painkillers. His nose was still bleeding and he tried stuffing it with tissues.

'I wasn't expecting you back so soon. Everything okay?'

He was removing his shirt and inspecting his face in the mirror not wanting to explain.

'What the hell happened to you?' His father demanded from the open doorway. 'Were you caught out in the rain?'

'I was out in town and ended up being probed by that bastard Cillian Connelly on Porthgwidden Beach. Fortunately Branna and Joe were there to stop him. Another fun day out for me in St Ives. This place never ceases to amaze me. What have you been up to?'

'Me? I'm fine,' he replied. 'I'm more concerned about you. You're soaking wet.'

'I've got some spare clothes in my room. Branna fixed me up after the mind probe. I only got away because Joe turned up and made us both go to sleep. But Dad, this is far worse. Branna flew to the Parsonage. The Connellys have kidnapped Joo. They've put a spell on her to forget who she is.'

'Sit down, Finn. You're making me nervous. You need to rest after that kind of attack,' he was rolling his eyes. 'One thing at a time and slowly this time.'

'That's why I came here. I didn't fancy driving to Penberth feeling like this.'

'Your nose is bleeding.'

'I know,' he said, pinching it between his fingers. 'It won't stop.'

'And you're blocking me,' Milton added.

'That's something I acquired in New York. Cillian Connelly knows about my soul light. I think you do as well and it's high time you told me everything you know about it. I need to understand what it is so that I can defend myself.'

His father was frowning. The memory of his beloved wife Phoebe dying had consumed him. 'Okay son, if that's what you want. Now is as good a time as any.'

'So you *do* know something,' he said.

'I suppose you can call it that but I kept it from you because it scares the crap out of me. Besides, you never asked me about it.

When your mother was seven years old, her grandfather Kingsley, wanted his two grandchildren to visit him on his deathbed. He chose Phoebe because she was his favourite. Her brother Robert never knew anything about it at the time and he still doesn't know. Before he died, he passed the soul light entity onto your mother. Apparently it's easy to move it into a child because they can absorb it easily. From adult to adult, it invariably leads to death. It's incredibly rare for soul light to be found, never mind in humans. It's raw spiritual energy, making the host powerful if they chose to wield it like a weapon.

'When you attacked Jared at Eternia Cottage last year, you used it to shatter his bones. I saw you doing it. You must have been angry because it made you stronger. In the wrong hands, it can cause a huge amount of damage. Most people can't contain it. You were a perfect genetic match for your mother so she passed it on to you before she died. Had she not done so, she'd have been forced into servitude as a Sentry guard. This is what separates you from other gifted spirits. All Sentries have soul light energy, but you have possibly many times what you would normally find in a Sentry. On its own, it's an ability but only if it resides in a mortal that's good and pure. Unfortunately when your mother died, she lost part of her soul when she gave it to you and she never went to *Etherea*.'

'What do you mean? Is she a ghost?'

'I don't think so,' he replied. 'I've never seen her. In this instance, she became a shadow – not a full spirit. It's anyone's guess what happened to her.'

'And you knew this and never told me?'

'How am I supposed to tell you that, Finn? You're my son. One day soon, you'll become a father. I hope like hell you have a better time of it than I did. I lost my best friend and my soul mate. I never wanted to tell you what happened because I have never come to terms with it myself. It still haunts me and I can see her face in you all the time.'

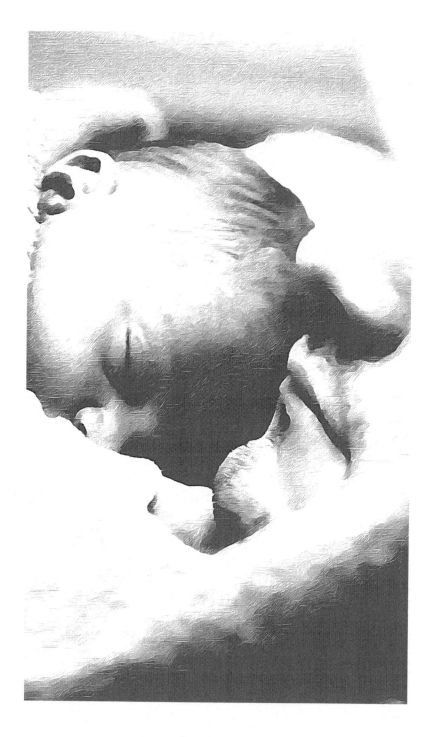

7

~~~

a living thing

August 1966

Finlay Milton was gardening outside with his wife Phoebe when the contractions started. They were pottering away in the pretty courtyard of a fisherman's cottage.

It was late afternoon when the young woman bent over crippled with abdominal pain. Finlay dropped his secateurs. Deadheading the dahlias would have to wait.

'Phoebe, Darling – are you alright?' He asked.

'It's the baby,' she said, and her waters broke. 'It's definitely on its way.'

'It looks like he's coming earlier than we thought,' he held her arm to steady her. 'I'll call the midwife, she'll be here in ten minutes.'

'The longest ten minutes of my life,' she said, creasing her eyes. 'Finlay, what have you done to me? How do you know it's going a boy?'

Finlay looked at his beautiful wife with bewilderment. 'I can sense it's a boy. I've always known. Come on let's get you inside.'

Soon a young midwife called Maryanne arrived, by which time Phoebe was already exhausted and soaking with sweat.

The midwife moved her into a better position on the bed and checked her over thoroughly. She instructed Finlay to boil some water and readied Phoebe for the imminent birth.

'He's coming,' Maryanne said softly. 'You are fully dilated. Are you staying for the birth, Professor Milton?'

'Of course I am,' he replied. 'I'm not missing this.'

Phoebe's long blonde hair was tied back and sweat was running down her face. It was a humid August night and the windows were wide open. The harbour was bathed in the fading pinks and blues of the sunset.

'I need you to breathe, Phoebe, like we showed you in the classes,' Maryanne said gently. 'It's going to be quick.'

She took short breaths, while he held her hand tightly. Her expression dulled and she looked into his eyes. 'Finlay, something's not right.'

'Hang on, Sweetheart. It'll be all over in a minute.'

'One big push,' Maryanne said. 'I can see the head.'

She pushed with all her might, the pain crippling her with every contraction. When the baby finally slid into the midwife's hands, Phoebe heard crazy, maniacal laughing. But no one else heard it. Finlay was reading her mind and something was seriously wrong. The newborn was wrapped in a soft blue blanket and passed into his mother's waiting hands.

'It's a boy,' Maryanne said. 'Congratulations to both of you. You did really well, Phoebe.'

'Look at him Finlay, he's my gift to you, Darling,' she said. 'You were right, we have a son. Isn't he perfect?'

He kissed her. 'Of course he's perfect, he looks just like you. What shall we call him, Sweetheart?'

'Finn George ... I don't feel so good.' She began to pass in and out of consciousness.

'Phoebe?' Maryanne checked her pulse.

As soon as the midwife realised she was deteriorating she hurriedly left the room to call the doctor. Finlay lifted the baby into his arms and studied his tiny face briefly before staring at his ailing wife.

Briefly she opened her eyes. With hardly any energy left, she said, 'I love you so much. I can't stop what's happening to me but I can protect him. Hold him up Finlay, please.'

He read her mind and his worst fears were confirmed.

She was dying.

It was all he could do to watch her slip away.

'You'll always be a shadow if you do this, Phoebe. Just because you *can* doesn't mean you should. You don't have to pass on this ability – not like this – not to our son.'

'Our son may need it one day, it's my way of being there for him. Part of me can live on in the soul light. You knew I would do this if I checked out before you. It will never hurt Finn. No one else can survive the process. I have to try or they'll force me to become a Sentry with this much power. My grandfather would've never given me the soul light, without good reason. I know everything is going to be fine. I had a vision. This way Finn can be more than you can ever imagine.'

'Vision or not, I can imagine a lot and I don't like it. Kingsley has a lot to answer for.' He was angry. 'Does this have to happen right now? Can't you wait sixty years and we can slip off together? I can't lose you Phoebe, not now, not like this – it just isn't fair!'

Phoebe: *Finlay, please don't cry.*

Finlay: *Phoebe, I love you.*

Phoebe: *I love you too.*

Tears were falling down her face as an arch of iridescent light began to pour out of her chest. For a moment the room was filled with bright light, made up of many colours, swaying like joined particles in the air. It glistened towards the baby where it began to disappear inside its body. Suddenly Phoebe's body slumped back and her spirit emerged – the detail derailing her husband.

He ran his hand through her and she came apart and back together again. She was perfect in every aspect until she began to fade. It happened so quickly and then she disappeared. The loving smile in her eyes would haunt him for years to come. He dropped to his knees and cried his heart out. Safe in his arms, the baby lay silently, not making a sound.

Returning to the room, Maryanne lifted baby Finn into her arms.

'She's gone,' he whispered with tears falling down his face. 'My Phoebe has gone. She was so healthy. What am I supposed to do now?'

'I'm so sorry, Mr Milton,' she said. 'The doctor is on his way. Is there anything I can do?'

'The boy, can you take care of him for me, just for a little while? I need some time with my wife.'

'Of course, we'll take care of everything. I can't believe it,' she said with sadness. 'This one's a little bruiser.'

'Thank you,' he whispered, grabbing a glimpse of his son, who was sucking his thumb. His crown of thick hair was almost white, similar to Phoebe's. His eyes were pale grey and he was watching his father intently.

Maryanne cared for Finn and left the young English major alone in the bedroom. The bright young woman had died so suddenly without any apparent reason.

He sat in shock rocking his wife's body in his arms, stroking her blonde hair and kissing her forehead. Her body was limp and unresponsive. There was an eerie atmosphere and he was breathless. They had been married less than a year. She had been only twenty-one years old. The child represented everything that was left of her. Something profoundly deep was shattering inside him and it hurt with a resounding passion. Finlay Milton was inconsolable as part of his soul died along with her.

1997

Finn empathised over the terrible burden his father had carried. He could finally come to terms with how she had died.

'I have lived with this for over thirty years. Did you think it was easy for me *not* tell you about your mother? I know it's inconvenient having this soul light but you're stuck with it. It was your mother's last wish. You can learn to control it but at the end of the day you should only use it for self-defence, Finn, nothing more. You have got to find a way of embracing it.'

'My mother knew how to move it into me. What did she use it for?'

'Your mother was a brilliant surfer and she used it in the water. Funny as it sounds, she was amazing. She used to glow, like you do, except you don't hide it so well. Branna and I talked about this while you were in New York. She would only discuss it with you once I explained it. I wish I knew more. I have no idea how Kingsley inherited it or where it came from.'

He was feeling uncomfortable. 'What happens if Cillian takes it all?'

'It will probably kill him.'

'But what will happen to me? If it broke my mother's spirit surely it will do the same thing to me.'

'I don't know anyone other than Branna who can possibly help with this now. I'm at a loss of what to tell you. It would be prudent to keep him away from you. Every time he takes it from you, it will make you weaker. Who would've thought someone like that would exist? He's like a vampire.'

'Branna's busy finding a ghost,' he said. 'I left Ellie in Penberth this morning in a right state. None of this is doing her any good. At least she's not on her own.'

'What are you going to do?'

'Joo is the priority now,' he said brightly. 'I hope she's alright. I must phone Ellie. She's not going to be too happy when I tell her where she is. I can't believe the day I'm having.'

⁓

Michael was sitting in one of the upright chairs reading a newspaper, boredom seeping through his pores like acid. The Parsonage was doing nothing to improve his mood.

'I'm not sure it was wise sending that note to the Praeds, Cillian.'

'Why?' He was picking at the skin around his fingernails. 'It's about time we got moving with this and I want to go home.'

Since the defeat on the beach he was itching to get his hands on Finn again. He longed to know more about the mysterious soul light. The feeling in his veins was new and he wanted more of it. He cared less about the consequences even though it was changing him.

His father had been cruel when he returned with the news of having found Finn and then subsequently losing him. He had received a solid punch in the face and had resisted the urge to thump him back. A bruise was forming on his cheek below the left eye. He thought of utilising the soul light and it began to heal, much to his surprise.

'What are you intending on doing with that strange woman upstairs?' Jarlath asked. 'She's got abilities, including telepathy and planing. I think you're making a big mistake. She could ruin everything.'

'I may take her with me when we head home,' he replied. 'Or I may not. She's so easy to bend and she amuses me.'

'What if it wears off?' His brother asked.

'It won't,' he said. 'She thinks she's in love with me.'

'You're crazy,' Michael said. 'You could have any woman you want and you go for that pixie?'

'She's cute and I like small women.'

'You make her sound like a toy,' Jarlath said. 'I don't think Mam will approve when you rock up with her.'

'Mam has nothing to do with this. Juliet's only here to lure Milton. When he gets here I'm going to torture him.' He smirked at his brother. 'It will be worth all the hassle, I assure you.'

'It's no more than he deserves,' Michael said. 'I can't believe Branna killed Logan. She'll pay for what she's done. When I get my hands on her, I'll kill her too. She deceived her own father and killed him in cold blood.'

'We're so close now,' he added. 'Jarlath, I want you to stay with Juliet until I call for you. I need him inside the house and then he'll be mine. He has no idea what I'm capable of and has forgotten most of his abilities. Milton will be a walkover because of how much he cares for her. As soon as I have full control of him, it will be over.'

'I hope you're right, brother,' Jarlath said.

'I'm always right, Jarlath.'

~~

When he phoned Eternia Cottage, there was no reply so he decided to call Joe at the barn, who picked up the phone right away.

'Hello Finn, how are you feeling? I was about to phone you.'

'I'm still at my dad's,' he replied. 'I'm feeling much better besides a nose bleed from hell. Have you heard from Serina?'

'The girls have gone out for a drive along the coast.'

'Oh okay.'

'She's in good hands,' Joe added. 'You don't have to worry. By the way, a few of the others are coming round shortly, I would like you to meet them.'

He dropped the receiver back in its cradle and glanced at his father. 'Joe's gathering some friends at his place so we can rescue Joo.'

'That sounds like a more sensible approach.' Milton said.

'I guess. I wish I could control the soul light better then I could stop him from taking it.'

'You only have to remember one thing: focus your energy for control. There's nothing you can't do when you are focused. You will be surprised what you can simply command from your thoughts. Maybe you can practise this at the barn. You're doing the right thing and soon Joo will be home.'

'I must adopt some of your optimism, Dad.'

When the front door of the barn opened, his curly haired cousin appeared wearing a big grin.

'How are you? I heard about what happened at the beach. It looks like Cillian Connelly has it in for both our brains.'

'I've had better days, Bastian. You look better than you did yesterday,' he responded.

'I'm feeling a lot better. Come in.' Bastian led the way into the circular sunken lounge. 'What are your immediate plans?'

'I'm back for good aside from fighting off any Connellys,' he said. 'I missed your sense of humour too much.'

'I suppose it does feel good having you here, even if you are a trouble magnet.'

He frowned at his cousin whose expression melted into a smile as he presented some of his oldest friends.

Joe was first to greet him. 'We can help you with your abilities, Finn, but first, we need some introductions.'

It wasn't easy to drop his guard because he wasn't used to it – especially around unfamiliar people with abilities. It was clear they wanted nothing from him but being the centre of attention pushed him out of his comfort zone.

'This is Simon Nancarrow, his brother Jerry will be here soon,' Joe explained. 'Jerry works at the bank. He can't stay long but he's dying to meet you.'

Simon Nancarrow was thirty-five years old, with dark brown hair and a tall athletic frame. A gifted surgeon, he lived in a large cottage in The Digey with his wife Chloe and their young son Toby. Raised single-handedly by their mother, Simon and Jerry were very close. They lost their father to Logan Connelly.

'Simon works with me at Treliske.' Bastian said. 'He's a bit of a wizard.'

'I think you drove us to a beach party once.' He shook Simon's hand.

'Yep, that was me. I thought you might have forgotten about that,'

'Not likely.' He remembered that night clearly as though it was imprinted on his mind. Fourteen years ago he met Branna Connelly and her brother Jared for the first time.

'Simon can produce lightning and can move very fast. We're all telepathic.' Joe said. 'And this is Tom Ellery.'

Tom was Serina's brother. Originally from St Ives, Bastian had known Tom since junior school. He had a black belt in karate and was a car mechanic. Married to Willow, they had two young children, Winter and Charlie. His crown was covered in blond hair and he looked like his sister.

'I think we'll get along, we seem to have a lot in common,' Tom said. 'Good to meet you, Finn.'

'It's only Jerry and Branna left. They can play catch up when they get here. Come on Finn, show us what you've got,' Joe pressed. 'I've set up a range in the garden.'

The meadow was neatly fringed with maples, pines and beech trees. It was drizzling and the light was fading. In the distance storm clouds were brewing. Joe had placed half a dozen used cans on a boundary fence. They all stood back as he closed his eyes and searched for his power.

Thinking about his father's words, he focused on striking all six objects at the same time. A stream of pure white energy flew from his hands. It felt stronger than anything he could recall. It sent the cans flying several hundred feet beyond. The force pushed the fence making it totter back and forth.

No one said a word when he turned around. Joe's mouth was wide open in shock. Tom and Simon looked surprised. For the first time he was sated. There had never been anywhere to practise such a dangerous ability. It hadn't scared him as much as he had anticipated.

'What was that?' Joe asked.

'Stand back.' He focused on releasing an invisible energy wave and held his hands outwards, his eyes fixed on the fence panel. The invisible wave flew towards the fence, lifted it from its posts and deposited it far into the next field.

'Holy shit, Finn. You'd better stop that now,' Joe said.

'Sorry about your fence. I'll get it fixed. I can definitely work with this now.'

'Don't apologise.' Joe gasped. 'Can you do bolts as well?'

'They're pretty lethal,' he was beginning to enjoy himself with his captive audience. Opening his palm a large glowing ball of white energy formed which floated above his fingers.

Concentrating hard, he propelled it upwards where it hung like a weightless white orb thirty feet above their heads. He caught a glimpse of their expressions before commanding it to explode into a wide arch made up of hundreds of white sparks.

'No more wasting money on fireworks.' A Cornish accent interrupted the moment and everyone turned to look. 'That's pretty impressive for a local lad.'

With shoulder length dark shaggy hair tied back in a tail and piercing blue eyes, Jerry Nancarrow owned a charm filled intensity brimming with self-confidence. He was decked out in a navy blue tailored suit and tie.

'Jerry,' Bastian said cheerily.

'Bastian! Look at you, buddy.' He slapped Bastian on the back and hugged him. 'Magic man, back from the dead. How on earth did you get out of that coma? They're going mad at the hospital, they think you've been abducted by aliens.'

'I had some special help from Branna,' Bastian replied. 'You do exaggerate sometimes. Finn, meet Jerry Nancarrow, bank manager extraordinaire.'

'I knew it had to be you. Impressive bolt, Finn.' Jerry offered him a firm handshake. 'Nice to finally meet the legend.'

He managed a brief smile unsure of what to say. Jerry's blue eyes were wide open with anticipation. 'So what did I miss? What happened to your fence, Joe? It looks a bit fubar to me.'

'Finn was giving us a demonstration before you arrived,' Joe said.

'He wrecked the fence?' Jerry asked. 'Now I *am* impressed. We've heard so much about you. I didn't fully believe in it until now but you're the real deal.'

Finn found the attention strange and sensed the black haired woman walking across the grass, dressed in a dark green linen jacket, long skirt and leather boots. Her hair was tied back. He smiled and gave her a warm hug. 'I can't thank you enough for saving my life again.'

'I need to help you moderate your abilities so you can control them better,' she said softly. 'You spoke with your father.'

'Yes, he explained soul light as best he could.'

'Moderate?' Bastian asked. 'What does that mean?'

'It means he'll be able to focus more accurately, more precisely than ever before,' she said. 'And he's still evolving.'

They were all staring at her. Even though Bastian had explained her part in defeating the Connellys, they remembered her family and their ways with terror. They all shared the same feeling of uncertainty. The fear was bubbling under the surface.

'My cousins have kidnapped Joo and they are holding her prisoner in the Parsonage,' she said. 'When I found her, she didn't recognise me because she's under a spell.'

'They want me and that's why they snatched her.' Finn added. 'They're using her as bait.'

'This was in the door when I arrived.' Jerry was holding up a folded piece of paper. 'It looks like they want an exchange.'

'Who's it from?' Branna asked.

'It says: *We have Juliet. If you want to see her alive make sure Milton presents himself by 7 pm at the Parsonage.*

'You can't go there, Finn.' Joe said. 'They'll kill you.'

'We don't know that for sure.' Simon added.

'That parasite tried to kill him on the beach. I saw him probing his mind.' Joe said. 'It's too risky.'

'I agree,' Branna said.

'We can't leave Joo there either,' Finn added. 'I have to go and get her. What choice do I have?'

'There has to be another way.' Bastian protested.

'If anything happens, we'll break into the house and spring you both,' Tom said. 'There's probably more of us than them.'

'I don't like it,' she said. 'Cillian's worse than Jared and I should know. I tried getting close to her but it was no good. She's been brain washed by one of Cillian's spells. He has complete control over her. I could break it if I could get close enough. You need to plant a familiar memory in her mind from a time before the charm was placed, using an older memory of Joo's. It's that simple.'

Joe said. 'Then Joo has no idea what's going on.'

'We've got to do something to help her,' Jerry said. 'I must go back to work and close up for the day, even though this is far more important. I'll come back at six. We need to regroup. I don't like the idea of Joo being in danger. If there's anything I can do to help, count me in.'

'Me too. I have to go but I'll be back with Jerry later.' Simon said.

There was a growing sense of intense concern among the group and Finn could not help but wonder what was going to happen later. All he could think about was rescuing Joo and bringing her home. The prospect of meeting Cillian again was upmost in his mind.

'You're going to go over there, aren't you?' Bastian looked at him.

'They'll know if I don't turn up alone. I can't leave her there.'

'I can plane along side you when you leave,' Joe suggested. 'I can be invisible.'

'Okay,' he said. 'But I don't know what we're going to do if Joo doesn't want to leave.'

'We have to get her out of there no matter what state she's in,' Jerry said. 'We can worry about the details later. Like you said, the charm is simple to break. We just need to get close enough to break it.'

～

Finn stayed with Joe for the remainder of the afternoon. He finally reached Ellie on the phone before Simon and Jerry arrived. 'How are you feeling? I've had a mad day.'

'I'm feeling much better,' she replied. 'We went on a drive to Porthgwarra for some fresh air. We seemed to escape the rain. Any news about Joo?'

He decided not to tell her about the aggressive encounter on Porthgwidden Beach. She was too fragile. Telling her about Joo was bad enough.

'It isn't good I'm afraid, Darling. Branna found Joo when she flew to the Parsonage earlier. The Connellys are holding her. They want me to go there tonight. It's looking like the only way to get her out of there is to find out what they want.'

'Oh heavens, no Finn. Has she been there the whole time?'

'I think so but it's different this time. I can fight. Since I saw you earlier, Dad has helped me to focus on my soul light. It makes more sense now. I've been practising in Joe's garden.'

'I couldn't bear to lose you after everything we've been through.'

'Hey, it's going to be alright,' he said. 'It has to be.'

'I know what that family did to you, they nearly killed you,' she stressed. 'I couldn't handle it if they hurt Joo as well.'

'I'm not going to let Joo down, I promise. I can't believe everything that's happened since we got back.'

'We haven't even unpacked and I've got loads of stuff at Eternia. Finn, I need to go home.'

'Soon, baby. How did we get so disorganized?'

'We? And I thought it was *you* all this time.' She said.

He knew she was only trying to lighten the mood. Talking about inane things seemed to help for a moment. 'I'm going to the Parsonage at seven.'

'You sound different,' she said.

'I think it's finally settled. I've finally got my mojo back. I thought I was going mad.'

'I can't read you anymore,' she said.

'I have to be able to block my mind. It's the only thing standing between me and that crazy fruit loop. By the way, I met the posse earlier.'

'They're a good bunch of people.'

'I'll bring Joo to Penberth later tonight. I have to do this, you do understand, don't you?'

'Just be careful, Darling. I love you so much.'

'I love you too.' He said goodbye, feeling drained but optimistic. With an hour to go before he was due at the Parsonage, he was feeling more concerned about Cillian.

He walked up the road alone. It was dark but he knew the way to the Connelly home, it wasn't something he could easily forget. Soon the tatty old house began to stand out from the others. Set back from the road and detached, it threw up a large gravelled driveway with dark ivy spreading across the brickwork. The spidery trees were coated in layers of dying ivy. A once grand house abandoned and bleeding with neglect.

He determined to escape with Joo. In truth he had no idea what was going to happen. He kept his resolve, rescuing her was what mattered. Joe had planed ahead and was waiting by the front door when he stepped onto the drive. His spirit was briefly visible when Finn knocked on the large wooden door.

Michael appeared and he recalled the last time he had been there. It had been a brutal experience. Although Michael was barely in the same power league as his cousin Logan, he was keeping his mind blocked shut all the same.

'Why don't you come in?' Michael said, looking past to check he flying solo. 'You came alone?'

'That's what you wanted, isn't it?' He replied coldly.

'This doesn't have to be complicated.'

He stepped into the hall and felt the cold damp air. Cillian was standing a few feet away with a gaze directed entirely at him. He remembered their earlier encounter but couldn't read either of them. Their eyes tore into him like needles. 'I've only come here for Joo.'

'Cillian, bring the girl downstairs.' Michael said.

'Why don't you come into the lounge, Finn?'

As he followed Michael from the hall, he felt sick as the memory consumed him: being beaten, kicked and sliced with a knife. He thought: *I can't do this.*

'If you want Juliet to live, you'll do as we say.' Michael shoved him into the middle of the lounge. There was hardly any furniture and there was dust everywhere. A sliver of sunlight crossed the room, leaving patterns in the air.

'I didn't kill Jared or Logan. I never meant for anyone to die.' He said.

'Because of you, they're both dead,' Michael said. 'Now sit down, Milton. This won't take long. I want you to understand there are consequences for messing with my family.'

He sat down on of the chairs but didn't feel comfortable. All the while he watched Michael and clenched his fists. He could sense Joe's spirit nearby. It encouraged him having him close even though he knew he couldn't do much to physically help him.

It took several minutes before Cillian emerged with Joo who looked radically different. She was wearing a long skirt and a white blouse, strange attire for someone twice her age. Her feet were bare, her hair flattened and she was wearing a vacant expression.

With no make up, she looked directly at him with an air of confusion. There was no trace of recognition at all. He was a complete stranger to her.

'Joo, are you alright?' He asked.

'Who are you?' She replied with another question.

'It's me … Finn.'

She shook her head, growing more uncomfortable.

'Do you want to take her away?' Cillian asked before leaning down to whisper in her ear. 'Juliet, do you want to leave with this man? Do you want to know how many members of our family that he's murdered in cold blood?'

'Murdered?' Her expression changed.

'He's lying to you. Don't believe him. It's not true.' He protested. 'What have you done to her?'

'Milton, it's no use,' Cillian said. 'Juliet's made up her mind and I agree with her. Murder is a heinous crime.'

'Release her from this spell, Connelly, immediately.' He insisted. 'You can't do this kind of thing.'

'Juliet's life is of no importance to me. She has fulfilled her task. You're here. That's all that matters.' Cillian let go of her hand and calmly approached him. 'She can leave right now if she wants to. She's always been free to leave.'

Finn felt a chill run up his spine. He was weighing up how he could contain the potentially volatile situation. Michael was watching although uninvolved. His eldest son Cillian was an unknown quantity and was taking the lead. He wondered who exactly was in charge.

'I need to finish what I started or my brother Jarlath will kill her,' Cillian said. 'Do you understand?'

He turned around to witness a third man with his hand fixed firmly around Joo's throat. Cillian was staring transfixed at him as though he was his next meal. His eyes widened and he was unable to read any of them.

'You're not going to read me again,' Finn said.

'How much do you care about her?' Cillian was stroking her hair. It only took a moment for him to close the space and slap his hand upon his forehead. 'Unblock your mind or Jarlath will break her pretty little neck.'

He could taste their hatred for him. Jarlath's arm was tucked tightly around her neck. All it would take was a swift turn and it would break. His thoughts turned to Ellie.

He was trapped in an impossible situation and would only open his mind if his hand was forced. He thought about Dennis' words to not surrender, no matter what the sacrifice or who it was. But how could he not?

'I know how much she means to you, Milton,' Cillian said. 'Do you want her to live or die? The choice is yours but remember you're the one who has to live with it. Her fate means nothing to me.'

He was defeated and looked at Joo. She had no notion of what was happening. Her innocence was clear. A moment later he reluctantly unblocked his mind.

Immediately Cillian plunged in, pushing hard.

He was lightly chanting some words into his ear but Finn had no time to translate them: *Et dicetis ad me plane aperta et animum. Revela monimentum. Da mihi anima tua lucem, Finn Milton.*

The spell forced his mind open, making it impossible for him to close it again. The pain was excruciating and Cillian wasted no time extracting more of the incredible bright light from his body.

A bright thin stream of iridescence left his mouth and was effortlessly sucked into the perpetrator's. Finn's eyes rolled back. Blood was pouring from his nose and the pain in his skull was overwhelming. He was becoming weaker with every second that passed and then he slumped to the floor. Sounds were muffled and he could hardly lift his head or open his eyes.

Cillian was clutching his chest. His eyes were glowing white and then he exhaled an enormous breath. He appeared to be in considerable pain.

'What the hell are you doing?' Michael demanded.

'What an amazing rush, I had no idea how good that was going to be. That was so cool.' Cillian's hands were glowing white and his breathing was erratic.

Jarlath asked. 'What did you take from him, Cillian?'

'Soul light, brother. Don't try it. See these lesions? I have them up my arm, it comes at a price.'

Finn began to groan and gather himself on the floor when something hard struck his head. Everything went black.

An uncomfortable silence filled the room. Jarlath and Michael were staring at Cillian.

'Your eyes are glowing,' his father said. 'What *is* happening to you?'

'Milton has something unique. I'm going to take it from him and no one is going to stop me.' Cillian announced. Guarding his prisoner like an angry dog, he snatched Finn's hair and dragged his limp body across the floor and into the hall.

'Milton likes it the hard way,' Cillian said. 'I respect that. Jarlath, lock the girl in the bedroom. I'm going to secure him in the vault outside. Don't try and stop me or I will use violence. He's mine now and he *is* going to die. By the time I finish with him he's going to wish he'd never lived.'

'I thought this was going to be difficult.' Michael said to Jarlath when he left. 'But I don't think it's Milton we need to worry about anymore.'

8

~y~

spider web

Joe's spirit rushed through the wall and flew over houses and roads until he reached his body lying on his bed in the barn. The next second, he was up and running into the kitchen.

'Joe, what happened?' Serina asked.

'It's worse than we thought. They've taken Finn prisoner. One of them was extracting his soul light. He was like a vampire. I never saw it coming. He's going to kill him.'

'What?' Bastian asked. 'How is that even possible?'

'Joo's under some kind of spell, she didn't recognise him at all,' Joe said. 'They threatened to kill her if Finn refused to unblock his mind. He had no choice and now Cillian has complete control over him. I never thought that would happen. Joo's acting very strangely. She seriously isn't herself.'

'Let's get over there right now.' Jerry said emphatically. 'We can't let them get away with this. It's madness.'

'How many were there?' Tom asked.

'Three,' Joe said.

'We can take them on, no problem.' Jerry was confident.

Joe added, 'I've got no idea how we're going to handle this without one of them getting hurt and they know it.'

'What do you mean?' Bastian asked.

'If we go round there, who knows what they'll do to them,' Joe replied. 'I never thought he would be so vulnerable. One of them has extreme mind control powers.'

'We can't sit here and do nothing.' Bastian said.

'You're right.' Jerry countered, rubbing his hands together. 'I vote that we fight our way in.'

'I'll see what they're doing and report back,' Joe said. 'They didn't sense me, so it's safe to assume they haven't. Besides I'm the only one who can plane. Branna will be here soon. Wait for me before setting off.'

Serina gave him a tight hug. 'Be careful, Darling. Don't get too close to them.'

'I won't,' he said.

Finn woke in darkness to the stench of rotting meat filling his nostrils. A sliver of moonlight seeped through a crack in the wall. It was impossible to move his arms because his wrists were bound behind his back with a pair of metal cuffs. Lying on the cold hard dirty floor, his mind was foggy. He recalled Cillian taking more soul light and shuddered. He felt drained of energy and had never felt more exhausted. There was a throbbing and agonising pain in his head. Blood trickled down his face from his nose causing the metallic taste in his mouth. He creased his eyes at a sudden illumination.

'So you're awake.' It was Jarlath, turning a bright torch in his face.

Branna had never mentioned a vault in the Parsonage. The tiny chamber had a low ceiling and was filled with old boxes and rubbish. The dank smell hung in the air as though something had died in there, possibly a long time ago. It was dark but behind him he could make out the shape of a large safe, half sunken into the floor. The entrance had a large Victorian iron gate with a massive chain and lock attached to it.

'What have you done to Joo?' He asked. 'She has nothing to do with this.'

'Don't worry about the girl. She was only leverage to get you here. Cillian is your only concern now. He's out of control and I'm interested in what he does with you next. I've never seen him so driven.'

'You're breaking the rules.'

'You're funny,' Jarlath said. 'We *can* break the rules. We flaunt and corrupt them. Our blood cloaks us. It makes no difference what we do, we have no conflict other than what we make. I thought you knew that about our family, we're cloaked and you're not.'

'Where's your brother?' He asked tentatively.

'Waiting for your friends to get here,' Jarlath replied.

'My friends?'

'Your gifted buddies are on their way and we've got a surprise for them. Whatever you were expecting from us, it hardly compares with what we have in mind for them now.' He turned off the torch.

'Wait,' he said. 'You can't do this.'

'Oh, but we can, Milton. No one is going to stop us, not even you. You're naive and think you're better than us but the truth is you are pathetic.'

Jarlath securely locked the heavy gate, leaving him alone with the foul air filling his lungs and a rotten pain in his skull. Thinking about his friends walking into a trap, he tried to imagine what would happen. He focused on his soul light and how to fight back before it was too late.

'Is he awake, Jar?' Cillian demanded when his younger brother returned to the house.

'Yes and he's very annoyed.'

'Excellent. He isn't going anywhere soon,' Cillian said. 'Let's catch a spirit. Is he back yet? They were stupid sending someone to spy on us when we are prepared.'

'I can sense him coming back.' Jarlath closed his eyes to concentrate.

'Once we've dispatched his friends, I can get started on Milton's soul. I'm beginning to have some fun, brother, and it's about bloody time too.'

'Do you want me to check on the girl?'

'Make sure she's securely locked in,' he said. 'I don't want anyone getting near her. She's mine.'

Cillian approached his father sitting by the fireplace.

'You do realise that they'll come here in numbers,' Michael said. 'Are you sure about this?'

'Yes. Do you have the spirit orb?'

Michael opened a steel box and a tiny ghostly sparkling sphere floated out of it. It grew in size until it was the size of an orange.

'I can sense him now.' Cillian directed the orb to the floor with his mind and concealed it beneath the chair Michael was sitting on. Joe had been watching them for a few minutes when his spirit was drawn towards them, as though he was trapped in some kind of spectral tractor beam. The orb rose into Cillian's hand and Joe's soul was unwittingly sucked into it. Cillian stared at the orb filled with tiny specks of swirling white light and smiled.

'What amazing technology,' Cillian said. 'Got you, Mr Praed.' He directed the orb to fly back into the box and Michael locked it securely.

'One down,' Cillian said. 'I think that's the only spirit trap we'll need tonight. Milton can plane so it might be a solution for him as well when the time comes. Twelve hours in a spirit trap and you fade. This one will be dead by morning.'

'Milton deserves to suffer before we kill him.' Michael said. 'I need to talk to Branna. We still don't know where she hid the bodies.'

'Don't worry, father, I know what to do,' Cillian said, scratching his arm. From his wrists to his shoulders a mass of pink and red ulcers were expanding. He rolled his sleeve down to the cuff. 'Milton will suffer before the end. I've something in mind for Branna which will be far more entertaining than killing her.'

Floating out of his body, Finn planed into the house. It was the simplest thing to do and he was drawn towards a small pane of coloured glass fitted in a downstairs window. Flying through it he found himself in a dark and dusty wooden stairwell. It was panelled on all sides and blocked off from the rest of the house. It twisted around to closed wooden doors at either end. A large hook was swinging from a rope in the ceiling.

Inaudible whispering filled his ears, which sounded like a conversation before falling silent. The air turned bitterly cold. He floated in the stairwell when a wind lashed past him suddenly. There was no obvious reason for it. He swallowed and rose in the direction of the first floor, which he found easily as a spirit since he could pass through walls and doors.

The darkened upper corridor of the house was dimly lit. There were abstract paintings of Gothic landscapes hanging on the walls. He couldn't imagine a more unpleasant atmosphere. Cobwebs hung everywhere.

A grey shadow passed by him and disappeared through the wall. He felt a cold wind whip past him like the one in the stairwell.

Ghost: *Finn Milton, what are you doing here?*

A faint audible female voice could be heard, distant yet eerie. He paused. The shadow reappeared and rushed through him once more down the corridor and out the far side of the house. Strange whispering followed.

He had never planed inside the Parsonage before and had no idea the house was haunted. He stared back down the corridor and the shape of a woman appeared, hardly visible to the naked eye. She looked young, no more than twenty and her neck appeared to be broken. Her eyes were like dark holes and a grim sadness hung about her.

Ghost: *Why have you come here? People die in this house.*

Finn: *My friend's trapped and I have to help her. Who are you?*

Ghost: *That isn't important. You should leave. She's coming back ... she's angrier this time ... she hates the fact that he is taking it from you ... she's so incensed because she can't do anything to stop him.*

Finn: *Who is she?*

But it was too late.

The ghostly woman vanished leaving him alone in the corridor with the strange revelation. He turned his attention to Joo as time was pressing. When he discovered her she was sitting on a bed, staring forward in a catatonic state. He pushed through making himself more defined until she could actually see him.

'What are you?' She asked.

Finn: *Don't you remember me, Joo?*

He pushed his spiritual index finger against her forehead. She didn't move and seemed too afraid to. He looked into her mind and could clearly see the charm working. It was blocking all her memories, replacing them with fake emotions and ideas. He channelled some of his own memories into her mind, ones where Joo was herself. All of a sudden she looked at herself in the mirror on the wall.

'Finn?' She spoke with hardly a whisper.

Finn: *Do you remember me?*

'How on Earth could I forget you? You're such a big lummox.' There was the start of a grin forming on her face.

Finn: *You could be a bit nicer to me. I can't believe I actually missed you while we were away.*

'What are you doing here? In fact where am I?'

Finn: *You're in the Parsonage and the Irish Connellys have abducted you. They've got my body locked in the vault. I came to rescue you but it kind of went wrong.*

'You're here too?'

Finn: *Afraid so but Bastian's on his way with his friends. We've formed a small posse. We had to play it their way and use me as bait to get you out of here. There's so little time.*

'They nailed the windows shut and locked the door,' she said.

Finn: *When they come back you need to act as though nothing's changed. You need to block your mind and have the same blank thoughts, this way Cillian won't suspect anything. Although if mind locking seems to break the spell, it can't be that powerful. I need to find a way out of the vault. They've got me chained to the floor. Stay positive and we'll get you out of here.*

'Cillian was the one outside our house. He put a spell on me after I found your dad – he was in such a bad state. Bastian was hurt as well. Are they okay?'

Finn: *Dad's fine and so is Bastian. When I heard the news from Caron, I called Branna and she healed them. I don't know what we'd do without her.*

'Thank goodness. I suppose I've been here all week. What the hell am I wearing?'

Finn: *Sorry but we didn't know where you were.*

'You ought to plane back or you'll be exhausted,' she said.

Finn: *You're right. We'll get you out of here tonight, I promise. Remember to pretend.*

'I'll do my best. Be careful and thank you.'

He darted out the window and straight into the garden. He didn't want to hang around and commune with another ghost even though he could sense more than one watching him. The pull of his body was strong and he slipped back in easily.

Cillian was standing over him and he felt his boot kicking him hard in the ribs. He doubled up in pain as his soul slid slowly into place.

'You ought to know something. I'm growing stronger with your soul light. You thought it would kill me but I'm learning to deal with it. You have all this power and you never use it. I know about *Etherea*. They won't be able to stop me now. By the way, one of your friends was foolish to come back as a spirit. Did you think we wouldn't notice him?'

'What are you talking about?'

'The Praed man,' Cillian said. 'He'll fade by morning.'

'What have you done to him?' He couldn't believe it and a forgotten memory popped into his mind concerning Sentries.

'If you plane again, you can join him,' Cillian said.

He knew he wasn't joking. 'You have a spirit trap.'

'That's very insightful. You should think twice about planing if you understand how it works.'

Cillian snatched his hair and looked at his face in the dim light. 'Jared was slightly impressed by you but I can't see it myself.'

'Why don't you let me go and I'll show you what I can really do.'

'I already know, I can feel soul light burning inside me. It's intoxicating. You can't block me, your mind is forced open to me now and there's nothing you can do about it. You can't fight me.'

Finn couldn't move his arms. His best abilities were channelled through them and he couldn't do anything about it. He could still move objects but there was little around him that offered an opportunity.

'I'm going to wait for your friends. Don't make me use a bolt on you. You should know, I want to take the rest of your soul light and I don't care if it kills you either. You deserve it.'

'It will kill you,' Finn said.

'I don't think so. You won't be in too much pain before you die but I can change that if you piss me off.'

Cillian raised his hands and made small twin glowing white orbs of energy. He made them dissipate beside his face before leaving. The heat from the orbs was hot. There was a persistent throbbing pain in his ribs. He couldn't warn the others unless he planed again. If they were watching him he'd be sucked into a spirit trap. For the moment Cillian wanted him alive and this gave him valuable hope. Desperately thirsty, he was beginning to wonder how he could escape.

He thought about his mother and how she may have used soul light. He closed his eyes and concentrated on the metal cuffs holding his hands together.

⁓

'Is it wise keeping him conscious? If his friends come through the garden, he could call out to them.' Michael said. 'He mustn't get free, he's far too dangerous.'

'He'll think twice about planing again but you do have a point,' Cillian said. 'Give me that spirit trap. It can go in the vault and Milton can go to sleep for a few hours.'

Michael passed his eldest son the box containing Joe's spirit and Cillian returned to the vault.

'I must be popular today.' Finn watched as he placed the box on the far side of the chamber.

'I wouldn't get your hopes up,' Cillian said.

'What's that?'

'Nothing for you to worry about.'

Cillian dropped his hand onto his forehead and began to probe his mind. Finn shook him off only to feel the full force of his fist ramming into his nose. He landed on his side, pain spreading to every corner of his face. 'Let me into your mind or I will kill you right now.' Cillian was furious.

Finn could feel him inside his mind and waited patiently for the right moment. Without any mental warning, he lifted Cillian off the floor using his mind and slammed him against the crumbling wall of the vault. He could imagine soul light changing the atoms of the metal cuffs. Suddenly it began to soften before crumbling to dust. It was a moment of clarity. His hands were free to channel an impressive energy wave. Cillian opened his eyes and suffered the full force of it, his skull striking the wall before losing consciousness.

Finn felt for the box on the floor and grabbed it, pushing the gate open with his mind. Standing free in the garden, his hands and eyes were glowing white with soul light.

~~

'Where's Joe?' Serina demanded. 'He should be back by now.'

'We should go over there now.' Jerry was itching to leave.

'I think we should all go together.' Branna said.

'Splitting up is no good, they'll pick us off like flies.'

'Really?' Tom asked. 'How would you know?'

'Believe me. You cannot underestimate any of them. Cillian can fire plasma bolts. He has strong mind powers and can cast spells by merely touching you. If he has taken more of Finn's soul light, it will only make him stronger. No one must take him on unless they can deflect bolts. Who can do that?'

'I can,' Jerry said, stepping forward. 'I can deflect energy waves, possibly bolts. I haven't had much field experience but I'm willing to try. Simon can make lightning.'

'But no one can make bolts.' Branna said.

'It'll have to do. We can't sit here and do nothing,' Serina said. 'We can all fight.'

'Milton can.' Bastian spoke up. 'He can make bolts.'

'Finn's dad?' Simon laughed out loud. 'I had no idea the professor is such a force of nature. Who would've thought it?'

'It would be best to not involve him,' Serina said. 'I don't think Finn would approve.'

'We'll have to make do with what we have.' Tom surmised.

'We are six. It has to make a difference.' Jerry zipped up his leather jacket. 'I'm ready.'

'As ready as we'll ever be,' Branna said.

The four men and two women began to walk down the hill towards the Parsonage. Once they were on the road, thoughts were passing between them. They had grown tighter as a group, wanting desperately to believe it would be enough to defeat the Connellys, but it was proving difficult.

Jarlath sprinted back to the Parsonage, slamming the door behind him. 'Six of them, incoming.'

'Six? Are they all coming at once?' Michael was peering out the window. 'That must be Branna. What's taking Cillian so long?'

'He's outside,' Jarlath said. 'Seeing to Milton.'

'Branna's picked sides.' Michael said. 'It's disappointing, I always had a soft spot for her. She was such a sweet child.'

'I don't want to fight my cousin,' Jarlath said.

'She stabbed Logan in the heart! She isn't family anymore. Get that into your thick skull, Jarlath.'

'This is Branna we're talking about. Are you sure she killed him?'

'She told Milton about it,' Michael said. 'Cillian read his mind.'

'They're here.'

The front door took off into the hall, blown completely off its hinges. The noise was loud and sudden. Jarlath entered the hall to be confronted by two tall dark haired men and four others following.

'Hello pond life,' Jerry said with a smirk before shoving a massive energy wave towards the young Connelly. It threw Jarlath off his feet, knocking the hog's head off the wall, which clattered with him to the floor. Simon stood beside his brother as Jarlath started firing bolts in their direction. Jerry deflected each one making them disappear, while Simon fired short bursts of lightning to slow him down.

'That's more like it,' Branna said, expressing her admiration for the Nancarrow supernatural handiwork and stepped past them into the lounge. 'Hello Michael, did you miss me?'

Finn could hear a commotion inside the house and thought it had to be the posse. Using his mind he unlocked the box and gently lifted out the spirit trap. It looked familiar. On tapping it, a spirit emerged.

'Joe, what on Earth happened to you?' He gasped.

Joe: *I don't remember but I didn't think I was coming back.*

'See if you can read one of the Connellys,' he said. 'We need to know where their talisman is or anything about James Connelly. I'm going to find Joo. I've managed to take care of Cillian, he should be unconscious for a while.'

Joe: *Good job that man, I'm on it and thanks for saving me.*

He smiled at Joe and turned his attention back to the case at hand: welding the lock on the vault using soul light like a blowtorch. He thought it might buy them some time with Cillian trapped inside and incapacitated.

Entering via the back door of the Parsonage, Finn discovered the concealed second staircase behind a rotting wooden door. He kicked it open when it refused to budge. As he ascended the damaged stairs, the air felt desperately cold and his footing almost slipped. He could see his breath in the air and paused to look up. A hook and chain were fixed into the wooden boards of the ceiling and it was rocking from side to side on its own.

Finn ignored it and pushed on. At the top of the stairs the door was sealed. Focusing enough energy he blew it into the corridor. The door had been wallpapered over on the other side. Strips of paper were torn from the walls when the door left its hinges.

After the ghostly events from earlier, little surprised Finn about the Parsonage anymore. The less attention he gave it, the better. He sensed the room where Joo was being kept prisoner. He thought of his father's words about soul light and mentally pushed the locked door inwards as though it was made of paper. He lowered his hands and found them glowing white. It was all about focus.

Joo was sitting on the bed, holding onto her knees. When Finn entered, she ran into his arms and hugged him hard. The relief on her face was insurmountable. Finn was pleased that no one had come back to plant a new spell in her mind.

'Finn, I thought you'd never come. I saw a ghost of a young woman – there's more than one ghost in this house. It's really creepy.'

'I know about the ghosts, Joo,' Finn said. 'Come on, we have to get out of this crazy house. Stick beside me and don't stop unless I tell you to. We're not out of this yet. The ghost story can wait for later.'

In the lounge, Branna faced her distant cousin for the first time in months. Michael mentally slammed the door shut and stared at her. The room was mostly in shadow, the drapes half closed and the smell of damp was overwhelming. There was little furniture and much dust in the air.

'Miss you, Branna? I hardly think so after what you've done.'

'It was necessary,' Branna said. 'You have no idea what happened leading up to my father's death.'

'You were stupid to come back here. I know what you did to him. Now you're here, it's time you were dealt with properly.'

'You must release Finn and Joo. Michael, you have no right to do this. They haven't done anything wrong.'

'You have no right to make demands or terms. You look like your father but you're nothing like him. You're a weak and dishonest coward.'

'Logan had it coming. You put Joe in a spirit trap and locked Finn in the vault. How could you? You knew what my father kept down there, you bastard.' Branna had been reading his mind, learning of what had happened since Finn arrived earlier.

'Do you think you're going to win this?' Michael asked calmly. Cillian was still absent and she was reading his mind liberally. Without his eldest son, he had exposed a severe chink in his amour. 'Stop reading my mind.'

'Never. You're evil just like Logan,' she said. 'You're all the same, only after your own self-interests.'

Michael Connelly was fifty-one years old and ruggedly handsome for his age. He was lord of a vast ancestral pile not far from Dublin. Father to two sons and a daughter, he ran a housing development company called Connelly Developments. Cillian ran an offshoot for their investors. Michael was wealthy with a faithful wife called Ciaran. His personal life was a world away from the shabby and spartan veneer of the Parsonage. He had no patience but had cared deeply for Branna's father Logan. Family meant everything to him.

'You can't fight me, Branna. You don't know how. You're just a child.'

'Yeah well, watch me.'

She mentally pushed him out of his chair. He sprang to his feet and tore into her, swiping his fist close to her head. She swiftly ducked out of the way and propelled him into the fireplace, where he sliced his forehead open on the granite.

'Does it hurt much?' She asked as he wiped blood from his brow.

'I'm going to kill you,' He spat, stumbling to his feet, determination etched on his face while she humiliated him. Michael had few abilities but using basic telekinesis, he aimed an old wooden coffee table at her. She held it steady as the legs skimmed the top of her head. Her plait of hair sliced through the air. She threw the table back at him with twice the force and it struck him hard knocking him off his feet.

Jarlath was beginning to overpower the Nancarrow brothers. Tom had been hit in the shoulder and had managed to crawl outside. Serina stepped in between Simon and Jerry to help. Bastian checked out Tom's injury as he stood in pain on the gravel drive in the dark.

'Come and join the party. There's room for more in here,' Jarlath laughed at them. 'Why don't you people give up?'

Jarlath began firing random bolts everywhere but they were fast and darted to miss them. One hit Serina in the leg and she went down. Bastian managed to pull her free and into the drive.

'I'm going to check the back of the house,' Bastian said. 'Try and get away from here. If I can get close enough to this bastard I can send him to sleep but we've got to find Finn and Joo.'

'Be careful, Bastian.' Serina said as he crept away into the dark.

'You're outnumbered,' Jerry said. 'Give it up, Connelly.'

'You're two down, I don't think so,' Jarlath replied.

Finn and Joo were standing behind Jarlath in the back doorway. Using the moment's distraction, Joe's spirit tapped Jarlath on the shoulder. He dropped unconscious to the floor like a heavy stone. Jerry and Simon sighed with much needed relief and took stock of the situation.

'Joe, good man,' Jerry said. 'Finn, Joo are you alright?'

Finn had his arm around Joo protectively when they stepped into the hall. His face was swollen, his nose was bleeding and his shirt was torn.

'We're okay. Where are the others?'

'Branna's in there with Michael,' Jerry said, pointing to the closed door of the lounge. 'Tom and Serina are outside, and Bastian's gone round the back looking for you.'

'Oh no, Cillian's back there,' Finn said. 'He's mad.'

'I'll go, you guys get safely out of here,' Jerry said, sprinting like the wind in the direction from where Finn had come. The garden was dark and full of creeping white mist. 'Bastian?'

'I'm here,' Bastian whispered. He was trying to prize open an old iron gate. 'Someone's in there.'

'Finn and Joo are safe, don't try and open this,' Jerry said. 'It's not a good idea, Bastian.'

'Why?'

'Because there's a nutter in there.' Jerry spoke quietly. 'We should go now.'

A low rumbling sound made both men stare at the gate.

The next moment it flew towards them with an almighty force.

'Run, Bastian,' Jerry shouted.

Without looking back, they ran impossibly fast around the side of the house leaving Cillian to quietly compose himself on the granite path.

Cillian: *Run away, you cowards. This feels too good.*

Serina smiled when she saw the spirit of her husband: *I was worried about you.*

Joe: *I'm going to help Branna. It's high time you all got out of here while you've got the chance.*

Finn and Joo were on the pavement near the Parsonage when Bastian and Jerry ran straight past them. They slowed down to check on the others.

'That was too close for comfort,' Bastian said, slapping Finn on the shoulder. 'Are you okay?'

'I'm fine but Branna needs our help,' Finn said. 'I'm worried about her.'

'You can't go back in there,' Jerry said. 'There's a crazy glowing man in the garden.'

Serina hugged Joo. 'You gave us all a terrible scare, Joo. How are you feeling?'

'Just confused,' she said. 'When I saw Finn earlier I'd forgotten everything. They didn't harm me but I can't remember much – just how happy I was to see him.'

'How's you leg?' Tom asked his sister, who was leaning into Bastian.

'Very sore, how's your shoulder?' Serina replied with a smirk.

'It's like being shot,' Tom replied. 'I can't believe how much damage those bolts can do. It bloody hurts.'

'Let's get out of here,' Jerry said.

Finn was trying to peer through the dirty lounge window. It was enough to see Cillian appear inside the room wearing an expression of pure loathing.

'We can't leave her there,' Finn said. 'Cillian's escaped.'

'Yeah and he nearly hit us with an iron gate,' Jerry said. 'I think we got lucky.'

'Finn, you've done all you can,' Simon said. 'I'm sure Branna can look after herself.'

Finn added, 'I don't know. She's not that strong.'

'You managed to get Joo out safely, that was the objective,' Jerry said. 'Let's go before they come after us. If you go back, who knows what's going to happen? You can't fight them like this. You're hurt too.'

Reluctantly Finn agreed with him, feeling his new bruises. The two Connelly men would be bearing down on Branna and there was little he could do to stop them. As the injured and ragged group walked back to the barn, not one of them said a word. Joo held onto Finn's hand like glue.

9

~

midnight blue

Branna ducked when Michael attacked, his fists primed to strike her face but he missed her again. Suddenly Cillian tore into the lounge and the pair froze. Michael nodded to his son and Cillian fell to his knees. He released a heavy force of energy, which swept across the room like a heavy gust of wind. It struck Branna, sending her body flying backwards. She banged her head hard on the wall and promptly passed out.

'And about time too. Where the hell have you been, Cillian?' Michael checked her pulse. 'She's still alive.'

'I was distracted but Jarlath's out cold.'

'What?' Michael tore out of the room.

Joe was invisible and unnoticed but hung close and read the unlocked layers of Michael's mind.

'What's the matter with him?' Michael asked.

'One of them has a sleep ability,' he replied. 'Did you have anything special in mind for Branna? She should pay for her crimes.'

'I didn't expect to have her at my disposal so easily. What about Milton? Is he still secure? I thought you had all this under control, Cillian.'

Cillian didn't want to admit he had failed to restrain him but had to share the truth. 'He escaped.'

What annoyed him more was that Finn had finally figured out how to use the soul light. Soul light he should have taken.

'That was stupid even for you,' Michael snapped. 'They've all gone except Branna.'

Cillian touched his brother to cancel the sleep spell and he woke, nursing a foul headache. 'What happened?'

'You let them get away. You're an idiot, Jarlath Connelly.'

'Looks like you fared no better. Finn Milton got away with the girl. I saw them leave. Where were you?'

'*How* did he do that?' Cillian ran upstairs to find the bedroom empty. 'Damn it to hell and back.'

'What *did* you have in mind for Branna?' Michael asked when he came back down the stairs.

'I'm going to find out exactly where she buried Logan and Jared. Then I'm going to plant a spell so hard to decipher in her mind that she will never be able to change it. After that, I'm going to let her go.'

'Let her go?' Michael blurted. 'Are you mad?'

Cillian said, 'I don't want to spoil the surprise but Branna chose the wrong day for a family reunion.'

While Branna was delirious, Cillian carefully read her mind and relived the moment when she stabbed her father in the heart. 'Logan is buried in the garden and so is Jared, behind the olive tree.'

Michael stared at his son. 'Both of them? I don't believe it. She should have given them proper burials.'

'We must call the police,' Jarlath said. 'You can control them, Cillian. Let them sort it out. She's the prime suspect and deserves everything she gets. '

'I have a far better punishment in mind. We're not calling the police. I realise we can make them do whatever we want but I've got other plans for Branna, something more befitting her crime. I need a moment's peace while I work on a charm, can you give me some space? When she wakes up, I'll handle our cousin. Don't worry, you're going to like it.'

They moved into the hall, closing the door to the lounge. Michael lifted the hog's head and hung it back on the wall. 'This isn't a home anymore. It saddens me that Logan is no longer with us. He was like a brother to me. Jared was so young and strong. This is the worst possible outcome.'

Joe was in the lounge watching Cillian pressing his palm to Branna's forehead and chanting some words into her ear: *Terminus enim vita et natura, cum Corvus iterum vertat manebitis corvus in perpetuum. Et oblitus es homo. Et oblitus es Branna Connelly.*

Joe could barely hear the words. Latin had been one of his better subjects at grammar school but *'you will forget'* were the only words he could translate.

Joe: *Forget what?*

Cillian heard Joe's thought and looked directly at his spirit even though he couldn't see him. He focused to make Joe reveal himself. Joe struggled against the vigorous mind control.

'I thought I'd put you away for good, Mr Praed.'

Joe couldn't fight it and as Cillian took control, he was reading his mind. 'James Connelly? Why are you so interested in him? What have you been up to?'

Cillian twisted his hand and soul light seeped into the air. The glowing particles crept towards Joe like a twisting snake. He held it steady, ready to attack but still reading Joe's mind.

'The almanac? You have been reading my father's mind and now you know far too much. Before I destroy you, I'll share something,' he said. 'When Branna wakes up and turns into a raven, that is all she'll ever know. She'll never be able to turn back into a human.'

Joe: *You can't do that, it's wrong.*

'But I can and I will leave no trace of you, Joe Praed.'

Cillian's expression turned dark and he targeted the iridescent soul light at the ensnared spirit and thought about destroying him. A blinding white light filled the lounge. Something tore at Cillian, pushing him away from Joe and throwing him right across the room. Cillian was unable to fight it. The faint outline of a tall white form floated before him. It was carrying a long spear.

Sentry: *You will not destroy this spirit.*

Joe's soul vanished along with the Sentry a second later.

Cillian: *Goddam Sentries.*

Joe had read Michael's mind and learnt information Cillian had known nothing about. He was incensed at how well his father had concealed it from him. There was an almanac of family history locked away in a safe, at home in Meath. His father had lied to him. Joe had been looking for a talisman — their talisman.

Branna stirred and swiftly healed the lump on the back of her head.

'Hello, Branna. Feeling any better?'

She leapt to her feet defensively and brushed herself down.

'What have you done?'

'Nothing much,' he replied with a wry smile. 'I was waiting for you to wake up and now that you have, you can leave.'

She looked at him with mistrust. 'You're letting me go? What the hell was all that about? Why did you hurt Finn so much?'

'That is none of your business. I know where you buried Logan and Jared. We're going to give them a proper burial, not dump them like you did without any care or respect. You're not part of our family anymore. You sicken me. Get out of this house.'

She hurried into the hall where she encountered Michael and Jarlath. They momentarily stared at her but nothing was spoken. Stepping through the gaping hole that used to be the front door, she headed for the road but the act was dubious.

Cillian was a master at spells, better than anyone she knew. It was hardly possible that all he wanted to know was the resting place of Logan and Jared. It made little sense. Even so, she ran to Joe's barn and never once looked back.

Finn was surprised when she appeared unhurt in the doorway of the barn. He gave her a tight hug and apologised for not stepping in to assist at the Parsonage.

'It was wise to not come back for me, Finn.'

The others were grouped in the kitchen comparing wounds and tactics when she walked in.

'How did you get away?' Simon asked.

'Cillian knocked me out and when I woke up they let me go,' Branna said. 'I got the hell out of there.'

Finn could see Joo rearranging her flattened hair in the bathroom with Jerry watching from a distance. Bastian was tending to Tom's shoulder. Serina was lost in thought. The only one missing was Joe. He was unsure about Branna. Something didn't sit right.

'Did you see Joe?' Serina asked her. 'He's not back yet.'

'Sorry, but I've got no idea where he is,' she replied. 'Your leg looks sore Serina. Here, let me have a look at it.' She rested her hand over the hole in her jeans and pressed it against the bolt scar. 'There, it's all fixed. Did anyone else get hurt?'

'Did you do that?' Jerry stared at Branna who gave a brief smile in response.

'One of my abilities is healing, Jerry. It comes in rather handy at times.'

Serina flexed her leg. 'Thanks, Branna. It feels much better.'

'No problem. Tom, let me check your shoulder.'

'Joe should be back by now,' Serina said.

'I don't think Cillian's going to give up,' Finn said. 'He wants my soul light and I'm starting to feel weaker.'

'I couldn't read him earlier, he was too strong,' Branna said. 'They know where Logan and Jared are buried but I can't go back to the Parsonage now. I'm surprised that's all they wanted to know.'

'We still need that talisman,' Finn said. 'I had no idea your old house was so haunted.'

'You could be right,' she said. 'Although I've never encountered any ghosts. That bruise looks nasty on your head, Finn.' The pain ebbed away when she touched it and she was rewarded with a smile.

'Haunted?' Jerry asked. 'Reenie, have you got any beer?'

'There's some in the fridge,' Serina said. 'Get me one too. I'm going to check on Joe. He could be sleeping.'

A moment later a tormented scream was heard coming from the bedroom and Tom raced after it. His sister was cradling Joe's limp and unresponsive body. 'Joe's dead, Tom.'

'He can't be.' Tom felt for a pulse.

'I've read his mind and there's no connection.' Tears were falling down her face.

'I don't believe it, we must wait. You know how this works, he will come back.' Tom reached for his sister's hand. 'Come here.' Serina buried her face in Tom's shoulder when Bastian entered the bedroom.

Tom: *Something's happened to Joe.*

Joe was being pulled along by an invisible cord. The illuminated vista of St Ives and Hayle lay below in all its glory. The Sentry let go of his spirit, allowing him to fly freely.

Sentry: *You're safe from them now.*

Joe: *Thank you for saving me. Why didn't you stop them doing those other crimes? These people are dangerous.*

Sentry: *Sometimes we depend upon mortals to assist us. A charmed talisman cloaks these people, that much is clear. I sensed your death so I intervened. Due to this man possessing soul light, I was able to locate him and single you out. I know you are working with Finn Milton and I've been watching him. When you see him, tell him we are watching and waiting. His visit to our portal was not a waste of time. He believes in us but we cannot reveal ourselves without good reason.*

My name is Guilar. I have helped Finn before. I am one of the few who believe a relationship with mortals is essential, especially at times like these. Find the talisman and we can fully assist. We don't want this man to strip Finn of all his soul light ... it would be catastrophic to say the least. You must return now, and quickly for your mortal link is fading.

Joe looked once more at the hooded spectre and threw himself into a vertical head dive, flying directly towards the barn. It had been the first time he had spoken to a Sentry from *Etherea*.

ᕄ

'Why did you let her go?' Michael demanded.

'Everything's under control, Father,' Cillian said. 'Don't worry.'

'You let her walk right out of here,' Jarlath added. 'Why?'

Cillian poured himself a whisky. 'The next time she turns into a raven will be the last time she transforms. She'll forget being human and be fixed as a bird. No one will ever get close enough to break it.'

'No way,' Jarlath said. 'You surprise me, Brother.'

'I couldn't bring myself to kill her. In some ways I empathise with her. Wanting to help others is a noble cause but she doesn't deserve a mortal life. She'll be a raven for the rest of her life. It's highly unlikely anyone will know who she is and she won't be able to break the enchantment herself.'

'That was less messy for a change,' Michael said.

'You should have more faith in me.'

'You should try earning it,' he added.

'There's something I need to know, Father. What do you know about James Connelly and an almanac?'

Michael had buried the memory making it impossible for his eldest to learn of its existence. The secrecy of the family almanac had been breached.

'Leave us alone, Jarlath,' Michael commanded and reluctantly his younger son went outside. 'I don't know how you found out about it but it isn't something I want to repeat to you or anyone else. It's my business and when I die, you'll inherit the almanac and our family history. It will be on your shoulders, and not something to share with anyone but your first born on your own death bed.'

'You're not going to tell me, are you? I figured you would respond like this and it's a great pity.'

Cillian played with the light sparking from the tips of his fingers, making it snake and seep through the air like mist.

'What is coming out of your hands?'

'Finn Milton is full of soul light. I thought you'd know that. I started to extract it but I was interrupted. It's intoxicating and I want more of it. Once I have it all he will die, which is what everyone wants. You see I am taking care of business as usual.'

'Your arms are covered in ulcers,' Michael said.

'It looks bad, I admit, but it's of little consequence compared with the power I can feel. You're going to tell me what the almanac is. You have never told me about our talisman. Where is it?'

There were dramatic changes in Cillian. He was developing an unfamiliar aggression. Soul light was gradually altering his physiology. His mind was sharper and more attuned to his senses. His eyes were glowing white and he was growing more impatient by the minute.

'I know what it means—soul light is pure energy. Finally, I've found something that agrees with me. I don't expect you to understand, you've always been weak.'

'You're a blind moth seduced by a powerful flame. If you don't cease this activity, Cillian, it will kill you. Your hair is falling out.'

'I've never felt better. You have no idea how it feels. Tell me about our talisman and don't spare me any details.'

'I don't know where it is,' he admitted.

It was the truth and had been made a long time ago for Michael's grandfather, James. He had in his possession a letter written by James months before his strange disappearance in the early 1940's. The letter had been sent to Michael's father Art and consequently placed inside the almanac for safe-keeping, over fifty years ago.

All it mentioned was the existence of a talisman, not its location.

'Impossible! You must know where it is,' Cillian said. 'How can it be safe if we don't know where it is? This is unacceptable.'

'I honestly don't know and while it's lost, we're alive. It's safe to assume that no one knows of its existence. I wouldn't know where to start looking.'

'So why was Joe Praed's spirit so interested in it? I'll force the truth out of you, Father and you will tell me.' .

'You *will* certainly not. I *am* your father and you will respect me.'

'Have it your way,' he said. 'I know where the almanac is, I don't need you anymore.'

Cillian focused his mind inwards and directed soul light at his father. He spoke the Latin words softly: *Et possidebo te in cinerem reddatur, Patre.*

'No, Cillian.' But it was too late.

A thin stream of iridescent light left Cillian's finger and touched his father on the shoulder. It disappeared through the cotton of his shirt and dug into his flesh. As the light encountered cells, each one was rendered to dust until the outline of his tall body was tottering upright. It had taken seconds. His eyes stared forward at his son, his mouth frozen open as his body transformed. The skin began to peel away until his body fell to pieces leaving a small pile of grey dust on the wooden floor.

'Interesting.' Kneeling down, he lightly ran his finger through the dusty substance. He rubbed some between his fingers and thought about his brother. The event would have to be classed as an accident. Jarlath would have to believe him and so would everyone else but that wouldn't be a stretch. It would be an elaborate spell. Having experienced spontaneous human combustion during a paranormal event, Michael Connelly had perished.

There would be a quiet family service in Meath, a wake, some predictable guests and the compulsory beige buffet. Eventually the mob would depart and Cillian would learn the truth about the almanac. He made the sound of an ironic laugh. Finally he would be the one in control and the rightful head of the Connelly family. It had been be so easy. He would go home and contemplate a plan. No one would stand in his way again.

Finn decided the safest option was for Joo to stay with them in Penberth. He offered to drop Branna home on the way back. They were all thinking about Joe and whether he would make it back. Stopping near Market Place, he turned to the dark haired woman and squeezed her hand.

'Thanks for everything you did tonight, Branna. Cillian isn't going to stop until he gets the rest of my soul light. I don't know how to stop him when he threatens those close to me.'

'None of this has been easy,' she said. 'I'll keep trying to find Duana.'

'She must be the ghost in the Parsonage. How old was she when she died?'

'Twenty-one,' she said. 'Very little is known about her and I have no family left to ask. Maybe you can talk to your grandmother. She might know something.'

Finn thought about his paternal grandmother, Heather Pengelly. 'I'll think about it. We've never been close but it might be worth a try.'

'Sometimes people can be enlightening when you least expect it,' she said, opening the car door. 'I'm so glad you're safe, Joo.'

'Thanks for your help,' she replied. 'I never want to see Cillian Connelly again.'

'I hope for your sake they return to Ireland,' Branna said. 'That would be one less thing to worry about.'

'I'm with you on that one,' he replied. 'I don't want to see them again either. Take care of yourself, Branna and we'll see you soon.'

She waved to them before stepping into Fore Street.

Joo clambered into the front seat. 'Are you okay, Finn?'

'I'm better than I thought I'd be. How about you?'

'I'm relieved,' she said. 'I saw him take something out of you earlier. What was it?'

'I've always had this light inside me. When I was born my mother gave it to me before she died. Since Cillian started taking it from me, I'm getting weaker. It makes my nose bleed. I have less energy and it's harder to concentrate. It gets worse every time he does it. I can't imagine what it's doing to him but it must be painful.'

'What do you mean?'

'It's dangerous. Soul light can kill, not to mention rot him from the inside out. He's a fool if he thinks otherwise.'

'Gross. I had no idea. You always have something going on, don't you? All this time and you still have secrets, Finn. I can't imagine what would've happened had you not come to rescue me. I've lost the last five days and I can't remember anything.'

'That's a good thing, Joo. Believe me, I wish I could forget the last five days.'

'I'm glad you guys are back, the house has been empty without you. Six months is far too long.'

He smiled finding her sentiment warm. 'We've missed you too and Ellie's going to be stoked when she sees you.'

'How is she?'

'Very pregnant and anxious to see you.'

'I bet she is,' she gave him a small smile.

On their return to Eternia Cottage, the reception awaiting them was filled with heightened excitement. Finn took a back seat while Ellie and Joo furiously caught up. Both of them cried tears when they greeted one another. Exhausted from the long day's events, he found solace in the kitchen with Rose and a bottle of single malt whisky.

'I can't believe they were so violent,' Rose said. 'Is Joe Praed missing?'

'I don't know what happened. He must have been caught out while I was rescuing Joo. I feel terrible because I asked him to help us.'

'Finn, sometimes things happen that we can't explain or understand.'

'But it was my fault.'

'Joe agreed to help you,' she said. 'He knew the risks. It could have happened to any one of you.'

'It doesn't make me feel any better. I need some air to clear my head. I'm going to walk to the harbour, can you let the girls know if they need me?'

Rose gave him a hug.

'Of course I will, Finn. Try not to worry.'

He followed the lane in the dark and approached the stone slipway. He was thinking about ghosts when something moved in the water. Small waves rippled against the slip as he moved in for a closer look.

A transparent swathe of mist suddenly erupted from the water and flew around him like a swarm of bees. He closed his eyes and relaxed. Whatever it was, it was supernatural and he wouldn't be able to fight it so he decided to remain calm. He could feel the cold air brushing against the skin on his face.

Finn: *Who are you, Spirit?*

He opened his eyes and a silvery shape formed appearing to hover above the wet stone floor. It didn't resemble anything he had seen before.

He extended a hand towards the mist but it moved further away to study him. A current of energy was flowing through his veins and his hands began to glow. The entity touched them and appeared to be charging itself on his soul light. The next moment it darted up into the darkness and disappeared.

Disgruntled with the outcome, he wandered back to the cottage. With Joo asleep under a duvet on the sofa, he turned off all the lights downstairs and ascended to the attic room with a glass of water. Ellie was lightly snoring so he opened the round window and perched on the narrow seat.

It was a moonless night and the garden was bathed in darkness. His mood was sombre with Cillian foremost in his mind. A low level headache refused to go away. With the advent of another bleed, he tilted his head back and pinched his nose.

He was convinced the strange mist was something he had encountered in the Parsonage earlier that evening. The ghost had given him a warning.

Quietly he climbed into bed. He stared at the sky until drifting off to sleep. It wasn't long before he began to dream.

He was walking along Porthmeor beach in the dark. It was deserted and the waves were crashing against the shoreline.

Behind him the streetlights were glowing through a strange blue translucent haze, which hung around like a fog.

Between the swell, he could make out the shape of something that appeared to be surfing.

His feet felt cold and wet in the water, which quickly rose to his waist as he searched for the strange entity.

Finn: Who are you?

The being rose from the water and darted around him. Concentrating he used soul light to grab it with his hands. On instinct, he inserted soul light into it. As the shape consumed the light, its physical appearance altered. He set it free and the being glowed with iridescent light. It resembled a human form but an intense anguish was emanating from it.

Ghost: More… Give me more.

He focused more energy at the spirit, until the ghostly outline of a woman appeared. He was startled at the transformation. For a while nothing was said but he couldn't tear his eyes from her face. She moved closer and stroked his face. It felt like a tickle. Her eyes were dark, her form white and transparent. She was a familiar young woman with long white hair. There was a look of warmth in her eyes that he had not experienced before.

Ghost: You must wake up, Darling ... wake up my boy... Finn...

He opened his eyes. For a moment it felt like he had travelled to another dimension where everything had been in minute detail. It felt like it had actually happened even though he knew it had been a dream. A sliver of moonlight cast a line across the bedroom floor through the open window. He was reeling with sweat and felt sick. His heart was pumping as though he had been running.

The memory of the beach was real. In his mind's eye, her eyes were still looking at him. Without making a sound he crept down the stairs leaving Ellie asleep in bed. Halfway down he paused to look at a group of framed photographs. Removing one, he carried it to the kitchen where he turned on a lamp. Looking curiously, he finally understood. The old black and white photograph depicted his parents on their wedding day in the 1960's. Something had touched him deep inside and his eyes watered involuntarily. She hadn't aged a day.

The mysterious entity had been his mother, Phoebe. He could hardly believe that she had made contact with him through a dream. A couple of tears fell down his cheek and he quietly laughed at the discovery, hardly believing his luck. He could still feel her love from their moment on the beach. It had touched him profoundly, bringing with it much sought after encouragement and hope that she was still alive.

10

~

threads

Branna woke early Sunday morning to the cool morning breeze on her face coming through the open window. She crept downstairs without waking her husband and turned on the coffee machine.

'Are you okay, Darling?' Minutes later, her husband Murray planted a kiss on her neck.

'I'm alright but we had a rough time of it last night.'

'What happened?'

'My cousins were predictably violent but everything worked out in the end. Finn managed to rescue Joo and she's safe. You never know what's going to happen with that lot. My relatives have their own agenda.'

'I don't know what to say other than I'm glad you're safe. It sounds terrible.'

'You don't have to say anything. It's over, that's the main thing. I'm itching to go out for a flight to brush away some cobwebs. You don't mind, do you? It might help settle the nerves I've been having since I got back last night. I don't feel right in myself.'

'For you, anything. Are you going to be long?'

'I'll be back for breakfast,' she smiled at him lovingly and stepped into the courtyard. 'It looks like it's going to be a nice day.'

'I love you, Branna.'

Still smiling at him, she quickly transformed into a raven. Murray watched as the bird took to the skies and flew out of sight. He grabbed some eggs, bacon and strong cheddar cheese from the fridge. Cheese and bacon omelette was her favourite. He touched the gold band on his finger and smiled, hardly believing she was his wife.

~~

'Finn, it's the phone for you,' Rose said. 'I'll leave it on the stairs.'

He half-opened the door and raised the handset into his open hand. 'Hello?'

'Are you good friends with Branna?'

'Who's this?'

'Her husband, Murray.'

'Murray? What's the problem?' There was anger in his voice and no shred of humour.

'I'm not used to this weird business you seem to have in common with my wife and I'm not too happy about it either. I'm assuming you know about her ability to change into a raven. So I'll make this simple for you. She flew off this morning and she hasn't come back.'

'I haven't seen her since I dropped her home last night. What time did she leave?'

'Three hours ago. She said she was going out for a quick flight. It's not like her to be this long without any word.'

'I'm sorry Murray but I have no idea where she is.'

'What exactly happened last night?' Murray demanded.

Finn didn't know where to start and suggested it would be better if he explained it face to face. A feeling of dread filled his soul as he hung up the call.

'Who's Murray?' Ellie asked, sitting up in bed.

'Branna's husband. She's missing.'

'I thought you dropped her home last night?'

'I did. Last night was strange, one minute the Connellys were holding her captive, then they let her go. It was too easy. Cillian is a master of spells, he could've planted something in her head.'

'What do you mean?'

'Something isn't right. Murray said she was only going out for short flight but she's been gone for hours. I don't know where she is. Darling, I know we were going to spend some time together today but I need to go over and talk to him. He sounds frantic. I need to call in on Serina as well and find out what happened to Joe.'

'Don't worry about me. We can catch up later. There must be a simple explanation. Branna doesn't play games. When are you going, Honey?'

He was already getting dressed. 'Now.'

He wanted to tell her about the weird dream and the strange encounter with his mother but thought against it. It could wait. Part of him knew it would happen again and right then he had more questions than answers.

Cillian explained for the third time what had happened to their father, blaming his death on the supernatural activity within the Parsonage. 'It's this house, it's unnatural. I can sense more than one spirit and none of them are friendly. He must have had a conflict with one of them.'

'I want to go home. This is unbelievable.' Jarlath was crying. 'What do we do about Logan and Jared's bodies?'

'They're not going anywhere soon, come on,' Cillian said. 'Let's get out of here. I'm not looking forward to telling Mam. She never wanted us to come to Cornwall in the first place.'

'Are we taking what's left of him home?'

'I've put his ashes in a jar.'

'I can't believe he's dead. There was nothing wrong with him.'

Cillian placed a brotherly arm around him. 'I know and I can't describe how much it grieves me too, Brother. When we get home I'll make everything right again.'

Jarlath's eyes were soaked with tears. 'How are you going to do that, Cillian? You don't look too good yourself. In fact, you look terrible.'

'It's only a temporary side effect.' He scratched his arm and flakes of skin fell away. 'Trust me, things are going to be very different from now on. With Branna out of the way, I'm gonna stake a claim on this house.'

'I thought you hated it here,' his younger brother said.

'It's growing on me. This house must be worth something, the grounds have quite a foot fall.' Cillian was walking around the house, writing notes in a small notebook. 'There's some valuable art upstairs that can definitely go.'

'I would burn it to the ground and get the whole area dug up. This place gives me the creeps.'

'You'll see, in time, everything will come right for us. I'll take care of matters from now on. Father never did have the stomach for it.'

❧

When Finn left the old pottery, he was none the wiser but Murray was on the verge of a full-scale panic attack. Unable to appease the situation he was left confused by her disappearance. It was early afternoon when he called in at the barn. He was expecting to find Serina on her own and traumatised but it was Joe who greeted him with a big smile.

'Finn, come in. Serina was beside herself when I woke up. She thought the worst.'

'Whoa… I bet she did. I thought we'd lost you. What happened?' He couldn't believe the relief he felt at finding him alive.

'The weirdest thing,' Joe said. 'I thought my number was up when something pulled me right out of the house. I was staring into the eyes of a huge Sentry. I never imagined that could ever happen. He was massive.'

'They must have been there the whole time. I take it you haven't encountered one before.'

'That was a first and I must say, I'm grateful,' Joe said. 'He saved my life. Do you fancy a beer?'

'That would be great but I can't stay for long. Have you seen Branna today?'

'Not since last night,' he retired to the lounge. 'Why?'

'I had a call from Branna's husband, Murray. She's been missing since breakfast time. I'm worried that Cillian cast a spell on her. She was alone with him before they let her go but I can't make any sense of it.'

'Last night I'm certain Cillian did something to Branna, but it's been wiped from my mind. I managed to read Michael after you escaped but I can't remember what I found.'

'Do you want me to read your mind? Sentries can mess with it. One of them scrambled mine last year.'

'Sure, why not?' Joe replied.

He searched his mind for ten minutes before uncovering the scene with Branna and Cillian in the lounge. Joe's presence came to Cillian's attention and he struck forward to attack him with soul light snaking out from his hand. Abruptly his spirit was torn through the layers of the house and into the night sky by a massive white light. He rewound the memory to the point when Cillian was holding a hand over Branna's forehead, softly chanting some words in Latin.

Due to learning Latin at school, he was able to translate it: *For the term of your natural life, when you change into a raven the next time, you will remain as a raven forevermore. You will forget you are a human being. You will forget you are Branna Connelly.*

A tiny speck of blood fell from Joe's nose. 'Sorry about the bleed.' Joe wiped it with a tissue. 'All par for the course, isn't it?'

'Unfortunately it can be. Murray said that Branna went out for a flight this morning.'

'She's stuck forever as a raven, oh no.' Joe said.

'It's her husband Murray I feel for. How do I explain that his wife has been cursed to remain as a raven? It sounds crazy.' He closed his eyes to take stock for a moment.

'You managed to break Joo's charm by mind-locking with her and reminding her who she is,' Joe said. 'Maybe it's a case of doing the same thing to Branna?'

'Have you tried catching a raven?'

'No, I haven't.' Joe half-smiled. 'It'll be another first but any of us can break the spell if we can get close enough. I'll make sure the others know what to do so that we can all be vigilant. It's no more than she would do for us. She's part of our posse and we must help her.'

'I'm glad you made it back.'

'I did have some spiritual help. I won't bad mouth Sentries anymore. Did you find the part about the Sentry? He was so cool turning up at the opportune moment.'

'Are you up for another probe?'

'Sure, knock yourself out,' Joe said.

Concentrating he found the memory where the Sentry materialised in the Parsonage lounge. Cillian was about to destroy him when the Sentry forced them apart, saving Joe's life in a millisecond.

'Guilar, I *remember* him.' Finn witnessed Joe's encounter. 'The Sentries know about us. I thought I was wasting my time but they *are* watching over us. I had no notion.'

'I had no idea they could be so friendly,' Joe said.

'Neither did I.'

'What are your current plans, Finn?'

'We want to move back home. I drove past the Parsonage earlier and the Connellys have gone, for good I hope. I saw them packing up their car.'

'That's a result,' Joe said.

'For now, it means we can move. Ellie needs some stability. It's not doing her or the baby any good.'

'I can give you a hand with your kitchen,' Joe said. 'Give me a shout when you're ready.'

'Thanks, Joe. I might take you up on that. The sooner life gets back to normal the better.'

❧

Walking through the harbour, Finn spied a large black raven flying towards The Warren. Ravens were rare in St Ives and he was certain it was Branna. By the time he reached the old pottery, there was no sign of the bird but he had to check if she had come home. Murray opened the door, wearing a strained expression of grief. He failed to conceal his mood. 'Milton, what do you want?'

'I saw a raven in the harbour. Has Branna come back?'

'No, she hasn't. What are you suggesting?' He asked with a modicum of aggression.

'I think she's been cursed.'

'Cursed? What the hell are you talking about?'

'Her cousin Cillian cursed her to stay like a raven.'

'Are you suggesting that someone cast a spell on my wife?' Murray seemed to be laughing but it was closer to anger.

'Exactly. It is possible.'

'Well, that's made my day, Milton. You'd better leave before I lamp you. We were happy before you came back to Cornwall. In fact, I was happy before Branna told me about *you*. You have provided us with nothing but grief. Have you ever wondered why you have hardly any friends? In future, unless you have something positive to tell me, I suggest you stay the hell away. Next time, I'll call the police.' He slammed the door in his face.

Finn was startled but took time to digest his words. Drama and violence had been his companion for as long as he could remember. Maybe Murray was right and he did cause nothing but grief to those around him. Branna was missing and it was his fault. He had invited her into his drama and she had joined in willingly without question. Guilt played heavily on his mind during the journey back to Penberth. The guilt would stay with him for some time to come. It had been months since he had taken his silver Porsche out for a spin but it scarcely eased his mind.

He couldn't stop thinking about her. If he could get close enough the spell could be broken but at the same time, finding the raven was proving to be impossible.

Cillian drove Jarlath out of Dublin towards County Meath. Pulling the car into the grounds of Róisín House, the brothers were confronted with acres and acres of grass and trees. At the far end of the drive was a traditional country house, with the original farm part of the estate. The front door of the house was framed with climbing wisteria and the buds of white roses.

'What are we going to tell Mam?' Jarlath spoke for the first time in hours.

'The truth.' Cillian turned off the engine and stared at his brother, whose eyes were red from weeping.

Ciaran Connelly approached her two sons, wearing a yellow apron over a white dress and a wide smile. It changed to an expression of witless apprehension when there was no sign of her husband. Both men appeared tired and disgruntled, neither one of them wearing happy faces.

'Boys, where's your father?'

Cillian stepped out of the car and embraced his mother. 'There was a terrible accident and Dad was killed. There was nothing we could do. It was over so fast we are still in shock, Mam.'

Ciaran fell to her knees and started shrieking. Jarlath tried to calm her but she shoved him away. 'How could you have been so stupid, Cillian? What happened?'

'After that journey, I need a whisky.' Cillian stepped past her and walked liberally into the house as though it was his. His first thought concerned the safe, located in the basement cellar. He tore the door off using telekinesis. The drink could wait.

'What are you doing in here, Cillian? Your father's still warm and you're already rooting through his things.' His mother found him knee deep in boxes filled with paperwork. 'You've literally gotten home.'

'Father's cold,' he gave her a wry smile, which was rewarded with a hard smack across his cheek. 'Good, this is what I need.' Ignoring her completely, he gathered several leather bound journals and retired to the study where he threw them down on his father's mahogany desk.

'What *is* wrong with you?' Ciaran demanded, following her son. 'What the hell happened in Cornwall?'

'Nothing is wrong with me but I did come to my senses. I like the place and I might even move there. Don't worry about Father's business. I'm going to take care of everything but I would appreciate some privacy, if you don't mind, Mam. I need my space.'

Ciaran gave him a filthy look. 'How dare you speak to me like this in my own home, Cillian.'

'Your home?' He laughed. 'Seriously? This is the Connelly family home and I am now head of the family which makes it mine.'

'You've lost your mind and look sick to me.' She turned and walked away with tears falling down her cheeks. Jarlath was busy making a doorstep sandwich in the kitchen, spreading the ingredients far and wide.

'What happened to Cillian in Cornwall? His hair's falling out and he's covered in sores. You *are* going to tell me everything, boy, or I'll beat you black and blue with an iron.'

'Cillian discovered soul light and it's making him crazy,' he said. 'I think it's best we do as he says.'

'Soul light? What on earth is that?' She demanded.

'I don't know but he's different and I'm keeping my distance. I suggest you do the same.'

'Were you there when your father was killed? Did Cillian have anything to do with it?'

'No, of course not. Cillian would never hurt Dad.'

'I can't believe he's really dead.' She sat down and began to sob, holding a white linen handkerchief to her nose. An hour later when her daughter, Kaitlin, arrived home and heard the news about her father, she broke into hysterics. Cillian did nothing to comfort any of them and locked them all out of the study.

A service of remembrance took place a week later for Michael. The few remaining family members attended including Irish cousins Liam and Gael and their sons, Desmond and Niall.

Not for one moment did Ciaran believe the gruesome fate of her husband. Cillian remained vigilant and refused to elaborate. The will left everything to Ciaran, except the almanac and some papers belonging to Michael. These were gifted to Cillian.

He found a quiet moment to read a specific letter when the leather box arrived from the solicitors. The almanac had been placed in a Dublin bank vault, only to be accessed by his eldest child after his death. There was little of interest to Cillian in the collection of papers, aside from a brief history of ancestral brothers Liam and Paul.

The letter was the prize because it mentioned the talisman. Sitting near the river opposite the ancient burial mounds, he opened the letter addressed to his grandfather and began to read it.

15 September, 1942

My dear son, Art,

I hope you're recovering from your recent wounds. I am glad to hear you're home from the front and on the mend. I hope to have news soon of your brother James, fighting for the Allies in Italy. I hope he makes it back safely.

I am presently staying with cousin Shannon in Cornwall. War has touched the small town of St Ives and even in Cornwall things are not what they seem.

I have instructed Shannon to create a talisman to protect our bloodline from Etherea. It is essential that we endure and to this purpose I am making a great investment in order to accomplish this.

Since your mother died, I have been a lonely man. Shannon's daughter Duana is proving to be a suitable match to bear children. I am going to ask for her hand in marriage. She is strong willed and a young beauty, I am sure you will approve.

She has a vast array of abilities including healing and telekinesis. Our children will be powerful beyond measure. If anything happens to me, I trust that you will show her kindness and support.

The talisman will be forwarded to Meath when it is completed. Shannon is working on it now. It is based on a necklace of extraordinary beauty and value. I do not wish to keep it on my person for fear of being robbed. We live in dangerous times.

Send my love to your sister Lara. I will be home soon with a new wife and all will be well again.

Yours affectionately
Your father, James C.

Cillian had no concept of Duana being the object of his great-grandfather's desire or affection. According to a further entry in the almanac, she died the following August, less than a year after the letter had been written. She gave birth to Logan and committed suicide. There was nothing written about James after that entry. He never returned to Ireland. It was as though he simply disappeared.

Art (Cillian's grandfather) died in the 1960's, fathering only one child, his father, but Michael had never seen the talisman. Something had happened to James while he had been in Cornwall, which meant the talisman could potentially still be there. At some point in the future he would have to search the Parsonage.

The ulcers on his arm were healing slowly, leaving ugly scar tissue in their wake, which resembled burnt skin. Vanity was not one of his many attributes and he dismissed the damage whenever his mother brought it up.

Returning home to organise the family business and consolidate his own affairs, had given him precious time to adjust to soul light. The gentle passing of time was making his body more compliant for the next time he encountered Finn Milton. Soul light was changing his mentality, making him more articulate and attuned to its power.

For the time being, Cillian had more pressing matters at hand, the running of his father's estate and keeping his mother's nose out of it. The next trip to Cornwall would have to wait until he had everything in place, which could take months.

In the mean time he was waiting on a response from a solicitor concerning Logan's will. His intention was simple: his name would be on the sizeable portfolio of property in St Ives.

11

~

hiatus

four weeks later

The waiting room in the hospital was fit to bursting point. The door opened and Finn entered wearing green scrubs and a killer smile. 'We have a healthy son. Mum is doing well too.'

'Congratulations.' Rose gave him a hug. 'When can we see them?'

'Ellie is expecting you guys,' he said. 'You can go in.'

Joo was beside Rose, equally desperate to see the new mother and baby. The two women leapt from their seats and bounded into the small room. Bastian passed them togged out in doctor's uniform having successfully delivered the baby.

'One at a time,' Bastian said, slapping Finn on the back. 'He's a little bruiser, just like his old man. That was an easy birth if ever I saw one.'

'Thanks Bast, I'm stoked it went so well.'

'I'm relieved I delivered him safely,' Bastian said. 'After all you've been through it was the least I could do.'

Serina and Joe greeted Finn with a hug.

Milton embraced his son and presented him with a cigar.

'Well done for making me a grandparent, Finn. You've made me very proud.'

Ellie was sitting up in bed with the precious bundle in her arms, wrapped in a blue blanket. Finn slipped in and sat on the edge of the bed. Her copper curly hair was loose around her shoulders and she was smiling from ear to ear.

'He's asleep, can you believe it?' She lifted the blanket so they could all see the baby's tiny face.

'He's beautiful, Ellie,' Rose said. 'I think I'm going to cry.'

'Have you decided on a name yet?' Joo asked.

'Samuel Bastian Milton, after my grandfather and my crazy cousin, of course.' Finn said squeezing Ellie's hand.

'That's a lovely name,' Rose said. 'Heather will be pleased.'

'Sam Milton's going to break some hearts,' Joo said. 'He's beautiful.'

Ellie held on tightly to Finn's hand. 'He looks like you, Finn.'

'He has your eyes. I love you, Mrs Milton.'

'Soon, I promise,' she whispered.

'*When* are you two getting married?' Milton asked from the doorway. 'And where is my handsome grandson?' Finn passed his son into his father's waiting hands. 'He's a chip off the old block. You've done us proud, Ellie.'

'Thanks Finlay,' she replied. 'We are going to get married.'

'You have my blessing. I always wanted to have a daughter.' He cast a wink to Finn who smiled back warmly. 'He's perfect and I can sense he has abilities. Ha, he's telepathic already.'

'You're going to have some fun with this one,' Serina said, with Joe at her side.

The next day, he drove Ellie and their baby home in the Porsche and in the five months that followed the couple learnt how to become a family. He rebuilt the damaged kitchen in a wooden contemporary style with Joe's expert help. His writing desk was installed in the studio where he finished working on Brett's script. His personal belongings were moved from Camden and he emptied the London flat, renting it out to a theatre colleague.

All that mattered was his family. Wanting to forget the reasons that had brought them back so abruptly from New York, he focused on making a safe base. Joo remained with them at his insistence. He had grown more protective since the kidnapping and wanted to keep a closer eye on her. An expensive alarm system was installed with new locks on every door. If anyone tried breaking in, he would know about it. The subject of the Connellys was given space for Ellie's sake. She loved being a mother, which made him adore her even more.

All appeared to be calm on the outside but he refused to believe their peace would last. Cillian was involved in a news story that created some heat for a few weeks before disappearing off the radar. The location of Logan and Jared Connelly's hidden bodies came to light, and Branna was conveniently accused of their grievous murders. The next headline was her body turning up in Ireland and then the case was closed. Of course, armed with the fantastical truth, Finn didn't believe a word of it.

In town whenever he encountered Murray, the jeweller always crossed the road to avoid him. He had been through the mill with the police. No one had seen or heard from Branna adding more fuel to the theory that she had been cursed. There had been no sightings of ravens, which left him with a constant feeling of helplessness. Whoever was being classed as the Branna in Ireland could not possibly be the real Branna, not in his mind anyway.

He wished things were different but all he could do was to keep on eye on any changes. Sometimes he would check on the Parsonage, which was growing shabby with no one around to maintain it. The ground floor windows had been boarded up to deter squatters. The front door had been replaced with wooden boards. Plants had grown wild almost concealing the entrance with brambles, vines and hog weed.

One morning he looked at the upper windows and gasped. There was someone looking back at him. Their eyes locked before the spirit moved into the shadows. He parked the car and hurried to the back of the house, searching for a way in but his way was blocked. The back windows were covered with wooden boards. Every time he ventured into the Parsonage something terrible happened so he headed home. He tried to forget about it but the image of the ghost stayed with him throughout the afternoon.

Ellie was nursing Sam at the table when he brought three full bags of groceries into the kitchen. 'Are you okay?' She asked. 'You have an atmosphere about you today.'

He was rarely quiet. 'Yeah, you could say that.'

'Have you been to the Parsonage?'

'Your telepathy's far too good, Ellie.' He was putting the milk in the fridge.

'So I'm right for a change.' Sam was falling asleep in her arms.

'I had a look. The place is haunted.'

'I don't want you going anywhere near that place.'

'I know. I won't. It's just …I think I saw Duana's ghost.'

'Who's Duana?'

'Logan's mother,' he replied.

'Ghosts, honestly Finn, whatever next?'

'There are ghosts in that house, ask Joo if you don't believe me. I need to talk to her but I'd rather go with your blessing than sneak around behind your back.'

She asked. 'Why is this so important?'

'Duana knows about the talisman. She might be able to help me find Branna. It's been six months since she disappeared. It wasn't her body they found in Ireland. We have unfinished business. Maybe I should talk to my dad or even visit my grandmother. Someone must know something. I can't sit here and do nothing!'

He felt subdued and put away the last of the groceries. It was clear she was unhappy with the subject, but he was tired of ignoring it. He watched her carry Sam to the bedroom to place the little boy in his crib.

When she came back he was staring out of the small window overlooking the lane.

'I know you too well, Finn Milton. You won't be happy until you plane to that house.'

'I only want to talk to her,' he replied.

'I want a normal life with you and Sam. Is that too much to ask? No magic, no witches, no spirits and no Sentries. I want us to be a normal family.' She stretched her arms around his waist, resting her face against his back. 'Maybe you should visit your gran. At least do this before you plane to the Parsonage. She has been around a lot longer than we have. Maybe she knows something, what have you got to lose?'

He had everything he needed but something was always nagging him. Something he couldn't fix. No matter how much time he spent looking for her, Branna was nowhere to be found. Cillian would be untouchable with a talisman even though it was lost.

Dennis' vision was always there. Not a day went by when he didn't think about its relevance or their uncertain future. It had become an obsession. She was right about wanting a normal life. He wanted one too.

'Thanks, darling. I'll go and see Heather first.'

'I asked Joo if she would babysit for us tonight,' she said brightly and he turned around.

'What did you have in mind?' He held her in his arms.

'Since Sam was born, we've been stuck in this house and I thought it would be good for both of us if we went out.'

'It's a good idea,' he said, stroking her hair.

'I want to plane with you.'

'What about Joo? Is she okay about looking after Sam? I don't want to impose on her because she lives here.'

'Joo wants to give us a break and has kindly offered. She knows we'll be zonked out when we get back, but I've always wanted to plane with you and this could be our chance.'

'Let's go when Sam goes to sleep later.'

Joo was watching a film on the television in the studio. Sam was sleeping soundly and the baby listening device was plugged into the wall next to his cot. Finn and Ellie lay down on their bed smiling at one another.

'I can't believe we're actually doing this,' she said.

'You've been pregnant the whole time.'

'That wasn't all my fault,' she smiled.

He found her hand and gave it a tight squeeze before closing his eyes. The next moment their souls were floating in the air above their bodies. She idly brushed her hand through his spirit and it parted and reformed. He smiled finding her thoughts easily in her mind. She would be able to read his for the first time in ages, which was partly why he agreed to planing in the first place. It would be simpler than having to tell her everything.

He tore up through the ceiling, pulling her spirit behind him. Below the town of St Ives was lit up with street and restaurant lights all around the harbour. He pushed on towards Porthgwidden beach with her flying close behind.

Ellie: *I want it to be just about us tonight, Finn.*

He drew up close and planted a kiss on her lips. They embraced and appeared to become one entity. He ascended holding on to her, all the while kissing her passionately. Their souls careened through lower lying clouds until a carpet of stars was revealed.

Finn: *I love you more than I thought was possible.*

Ellie: *I love you too. This is amazing. Why haven't we done this before? I feel free for the first time in ages.*

Finn: *It was good of Joo to do this for us. She seems a lot better nowadays. I thought she might have been scarred from her ordeal but she's a right little trooper.*

Ellie: *She's a survivor, like you.*

Finn: *She needs to find herself a partner, that's what she needs to do. Why is she always single?*

Ellie: *She's never found the right guy and won't take second best.*

Finn: *So who is this Mr Right? Do we know him?*

Ellie: *You do know one of them but you mustn't say anything. If there's one thing I've learnt, these things work themselves out in time.*

He read her mind and learnt the truth. Joo was holding a torch for one of Bastian's close friends. He smiled because he knew more. Although it appeared unrequited at face value, both parties were actually interested but neither one was aware or making a move. She caught his thoughts and broke into a grin.

Finn: *I'm not getting involved, not even remotely. Don't give me that look. Do you fancy flying to Godrevy lighthouse? Come on, I'll race you Mrs Milton but you won't beat me.*

Ellie: *You really know how to show a girl a good time.*

During the past six months, Cillian had been working extensively on a plan to how he could acquire the large St Ives Connelly estate. Theoretically it belonged to Branna, being the only living descendant. He had designed an elaborate plot making her responsible for murdering her father and brother. After several long phone calls, the local police unearthed two bodies buried in the Parsonage garden. Jared and Logan were duly identified and their deaths officially registered. The press splashed the story across the front page of local newspapers with glee, publishing the potential murder story for all to read. Cillian painted a dire picture of Branna, accusing her of murder and running away to avoid being caught by the police. Due to her cursed absence she was unable to defend herself. The situation fell hard on Murray, who had to deal with awkward interviews with the police. Within hours the persistent press set up camp outside his house, haranguing him every time he opened the front door.

With each piece of his plan falling in place, Cillian played his final card.

Finding a woman in her late twenties, who resembled Branna's shape and size, wasn't difficult. A Dublin hotel receptionist called Carrie Mullen served him when he booked himself into a suite in the city. In size and looks, she was Branna's double, even down to her long lustrous black hair. After a few drinks, she was persuaded to spend the night with him. Carrie was single with no local family. No one would miss her.

He invited her home for the weekend but she never made it to the family estate. Probed mentally to death, he began transforming her corpse into his cousin.

The next day, with Carrie unrecognisable, he called the police. Having planted a charmed scenario in his family's minds about Branna visiting and causing threatening behaviour, the authorities believed the lie and issued a report. The fake Branna Smith was officially pronounced dead and her body swiftly cremated, thus destroying the vital truth.

The development reached the St Ives constabulary and a policeman visited Murray. Reluctantly he had to listen to the story of his wife attacking her Connelly relatives in Ireland. His heart was broken when he heard the accounts surrounding her death.

Cillian had written a statement of accidental death in self-defence, whilst protecting his family. Amazingly it stuck and Murray fell to pieces.

Some time later when a local solicitor finalised the probate details of the Connelly estate, the sole heir became apparent. The point Cillian had failed to consider was Branna taking a husband. Everything, including Jared's nightclub, the Parsonage and three retail properties, was left to Murray Smith.

A letter arrived at the Meath estate explaining the beneficiary. Cillian saw red and made steps to contest the will immediately. After months of legal wrangling, it was time to make travel plans.

On his father's advice, Finn decided it was high time he visited his paternal grandmother Heather Pengelly. She had known the Connellys during the 1940's when war had touched the people of St Ives. Walking along the harbour front to the Digey, he recalled an earlier conversation he had shared with his father.

'Shannon Connelly lived in the Parsonage with her daughter back then. I think Heather knew the daughter but she died very young. If you decide to see her, please don't mention your mother or your visions. She might have a heart attack. Heather always asks after you and once you get to know her, she will surprise you. She constantly surprises me but she isn't a conventional woman.'

'If Heather can help me find the talisman, and I can destroy it, Cillian will no longer be a threat. Ellie and I will always live with the fear of him coming after us otherwise. Even though I know they've gone, he will come back for me. How can we raise a child safely under these circumstances?'

'If you find it, you'll have to run the gauntlet again. Have you considered this?'

'Yes, Dad. It feels like I have found a new vocation in the underworld. One I won't be able to remember.'

He arrived at the old cottage in The Digey having second thoughts. Guilt played heavily because he had never known his grandmother. Their estrangement had been another symptom of the Connelly curse, following the moment of his birth and the death of his mother, Heather's only daughter.

Desperation had forced the visit, like the one he had made to see his great grandmother the previous year. Deep down he prayed Heather would be as generous with her time and knowledge as Jessica had been.

Nervously he knocked on the tiny blue wooden door. There were symbols carved into the wooden door frame and his finger traced the shapes while he waited. Instinctively he thought about protection symbols. He had made an effort and dressed smartly in his best black jeans, white shirt and black tie, topped off with a black jacket.

The door opened marginally and a short, white haired woman peered out. 'What do you want?' She demanded.

'I'm Finn, your grandson.' He assumed he was the last person she was expecting to see.

Her expression melted suddenly like a soft breeze, as though she had turned into someone else.

'Finn? What are you doing here?'

She raised her glasses, hanging around her neck on a chain, and stared at him.

'I need to ask you a few questions if you don't mind. It's important.'

Heather studied his face through her thick-rimmed glasses. His hair was coppery brown with a prominent white streak. His eyes were pale grey, like his mother's. Her eyes were watering because he looked so much like her late daughter Phoebe.

'You'd better come in, it's going to be a cold one today.'

She smiled and he lowered his head to follow her through the small doorway. The dimly lit sitting room was decorated with patterned lime green wallpaper. All her belongings were neatly arranged, the room furnished from another era. Family photos graced the walls, including ones of him as a child. There were several of his mother and her brother Robert as children.

A framed wedding photograph of Jessica and Kingsley, taken in the 1920s, prompted him to look closer. He could hardly believe how pretty Jessica had been in her youth. No wonder Kingsley had married her. She had been a stunning woman.

'Jessie was beautiful when she was younger. Your father talked to me over the years about your plight. I can't believe how much hatred can come from love. Would you like some tea?' She asked.

'Yes please. I'm sorry we never knew each other. I'd like to change that.'

'Maybe a change is in the air, I felt it when you came in.' Her Cornish accent was soft and her tone knowing. 'You have so much of your mother about you. I can sense it as though she's with us right now.'

'I wish I'd known her.' He thought about the possibility of having part of his mother inside him due to the soul light—part of her soul. *Maybe it isn't such a stretch*, he thought.

'She was a beautiful girl, my Phoebe. I miss them all—especially her. And you Finn, you've become a father.'

'I'm sorry I haven't been to see you.'

'You're here now, that's the important thing.' In the kitchen she placed a kettle on the Aga to boil some water. 'Your father told me about the baby, of course. He's so proud of you. Can you reach for those two mugs?'

The kitchen was so small that his head brushed the ceiling. Aside from the Aga, the kitchen housed a hand carved wooden table, four chairs, a modern fridge and a Belfast sink. The back door led into a small courtyard with an outside toilet.

The space was rammed full with flowering spring flowers and pot plants. He smiled at how perfectly she fitted into the tiny space. She had done for years.

'I had no idea these cottages were so small.' He placed the mugs on the table.

'I prefer the word 'compact',' she smiled. 'Shall we go into the lounge? I think we'll be more comfortable in there. When I married your grandfather, we raised two children in this cottage. Hard to believe, isn't it? You should see how tiny the rooms are upstairs. But so much time has been wasted, Finn. What's the real reason you came to visit me?'

'I'm here because of the Connellys,' he said.

'Ah yes, the Connellys, the oldest blight on my world. Why are you bothering with them? They are all gone now, thanks mostly to you.'

'Not all of them are gone. I need to ask you something from the time of the war if you don't mind,' he said. 'Did you know James Connelly?'

She fell silent at the mention of his name. Out of her comfort zone she reached into the drawer of an oak bureau and dragged out a cardboard file. Inside were old newspaper clippings, and rifling through them she picked one out and handed it to him.

The clipping was from a faded old copy of *The Cornishman* newspaper, dated 1943.

'It was such a long time ago. This might help to explain it. Ah, how do you like your tea?' On hearing the kettle whistling, she disappeared back to the kitchen.

'White, no sugar please.'

He turned his attention to the clipping. The article listed Duana Connelly as having committed suicide at the family home, The Parsonage, owned by her mother Shannon. There was a short eulogy but no details of a funeral.

There was a faded black and white photograph of Duana and he shuddered.

'You've met her, haven't you? I can tell. You recognise her.' She passed him a mug of hot tea and a plate of plain biscuits. 'I only have Garibaldis, I'm afraid.'

'Thanks.' He sipped the tea and bit into a biscuit. 'I saw her ghost standing in the window, upstairs in the Parsonage the other day. I want to astral plane and actually speak to her. Back in March, I was involved in an issue at the Parsonage and I was planing. I met her then and she spoke to me. Unfortunately I haven't been back because Ellie doesn't like it.'

'Astral Planing, huh? And you can see ghosts and commune with them. That's an interesting ability, Finn. Not many people can do that but you have spent time with Sentries. That alone can permanently change your perception. I know Ana haunts St Ives because I've seen her too. She never had a proper burial and died not long after giving birth to that bastard, Logan. In the end something bad happened to her, I'm sure of it. Shannon raised that monster and poured all her hatred into him. I should know because he killed my husband, Sam.'

'I'm so sorry to bring this up but you actually believe me, part of me thought you wouldn't,' he said. 'It sounds crazy but I'm friends with Logan's daughter, Branna. She believes Shannon made a talisman for James but it's been lost for years.'

'James disappeared not long after Ana died, leaving Shannon alone to raise her baby,' she continued. 'He came to Cornwall to find a new wife, the previous year, since he had been recently widowed. The trouble began when James became interested in Ana but he was far too old for her, in my opinion. People talked about Ana seducing James with witchcraft but that was a lie. She was as harmless as a butterfly and just as fragile.'

'You knew Ana.' He deduced from the poignancy of her words.

'We were friends for a while and even had our pregnancies at the same time. For a while Ana was in love with a handsome soldier called Thomas. He was posted here with his unit before the D-Day landings during the war. He had one of those Clark Gable moustaches. She was excited about their relationship and talked about moving to America after the war but he perished in France like so many others. I remember James. Ana told me about his enchantments and how he took advantage of her. He could even be Logan's father. I only saw her once after she split up with Thomas. We lost touch around the time James came to live with them. That's what happens sometimes, you drift apart.'

'Do you know what happened to James?'

'All the answers you seek are in that house, Finn. There are some ghosts with unfinished business, ones that never had burials. Since you can commune with ghosts, I suggest you do that. One of them knows the truth.'

'I thought as much,' he sighed. 'Our lives always seem to be affected by that family, one way or another.'

'Don't be scared of the wind spirit,' she said, resting her hand over his. 'Your mother has no control over her actions but you can help her with that.'

'What are you talking about?'

'When you were born, your mother gave you something very special … a tiny part of her soul. It's time for you to give it back to her. It's not your fault, but the time is approaching.'

'How do you know?'

'It's written all over you. I can read you like an open book. She has reached out to you in your dreams, hasn't she? I knew she would, one day.'

He was startled. She was more powerful than he imagined and he had so many questions. 'Dad doesn't believe me. He told me not to mention it. But I can't hide anything from you, can I?'

'No,' she smiled. 'No one chooses to be born like this. I've made mistakes in my life but one of them is looking much healthier now you're here.'

'Thanks, Heather.'

'Do one thing for me, Finn. Please don't lose any more of your soul light.'

'I had no choice.'

'It makes no difference in the end if you have to make sacrifices. If he takes it all from you, he'll not only kill you but it will spark off the demise of our world. He has no idea what he is dealing with. Very few people understand what is at stake. So much of our history has already been lost.'

He was reminded of Dennis' vision and how similar her words sounded to his warning. 'What do you know about soul light?'

'I know it's not of this earth and capable of giving the host immeasurable power.'

'Where did it come from?' He asked.

'You have always looked to the stars. Where do you think it came from? It made Sam's father Kingsley very powerful. He used it to build an amazing house, on his own, but that was a very long time ago.'

He was lost for words. The idea that he carried alien matter inside him made him retch. His hands began to glow. She held them steady in hers. 'For you, this is a gift because you have a good heart. Whatever it takes, you must stop him from taking any more.'

'I'll try but what if he forces me again, against my will? He threatened to kill one of my friends when I refused him. What can I do if he blackmails me again?'

'I understand sacrifice too well. The fate of your soul light is the most important thing. You must guard it from this moth with your life. It's your flame, Finn.'

Heather knew everything Dennis had shown him because she had experienced the same vision. She was referring to him as a Flame and he was playing host to an energy that would prove unstable in the wrong hands.

'The future *can* change, Finn. It's not been written yet. Here, let me fix your telepathy. Who knows how this is going to play out. Our family has a history of receiving visions, and every now and then the warning is enough to change the outcome.'

She touched his forehead and closed her eyes. The next moment he could block his mind again. They looked at each other before she simply smiled.

'This visit has been long overdue, I'm sorry it took me so long to realise.'

'You're here now, that's all that matters, Finn. Bring Ellie and Sam over, I'd love to meet them both. At times like this we need each another more than we care to admit.'

He embraced his grandmother and was surprised at her warmth. It was unexpected. He was still reeling at her revelations when he stepped out into the lane.

'You don't have to say anything,' she said.

'It was lovely to see you, Gran.'

'You know where I am if you need me. Good luck finding the talisman. There are forces at work that are on a much larger scale than you can possibly imagine. You never know, maybe Ana can help you to find your lost friend as well.'

It was a cold November morning when Cillian knocked on the door of the old pottery. Murray was confronted with a sickly looking man with thinning hair on opening it.

'Hello, I'm Cillian Connelly. I'm related to your late wife. I was wondering if I could steal a moment of your time.'

Murray allowed him to come in and turned on the kettle to make some tea, all the while saying nothing to the weird looking stranger who was peering around.

'I was so sorry to hear about your wife. I knew Branna but not very well. She was such a beautiful soul.'

'Why are you really here, Cillian?' He asked curtly. 'Let's cut the bullshit, shall we?'

'I'm one of Branna's closest living relatives and it appears that you, Murray, have been bequeathed the entire Cornish estate. I've tried contesting it, but it's proved difficult.'

'So it's you. What do you really want?' Murray asked.

'I want the land which belonged to Logan Connelly, including the Parsonage.'

'You can't have it,' he replied. 'I don't believe any of those lies about Branna. She never hurt anyone, never mind her own twin brother.'

'What little you know, Murray! The truth has finally come out about that witch. Branna was no different to her father and she murdered him in cold blood. We all make choices and she betrayed her own blood. Didn't you know your wife? How very careless of you.'

'You're the one spreading those lies about her,' Murray said.

'And why would I do that? I feel nothing personal towards her, but like I said, we were never close.'

'And is that why you cursed her to remain a raven? She's still alive, isn't she?'

'You've rare insight for a man with no abilities but then Finn Milton probably told you that. He has an uncanny gift for uncovering trails of deceit but then again, he's a pathfinder. So Murray, how does it feel being so ordinary in such a strange place among so many gifted individuals?'

'Oh, Mr Connelly, I've many abilities and one of them is making you leave my house. Get out. You're getting nothing from me. I've no interest in helping anyone who's hurt my wife and don't you ever mention that Milton name in front of me again. He's nothing but trouble.'

'You think you can actually outwit me?' A twisted laugh left Cillian's mouth. 'You're pathetic. I was hoping you'd be more forthcoming but you've left me with no choice.' He focused a telepathic charm on Murray, who was immediately taken off guard and unable to move.

Murray Smith, scribe aliquid et ponam in conspectu vestro. Et tu confidere fecisti mortiferam et mortuum est, a timido ariolatus est. Et mandata mea non interrogabant.

Once the words were spoken, Murray was locked in a catatonic state unable to talk. Cillian withdrew a brown envelope filled with several papers. He made Murray dutifully sign each one, giving away ownership of all the Connelly properties.

'Obedience is underrated, Mr Smith. In five minutes you'll be yourself again, well sort of. You will not remember this visit but you will accept that I, Cillian Connelly, am the sole heir of Logan Connelly's land and estate. You will never question the fate of your wife. She died a murderer and you can consider yourself free of that legacy. She never loved you and used you to hide her true identity.

Oh and while we're at it, you can forget your history with Finn Milton. When you next meet him you will not remember him in the slightest which will wind him up no end. Call that my sense of humour, if you like, Murray. I'm a twisted prickly fellow, as I've been told on many occasions. I bid you farewell. You've made my day, hell you've made my year and I can't thank you enough for your assistance in the matter. It's been so much fun.'

Cillian bowed theatrically then departed clutching the brown envelope with glee. He was feeling victorious and walked in the direction of his solicitors with a spring in his step.

Five minutes later when Murray snapped out of the trance, the kettle was howling. He had no idea why he was sitting in the lounge. One thing was clear though, Branna had been revealed as a cold-blooded murderer and not the person he believed she was. Tearing off his wedding ring her threw it with force into the unlit fireplace. A single tear fell down his face. He had lost something very dear to him but had no idea what it was or when it happened.

Sam was sitting in his high chair, eating his breakfast. Ellie was spoon-feeding him and Finn was engrossed in the local newspaper, drinking coffee. The couple had fallen into an unfamiliar but simple routine. She had resumed her painting and he had started writing a novel. All was calm.

'Sam looks so much like you,' she said. 'I can't believe he's six months old already.'

He glanced at his son and Sam smiled back. The boy was impossible to ignore and he ruffled his tiny patch of blond hair. His eyes were dark green and his smile was infectious.

'The strangest thing is being able to read his mind. Who would've thought that babies could be so intelligent and focused? I imagined we'd have to wait a while longer before we knew what he wanted.'

'He's a chip off the old block,' she said. 'Are you going out for your walk?'

'Yeah,' he said. 'I've got to keep looking for her.'

'She was a good friend but I don't believe those lies. I can't imagine how Murray's handling it.'

'I know, Ellie. It's been months since that story broke and it still feels wrong.'

Every day he would take the same walk along the harbour front, across to Porthgwidden and Porthmeor Beach before climbing Porthmeor Hill, and strolling along Alexandra Road to the Parsonage. He would walk home via Higher Stennack but there was never any sign of the raven. He spotted Murray out on many occasions but his stern expression was always primed to keep his distance. But on that particular morning near The Sloop Inn, Murray behaved as though he didn't recognise him.

He decided to approach more out of curiosity than anything else. 'Murray, how are you?' He was greeted with a look of confusion.

'Do I know you?' Murray asked.

'You don't remember me?'

'Should I?'

On reading his mind there was an unexpected yet familiar pattern. Murray had been charmed. His beliefs had been altered radically. His recent memories were plain to see and Finn shuddered to the core when he realised who had returned. Only one person had the ability to make charms of that nature. Cillian had visited Murray and taken advantage of him.

He could hear distant laughing as though it had been primed especially for him. It gave him a chill.

When her body turned up in Southern Ireland, Branna was confirmed as the Connelly murderer. The murder case had been closed. At the time he hadn't believed a word of it but a charmed Murray was convinced like never before of her guilt and fabricated deception.

Breaking the charm would bring Murray and Cillian back together, which would only end badly. It was safer for Murray to remain oblivious, at least until he knew more. Suddenly he thought twice about fixing his mind and said, 'I must be mistaken. I thought you were someone else.'

Murray grumbled and carried on about his business.

Finn headed for the Parsonage, watching his back all the time. When he drew closer, he could see that the boards over the front door had been removed and a white van was parked in the drive. A serviceman was installing a new door. Boldly, he decided to approach.

'Excuse me, is anyone living here now?'

'The new owner arrived yesterday.' The workman had a strong Cornish accent. 'He's gone to Truro on business. You can catch him later.'

'What's his name?'

'Cillian Connelly.'

Finn nodded and walked away. Logan and Jared's deaths had been registered. Branna would have been the sole benefactor. With Branna confirmed dead, her husband Murray would have been in line to inherit everything, which explained Cillian's motive for greed. He had charmed Murray out of the entire Connelly estate. More than ever his thoughts moved to Duana. It was time to pay her a visit.

Concerned, he arrived home to find Ellie painting on a large canvas in the studio. Joo was working a late shift at the salon and Sam was having a nap on a blanket on the sofa.

'Hello, beautiful.' He kissed her on the cheek.

'Good walk?'

'Someone has moved into the Parsonage,' he replied.

'Anyone we know?'

'Cillian.'

'Are you sure?'

'Yes and I told you this would happen.'

'Finn, please be reasonable,' she said defensively.

'I *am* being reasonable. I want to protect you and Sam but the reality is – I can't. I have to find that talisman and destroy it. Cillian's a real threat. Without the talisman, he's too powerful.'

'Can't you ask Joe to help?'

'Joe had a narrow escape last time. I can't ask him again, it's not fair.'

'I don't like this at all, Finn.'

'Don't worry, I'm going to plane. He won't see me. I need to summon one of the ghosts. I can't ignore it anymore. I must talk with Duana.'

'No sign of Branna then?'

He had refused to give up on her, even though locally her name was mud and her reputation in tatters. 'No, but I don't think it was her body they found in Ireland.'

She gave him a tight hug. 'I feel the same way, poor Murray.'

'Bolt the door when I leave. I don't feel comfortable leaving you on your own, even with Joo. I'm going to call a few of the guys and get them to come over, do you mind?'

'Of course not. Are you going to be long?'

'I have no idea. As long as it takes, I guess,' he said. 'Either way I must go.'

❧

When he planed to the Parsonage his spirit body was pale and well defined. He paused outside the ominous stark building to listen. Cillian had not returned but there was a white van parked in the drive. He could hear the noise of a radio and the muffled sound of a conversation from workmen brought in to fix up the house. With silent determination he darted through the first floor wall and came to a stop in the upstairs corridor. The space was freezing cold.

The air was stale. A glowing light began to form at the other end of the corridor. He was close to the hidden back stairs where a new door had been recently hung. Beyond it, something was clanking loudly like chains.

Floating through the door, he hovered at the top of the old twisty wooden stairwell. Glancing at the ceiling the clanking sound stopped. There was a large unmoving metal hook. Something supernatural rushed through him making him shudder involuntarily.

Finn: *Wait a minute.*

Ghost: *You shouldn't have come back here, Finn Milton. He's back and wants your soul. He won't stop until he has taken everything from you.*

Finn: *Duana, please show yourself. I mean you no harm. I must talk to you. I have no one left to turn to and I am running out of time.*

The form of a young woman emerged, her face etched with sorrow. Sensing her pain he tried to shield himself from her emotions but they were intense. Her mind was repressed, her memories shattered and he was unable to make any sense of them.

Duana: *You cannot read me, Finn. No one can.*

Finn: *I need your help. There must be some way I can help you.*

Duana: *No one can help me. I'm lost.*

Finn: *You're wrong about that.*

Duana: *What gives you the arrogance to think you're different?*

Finn: *Because I am different and I need you.*

Duana: *There is nothing I have that could possibly be of any interest to you.*

Finn: *You're so wrong about that.*

Around her neck were sixteen precious stones laid in a row with smaller ones in between. It was a necklace from the last century and the prospect consumed him.

Duana: *You want this? You can't have it.*

Finn: *Duana, please – are you wearing the talisman?*

Duana: *It makes no difference if I am. I'm forever lost.*

She suddenly shrieked and disappeared. He was left wondering if he had scared her away completely. Either way, he was left alone wondering if the potential opportunity had been wasted.

2nd Ghost: *You shouldn't ask too much of her.*

An unfamiliar female voice entered his mind and he followed it back along the corridor. Standing upright with her feet brushing the floor, and wearing what looked like a long white dress, the woman was quite different to Duana. She had short hair and wore a strict expression.

Finn: *Who are you?*

2nd Ghost: *Melandra is my name.*

Finn: *What happened to you?*

Melandra: *I was pushed down the stairs and the fall broke my neck. After I died, my spirit was trapped in this house. I don't know how to move on.*

Finn: *Who did this to you?*

Melandra: *My husband, Logan.*

Finn: *You're Branna's mother?*

Melandra: *There are many mothers in this house. We have all lost our children. You were lost to one and she is tormented beyond belief.*

She was referring to his mother Phoebe but as much as he wanted to know more, he had to focus on the talisman.

Finn: *I must find Duana.*

Melandra: *She won't come to you because she's scared.*

Finn: *Why?*

Melandra: *Because you only want something from her.*

Finn: *This is different. I need the talisman that Shannon made for her cousin James. Without it I fear more people are going to die, including myself.*

Melandra: *Do not mention that name in this house. That man was one of the worst offenders.*

Finn: *What did he do?*

Melandra: *He hurt Ana the most. Do I have to spell it out to you? I can sense you're not here to harm her. If I were you and still mortal, and free of that indomitable curse, I would stay away from this place. However, you're not about to give up or listen to the warbling of an old ghost. Logan hurt you too. We all have this in common, Finn. His mother's here but she has suffered so much. I fear you are not strong enough for what lies ahead and you will fail trying.*

Duana materialised next to her in the corridor. He wondered if she had been there all along. The two female ghosts were staring at him intently.

Duana: *Do you want to hear the miserable story of my life? You're a determined man and you're risking everything for her, your love. You love her so much. It's hard to believe a man can care so much for an old talisman.*

Finn: *It must be destroyed for my family to be safe. Cillian can conceal his violence and crimes using his abilities and he is growing stronger. The talisman is protecting him and I must stop him. There is little time. I fear you are the only one who can help me.*

Duana: *I'm warning you, Finn... if Cillian becomes aware of your soul, you must be prepared for flight. He can disperse your soul with a single thought now he has soul light. I will shield you from sight when we mind lock but you won't like what I'm about to show you. No one has had the guts to come this close to me before and I like your soul light. It calms me. It's beautiful and strangely enough, it gives me hope that there is still good in this world. This is why I will help you.*

In 1942, I was a young woman about to start her adult life. Everyone called me Ana. It was less mysterious than Duana, what with my mother being an unpopular witch, it raised fewer eyebrows. It was an ordinary summer's day when he arrived at the Parsonage, a day I'll never forget. It started a chain of events that led to my untimely and violent demise.

12

〜

the unexpected visitor

August 1942

The heat from the midday sun was burning her fair freckled skin. Ana pulled the straw hat over her head to shade her eyes. A recent addition to the Parsonage garden had arrived and she was preparing to plant it in the hard ground with her mother's help.

'I love olives,' Shannon said. 'I hope it thrives in this field of a garden.'

The tree-lined garden was very secluded, without any close neighbours to watch over their activities. The two women looked at one another. The same height and build, they looked like sisters to a stranger. Shannon raised her hand and focused on the olive tree resting in its large pot. Slowly it began to rise as though by itself. The two women walked behind the floating plant along the gravel path to the tip of the lawn as though it was the most natural thing to do in the world.

At the end of the generous tree-lined garden was a cultivated vegetable garden designed by Shannon's late mother. Everything was laid out in neat raised beds with ample drainage. Precious water was collected in makeshift barrels.

Since Shannon and Ana were both able to wield telekinesis, the ability to move objects with their minds made gardening an enjoyable chore. The vegetable harvest was due. It was essential in wartime. Ana had planted potatoes, onions, carrots, cabbage and green beans.

With rationing in place, any home grown food was a bonus. A pigsty housed two large fat animals.

'I want the olive to be in the centre of the garden,' Shannon said and Ana wielded telekinesis expertly in order to move the sapling. 'In front of the raised beds.'

A male voice interrupted their activity. 'Would you like a hand with that?'

Both women were alerted to the new company. Ana dropped the tree gently to the ground where it stood upright on its root bag.

The sound of a man had been absent from their lives for a long time. The sun blinded Ana but she could make out a tall shape standing near the garden gate. He was wearing a short bowler hat and a three-piece tweed suit.

Shannon pulled off her gardening gloves.

'Can I help you?'

'What if he saw me moving the olive?' Ana whispered.

Her face changed when she recognised her cousin, James Connelly: *Ana, he's family, no need to worry. He's just like us.*

Their clandestine abilities had been passed on from their ancestors. They made particular care to conceal anything out of the ordinary to not attract any unwelcome attention. There had always been plenty of rumours. Shannon was considered to be a witch by many, yet she continued to live by her own rules. No one was going to tell her what to do.

'Oh my, James,' Shannon said with a flirty smile, her demeanour changing radically. 'Is that really you? It's been so long.'

'Shannon, you look well,' James said, taking off his hat to reveal a full head of tidy black hair.

Shannon was in her forties and carried herself with an air of arrogance. Her long dark hair was tied back with an art deco silver clip. Her pale skin and clear blue eyes made her striking to almost any man that came into her company. She was wearing khaki linen trousers and a white shirt, tucked in at her narrow waist. Where Shannon lost out on height, she made up for by having a perfect hourglass figure.

James looked younger than his years.

He had lost his wife, Caren, to consumption two years before. It was the first time he had seen his cousin in years.

Ana stepped out of the sun and studied him. James looked her up and down as though she was a commodity to be traded with.

She closed her mind to stop him from reading it.

'Ana, meet James,' Shannon said. 'My first cousin from Ireland. The years have been kind to you, James. I was so sorry to hear about Caren. Life can't be easy without your loved ones close to you.'

'Thank you, Shannon, you're too kind,' James said, instantly distracted by Ana who had approached them. 'This must be Duana. You've blossomed into a real beauty, my girl.'

James took her thin hand and kissed it, using the opportunity to smell her skin.

She shirked away from him. 'It's Ana.'

'Ana, what a beautiful name,' James said.

'What are you doing here?' Shannon asked.

'I'm visiting my kin in Cornwall, is there no shame in that?' He smiled and displayed a perfect set of teeth.

'Where are you staying?' Ana asked him.

'I was rather hoping you could put me up,' he replied. 'But only for a short while.'

'That would be my pleasure, James. Ana, put the kettle on and make some tea. We'll prepare a room for you. So, how are your boys? I hear your eldest, James, is in Italy.'

'He's fighting at the front. Art wasn't so lucky. He was hit by shrapnel and has some lodged in his leg. He came home last month. He's lucky to be alive since most of his unit were killed.'

'It's a bad time for everyone. Why don't you come inside?'

Shannon led the way into the house, which was furnished with some of the best pieces of arts and crafts that Cornwall and Devon had to offer. The feel of the house was light and airy. Modest and tidy, the walls were decorated with exquisite handmade wallpaper.

James found himself at home immediately and eyed Ana with an ardent passion. This was not lost on Shannon, who ensured Ana spent as little time with him as possible.

'How old is Ana?' James asked over brandy later that evening.

'She's nineteen and going to university in London when the war is over,' Shannon replied hastily. 'She has plans to be a teacher and wants to study in one of the best places.'

'Not getting married? What a waste of a young woman, her place should be working in the home, not for someone else. Incidentally, I was hunting in Meath and killed a hog with my rifle. It was an extraordinary beast. I've had it stuffed. It will look splendid hanging in your hallway. It should arrive tomorrow.' James was expressing too much pride and enthusiasm.

'Thank you but you shouldn't have done that.'

'I wanted to. I've heard stories about you, Shannon. Is it true you can make a talisman that will shield one from *Etherea*?'

'You don't mince your words. Do you want me to make you one?'

'That would be fantastic,' James said. 'How can I ever thank you?'

'You're family, you don't have to,' she replied.

Ana hurried up the stairs having listened to their conversation. In her room she climbed into bed and was unimpressed by the mysterious cousin visiting from Ireland. She shared her mother's distaste of the stuffed hog. However, without disrespecting James, she would show interest and flatter him.

In the following week, James made himself more at home. He had no intention of leaving and Shannon appeared to be perfectly content with the arrangement.

Working a part-time job cleaning local offices and local landowner's homes, Ana grabbed any opportunity to earn money. It provided her with a small income and more importantly, time away from the Parsonage.

She had few friends in St Ives, although two years her senior, Heather Trevaskas was someone she had grown close to in the previous year through working together. Heather had become engaged to her boyfriend Samuel Pengelly and their wedding was planned for early November.

There had been a big change in St Ives since the US Army personnel had arrived almost overnight. There was a constant threat of gunfire from the skies. At night there were curfews. For the past few weeks, Ana had been secretly dating an American soldier called Thomas Janet. They were the same age and after a dozen hand-written letters, she agreed to meet him for tea one afternoon. On every afternoon since their first date, they met for an hour to walk near the beach, which was fenced off with barbed wire.

Ana was leaving work when she caught sight of Thomas and waved to him. The handsome young soldier's face transformed when he saw her. He was tall with dark brown hair, a skinny moustache and deep blue eyes. 'Ana, are you still working?' He planted a kiss on her lips.

'I've finished. What are you up to?'

'I have to report to my barracks,' he said. 'Do you fancy going to the cinema tomorrow afternoon?'

Ana pulled out her diary and checked. 'I should be free by three o'clock.'

'Excellent.' He kissed her again. 'Shall I meet you there?'

'It sounds like a plan.'

'When this war is over, I want to take you to the States,' he said. 'You'll love California, it's hot like this every day.'

Ana watched the handsome GI walk away and smiled. However much she tried to deny it, she had fallen in love with him.

The morning of the 28th August 1942 was nothing special. The weather was dull with a leaden yellow overcast and the humidity was high. People went about their business as usual. Ana had completed the Parsonage chores and was due to clean one of the offices on Fore Street. James had pursued her earlier in the house but she had managed to slip past and leave without him noticing.

When she arrived at the office, Heather had already started cleaning the windows.

'How's the house guest, maid?'

'The same old creep,' Ana replied. 'He has a morbid curiosity about me – I wish he'd go back to Ireland.'

'Older men can be predatory, especially when they are widowers. Are you meeting Thomas today?'

'We're going to see a movie this afternoon.'

'He's a lovely man, Ana.'

'I know, I can't stop thinking about him.'

It was before three when Ana walked to the cinema in Royal Square. It had opened three years before, a grand cinema with over 600 seats. Thomas was running late so she waited for him on the granite steps. Heather was approaching when a droning noise was heard in the skies above. It sounded like a plane. It came from the west and the next thing, a loud explosion could be heard as a bomb was dropped on the town. Ana ran towards her as machine gun fire was heard growing louder with every second.

'Ana!' She shrieked.

'Get down, we're being attacked,' Ana shouted over the din.

Smoke was rising all over town as a barrage of bullets showered down over the road and the cinema. The women tried to dodge the bullets but one struck Heather's leg. Suddenly Ana looked back at the cinema. It was peppered with bullet holes and lying on the steps was Thomas, clutching his stomach.

'Thomas!' She rested her hand on Heather's leg and concentrated hard. The next moment the bullet came free in her hand and the wound was healed. 'Get under cover, I have to check Thomas.'

The skies grew quieter. The plane had gone, having bombed the gas works and wrecked a few houses. She reached for Thomas' hand and squeezed it. 'Are you okay?'

Thomas was losing consciousness. There was an entry wound to his chest. Ana tore his jacket open, followed by his shirt, which offered the bloody menacing hole. Blood was pouring out between her fingers and Thomas was turning grey. 'Ana … what are you doing?'

'I'm going to save you, Darling,' she replied, pushing her hand against the wound.

'You can't, it's too deep… Are you hurt?'

'I'm fine,' she said.

Seconds later Thomas sat upright, the healed wound leaving only traces of blood behind. He looked at Ana warily. She had done something impossible. Heather approached and caught his eye.

'What did you do to me?' Thomas demanded. 'You're a bloody witch, Ana. You probably charmed me to fall in love with you too.'

'No, I didn't.' Ana was trembling at the change in the tone of his voice. 'I can heal. I couldn't leave you to die when I could save your life. I love you.'

'It's not right that you can do this.' He stood up. 'I have to report back. I don't think we should see each other again. You're not right.'

'No, Thomas, please don't say that.' She was beginning to cry.

'I don't know you anymore,' he said adopting a distant expression. 'No one can do that sort of thing. No one.'

'Thomas, please … you don't understand.'

'You're right. I don't understand *you*. Please leave me alone, Miss Connelly.' He gave her an unsavoury look and walked away. She watched him disappear and her heart sank to a new level.

Heather took her hand. 'Come on, Ana. There are others. We must help them. Don't worry about Thomas, he's upset.' People were running around amid the chaos. Smoke filled the air and panic had set in. Frantic young children were aimlessly looking for their mothers.

Ana helped out until the ambulance men arrived and was careful not to expose her ability even though it meant saving lives. A new field hospital was opened and most of the fifty or so injured were taken there. Two hours later she found herself walking home to the Parsonage, on her own and without any further word from Thomas.

The shock of the afternoon was only starting to sink in. Her tea dress was covered in bloodstains and her hands were grouted with dirt and blood.

Talk at the dinner table had been purely about the bomb attack. Ana retired to bed early without so much as a word. When she turned off the light, something was out of sorts. Someone was hiding in the shadows and staring at her.

'Who's there?' She asked.

'Only James.'

'What are you doing in my room?'

'I wanted to see you.'

'Get out,' she snapped.

'Come on Ana, you don't mean that? I've seen the way you look at me. You are a very handsome woman and will produce excellent children. I'm looking for a wife and you are perfect.'

'You're imagining things,' she said. 'You're far too old for me.'

Before Ana had a chance to move, James had placed his hand on her forehead. He was probing her mind and planting a spell, spoken in Latin:

Et obeditis mihi, in omnibus Connelly Duana. Interrogabo te, et non convenit aliquid in uxorem meam amodo vobis faciam. Meus es tu.

Her mind misted over and she fell silent. James removed her nightdress until she was naked on the bed, unable to move. He slipped in next to her, running his hands all over her body.

The next morning Ana repeatedly threw up in the bowl in her room. James had risen two hours before. She dressed alone and slipped out, running into town, anywhere but remain in the Parsonage. She found Heather in a café near Porthmeor Beach.

'What's the matter with you?' Heather asked.

'It's Thomas, he doesn't want to see me anymore,' she said.

'You pulled a strange stunt yesterday. People are talking about you. They think you're a witch like your mother. The yanks don't like it. It's spooked them like a bad omen.'

'I'm not a witch, Heather. I'm not evil. I was born this way. You have it in your family too. Honestly, people overreact all the time.'

'I know but it's unspoken what abilities we have. I understand and sympathise with you but I don't know how to help. It might be better if you lay low for a while, at least until people have forgotten. You must know how it's been with your mother in the past.'

'How long will that take?'

'I don't know, a few weeks maybe.'

'My Irish cousin is taking advantage of me,' Ana admitted, changing the subject.

'James? I met him the other day, he's charming.'

'Those are not the words I would use.'

'Tell him you aren't interested.'

'It doesn't seem to stop him,' Ana said. 'I must go home.'

'Ana? Thank you for fixing my leg. You saved Thomas' life as well. He knows what you did. You must understand having special abilities isn't normal to these people. Not like it is for us. It scares them half to death.'

'I blew it with the one man I was meant to be with – by saving his life. I can't believe it, Heather.'

Ana had to face the responsibility and consequences of her actions. It was too small a community and her mother was more despised than liked. She was on her own and vulnerable. Their friendship was dimming. In the months that followed, she had never felt more alone.

The next time they encountered one another, the young women were both heavily pregnant. Ana was subdued and hadn't noticed Heather waiting in line at the midwife clinic. Ana turned her head, but the look in her eyes said it all. She was a ghost of her former self. Her eyes were sunken and grey shadows lay beneath them.

Any humour had long since vanished from her face. She had aged ten years in the last eight months.

'Ana, is that really you?' Heather took the seat next to her. 'I haven't seen you for months, and you're expecting as well?'

'So it seems. I heard you married Sam.'

'Yes, I'm sorry you didn't come to the wedding. I sent you an invitation.'

'James wouldn't allow it,' she said. 'And my mother has a thing about the Pengellys.'

'James?'

'My husband,' she replied with words void of emotion.

'I had no idea you married him,' Heather said with surprise.

'He made me. He rapes me, I can't stop him.' She spoke softly under her breath, less than a whisper. 'He controls me.'

'Are you sure?'

'This is his child in my belly. I don't want to give birth to his bastard. It will be a monster.'

'Does your mother know?' Heather asked.

'She does nothing to stop him. James always has her approval with everything. She does whatever he says.'

She raised her hand to Ana's forehead and searched her mind. 'You have a spell on you, Ana.'

'He makes me do things to him and I can't control myself.'

'I want you to stop thinking for a moment,' she said. 'I have an idea. Can you read my mind?'

'No, I have no abilities anymore, he took them from me.'

'That's not true. He made you forget them. I'm going to remind you of who you used to be, Ana. You'll see, this can be changed.'

Heather began pouring memories into her mind – memories of a time before James, before Thomas. It was her own memory of the young woman, when Ana had last been herself. In an instant the spell broke and she thought freely for the first time in over eight months.

Her hand dropped onto her extended belly and she began to cry inconsolably. 'I can remember everything he does to me, Heather. Oh my God, he rapes me every night. I have no control over anything. I want to die.'

'Are you alright, Mrs Connelly?' One of the midwives asked, placing a caring hand on her shoulder. 'You seem very upset today.'

'I'm fine.' Once the young midwife walked away, she turned to Heather. 'I must leave. I can't stay here. I have to run far away until I don't know anyone anymore.'

'You can't, Ana. Wait a moment.'

Tears filled her eyes. 'I don't want to live in this world anymore, it's too cruel.'

'Don't do anything foolish, Ana, please,' she said but Ana was already leaving. She followed her outside but Ana insisted on heading home. 'When is your baby due?'

'Next week. It's a boy, I can sense him but I don't think I can ever love him. He was made from violence.'

'I'm living in the Digey, here's my address,' she quickly scribbled it on a scrap of paper and handed it to her. 'I'm here anytime you need me. Just say the word.'

'Thank you Heather, you have opened my eyes and I'll never forget you, my friend.'

Ana walked up the road towards the Parsonage. She could hardly walk being so pregnant. A week later she gave birth at home to a healthy screaming baby boy with a shock of black hair and five teeth. James and Shannon were overjoyed but Ana had no emotion left in her soul. James announced plans to return to Ireland with his new family but Ana had other ideas.

She waited for him that night, hiding a knife under her pillow. James climbed in beside her and planted a kiss on her cheek. 'I want to have many more children with you Ana.' He reached his hand to her belly. 'Logan is a healthy boy and will grow to be strong. I'm very proud of you.'

'I don't want any more children with you,' she said firmly. 'I never wanted this one.'

'You don't have a say in this, my dear wife. You made a vow to obey me and you will.'

'You're wrong, James.' Ana drew the knife to his throat.

'I had no idea you are so plucky, Ana.' There was a glint of a smirk on his face.

'I want you to die,' she said, piercing the skin on his neck.

'Go on then, kill me … if you can.'

There was no fear in his eyes and for a moment it was a distraction. Ana tried pushing the knife in but she couldn't move her hand. James removed the blade from her hand, twisting it, making it drop to the floor. His eyes darkened. 'You have left me with no choice, Ana, which is sad in my eyes.' James was calm as he pulled on his dressing gown. 'Get up.'

She had no choice but to obey him and climbed out of bed, wearing a long white night dress. James pulled her hair away from her neck and placed an amethyst necklace around her neck.

'It truly is beautiful on you. You will always wear it, in this life and the next.' James grabbed her hand and pulled her into the corridor.

'No, I won't go with you,' Ana protested, dragging her heels. 'Let go of me. I don't want to wear this necklace, it's enchanted.'

'You will do as I say,' he said. 'I am your husband and you *will* obey me, Ana.'

He led her to the closed door at the end of the corridor, unlocked it and pressed her against the wall.

'When you wake up, you'll think again on what I've offered you. Now go to sleep, my Darling.'

Ana fell unconscious into his waiting arms.

When she opened her eyes, her hands were tied behind her back and she was tottering on her feet on the top step of the back stairs. A rope was attached to a hook in the ceiling and extended to a noose around her neck.

It was pitch dark and when the moon emerged from behind the clouds, the light filled the stairwell.

'Ana, my lovely Ana. I wish I could trust you.'

'What are you doing?' She asked, unable to see him. 'Let me go, please.'

James was holding the other end of the rope and standing behind her. 'I'm helping you into the next life, my dear. Why on earth would I let you stay? If I can't tame you, no one will.'

With one short push Ana lost her footing. She slipped and fell, the rope around her neck tightened and stalled her. She couldn't breathe as it painfully strangled her. Her body swayed back and fro from the hook in the ceiling making a terrible sound until her last breath left her body.

Ana's spirit left her body instantly and she stared at the man who had betrayed her. James was unable to see her or even sense her. The necklace around her neck made her invisible to the Sentries. She was able to follow future events without anyone being aware of her. Only the spiritually aware would come to understand but that would take a very long time.

'You should've trusted me, Ana,' he whispered without remorse. 'Now you'll be forced to remain here in limbo forever while you wear my talisman.'

James slowly loosened the rope and her body dropped like a stone to the bottom of the stairwell. He lifted her into his arms, returned to the bedroom and laid her on the bed. Removing the noose and checking the necklace was still there, he wrapped the body in a blanket. He opened his packing trunk and stuffed her inside, locking it with a key. The trunk had only squeezed in through the opening but it was hidden and out of sight. He would lie to Shannon. Ana had drowned in the sea. Her body was lost. She was gone forever.

It was raining the next morning when Shannon opened the front door to find Heather Pengelly standing on the step. Her face contorted when she read her mind and learnt to whom she was married, the son of her nemesis, Jessica Pengelly. It made her angry.

'What are you doing? You have some nerve coming to my house, Pengelly.'

'I'm asking after Ana, is she alright?' Heather asked.

'Of course she is,' she snapped. 'Why shouldn't she be?'

'I saw her last week, she was so worried about James… She told me he was abusing her.'

'That's impossible, I would know if he was.'

'Mrs Connelly, I must warn you that you have a spell on you as well. I managed to break Ana's. I can help you to see things more clearly.'

'Get off my doorstep, how dare you come to my house telling me what I should do! You know nothing about my family.'

'You're wrong about that, James is not who he says he is.' Heather said but the door was slammed shut leaving her outside and alone. She headed back to her life with her husband and their new baby Robert. She never ventured to the Parsonage again.

Shannon opened the vault below the house where she kept her valuables. The entrance was by the house in the back garden, by way of a small and elaborately designed Victorian wrought iron door. In the safe was a small metal box.

Inside was her talisman: a gold bracelet with a large ruby in its side, hieroglyphics adorning its inner walls. She placed it on her wrist and systematically it broke James' spell.

'Damn those Pengellys,' she said aloud, returning her talisman to its box. Venturing upstairs, anger was boiling in her veins. There was no response when she called for her daughter. The stairwell door was open, which was normally locked. Looking closer she exhaled. It was cold and she could see her breath in the air. The baby began to cry. She entered the bedroom but there was no sign of her daughter or James.

'Logan, where's your mother?'

She picked up the hungry baby. His nappy was soaked through so she changed him and fed him with some warmed homemade formula found in the fridge. Ana had made it from evaporated milk, Karo syrup and boiled water. Since Ana refused to breast-feed Logan, she had made up her own recipe.

By the time James returned three hours later, there was still no sign of her daughter. She waited for him in the lounge. His son Logan was asleep in a small crib beside her.

'James, have you seen Ana?'

'No, I've been out looking for her,' he said. 'It appears as though she has run away.'

'Why don't you tell me where she is? And while you're at it, explain exactly what you have been doing since you arrived at my house.'

'What's the matter, Shannon? You seem different today.'

'Do you think I'm stupid?' She flicked her wrist and a small bolt of light fired across the room hitting him in the eye. James cried out in shock, clutching his face, his eye bleeding from its socket. Blood trickled down his cheek.

He was suffering immeasurable and unexpected agony. 'Why are you attacking me?'

'You know why. Where is my daughter? Do you want to be blinded in both eyes?' She was perfectly still with her hand poised. 'Well?'

'She's dead,' he admitted.

She almost lost her breath. 'What did you do, you bastard?'

'I was too late. She hung herself. I found her last night. I didn't want to upset you so I buried her in the garden.'

'Liar! Where is she?'

'In the earth,' he replied with a lie.

'It's a better place than the one you're going to,' she seethed.

The second bolt blinded him completely. He was screaming in pain when she snatched his hair and dragged him across the wooden floor to the back of the house. Blood poured down his face from his ruptured eyes, which he clutched with both hands. She used telekinesis to overcome his body weight. The loathing in her soul was overpowering her senses… she wanted to beat him to death.

Kicking the back door open, she moved him across the granite slabs to the outhouse. He was in terrible pain and protested as his eyes continued to bleed out. Without giving any warning she raised a heavy spade and slammed it on the back of his head.

James Connelly died beside the gate of the pigsty. She mentally pushed his body inside the muddy interior and closed the gate. Two enormous pigs began sniffing at the new meal. She went back inside the house and locked the door, thoroughly washing her hands in the kitchen sink.

The baby began to cry. With her daughter gone, he would need a mother. It was wartime and there were orphans arriving every day to escape the cities being bombed. Another mouth to feed, no less, but Logan was her grandson. He would endure and learn everything she knew about magic and spells, growing up to be a strong and dangerous man. In time he would protect her, become her legacy and have a family of his own.

Logan would never learn the truth about his mother's body wearing a valuable talisman, packed away in an old trunk hidden in the loft or the identity of his real father consumed by two large pigs in the Parsonage garden.

Not a trace was left of James and the only person who knew of his fate was Shannon. She made it clear to anyone who asked after him that he had simply left town. The secret of his death died with her in the mid 1960's.

Afraid of heights, Shannon never ventured into the loft or discovered the truth of what happened to her daughter Duana. In the end she died of a broken heart, ruthlessly challenged on a daily basis by her violent and unruly grandson, sated only by the solace found in a bottle of single malt whisky.

13

~~

back to life

Ana: *Finn, come out of this now.*

Finn: *Ana?*

The Parsonage transformed into its familiar dingy state before his eyes. Gone was the clean and fresh veneer, to be replaced by the dark corridor and damp odour. His mind adjusted to the change. Ana's ghost was floating beside his animated spirit.

Finn: *Your body's in the loft.*

Ana: *It's always been there. James hid my body thinking no one would ever find it. No one knew, not even my mother.*

Finn: *All this time and it wasn't suicide, Ana. It must be the talisman stopping you from moving on. I can't believe what James did to you. Surely with James being Logan's father then his talisman should have protected Jared.*

Ana: *I was there when my mother made the talisman for James. It was her way of training me in the dark arts although I was never that interested. I never had the appetite to con people or control them. James stipulated and named only his living bloodline to be protected. It never shielded Logan or any future offspring, but they bore the spoils of Shannon's talisman. I was here the night Logan died. I saw him take his last breath. Seeing your child die like that should have some effect but I felt nothing. I never loved him. He was a living beast in my eyes, a product of rape. Branna had no idea I was watching her stab him in the heart. It would've been so easy to stop her but he was so like my mother in the end. I could've revealed myself to her right in that moment but Logan had to die. As for Shannon, she never got over my death. She was full of hate and bitterness. It's not surprising really. I never hated her and she did love me. I'm sorry about your curse but it was put into motion long before I was born.*

Finn: *Your death needs to be properly registered and then we can hold a funeral for you. I don't want to get the police involved but I can't see how this can be resolved otherwise.*

Ana: *I'm wearing the talisman around my neck. If the police come to the house, Cillian will find it. That can never happen.*

Finn: *I know. I understand how reluctant you were to share the truth with me but it's time to change things. I'll try and come back tomorrow and retrieve your body.*

Ana: *Before you leave, can you to give a message to Heather? I know she's your grandmother. She always had a good heart and tried to do the right thing. Tell her I never meant to push her away. I was trapped and if she hadn't found me that day, my life could've turned out much worse.*

Finn: *Worse than dying?*

Ana: *Believe me, free will is much better than no will. My life would've been intolerable with James. Heather was my only true friend and I cared for her deeply. It is only fitting that I make amends by helping her grandson.*

Finn: *I'll make sure Heather knows. She told me about your ghost. Nothing gets past her, it seems.*

Ana: *Heather is a very wise woman. You're lucky to have her in your life. You should spend more time with her.*

Finn: *Thank you Ana. I know what I have to do now. I don't know if you can help me find Branna. She has been missing for months and we have no idea where she is. Cillian cursed her to stay like a raven.*

Ana: *It matters to me that you and Branna have become friends, that we can cross the generations and do the right thing. She has a good heart. I have an idea that might help her to find you. You can break the charm and she can turn back into a woman. Leave this with me and I'll do anything I can in the time remaining. I'll only be able*

to help you until the talisman is removed from my neck. After that,
Etherea will become aware of my existence and a Sentry will come for
me. Keep your eyes and ears open. There is always hope, my friend,
when we fight evil of this nature. I will see you again when you recover
from your fatigue.

He flew out of the house to find the first rays of sun dancing
across the town and out to sea. Many hours had passed since he
found Ana. Finding home, he entered his body and woke up seconds
later. He was exhausted and drank water from a glass beside the bed.

Ellie walked into the bedroom carrying Sam in her arms.

'Finn, when did you get back?'

'Literally just now.'

'You look exhausted.' She laid Sam down in his cot.

'I'm absolutely knackered, Honey.'

'You were gone for almost a day. I was concerned. Did you find
what you were looking for?'

'Yes, the talisman is hidden in the Parsonage. I had an amazing
conversation with a ghost. I'll tell you everything when I wake up.' They
exchanged a lingering kiss before he closed his eyes and passed out.

Finn woke up late afternoon and stumbled his way into the
kitchen to be overwhelmed by a crowd of familiar faces sat around
their large oak dining table. Their talk stopped immediately when
he made his appearance barefoot in a grey dressing gown with a
mass of bed hair. 'To what to I owe this pleasure?'

'We're here to help you on your latest quest,' Joe said, sitting
beside Simon and Jerry Nancarrow, Bastian and Tom. Serina was
fussing over Sam while Ellie and Joo served copious cups of tea to
everyone.

'The Posse's here,' he added with a little enthusiasm.

'Park your bum and fill us in on what's been happening of late in the Flame drama,' Jerry said. 'It's been a while since there's been any action. I was beginning to think you'd retired from the world of the paranormal.'

He pulled up a chair and Ellie poured him a mug of hot black coffee. He gave her a disapproving look that melted into a smile. 'I planed to the Parsonage and spoke to the ghost of Branna's grandmother, Ana. I have a really good ghost story if anyone wants to hear it.'

'So the Parsonage *is* really haunted.' Jerry said.

'Big time,' he replied. 'There are at least three ghosts.'

'Ghosties.' Joo said, looking intently at Jerry who pulled a ghoulish face making her smile.

'I persuaded Ana to tell me her story. She was murdered. James Connelly placed his talisman, a necklace, around her neck and hung her in the back stairwell. He hid her body, still wearing the necklace, in a trunk in the loft. The talisman prevented her soul from moving on. She is, in effect, trapped in limbo and has been for over fifty years. Now I need to go back and retrieve the trunk.'

'Her body's in the loft?' Bastian asked. 'Could it be the same trunk I saw last year when we stole Logan's talisman?'

'Yes,' he replied. 'Quite possibly.'

'Yuck,' Jerry said. 'Dead bodies, talismans … how are you going to break in if he's back?'

'I haven't worked out that part yet, I'm guessing that's why you're all here. We need a plan. A few days ago, I ran into Branna's husband Murray. He was behaving so strangely I decided to read his mind. Cillian charmed him into signing the whole Connelly estate over to him. With Branna officially dead, the inheritance was left to Murray because they were married. I didn't break the spell because I thought it would only leave him vulnerable, considering what happened to Branna.'

'Cillian doesn't waste time with his spells,' Joe said. 'Poor Murray has no idea. This Connelly has some nerve taking anything he wants.'

A tapping noise in the distance distracted Finn. No one else heard it. He concentrated above all the other noises coming from the house until he could separate it. Fortunately the sound persisted and he decided to pursue it.

'What is it?' Ellie asked when he began walking away.

'Can't you hear it?' He asked, climbing the steps and opening the door to the studio. The tapping noise grew louder.

'No, I can't hear anything,' she said hurrying after him.

The others followed to see him command the window to open. A huge black bird flew wide into the space. Using telekinesis, he drew the raven into his waiting hands before it had a chance to escape. The bird settled in his grip easily and he glanced at the others with a wide smile.

'It's Branna. Ana must have found her.'

Swiftly he filled the raven's mind with a memory of the last time it had flown into the studio. A memory of the raven being a tall dark haired woman.

Finn: *Remember who you are, Branna … and wake up.*

He placed the bird on the floor and moved to where everyone was watching from a safe distance. The bird was shaking its head very fast. A thin wave of blue mist exploded from the raven, blasting its way to each corner of the room. Suddenly every fuse blew in the house. Light bulbs smashed in their sockets. A wild storm of black feathers flew around the large open space striking the others as they watched the weird spectacle with awe.

'What's happening?' Jerry asked.

'I must have broken the spell,' he said.

A crackling noise followed and Branna lay on the floor unconscious and unclothed. Finn grabbed a throw from the sofa and covered her body to save her modesty. She remained still like a corpse and no one said a word. He rested his hand against her cold forehead, closed his eyes and read her mind.

Finn: *Branna, can you hear me?*

He poured more memories into her mind until she opened her eyes and stared back at him. Tears fell down her cheeks as she woke up to her own mortality.

'Finn?' She touched his hand and squeezed it. 'Oh, I don't know why I flew here. I must have known you would be here.'

'You've been missing for months.' He said softly. 'Here, let me help you.'

Finn assisted her to the sofa while Ellie brought her clothing.

'Murray must be going mad.' She managed a smile. 'Cillian cast a spell on me when we were in the Parsonage. I was too weak to stop him.'

'He's very good at that,' Joo said.

'He's back, isn't he?' She asked. 'I can't explain it, I just know.'

'He *is* back,' Joe said. 'But not for long if we have anything to do with it. We need Murray on side. Finn, you must break his spell so he remembers Branna.'

There was a common sense of relief in all their minds and Finn couldn't help but smile at her.

'I don't think Cillian will find the talisman by himself. Even so, I'm going to feel a lot better once it's safely in my hand.'

'You've found it?' She asked.

'It's in the loft above your old bed along with the body of your dead grandmother.'

'Oh heavens, Finn, that's terrible,' she said. 'I had no idea.'

'She didn't want you to know.'

'You've spoken to her?'

'Yes, and I'll tell you everything in time, I promise,' he replied.

'All this time and you only just found out where it is? Can one of you please walk me home?'

'I'll take you,' he said.

'Why don't we all come with you?' Jerry suggested. 'Murray might take this more seriously if we're all there to back you up. That is, after his charm is broken.'

Branna said nothing on the way to the old pottery. They were all behaving in a protective manner towards her. Although weak, she was safe among them.

'There's a lot you should know,' Finn said. 'Cillian's been busy since you disappeared. He framed you for murder and faked your death with someone else's body. He put a spell on Murray to make him forget you, the way you truly are and then forced him to sign over your father's estate. I have to break the spell before he sees you or it will be disastrous.'

'Framed for murder? More spells?'

'It's been all over the papers, the police found Logan and Jared's bodies,' Joe said. 'I'm sorry Branna, but you're going to have to lay low until all of this is sorted.'

'I'm a wizard with law, so leave this with me,' Jerry said. 'I have an idea that might clear your name and restore your inheritance.'

'Thanks Jerry,' she sighed. 'Cillian won't be expecting me to be back. If he has acquired everything that belonged to my father, he may go out to check on the other properties.'

Finn said, 'I don't think you should count yourself in this time. We can handle it without you.'

He knocked on the door and seconds later Murray opened it. He looked out at the seven people standing on his doorstep. 'Yes? How can I help you?'

Finn extended his hand. 'I would like to introduce myself. I'm Finn Milton.'

Murray hesitated for a moment before he caved in and passed his hand over. Finn held onto it firmly and closed his eyes, tracing the spell and squashing it with an older memory of Murray. It took seconds for him to wake up to his senses. He shook off his hand immediately as though it was red-hot. His face contorted and started to turn red.

'What the hell are you doing here, Milton? Have you lost your mind? I told you to stay away from me! How dare you come to my house! If it wasn't for you Branna would still be here.'

'I've brought your wife home, Murray.' He stepped aside to let her move to the front. It was a line he had wanted to say for the longest time. Branna lowered the sweatshirt hood to expose her face. Murray absently pushed Finn out of the way and swallowed her into his arms.

'Branna,' he said quietly stroking her hair, holding her tight. 'I thought you were gone forever. It broke my heart.'

'It's alright, Darling.' She raised her hand to his cheek. 'These people are my friends and you *must* trust them. They brought me back. I don't have a spell on me anymore.'

Murray raised his eyes to Finn. 'You'd better come in. *All* of you.'

Finn was so relieved he couldn't stop smiling. With Branna's return, his self-esteem had come back in spades. Unsurprisingly, the main topic of conversation was about the lost talisman. After Murray made a pot of tea they retired to the lounge. Branna sat comfortably with Murray's arms wrapped around her on the sofa, listening contentedly as Finn explained his plan.

'Ana cannot be not detected by Sentries because she is still wearing the talisman. Once it's removed they'll find her and she'll ascend to *Etherea*. I promised I would arrange her a proper burial.'

'I had no idea she was called Ana, I honestly thought she'd committed suicide.' Branna said.

'It was all James' doing.'

'That explains the coldness upstairs and why the door was papered up. We weren't allowed to use the back stairwell,' she said. 'As children, my father would berate us if we tried. So Ana died there. I don't understand why she came to you, Finn, after all this time, and not me.'

'She was the all seeing eye in the Parsonage for over fifty years. She knows everything that happened there but she wanted to shield you from the awful truth.'

'James fathered Logan,' she said. 'He was also grandfather to Michael and me. It's so messed up. Logan and Michael were about the same age. No wonder it never got out. I guess they never knew the truth either.'

'She's not the only ghost,' he said.

'Who else is there?' Murray asked.

'Branna, your mother Melandra cannot move on. Once this is over, you could help her. Her body must be hidden somewhere in the house. The third one is my mother.'

'Have you communicated with her?' Bastian asked.

'Only in a dream. The first time I felt her she was like a gust of wind. There must be a way to save her and a reason to why she's here.'

Branna added, 'you must have some kind of animal magnetism when it comes to ghosts, Finn. They never revealed themselves to me in all the time I lived there.'

'They didn't want to scare you. When we have a moment, I can mind-lock to show you what happened to Ana. She was right in the thick of it when St Ives was bombed in the war. She showed me everything including a soldier she fell in love with.'

Branna said. 'It sounds intriguing.'

'I'm going to take the talisman to *Etherea*,' he said.

Every one had considered this. It was the only way to be certain that the talisman would be destroyed. What with the danger of surviving such a trip, he was the only mortal who had ever been allowed to leave *Etherea*. He was the only one qualified to do the task.

'Ellie, Sam and Joo need to be somewhere safe,' he said. 'Penberth is the best option. I'll plane from here to the Lizard. Only then can we safely take on Cillian.'

'It took a long time to destroy the last talisman. You nearly died,' Bastian said. 'Is this the only option?'

'I have to be planing for it to be removed by a Sentry. It must be around my neck before I set off, it's the only way it will appear on my spiritual body.'

'The bracelet was burnt off your wrist. Imagine how painful that necklace is going to be.' Joe said.

'That's where I come in,' Branna said. 'I can heal you.'

'We need to steal the talisman first,' Jerry said. 'We can take turns watching the house. When he leaves, we'll break in.'

'Tomorrow morning,' Finn suggested. 'I'll take the first watch.'

'I'll leave my car nearby,' Joe said. 'So we can get away quickly.'

'I had no idea all of this was going on right under my nose,' Murray said. 'You all have abilities I simply cannot comprehend.'

'Don't worry, Honey, you're not alone,' she said. 'No one can find out and it must be handled delicately.'

'How are we going to clear your name?' Simon asked. 'If the police discover you're back, it could turn out to be very messy, especially if Cillian is involved.'

'Let me worry about that,' Jerry said. 'Keep a very low profile, Branna, at least until I've sorted a few things. I have a QC friend called Verity, let's say she owes me a favour.'

'There are enough character witnesses to clear your name,' Tom said. 'We can all testify for you.'

'Which is why it will work,' Jerry added with an air of confidence.

'I *did* kill my father,' Branna looked at her husband. 'He gave me no choice. I had to stop him. He was going to kill Finn and Ellie, he was completely mad.'

'This world is part of who you are,' Murray said. 'I need time to get used to it but I'm over the moon you're home safe and sound. I never want to go through anything like that again. I hated losing you, Sweetheart. It was the worst feeling in the world.'

At daybreak, Finn was sitting in Joe's car on the opposite side of the road to the Parsonage grounds, wearing a beanie hat and a warm padded jacket. It was a cold November morning and he could see his breath in the air. Armed with a flask of hot coffee, he settled in to watch the house. Joe was expected to relieve him after a couple of hours.

He wondered how it would affect Ana once the necklace was removed. He wanted to commune with her one final time before she was whisked off to *Etherea* and the afterlife she had been so cruelly denied. There were so many unanswered questions, mainly concerning his mother. Melandra had been coy and not divulged anything specific but he assumed both spirits knew about the fate of Phoebe Milton.

He briefly visited his father the night before and explained his plan. For once Milton did nothing to deter him from carrying them out. Deep down, they both wanted nothing more than what was coming to the young Connelly. There was no hidden love going on and his father was standing by in case he needed him.

He could finally concentrate on the matter at hand, waiting for Cillian to leave so that he could snatch the trunk containing Ana's remains. After growing restless, he poured himself a black coffee from his flask. Joe lent through the open window and took the coffee from his hand. 'Thanks Finn, no sign of Connelly yet?'

'No, it's still early. I might wait a bit longer with you.'

'Cool,' Joe replied, climbing into the passenger seat. 'Have you thought about what we're going to do if he sees us?'

'I'm hoping that won't happen,' he said, pouring himself a second cup. 'He's after my soul, so we need to be one step ahead of him if this is going to work.'

'When are you guys getting married?'

'That's a good question,' he replied. 'I had so many plans before we came home but everything's kind of gone out the window. Once this is over, we will plan our wedding. Who would've thought I'd become some kind of supernatural bounty hunter? The only reward I get is to live in peace, it's nuts.'

'I've never met anyone with so many problems,' Joe said.

'Sometimes I wonder what it would be like to be normal, to live without any powers.'

'Life would be so boring, wouldn't it?' Joe smiled.

He managed a small laugh. 'You're right, I keep thinking one day I'll wake up and feel blessed to have them.'

'You *are* blessed. You have a lovely woman and a beautiful son.'

'I did strike lucky there.' He admitted.

'Luck had nothing to do with it. It was fate. You guys are meant to be together. Some things are meant to happen. I believe in that logic.'

'Look Joe, the door's opening.'

Cillian locked the front door and climbed into an expensive black sports car. A minute later he sped off in the direction of town.

'Let's get that trunk,' Joe said, opening the door.

He turned to him seriously. 'Joe, once we start this, there's no going back.'

'I know, that's why I'm here. Did you think you were the only mad one around here? You have a lot to learn, Finn Milton. Don't you know? We're all as bonkers as you are.'

They approached the back of the house where he melted the lock on the back door using soul light. Once inside, he ascended the twisting back stairs closely followed by Joe. There was barely any light and the old wooden steps creaked precariously underfoot. At the top, the door was open. They stepped into the first floor corridor to be confronted by a darkened passage framed with cobwebs. The temperature was below zero.

'We have to find the room where they were holding Joo,' he said. 'It's along here. Every time I come here it looks different.'

'It's bloody freezing,' Joe said as they shuffled slowly along.

'The ghosts make it cold. The best thing is to not show them any fear and they won't bother you.' He led him into Branna's old room and stared at the loft opening in the ceiling. 'It's up there.'

Moving a wooden bench under the hatch he pushed it open. Clambering into the cramped space, he found the old dusty trunk exactly where Bastian had described. He pushed it towards the opening where Joe was waiting. Cautiously he lowered it down to the floor.

'It's locked,' Joe said, inspecting the old packing trunk. 'Your hair's white, Finn. Are you going to open it here?'

He swept the cobwebs from his hair. 'Joe, she's right behind you.' He was looking warmly at Ana's spirit who had been watching them the whole time.

'Who is?'

'Ana.'

'What?' Joe turned around and could see her so clearly he nearly bit his tongue. The white ghost of a beautiful young woman was floating, wearing a silky dress. She was shimmering in the half-light and the enchanted necklace lay around her neck.

Ana: *Don't be afraid of me. I won't harm you, Joe Praed. The Sentry who saved you, he made it possible for you to see spirits. Finn, open the trunk and remove the talisman and then I'll be free of its magic.*

'Now let's see how easy this is going to be to open.' He closed his eyes and touched the cold metal of the lock with much concentration. The metal clips started to move by themselves before pinging open. He slowly raised the lid when a rush of air blew out that smelt of another era, musky and dank. They both screwed up their faces. The content of the trunk was laid bare for the first time in over fifty years.

'Thanks funky,' Joe coughed.

A physical mound had formed under a dark and dusty blue blanket. Kneeling, Finn lifted the material back delicately and lent on his haunches, raising a hand over his mouth. An expression of sadness mixed with horror crossed his face and his eyes began to water. The small female skeleton had calcified. The bones had completely gelled together. Her long brown hair was fine and brittle. He touched the amethyst necklace and carefully opened its clasp, without touching her remains. He pulled it free and Joe closed the lid on the trunk.

Finn was holding the solid necklace between his fingers, crafted with large amethyst stones and gold. While she smiled warmly, a blue light arched from her spirit and the necklace disappeared from her ghostly neck.

Ana: *It's been so long. I had forgotten what it feels like to be free of that damnable thing. Oh thank you. You have restored my faith in human nature. You're a man of your word and I'm in your debt.*

Finn: *You're free and we'll arrange your funeral, it's the least we can do. I wonder how long the Sentry will take to get here.*

He wanted to talk to her for longer but knew it would be only a matter of precious moments before her soul's existence would be revealed to the spiritual underworld. Sentries had a sixth sense when it came to finding spirits who were ready to cross over.

A tall ghostly soldier appeared and Finn urged Joe to stand as far back as possible. Their breath was visible in the air and the room had become even colder. The Sentry stared at the two mortals, and then the fifty-year-old ghost finding unusual activity.

Sentry: *What has transpired here? Both of you mortals can see me.*

Finn: *We have both seen Sentries before.*

Ana: *Finn Milton removed a talisman from my remains.*

Sentry: *This mortal has a talisman? I cannot see it.*

Finn: *It's in my hand.* The talisman was still cloaked and no matter what, the Sentry could not see it. *You have to believe me.*

Sentry: *This makes little sense to me. I do not understand how this spirit has been trapped here for so long without us knowing about it.*

Finn: *I will bring it to Etherea and it will make sense.*

Sentry: *In that case, Finn Milton, you will be expected. Come, Duana, it is time for you to leave. This is no place for a lost spirit. I fear you have been here far too long.*

Ana: *Goodbye Finn and thank you. There is one more thing.*

Sentry: *Do not speak of these matters, it is forbidden.*

Ana: *But why? He has the right to know.*

Sentry: *It is too late.*

Finn watched in amazement as the Sentry gently clasped her tiny hand. In the split second before they disappeared, he was certain he heard the following words in his mind: *Phoebe's spirit is here.*

The temperature in the room had chilled considerably. He looked at Joe. 'Did you hear that?'

'Hear what?'

'I heard her say that Phoebe is here. It must be true.'

'What are you talking about?'

'My mother is here.'

'She died when you were born,' Joe said. 'How can she be here now?'

'When she gave me her soul light it broke her spirit and she never crossed over. She has been trapped between our world and the spirit world. There has to be a reason why she's still around, it must have something to do with Cillian. I've been having strange dreams about her for some time.'

'Have you seen her ghost?' Joe asked.

'Not exactly but I have felt her presence, if that's what it was.'

'We should get the talisman out of here and take the trunk as well.'

'You're not wrong, Joe.'

'That was weird with the Sentry. Is this what happens when we die?'

'Yeah, when our bodies die... I never get used to being around them.' Finn dropped the necklace into his jacket pocket. 'I hope this is the last time I come here.'

'Me too,' Joe replied.

Finn drove back to the house and they placed the dusty old trunk on the wooden floor in the studio. Bastian and Jerry were waiting for them with Ellie and Joo. They all drew closer to inspect it.

'Was there any trouble?' Ellie asked, giving him a kiss.

'Luckily, nothing. When Cillian left, we broke in through the back. The trunk was in the loft, and this.' Finn withdrew the amethyst necklace from his pocket. 'We don't need to open the trunk. Not long after the talisman was removed, a Sentry appeared and took Ana's spirit which was pretty bizarre.'

'I think we've seen enough dead bodies.' Bastian looked keenly at the necklace. 'So this is what all the fuss has been about.'

'It looks valuable,' Joo said.

'It is,' Finn agreed. 'But for all the wrong reasons.'

'What happens now?' Jerry asked.

'I'm going to take this piece of junk to *Etherea*.'

'Cool.' Jerry said.

'We're so close to ending this.' Finn put his arm around Ellie.

'Let's hope they're grateful,' Joo said. 'I can't believe what we've been through over this.'

'I'm going to wait until later. Talisman's have a habit of glowing brighter than yourself.'

'As long as you come back in one piece,' Ellie said. 'That's all I care about.'

He kissed her. 'There's light at the end of the tunnel. Once it's done, the Sentries will be on our side and Cillian won't stand a chance. I wouldn't have gotten this far without all your help. I am weaker than before I met him, but I only have one shot at this. Ellie, please tell me you're going to Penberth with Sam and Joo. I need to know you'll be far away from here when this starts. If any of that vision comes true then it will light up St Ives like never before. It will draw attention to our world and unfortunately everyone will see it.'

'After I feed Sam,' she said. 'I promise, Joo and I will set off right away. There's a storm coming in, I'm happy we're going to the other coast. It's going to be blowing a Hooley here.'

'I love you so much,' he whispered.

'I'm staying here with your body while you're visiting *Etherea*.' Bastian said. 'It's not a wise move leaving it unattended.'

'Bast, no one saw us leave the house. Cillian has no idea what we've done. He won't be expecting me to be planing to *Etherea* either.'

'After last year, I'm not taking any chances. The one time you decide to do this alone will be the time he comes for you. I've seen this happen too many times, cousin. You must never underestimate him. He has an agenda and won't stop.'

'Call me when he sets off and I'll come round and keep you company,' Jerry said. 'That is, once I've battened down the hatches at work and laid out a few sand bags. I can't say I'm looking forward to what's been forecast.'

'What are you going to do with Ana's remains?' Joo asked. 'We can't leave them here.'

'I don't know right now,' he replied, looking at the old trunk. 'At least she's free of the Parsonage. I'll ask Branna what she wants to do, Ana was her grandmother after all.'

A little while later Ellie packed Sam into his car seat in the front of the Porsche and Joo was crammed into the back seat. Finn was standing near the front door of the house watching the activity as the skies grew darker.

'Take care of yourself, Honey,' she said. 'If anything goes wrong …'

'It won't. It must work, Sweetheart. When it's destroyed, he'll have no way of hiding his crimes from the Sentries. It'll be over.'

'Come back to me, Finn… that's all I ask.'

'Ellie, I will always find you no matter what happens to me, you know that.' He swept her into his arms and kissed her.

'I don't want to let go of you.' She said with tears pricking her eyes. 'I love you.'

Finn: *I love you more.*

14

moirai (fate)

There were many items left behind in the Parsonage. Rummaging through Jared's personal belongings in his bedroom, Cillian found the keys to his nightclub in a leather jacket hanging up in his old wardrobe. Since Jared's demise, the club had been looted and decorated extensively with explicit graffiti. Maintenance was required in every direction but he wanted it sold and timed the visit with a local estate agent who promptly listed it for sale.

Upon his return, the door to the back staircase was ajar. Outside the light was fading and a thick mist was rolling in off the sea. The wind was picking up speed. Dark rain clouds were forming making visibility poor and distant rumblings threatened more bad weather to come. There was an unnatural chill in the air and he pulled his scarf tight around his neck. Looking closely at the door, the lock had been destroyed but no ordinary tools had been used.

After Ellie, Joo and Sam departed in the Porsche, Finn prepped himself mentally for the astral journey to the Lizard. Branna, Joe and Serina had visited earlier to wish him luck.

Bastian was the only one remaining. 'I can't believe you're going back.'

'Needs must,' he smiled. 'The necklace feels different, maybe it won't burn me this time.'

'It *has* to be removed.' Bastian reminded him.

'Yeah, right.' He glanced at the scar on his wrist that bore closer resemblance to an Egyptian tattoo than a burn.

With trepidation he held the necklace, which had trapped Ana and caused so much pain to his family. Whatever crimes Michael's family had committed using supernatural abilities, the necklace had hidden them from the Sentries of *Etherea*. By use of corrupt magic they had been able to hide in its shadow. The talisman, created over fifty years ago by Shannon Connelly, was a supernatural cloak from the underworld. The necklace would rest against his skin. It would become a part of him, albeit a temporarily spiritual part. There was no apparent life force attached to the necklace. It behaved like a normal piece of jewellery, yet there was nothing normal about it, or what he had to do with it in order to destroy it.

He moved into the bedroom, unbuttoned his shirt and placed the necklace around his neck. Lying on the bed he looked at his cousin standing in the doorway with a straight face. 'It's now or never, Bastian. Let's hope it works. They *are* expecting me this time.'

'I'll be here, Finn. I was hoping we'd miss that storm coming in off the Atlantic but with that spring tide, it's not likely. Take care with those Sentries, Cousin, and come back to us.'

'As if I'd forget.' He offered a small optimistic smile and closed his eyes.

His spirit emerged from his body and floated over the bed. He was glowing with a limited amount of soul light, seeping from his soul. Around his neck shone the amethyst necklace with a bright intensity.

Finn: *See you later.*

Bastian: *Good luck.*

His spirit darted through the ceiling and out into the sky. The town was being enveloped in thick sea mist. Creeping through St Ives and beyond, the light was luminescent. Rising waves were bashing over Smeaton's Pier with growing force. Dark clouds were closing in extinguishing the remaining daylight and rain lashed down in sheets. Despite the harsh conditions he rose higher and headed overland in the direction of Penzance. When he flew over the old engine house at Trencrom the moon escaped from behind the clouds to drape a silvery shadow over Mounts Bay in the distance. The faint outline of the coast leading to the Lizard peninsula and *Etherea* was laid out before him before vanishing in the mist.

Cillian marched through the Parsonage to check for anything out of place. He stopped in the old room where he had kept Joo prisoner, turned on the light and spotted a pile of dust on the floor. Looking up, he noticed the hatch in the ceiling. Standing on a stool, he lifted it and peered inside. The space was dark and beside the entrance, grooves in the dust were visible on the boarding, where something had been moved. To his right was a space showing the perfect outline of a large rectangular box or crate. It must have been there for years because the dust around it was considerable. The space where it had been lying was pristine.

Jumping back down, his hands were glowing with white sparks. Incensed, he threw on his jacket and grabbed his car keys. It was dark when he drove into town and difficult to drive in the bad weather. For the first time he knew exactly where to find his family's lost talisman.

Finn pushed on through the dense fog and sea mist, finding it harder to stay on course. The coastline was barely visible and he kept losing his bearings. The waves were crashing against the rocks at Kynance Cove, sending up sheets of spray and water. The light from the Lizard lighthouse appeared like a hazy glow then disappeared. As he grew closer, four identical ghostly white beings materialised above the Lion's Den and circled his spirit. In size alone they dwarfed him.

Sentry #1: *Do you have the talisman?*

Finn: *I'm wearing it.*

Sentry #1: *We have been informed about your imminent arrival. It is imperative the Council removes it immediately.*

Finn: *You're taking me to Etherea?*

Sentry #2: *Where else were you thinking of going, young mortal?*

The Sentry grabbed his spirit by the wrist and dived into the earth, trailing him behind. There was no going back. He closed his eyes and prayed the ordeal would be over quickly. All he could think about was whether he would see Ellie and Sam again.

Cillian parked carelessly in the small yard, knocking over a large plant pot. When he climbed out of the car, rain was pouring down and he was soaking wet. Huge gusts of wind knocked him almost right over but he regained his footing and looked up. One of the studio windows was ajar and rattling. He summoned soul light to jump to the first floor, where he climbed inside. Closing the window, he silenced the howling wind.

The lights were dimmed down low but there was no one around. An old packing trunk sat in the middle of the floor. Rubbing the surface exposed a copper nameplate with the words *James Connelly* engraved upon it. Cillian groaned his disgust. A chinking sound from another room caught his attention followed by the soft humming of music. He crept to the door to get a better look into the next room and was presented with a short staircase. It led past a couple of closed doors, so he followed the steps down.

In the kitchen Bastian was making a sandwich and the radio was turned on low. He turned around and consequently dropped the snack when he noticed Cillian.

'Hello, Bastian, I'm surprised to see you here.'

'Not as surprised as I am to see you.'

'Where's Finn?'

'Finn? You've got to be kidding me,' Bastian said.

'You're on your own, how foolish. Did you think it would be that easy to steal my talisman?'

Bastian was too slow. Cillian had him in a headlock before he had a chance to think and liberally read his mind. Swiftly the truth was revealed about Finn's plan. Bastian was charmed to sleep and promptly fell to the stone floor.

Finn's vacant body was lying motionless on the bed and he was wearing the lost talisman around his neck. Cillian wanted to kill him using the knife in his back pocket but the hunger kicked in with an acute intensity. His fingers twitched. His physical body was screaming out for soul light but he needed Finn's soul. Keeping his body alive would be on his terms so he carelessly dragged him by the hair from the bed. The body thudded heavily across the floor and down the stairs until he pushed the front door open. Outside in the lane the wind was tossing anything loose around like a small tornado. It was hard to stand straight in the driving rain. The trees were swaying and the noise coming from the sea was deafening. Aggressively, he dumped the body into the boot of his car, jumped into the driver's seat and slammed the door shut.

He pulled Finn's loose hair from between his fingers while he waited for the engine to warm up. Chunks of grey skin were peeling from the sides of his hands making the skin underneath angry. He rubbed them, winced from the sharp pain and pulled his jacket sleeves down to cover the sores.

Cillian understood that Finn's spirit would be impossibly drawn to his body so he drove back to the Parsonage. He was going to enjoy ending his life by springing a trap to consume the last of his soul light. It was coursing through his veins invigorating his appetite, even though it was rotting his skin.

His once luminous black hair was falling out in clumps revealing bald patches covered in more weeping sores. He was transforming but it felt good to him in a strange way. He turned on the headlamps and windscreen wipers and reversed into the lane. There was no going back.

The glass arena was vast and carried on for miles in every direction. Finn failed to recall the previous visit to *Etherea* but was mesmerized by its spiritual spectacle. Having travelled through gaseous tubes and fallen for what seemed miles and miles, he could hardly believe there would be so much light at the end of it. Higher up were rows and rows of spirits, which he later learnt, made up the High Council of *Etherea*. A Sentry guard drifted down from the council and stopped beside him.

Beside the Sentry was a soul he recognised. Ana was smiling and he could hardly believe how much she had changed. Her soul was glowing pure white and everything about her rang peace and serenity.

Ana: *I told them everything, Finn. They will release you after the talisman's removed. We may meet again one day, they want me to become a Sentry.*

He looked into her eyes when the Sentry clasped a pair of enormous hands on his shoulders. He never took his eyes from her while his spirit was forced into becoming more defined. The task was agonising. The Sentry poured more raw energy into him until he could barely handle it. His body was glowing intensely and he screamed out in agony. Only when his soul was visible in minute detail did the Sentry place his fingers on the necklace. He thought he was going to die. Every part of his soul hurt with a passion.

Cillian slammed on the brakes and skidded on the gravel in the dark driveway. Through driving rain he grabbed Finn's body from the trunk and marched around the side of the house.

When he dropped his lifeless body, his head struck the hard granite path making a low cracking sound and blood started to run from his nose.

Turning on a switch in the kitchen, light flooded into the garden and beyond. Turning his attention back to Finn he knelt down to remove his ancestor's necklace from his unconscious body. The precious stones felt hot. The skin under the necklace was burning. He grappled furiously with the talisman but was unable to touch it. It was fused to the skin then it vanished a second later. His skin was burnt in the exact shape of the necklace, leaving behind a seething burn several layers deep.

'No! This can't happen to me.' He cried out through the rain. 'You're going to pay big time for this, Milton.'

Finn's spirit was weak. At first there was relief, which quickly turned to panic when his soul began to fade. The Sentry was holding the enchanted necklace in his long wispy fingers. A second Sentry tapped him on the shoulder. Delirium set in and the arena faded before his eyes. A soft humming filled his ears and then nothing.

Sentry #2: *Do not concern yourself, Duana. The shock of removing a talisman is dangerous. In order for Finn to recover, his soul must recuperate. This won't take long and then we will let him go.*

The Sentry approached the Council with the ghostly piece of enchanted jewellery. The High Leader inspected the necklace and made it disintegrate. Rising up above all the spirits, she addressed her realm.

Clinthia: *The Realm of Etherea, I salute you as your leader, Clinthia of Centauri. A new talisman had been brought before us.*

Using its magic, mortals have abused their abilities and forged a new threat to our existence. Due to the actions of this selfless mortal spirit, Finn Milton, we are able to reveal the evil once more. The talisman has been destroyed and the cloak has gone. Sentries: Dispatch the first wave, find the perpetrators and disperse them – all of them. Do not stop until they are all dust. These Connelly crimes are stacking up. Sentries, you must investigate all gifted mortals named Connelly. Report back anything suspicious. This breach of the Dark Domain is unthinkable and must never be allowed to happen.

Clinthia regarded her Council with a stern gaze. High spirits were seated all around her, hanging off every word she spoke.

She was the highest-ranking elder spirit among them. She glowed white then bright cyan blue.

Her determination never once wavered.

In mortal years she looked to be no more than thirty years of age with striking features and piercing eyes.

Below the vast collection of spirits listened silently and patiently.

In the vast realm of *Etherea* she was considered an Empress.

Clinthia: *Strangely, this mortal has become less powerful since we were last graced by his presence. I am tempted to keep him but the council has made a promise. I hope this is not a promise we will live to regret. Sentries, you must watch him more closely in future but keep your distance. Sentry Guilar, take the spirit trap and open it near his home. Have more Sentries ready to act. Deal with this moth named Connelly, the perpetrator. Destroy him swiftly for I fear Finn's life is in danger. Connelly must not be allowed to extract any more soul light or it could be the end of everything we hold dear. If he is able to wield soul light at us, it will be all for nothing. At this rate, Finn is on his way to becoming an honorary Sentry. This would make him the second human to ever achieve this. Protect his soul at all costs. I pray the omen is wrong this time.*

Joe and Jerry arrived later than planned due to the worsening weather. The front door was swinging in the wind, slamming against the frame with the lock pulled back.

Pulling back the hood of his raincoat, Jerry sprinted up the stairs to discover Bastian lying on the kitchen floor with his eyes open and unresponsive.

'Bastian, are you okay? Joe, check on Finn,' Jerry said, trying to work out if Bastian was alive. He quickly tore off his jacket to administer first aid. 'Come on Bast, wake up Buddy… come on.'

Joe returned to the kitchen with a look of confusion.

'Finn's gone.'

'Are you sure? Ah hell, you don't think Cillian's been here, do you? Bastian was right. We should've stayed with him.'

'Do you think he's taken Finn's body? You can't be serious, Jerry.'

'Finn would never leave Bastian like this. He's unconscious. I'll put him on the bed and call Simon. Cillian *has* probably gone back to the Parsonage. Without his spirit, Finn's body is vulnerable to say the least. We must get over there and fast before his spirit returns from *Etherea*.'

'Sometimes you really surprise me. All the time you're joking, you're actually ahead of everything.'

Jerry smiled at him warily. 'I'm not just a pretty face, you know. I have a fast processor inside this brain of mine. I know what's going on, well, at least I think I do.'

'Well, *Brains*…for now the roads are pretty bad, I'm going to call Branna,' Joe said. 'Maybe she can get there before we can.'

The Sentry Guilar accepted the floating white orb and journeyed into the skies above The Lizard. The being flew on to St Ives in the dark and stepped on to the sand at Porthminster Beach. He withdrew the glowing spirit trap and tapped it with his long white finger.

Huge waves crashed on the shore but the Sentry was unmoved by the storm as it lashed on around them.

Finn opened his eyes and became aware he was no longer in *Etherea*. He was confused to how he had managed to arrive above a long wall of sand but his senses were slowly returning. The beach was being carved up by torrential winds, wild frothy waves and heavy rain. The storm had intensified and right in the centre of the melee floated the vague image of a tall ghostly spirit.

Finn: *Are you Guilar?*

Guilar: *Yes, I am he. I have brought your spirit home. The talisman has been destroyed and you are free to go. Our leader extends her highest gratitude for presenting the talisman. Your work will not be forgotten. Stay safe, young mortal.*

The Sentry was gone before Finn had the chance to respond. Checking his bearings he flew on alone towards town and their house. When the tug of his life cord changed course, his soul was unwillingly drawn to the farthest side of town. He couldn't understand what was happening and couldn't stop himself.

It soon became clear, when he flew over the Parsonage garden and spied his body lying inert and soaked on the sodden grass, that somebody had moved it. The pull to connect was overwhelming but he held his position using as much energy as he could muster before recognising the fateful scene. He had seen it in a damning vision whilst planing in New York.

Desmond had said the visions were rarely wrong. It would take everything he had if he was going to survive the ordeal that appeared to be mapped out right before him.

While waiting for his brother Simon to arrive, Jerry decided to read Bastian's mind. He planted the memory of earlier that afternoon when they had been together in the studio. Seconds later

Bastian woke and sat bolt upright. His eyes were wide open with fear and concern. 'Finn! He's here.'

'What happened to you?' Jerry asked.

'Cillian was here … is Finn okay? He must've knocked me out. He just wanted Finn, I don't remember anything else.'

Jerry said. 'Finn's gone, Bastian.'

'Oh no, Cillian's taken him to the Parsonage,' he replied. 'He was too fast for me. Everything's coming true from his vision. We have to stop him.'

'You were right to be concerned,' Jerry said.

'Branna is flying there ahead of us,' Joe said, withdrawing his mobile phone from his pocket. 'I'm going to call the others now you're awake.'

'Good plan,' Jerry said.

'I'll call Finlay, he should know what's happening,' Bastian said, 'and Ellie.'

'She called me when she couldn't get an answer from you earlier,' Joe said. 'We came over straight away, we would've been here sooner but the roads were flooded. She was worried something might have happened. I told her to stay where she is but knowing Ellie, that was like a red rag to a bull.'

Cillian was pacing up and down in the shadow of the house, close to where he had dropped Finn's body. Waiting for his spirit to return, his eyes were glowing. His hands were stinging from where he had been picking at the ulcerating skin. His skin had turned grey with darker slits appearing, one covering half his face. Skin flakes were coming away leaving sores in their wake. His teeth were falling out. The rain was lashing down flooding the garden. Several of the trees had fallen over and leaves flew everywhere. Lightning forked in the distance and seconds later thunder rumbled.

Cillian tore off Finn's unbuttoned shirt leaving him naked from the waist up. The terrible burn shaped necklace was exposed across his sternum and neck. He stared up into the sky and shouted. 'I can sense you. Show yourself, Milton. It's no use. You can't fight the pull of your own body. Your fate is entwined with mine now. You cannot resist it. Your soul is mine. The Sentries can't help you even if you have destroyed the talisman. I can sense them and I *will* destroy them too. The sooner you give in the better.'

Finn was exhausted and knew he was losing. His spirit could no longer fight the pull of his body. It was too strong and Cillian was right on the money. When he opened his eyes, two large hands were twisted tightly around his windpipe making it impossible to breathe.

With consciousness came the pain. The severe burn around his neck was intolerable. He couldn't move his legs. His head hurt more than anything, an excruciating pain from a cracked skull. The fatigue from astral planing consumed him and his eyes glazed over from the complication of ailments. The cold winter night's temperature dropped even further making him shiver and convulse involuntarily. His half-clothed wet body was blazing from the dozens of bruises Cillian had bestowed on him and then there was the small matter of being strangled.

'Hello Finn, I've been waiting for this moment for months. It makes no difference because I'm going to end it right now and no one will be able to stop me. I will be invincible with all your soul light. They will bow to me or die.'

'You can't …' He made barely a whisper.

'Like you're going to stop me.'

Cillian's body was glowing white when he telepathically plunged into his mind. A thin stream of iridescent mist poured out of Finn's body. The pain was excruciating and he suffered a seizure. Cillian sucked it in and soul light spread through his veins like alcohol. Finn convulsed erratically as the last of it was taken, leaving him completely paralysed on his back. The pain coursed through him like hot irons. Blood trickled from his nose as a strange numbness crept over him in waves. It happened so quickly all he could think about was Ellie and Sam. He began to cry without making a sound. His broken spirit was challenging his mortal body to let go. The damage had been done.

Cillian rose into the air flexing his mutated abilities, glowing like a beacon. From his almost hairless head an arch of light fanned out. His body jerked and adapted randomly to the radical and physical mutation. Half a dozen Sentries suddenly illuminated the garden. They had come to dispatch him, and with the talisman destroyed, the truth behind his intentions were laid bare.

Lightning poured out of him like a laser beam arch and the Sentries were pulverized as soon as they flew towards him. For a moment the only light came from Cillian and soul light. His body was glowing white and sparking energy. Many bright Sentries materialised on every side of the garden, identical in appearance and over eight feet tall.

'This is brilliant,' he said, counting the number of Sentries. 'I can fly and attack at the same time.' He dropped down beside Finn to gloat.

'Soul light will kill you,' he whispered.

'Are you feeling cold, Milton? Don't worry, it won't be long and you'll be dead. It's a pity you're going to miss the show. It's been my pleasure entirely. I'll send my condolences to your sad family, don't you worry about that. Oh, and I almost forgot the best part... when your soul leaves your body, it won't be in one piece. Ha, you are never coming back from this. Logan would be so proud of me.'

Cillian was laughing demonically and tore up into the sky. All Finn could do was watch as the garden lit up once more. A troop of over a hundred Sentries appeared and their intensity appeared like daylight as they gathered in a circle around the glowing human. Each one dropped their hood, revealing a troop of eerie spirits with darkened hollows for eyes, and focused their attention on the dangerous mortal. In amongst the lightning it was impossible to tell what was natural and what was spiritual. Thunder rumbled and the ground felt like it was shaking.

The energy leaving Cillian's body struck the spirits and carried on, blasting into the walls of the Parsonage. The force smashed into the brickwork and windows, sending rubble and dust crashing to the garden below, dangerously close to where Finn was lying in a helpless state. One of the turrets toppled and smashed on the ground missing him by inches. Mentally he tried to nudge the approaching debris as clouds of dust and broken bricks fell about all around him. He created a safe space but his commands were sluggish as his powers grew weaker. When the dust cleared the abomination rose again and approached another large party of Sentries. Finn could sense every one of them and feared the outcome but had nothing left to give because he was dying.

He alone was responsible for arming Cillian with a weapon that could destroy them all. The Sentries had once been mortal and each one of them carried a tiny fraction of soul light energy. Some were old and had served *Etherea* for thousands of years. They each had one thing in common: fighting corrupt, evil and demonic forces. Each time a Sentry came forward, it was obliterated into tiny specks of light. There was nothing the Sentries could do as Cillian attacked each and every one of them. Finn feared the worst was yet to come and drifted out of consciousness.

An hour earlier at Eternia Cottage in Penberth, Sam had fallen asleep in Ellie's arms. She gently laid the boy in the travel cot in her old room, tucked a blanket around him and placed his small blue teddy bear close by. She checked the listener was working and stared out the window into the darkness wearing a blank expression. The atmosphere was completely still. Minutes earlier the rain had been lashing hard against the glass. Thunder rumbled in the distance and the lights inside the house flickered.

Joo and Rose were downstairs in the kitchen making dinner. She had phoned Joe because Bastian had failed to give her an update. Joe had promised to check up on him at the house. During those long minutes, she had been unable to think about anything else. She could not question the overwhelming desire to drive to St Ives so she grabbed her jacket, pulled on her leather boots and hurried down the wooden staircase.

'Rose, can you look after Sam for me? I have to go to St Ives,' she said. 'Here's the baby listening thing, I'm sorry but I've got to go now.'

'What's wrong, love?' Rose asked.

'It's Finn.' She didn't stop to explain, merely grabbed the Porsche keys, opened the front door and was gone.

A few seconds later Joo was standing in front of the car. 'You're not going alone, Ellie. I'm coming with you. Besides the storm's hit town and it's mental over there.'

'Something's happened to Finn, I can feel it in my bones. I don't care about the weather, Joo. I'm not going to lose him now, not after everything we've been through.'

As soon as they passed Zennor and followed the road on, the view of St Ives was offered up to them. In the distance a large glowing orb of white light was illuminated over Higher Stennack. The town was submerged in a thick fog, so eerily bright with everything defined by weird shapes.

It was bright like the middle of the day.

'What on Earth is that?' Joo raised her hand to her mouth in shock.

'It's Cillian, it's started.'

'What are you talking about?'

'Cillian has taken all of Finn's soul light. We're too late and that, my dear friend, is a mass of Sentries.'

❦

'What the hell is that?' Bastian blurted when they approached the Parsonage. A patch of glowing daylight was basking around the vicinity of the old Connelly house. Everywhere was carpeted in fog. 'It looks like an electrical storm.'

Jerry said. 'Are those Sentries? I hope we're not too late.'

'There are hundreds of them,' Joe replied.

Half the town were witnessing the freaky supernatural event as it grew larger in scale on the night of one of the worst storms in living memory. A siren began screamed in the distance as the authorities moved in. Joe, Jerry and Bastian found themselves caught up in a torrent of local people heading in the same direction. No one understood what was going on and as they stared up at the sky, Tom and Serina found them.

'I hope Finn's alright,' Bastian said. 'It looks like Armageddon's arrived.'

'This is what Finn predicted,' Serina said. 'What happened to you, Bastian?'

'Cillian broke in and knocked me out. He must have taken Finn's body. We don't know if his soul has made it back from *Etherea*.'

Milton located them easily after walking across from The Warren. 'What's causing this to happen?'

'Cillian Connelly.' Bastian replied.

'Where's Finn?' He asked.

'We think he's in the garden,' Joe said. 'But he could be in terrible danger. I never thought that bastard would actually steal his body. I have no idea what we can do to stop this. The Sentries are being pulverised.'

'What about Ellie? Has anyone called her?' Milton asked.

'She's on her way,' Bastian replied.

'Milton,' Joe said. 'What are you thinking?'

'There must be a way into the garden,' he replied. 'I'm going to find it.'

'What about Branna?' Jerry watched Milton disappear into the crowd surging closer to the old building. 'This is utter madness. It could be dangerous in there.'

'Branna's flying, I spoke to her five minutes ago,' Joe said. 'Right now, she could be Finn's only hope.'

'Let's hope she makes it in time.' Jerry added. 'I thought she'd be here by now.

Finn was conscious.

The Sentries had ceased their movement and appeared to be hanging motionless in the air. The troop formed a large perimeter ring around Cillian when a black raven landed on the grass. The wind had completely dropped off and the clouds were parting above the garden.

Branna transformed and immediately felt Finn's wrist for a pulse. He found it difficult to breathe and was shaking from the cold. He could feel her pulling a jacket around his upper body to stave off the dropping temperature but it was far too small for him.

His organs were failing and he struggled to think straight. Part of his soul was severely damaged. He could feel her dragging him away from the masonry falling off the roof.

The countless Sentries surrounded the glowing nucleus that barely resembled a human being. Cillian was glowing like a beacon wielding his powerful weapon. He was using his mind and soul light to destroy the ghostly soldiers. Powerful beams of light were streaming from his body striking anything in its path.

They were being slowly annihilated.

A sudden rush of wind blew through the garden. Branna froze momentarily as a spiritual hand passed right through her. The strange entity hurtled off in another direction but it attracted the attention of the Sentries.

Finn could feel her holding his cold hands and rubbing them between hers. His mouth opened slightly and his spirit emerged.

He could no longer stop it.

To begin he was well defined but there was barely any light emanating from him. His mental state was slight, hardly registering at all. Random thoughts entered his mind but it was hard to form any sense. He glanced down and could see his eyes were closed on the motionless body laid out on the grass, the body that used to be his. Dennis had been exact in his description.

'Finn, what happened to you?' She asked his spirit in horror.

Finn: *I* …

'Finn, no! Don't leave us. You can't die, not like this.'

Finn spirit faded until he was almost invisible but his eyes were still looking upon her. She was transfixed. His eyes conveyed a deep sadness. He had fast moments of clarity then nothing. His broken soul jerked and twisted, transforming into a light gust of wind and was gone.

Tears ran down her cheeks and she cradled his dead body in her arms. Blood from his head wound covered her hands and she whispered, 'no, Finn, you can't die.'

15

～

Phoebe

The remaining band of Sentries formed a wide circle around the glowing man. Marcio and Guilar commanded a troop of senior guards who were overseeing the battle.

Marcio: *Finn Milton has been defeated, Guilar. His spirit is broken and out of control. I never imagined he could be defeated so easily. He was weak and his passing is a complete waste. If only he had owned a warrior soul, he would have never allowed this to happen, especially when he was warned about it. The Connelly mortal is stronger than we are. How are we going to stop him?*

Guilar: *You are wrong about Finn, he was not weak...he only lacked experience. There is another soul. I can sense a female. Her spirit is broken but it has a strong connection with Finn. I can feel it. It could be his mother. Her soul was never found.*

Marcio: *This is hopeless, Brother. Connelly will unleash terror onto the world and we will be responsible for allowing it to happen once he destroys us. If he joins ranks with the darker ones he will be unstoppable. I fear our leader was right ... we are approaching a new Dark Age of man.*

Guilar: *The solution lies with one of those lost souls if I can catch one. I believe they are connected. There is more soul matter residing inside Connelly. It does not come from one soul alone. I can sense the broken parts of at least two others inside him. He is growing evermore unstable as he adapts to soul light. It is tearing his physical body apart. We have to do something before he destroys us all or worse, explodes... there could be a massive fall out.*

Marcio: *I cannot afford to lose you, Guilar.*

Guilar: *Marcio, pretty soon there will be nothing left.*

Marcio: *Please exercise caution. We have lived far too long to die at this juncture. The world needs us to remain alive. We have lost too many tonight.*

Guilar: *I will be careful, Brother, do not concern yourself with my plight. I fear this is the only course of action left to take.*

The rogue female spirit flew out of control and wisped like a dart past Guilar. He chased it, ducking and diving, matching its projected path at every turn. It left the grounds of the Parsonage and disappeared into the thick sea mist. The Sentry flew after it through town, down alleyways and tight lanes, not losing his sense of the strange entity for one second. He predicted each move and judged its path, waiting until it turned direction again, and extended his hand to snatch the being as it whizzed past him.

Guilar: *Got you.*

The half-spirit struggled and screamed in his grasp, wriggling desperately to be freed. It had hardly any control over its sentient part. Guilar held on to it firmly and flew back to the Parsonage, all the while learning of its lost identity.

Ellie parked the Porsche in a space half a mile from the Parsonage. The police had closed most of the roads into town due to downed trees and the Stennack flooding.

The two women ran down the hill, passing groups of aimless spectators made up of men, women and children. More police were arriving in vans with sirens blaring. The cold mist was everywhere but a bright light from above lit up all their faces. The luminous Parsonage was crumbling and slowly being destroyed. The rain had petered out to a light drizzle. A second later Ellie and Joo ran into Serina, Joe and the others quite by chance. After their initial greeting Jerry explained everything.

Tears pricked Ellie's eyes. 'Cillian's taken all of Finn's soul light. This is why he has become so powerful. It can only mean one thing... Finn must be dead.'

'No, Ellie, we don't know anything yet,' Joe said. 'Try to be positive, Sweetheart.'

'Finn was convinced this was going to happen,' she said. 'I should've listened to him.'

'The police have stopped anyone trying to get into the garden,' Jerry said.

Ellie looked at Joo who was holding her hand, squeezing it tight. Both their eyes were watering at the prospect of never seeing Finn again.

～

Guilar: *Let me read you, spirit. Your name is Phoebe.*

Phoebe: *I am no one. I am lost ... let go of me.*

Guilar: *I can end your suffering if you let me help you.*

Phoebe: *There is nothing you can do to help me.*

Guilar: *You are wrong, child. I can revive you for a short time. You are severely damaged but there's something important you must do. You can save your son and maybe all of us. You could be the catalyst to end this battle.*

Phoebe: *What are you talking about?*

Guilar: *Can you see that abomination before us? See the soul light he is wielding? Do you remember soul light, Phoebe? Do you remember it?*

Phoebe: *I gave soul light to my baby but it was so long ago.*

Guilar: *It is the same soul light. This monster, reeking havoc before us, has stolen it from your son. You can fly into the light and absorb all that was taken. That is all you have to do. It will be a natural process because it knows you, Phoebe. Soul light used to reside inside you and it can again. It remembers. It is a living organism. Its energy will make you whole again. This human abomination stole part of Finn's soul and now your son is broken like you are. You must touch the soul light and make it work for you. You will find the missing part of your soul for it has lain dormant inside Finn since you died. When Cillian stole Finn's soul light, he absorbed part of his soul and what was left of yours. Fulfill your destiny, Phoebe, and stop this once and for all. You are the only one who can defeat him and save your son.*

Phoebe: *He will destroy me and render me to dust.*

Guilar: *Only if he is aware of you. I'll distract him, he will not be expecting it. I'll push you as close to him as I can. We only have one shot at this and you will need all of your strength to do this. You must fly right inside him. Phoebe, you must embrace the light and live again. We must do it now.*

Guilar broke ranks and approached the glowing heart of the garden concealing Phoebe's spirit behind him. She accepted she had no choice concerning his crazy idea. Her reflexes were slow to non-existent. He released her as they became dangerously close and swung her spirit towards Cillian like a shot bearing. Her broken soul hurtled towards the glowing mass unable to stop even if she wanted to.

Noticing the lone Sentry only feet away from him, Cillian fired a lethal stream of energy. The moment distracted him long enough for Phoebe to plunge her spirit inside the young man's glowing body. She disappeared into the seething mass and Guilar was greeted by his imminent sacrifice.

His life force was extinguished into many specks of light until there was nothing left of him. Witnessing the full horror, Marcio screamed a long painful lament for his lost brother. For over two thousand years they had never been separated.

Phoebe's damaged spirit stopped inside Cillian's glowing form. His physical body was ravaged by decomposition. A single particle of light forced itself away from the main entity and fused itself to her spirit. The process was rapid and brought a strange stillness to her soul.

Memories began to circulate in her mind, followed by sense and logic. She grew stronger and her consciousness cleared. For the first time in years she could form legible thoughts.

The sensation was like a powerful magnet attracting all the spiritual matter to her soul. She had no control over the process once it started. The iridescent light seeped into the fibre of her spirit, giving her maximum strength and form. There was enormous power at her disposal but she remained resolute and calm. The familiarity of the scene: she had seen it before in visions she was remembering.

As a mortal, she had experienced clear visions of the future, ones she had never been able to change. She had seen her own death and that of her son many years before it happened. Her fate had been tied to a curse like Finn's had been. As a consequence of being his mother, she had been cursed to die following his birth. She was remembering the vision she had seen of his death and how there was still a part for her to play in his fate... of further events that hadn't happened yet.

It was undeniable that Cillian's powers and abilities were drastically weakening. The light around him was fading and the lightning from his fingers reduced to no more than a spark. The result of being stripped of soul light meant his organs and muscle tissue were failing rapidly.

She revealed her ghostly shape in the growing darkness when she left the confines of his body. Her features of a young vibrant woman were striking and detailed. She had long blonde hair and her face was beautiful. She smiled into Cillian's wistful eyes before tapping him on the head.

Gravity took hold and his body dropped like a stone to the ground below. Hitting the granite path two seconds later, his spine broke in several places.

Blood trickled from his mouth and he was paralysed. Without soul light or a talisman to protect him, his soul was breaking apart. The surviving Sentries were gathering like vultures preparing to pick over a carcass.

Reborn, she continued to stare at the tragic looking corpse with rotting grey skin and ugly seeping callouses. Her spirit glowed brilliantly with iridescent colours.

Cillian coughed up blood and struggled to lift an ulcerated hand towards her. 'Who are you? How did you do that? You stole it from me...'

Phoebe: *Soul light was never meant for you. You would have destroyed everything. I had to stop you, Cillian. No one should use soul light to kill.*

'But you're just a girl,' he replied.

Phoebe: *That's true but I've also been dead for over thirty years. I've been waiting for you. Part of my soul was inside Finn. When you robbed him of soul light, you brought that part of me along with it. The soul light used to be mine before I died and it remembered me. I simply took it back. Your talisman was destroyed by my son. That's right, I'm Finn's mother. You never saw that one coming, did you? I can see into your pitiful mind, Cillian Connelly. No child should ever murder his father like you did. I can see what you did to Finn, Finlay and Bastian and I would kill you right now if I had the authority.*

Phoebe moved aside and Marcio swept down. She watched as he tore Cillian's damaged soul out of his broken body in an instant and dragged it back to the band of Sentries. Each one was baying for his blood and the end to his pitiful existence. It took seconds to tear his soul apart.

Marcio: *Are you going to come peacefully, Phoebe?*

Phoebe: *I have to do one thing first.*

Marcio: *If you successfully give soul light to him, Finn will always be vulnerable. Is that what you want for him? Isn't it better he fades naturally?*

Phoebe: *Of course not. It was always meant for his protection. I must give it back to him.*

Marcio: *Soul light will not save him. He's gone.*

Phoebe: *I must try. The other Sentry was prepared to help and he died trying.*

Marcio: *You speak of my brother, Guilar. He was a wise soul and he loved mortals. If it was his wish then I will help you but you must be prepared for the worst because we may never find him.*

Phoebe: *Please give me a few moments and I will come with you.*

She dropped down beside Finn's body and looked into Branna's face. For a moment she read the dark haired woman's mind. She had strong feelings for her son and was capable of being a powerful witch. At the same time, her intentions were good and she had no fear. Briefly she conveyed a message.

'You are Finn's mother,' she said.

Phoebe gave no verbal response and looked upon her son. He lay with his eyes closed, his face bruised and swollen. Blood from a head wound ran down his neck. As a grown man he resembled his father. In the sky above, the Sentries had disappeared and everything had returned to relative normality.

She looked upon Branna briefly and allowed her to read her mind. Then she rose into the air and held a firm gaze over the people spilling into the garden. The sound of one of them caught her immediate attention.

'My son is over there, get out of my way.'

Professor Milton pushed through a line of police officers. There were others in uniform with torches searching the garden. 'His life could be in danger.'

She watched her living husband tear across to where Branna was kneeling on the ground. Milton grabbed Finn's hands and held his limp body in his arms. Tears were rolling down his face. The grief she could feel was intense and painful.

'No, Finn why did you have to die?'

She made her spirit turn invisible. Milton had aged well in the last thirty years and she could feel the love she used to have for him but didn't want him to see her. Suddenly he looked up to right where she was floating. There was an expression of sadness and confusion on his face as though he knew she was there. Her spirit rose thirty feet in the air because her emotions were running wild and she needed some distance to understand them.

Two policemen were inspecting Cillian's dead body, lying on the path. His body was grey, his skin torn and severely ulcerated. A third officer approached Branna. She was holding a torch and flashed it in her face. 'What are you doing here? Who are you?'

'Branna Smith.'

'You'd better come with me.'

'Wait, Officer,' Milton said. 'She's done nothing wrong. The real murderer is over there.' He pointed to Cillian's body.

Branna stepped aside as the policewoman cuffed her hands. 'It's alright, Professor. They have to do this. It's part of their job.'

'But they can't arrest you,' Milton said. 'Officer, please.'

'I have identified her as the murderer of possibly five people after tonight's count,' the policewoman said. 'You need to keep your opinions to yourself Professor Milton. It looks like this one is dead as well. We will find out what happened here tonight. It looks like a double homicide with some special effects. Another body, Cooper.' She shouted to a colleague. 'It looks like a bloodbath.'

'Finn is my son, not another bloody body.' Milton was angry. 'You can't take him away! I'm his next of kin. I have rights. I can't believe you're doing this.'

'Are you going to be a problem, sir?' The policewoman asked. 'It's our job to contain the situation. There are crowds of people out there demanding answers. Maybe you should go and talk to them.'

Milton remained silent as more uniformed people swarmed around them.

Branna: *Don't let them know what happened here, Milton. They don't have any evidence. I haven't been here, remember? I'll be fine once they realise I'm innocent. Don't let them cremate or bury Finn's body. Keep it safe. There's still time to save him but you're going to have to trust me.*

Milton: W*hy?*

Branna: *Because his mother's searching for his soul and she's going to try and save him.*

Milton: *You saw Phoebe? She was here? I thought I could sense her for a moment but it was too much to hope for after all this time.*

Branna: *You're right, Professor. Phoebe is very much alive and she was here. She spoke to me.* She wore a small smile, before being pushed along by the policewoman. Milton could not help but manage to return a smile and his eyes were watering.

Finn's body was lifted onto a stretcher and placed inside a black body bag. There was blood oozing down his neck. One of the men zipped the bag shut and Milton watched the officers walk away carrying it between them. Bastian suddenly appeared at his side.

'Is Finn alright?'

'He's gone, Bastian,' Milton said. 'My boy's gone.'

'What are you talking about?' Bastian asked. 'Where is he?'

'Cillian killed him. They're taking his body away now. No wait a minute...'

'Is that Finn's body on the stretcher?' He asked.

Milton brushed past his nephew and raced after the men with the stretcher. 'What are you doing with my son's body?'

'We're taking it to the morgue for an autopsy. It has some strange burns on it and a head wound. This is usual procedure.'

Milton turned back to his nephew: *Bastian, don't let anything happen to Finn's body. There's a slim chance his soul is still out there. I can't explain it right now but trust me. Finn's mother is searching for him. Find a way of getting his body to Joe's barn and we can make a plan from there. No matter what, they must not do an autopsy on him.*

Bastian gave his uncle a look of abject surprise then managed a brief nod of understanding before heading after the policemen.

'I'm Doctor Bastian Pengelly and he's my patient. I need to inspect the body.'

'He was pronounced dead at the scene, there's nothing more you can do for him. The other one is dead as well.' The policewoman added, ushering Branna towards a police car. 'I suggest you let the professionals do their job, Doctor Pengelly, and you do yours. This a police matter now.'

'I would like to offer a second opinion,' Bastian insisted.

'Fine, go with him, I'm not going to argue with you,' the policewoman said before pushing Branna by the head into the back seat of the police car and slamming the door.

'What are they doing with Branna?' Jerry appeared beside Bastian, having squeezed his way forward through the crowd. 'That copper was definitely man-handling her.'

'They've arrested her,' Bastian replied. 'I wasn't there when it happened.'

'There must be something we can do about it,' Jerry said. 'She's innocent.'

Bastian: *Jerry, I agree with you but this has to wait because right now what I am about to ask of you is far more pressing. I'm going in the van with Finn's body. I'll call Caron and tell her you're on your way. I need you to grab one of my motorbikes and catch up with me. I'll call you on your mobile when I need you to intervene. We have to keep his body safe because there's a slim chance he can be saved. I want you to stop the van and I'll send these guys to sleep. It looks like they're taking his body to Truro.*

'Bast, of course. I'm on it.' Jerry said and nudged his way through the crowd until he was free to sprint down the hill to Porthgwidden and Bastian's garage.

Professor Finlay Milton numbly walked to the front of the Parsonage to be confronted by many confused faces. A familiar heaviness pressed hard on his heart.

Time was standing still. His heart was shattering.

He recalled holding his wife in his arms shortly after she died. It was the same feeling of hopelessness. There were muffled voices of people, confused and alarmed. His son was dead and it was unlikely he could be brought back.

'Excuse me.' A microphone and camera were suddenly rammed into his face. 'Can you make a statement about what happened here tonight? Was it an alien invasion? Do you know what it was about?'

Milton turned to the reporter, standing in the thick of a surging crowd of people. Everyone was desperate to understand the weird event. 'All I know is that it's over.'

'But what was it?' The young male reporter asked. 'The mist disappeared as soon as it was over. Was it some special effect? The weather was crazy. There were bodies…'

'I have no comment for you.' He pushed forward refusing to say anymore.

'Hey buddy, leave him alone,' Joe said, forcing his way towards him. 'Milton, come this way. Are you alright?'

'I'm fine,' Milton replied.

'I don't think you are,' Joe said.

A moment later, Ellie and Joo were standing before him. The tears were falling down Milton's face. His shoulders were hunched.

Milton: *I'm sorry Ellie but we were too late to save him. He's dead and so is Cillian.*

'No, Milton, please don't say this.' Ellie was able to read his mind and learn the painful truth. 'It can't be true. I can't believe it.'

'What happened?' Serina put her arm around Ellie who was becoming hysterical.

'I know you all cared for him and I want to thank every one of you. Cillian Connelly killed him and paid for it with his own life.

The Connelly family has taken everything from me. I can't believe I'll never see my boy again.'

Phoebe knew what the Sentry was thinking. In spirit form and with so much soul light inside her, Marcio could not stop her from reading his mind. Their thoughts had been crossing over without any conversation.

Marcio: *What do you expect will happen if you find him?*

Phoebe: *I will give him back his soul particle and he will be whole again.*

Marcio: *You can't do that on your own. You will need my help.*

Phoebe: *But you're not prepared to help me, are you?*

Marcio: *He could be anywhere. This is hopeless.*

Phoebe: *Only because helping mortals is not in your damn code. Finn is just as important as all those souls down there. He's been fighting evil all his life, and on his own. You thought he was weak. You must understand his innocence in all of this.*

Marcio: *I do not deny his innocence but what will you do for me if I help him? For every action there is a cost involved.*

Phoebe: *Fine, I'll come to Etherea, if that's what you want.*

Marcio: *I want you to come willingly. There is nothing for you up here with the mortals. Can't you see that your time has passed?*

Phoebe: *I have a grandson. I would like to see him before I go.*

Marcio: *Come on, Phoebe, you know how this works. The priority is to find your son and then I'm taking you to Etherea.*

Bastian was sitting uncomfortably between two body bags and two officers in the police van en route to the morgue. On reading their minds, it became clear they were not going to sit about all night. They were tired and wanted to go home so he waited for the opportune moment to reveal itself.

It came quickly and he tapped them both on the shoulder at the same time. The two officers slumped over and fell asleep where they were sitting. His unusual ability came in handy at times although it could yield consequent issues. Unzipping the body bag beside him revealed his cousin's unmoving grey face. Blood from his head wound had dried over his face. He swallowed and pulled out his mobile phone to call Jerry.

'What took you so long?' Jerry answered his handset from a siding near Lelant.

'I had to wait for the right moment,' Bastian said, looking out the back window. 'We're approaching Hayle. You can intervene anytime you like, Buddy.'

'Cool,' Jerry replied, slipped his phone into his pocket and dropped his visor.

A minute later the roar was heard of a loud motorbike cutting across the police van's trajectory. The driver swerved to miss the motorbike and pulled fast onto the hard shoulder of the A30 road between Hayle and St Erth. The bike came to a stop a few feet ahead.

The police officer tore out of the van and burst a load of expletives at Jerry. 'What the hell are you playing at, you idiot? You could've killed someone. This is a dangerous road.'

'Sorry but I lost control of the bike.' Jerry replied, slowly removing his helmet. With his attention caught up with Jerry, Bastian crept up behind the driver and tapped him on the shoulder. The man crumbled back into his waiting arms fast asleep. Between them, they eased the policeman to the side of the road and laid him down on the grass verge. 'Are there anymore in the back, Bastian?'

'Two,' he replied. 'This is making me nervous.' Several cars whizzed past on the dual carriageway and rain poured down making the roads slippery.

Jerry hurried to pull out one of the sleeping officers, followed by Bastian with the other until there were three unconscious policemen on the side of the road.

'I suppose it's a different way to spend the evening,' Jerry said with a grin. 'I mean with Finn around anything can happen even when he's dead. It's not like every night you get to see three real sleeping policemen.'

'Jerry, that's not funny. They'll wake up in a few hours time and won't know what happened to them. Talking of Finn, I hope Branna's right. It might be an idea to ask her to heal his wounds after you get her out of jail. What a hell of a night this is turning out to be. I can't believe Finn's actually dead. I'm not allowing myself to take that on board yet. I can't deal with it right now.'

'I know, it's mental,' Jerry said. 'Do you think he can be revived?'

'If Finn wakes up tomorrow, it wouldn't surprise me. He's done it before. Then again, it does freak me out.'

'I never thought I'd see anything like that in St Ives,' Jerry said. 'It looks like half the Parsonage has been knocked down.'

'Strange things have always happened in St Ives. Come on, let's get out of here.'

'I'll follow on your gorgeous bike, Bastian. I can't believe you let me borrow it. It's so bloody fast and your leathers fit me like a glove, I may have to borrow it again.'

'Jerry, please look after her.' He rolled his eyes. 'She's my pride and joy. Sometimes I find it hard to believe you're a bank manager.'

'What are you talking about? It's me.' He grinned.

Pulling on the helmet, he mounted the Japanese FZR750 motorbike and started her up.

Bastian headed back to St Ives, listening to Jerry Nancarrow driving the nuts off his beloved street fighter. Large knots were forming in his stomach. In the back of the van, his cousin lay dead in a black plastic bag. In the other body bag were the grim remains of Cillian Connelly. The whole business was making the doctor feel uneasy.

❧

Branna had been locked up in custody for nearly an hour before someone came to talk to her. They had placed her in a plain room with two chairs, a large wall mirror and a table.

The young officer was dressed in a tight grey wool suit and was sweating. He sat down opposite her and opened a thick file, packed with paperwork and photographs.

'Mrs Branna Smith, I'm Detective Parker. You're going to be moved to another station. Do you wish to make a statement now?'

'A statement?' She asked. 'Where should we start, Detective Parker?'

'How about the identity of the young man in the garden.'

'Which one?'

Parker rolled his eyes. 'The one with the broken back.' His voice was becoming tense. 'I don't like playing games, Mrs Smith.'

'Cillian Connelly was my cousin,' she said. 'He framed me for murder and killed Finn Milton.'

'That's all very well, but you have no evidence to back this up,' he replied.

'But there is evidence,' she lent back in the chair. 'Put me before a jury and I'll prove my innocence. I had nothing to do with any of these murders. Finn was my friend and I have witnesses to back this up.'

Parker began to laugh. 'You're something else. You were found at the murder scene and your hands were covered in blood. I suggest you use this time carefully to consider your limited options, Mrs Smith. I *will* come back.' He left her alone in the room.

❧

The splintered group assembled at Joe and Serina's barn. Although it was late, any news was highly anticipated when someone knocked at the door. Ellie answered it to find Milton on the doorstep.

'Milton.' she said. Her eyes were soaked with tears.

'I'm sorry for losing Finn.'

'It wasn't your fault, Cillian was too strong.' She replied.

'Bastian and Jerry are bringing his body here,' he said.

'I know.'

'There's a chance to save him, his soul could be still out there.'

'We can only hope,' she said. 'I can't accept it's over, it's been too much of a shock.'

'Where's Sam?'

'With Rose,' she said. 'I had to come over earlier, I had this feeling something was happening to him, I can't explain it, I just knew.'

'I don't blame you.'

Joe approached Milton and shook his hand. 'I can help by planing to search for Finn's spirit.'

'If Finn is still out there, I want to help too,' Ellie said. 'There's no better way to find a spirit. I'm definitely coming with you.'

Joe said, 'I thought you'd stopped planing. No one would blame you for not going, Ellie.'

'Just try and stop me, Joe,' she replied. 'Serina, can I use your spare room?'

'Of course,' she said. 'Joe, are you going or not?'

'Wife, sometimes you can be too much,' he grinned, slapping her on the bottom. 'You know I can't resist a good flight, especially at night.'

'Damn, and it's at times like these, I wish I could go with you,' she replied with a wink. 'Only I can't plane.'

'It might give me time to prepare myself for when I see his body later,' Ellie said. 'I can't handle it right now.'

After Ellie and Joe flew off into the night, Jerry pulled up outside the barn on Bastian's motorbike. Bastian parked up beside him and left the engine running in the van. 'I'm going to hide the van. We don't want the police finding out what we've been up to.'

Joe came outside when he heard the noise of the motorbike. 'Guys, what's happening?'

'We managed to get Finn's body away from the police,' Bastian replied. 'I need to ditch the van. Cillian's body is still in there.'

'Park it in the empty garage at the end of the lane, Bastian,' Joe said. 'We can move it tomorrow.'

'I'm going to leave it near the Parsonage and I'd rather do it right now because it's dark.' He replied somewhat agitated. 'I don't want anyone or anything linking this to us. I need to wipe down any fingerprints as well.'

Between them they lifted Finn's body into the barn. Bastian was gone for twenty minutes before he came back on foot. 'Where did you put his body?'

'It's in the conservatory, Bastian,' Serina said. 'I don't want to really look at him like this, I'm sorry. I know he means a lot to you but he's kind of dead.'

'Yeah, I know he is right now but he won't be later,' he replied.

'You should hear yourself, Bastian.' Jerry said. 'Hanging out with you is seriously messing with my head. Your optimism is off the chart.'

Serina: *Not the best timing, Jerry.*

'I feel as bad as everyone else, I'm only trying to lighten the mood,' Jerry said. 'Have you got any beer?'

'There's some cold ones in the fridge,' she said. 'Are you alright, Bastian?'

'I don't know what I'm going to do if this is it. If he's truly gone, I never said goodbye.'

'It's not over yet, there's still time for a miracle,' she said with her arm around him.

Bastian half-smiled. 'Finn almost died before. I don't want to believe it's happening for real this time.'

'Would you like a drink?' She asked. 'I have a rather nice single malt.' She grabbed the bottle and a few glasses.

'That will do,' he sighed. It was Finn's drink. When he tasted the first mouthful, it took everything he had not to cry.

'There is one thing you can be certain of, Bastian,' Jerry said.

'What's that?'

'How unpredictable Finn can be.'

'I'll drink to that,' Bastian raised his glass through the falling tears.

'To Finn,' they all said together. In the kitchen Serina, Tom, Simon, Bastian, Milton, Joo and Jerry looked at each other soberly and drank it down in one.

'Now that we've brought the *Flame* back safely, we need to concentrate on getting that bird out of her police pickle,' Jerry said. 'She's not going to manage it on her own.'

'Do you have a plan in mind, Mr Nancarrow?' Serina asked, clearly amused by Jerry's references.

'I do, as it goes,' he replied. 'Law degrees do come in handy. I need to go home and crank up my top of the range crap computer. A good friend of mine has been looking into it for me. I'll be back with the paperwork. Bast, can I borrow your bike?'

Bastian nodded. 'Sure, help yourself.'

Minutes later, Jerry Nancarrow had gone, still wearing Bastian's bike leathers.

16

~~

spirits having flown

A couple of hours passed before the detective returned to Branna's cell leaving the door wide open.

'You're free to go, Mrs Smith.'

'What?'

'We have four signed affidavits proving you had nothing to do with the murders. I don't know how you pulled this off Mrs Smith, but I'm impressed. You must have an expensive lawyer or just a lucky face. I can't decide.'

Branna thought: *But I don't have a lawyer.* 'In that case, Officer, I'll be off. Thank you.'

On the pavement outside the police station waiting and consequently cheering for her were Murray, Milton, Jerry, Bastian, Joo, Tom, Simon and Serina.

Overcome with emotion Branna hugged her husband Murray first.

'How did you do it?' She asked. 'I never expected to get out of there so fast.'

'Jerry's a wizard with these things,' Bastian said nonchalantly. 'And he has his connections.'

'Jerry!' She gave him a tight hug. 'I can't believe you would do that for me. Thank you.'

'It was a hunch that worked, what can I say?' Jerry was looking a little smug at the result. 'Besides, the posse needs you out here, not locked up in a police cell. Your inheritance will be rescinded as well.'

'That's brilliant news. Thank you so much. Now let's get you home, Mrs Smith,' Murray said. 'That's enough excitement for one night.'

She turned to Jerry. 'Thanks for coming back for me.'

'You're one of us and we help one another.'

'Where's Joe?' She asked.

'Chasing after Finn's soul,' Serina replied. 'He's taken Ellie with him and they're planing.'

'Let's hope they find him,' she said. 'You've saved Finn's body? You and Jerry are quite something on your own.'

'Yes, and so it seems are you… at mind reading.' Bastian replied with a modicum of sarcasm. 'His body is at the barn.'

'I can take a look at his wounds.' She suggested. 'But I want to have a look around the harbour first.'

'I want to take you home,' Murray groaned.

'I'm sorry, Darling, but there's something important I have to do first. I'll meet you all at the barn.' She gave her disgruntled husband a kiss, transformed into a raven to the delight of all her friends and flew off into the darkness.

The night became still after the storm surge and a strange play in the light near the end of the pier provided a distraction. The sea mist had completely cleared and the moon draped its light on the small boats in the harbour. Branna landed on the wall and looked around. The place was completely deserted. The only sound was coming from the chinking of the boats as they moved in the water.

A transparent shape emerged then disappeared only to reappear. It was spinning around in the air and dashing towards the lifeboat station, before flying back to Smeaton's Pier. It had no real thoughts, purpose or direction but there was a definite presence of something supernatural in the air. It remained for twenty minutes before disappearing.

Finally she decided to head back to the barn to attempt to heal Finn's injuries.

~

Ellie and Joe flew for half an hour in the pitch dark. Sensing two other souls they kept a safe distance before the spirits approached them. As they grew closer, one of them turned out to be a large Sentry.

Marcio: *You are looking for Finn Milton's spirit. We have not seen it and it is unlikely we will find it now. It has been too long.*

The second spirit had white lustrous hair, long and billowing out behind her.

Ellie: *Are you Finn's mother? Will you help me find him?*

Phoebe: *We have been looking.*

Suddenly a short blast of wind flew past the group of spirits, which dispersed Ellie before her soul came back together again. It touched her intimately. Immediately she took flight chasing it, leaving the others standing in mid air.

Joe: *What was that?*

Phoebe: *We should follow her, Joe Praed.*

She darted after Ellie who was stepping onto the sand at Porthminster beach. The broken spirit was attracted to her soul. Ellie was encouraged and stood silently waiting for the being to fly by once more. She raised her hands as it skimmed past several times, before being joined by the others.

Ellie: *It's Finn. He's right here.*

Phoebe: *He's attracted to you but then it's hardly surprising, you are his soul mate.*

Marcio focused on his soul, twitching and flicking randomly here and there without any sense or guided direction.

Finally, the Sentry's long fingers latched onto the spirit as it careened away once more.

Marcio: *Got you, Mr Milton.*

The broken desperate spirit lashed and fought to free itself, wriggling and twisting in Marcio's grasp but it was hopeless. The

Sentry fed energy into the broken soul and they all heard a weak telepathic voice: *Let... me... go.*

Ellie heard it, although it was faint and barely audible: *Finn, let them help you. I'm here, you have to trust them.*

Finn: *No... use, I... am... brok ...en.*

Ellie: *You must fight this Finn. Sam and I need you.*

Finn: *Ell... eee... so... so...rry... I ... let... you... down.*

Ellie: *No, Sweetheart, you could never do that.*

She approached Marcio and stroked her hand through Finn's weak spiritual body. He closed his eyes momentarily and stared back at her. It took all he had to remember.

Marcio: *Where is his body, Ellie?*

Ellie: *I can take you there right now.*

Marcio: *Good, I can see no reason why we can't commence the procedure. Do not be alarmed by what I am about to do.* The Sentry opened a spirit trap and Finn's soul was sucked inside.

Marcio: *Phoebe, let me touch you.*

Phoebe allowed the Sentry to search her soul for the missing part of Finn's soul. She was glowing with many rich iridescent colours. During the altercation with Cillian, she had managed to find not only her own missing soul particle but that of Finn's. At the same time, she had acquired some of Cillian's spirit.

Marcio found the foreign particles easily. First he withdrew Cillian's matter and destroyed it. Then he withdrew the tiny speck of Finn's soul and carefully dropped the glowing particle inside the spirit trap. It was left to fuse with the rest of his soul.

Marcio: *Once his soul has recovered, I will talk about the transference of soul light. You must never discuss what happened here.*

Joe: *Your have our word.*

Ellie: *How long will it take?*

Marcio: *Sometimes a moment can fly by and great things can come to pass. At other times much time must pass before results can be yielded. You should know this more than anyone, Ellie. One small event can have massive repercussions. Finn's soul is safe and will not fade. I can hear his thoughts and there is improvement but it can be a slow process.*

We lost many Sentries tonight but for now the threat has passed and we will endure again. We must work together to chase evil from this world. If we fail to revive Finn physically, he will endure in the afterlife. If the resurrection is successful, he may not be the same as a mortal. You must exercise patience with him, Ellie, when the time comes. It is important to remember this.

The Sentry was wise in years and tone. Ellie and Joe could not stop staring at him. The small orb was clutched tightly in his long ghostly fingers. Finn was caught up inside, fusing together and recovering.

Marcio: *In your mind, Ellie Morgan, I can see the location of Finn's mortal body. Now depart and fuse your souls back to your bodies. Do not fear for we will return soon enough. There is business to complete in Etherea, business I am not at liberty to discuss with you.*

Branna was working on Finn's wounds. Jerry was fascinated watching her work although she was becoming less optimistic about it being effective.

Serina had been supplying them with copious amounts of tea. Bastian was catnapping in a chair and Joo was asleep in the other lounge. Milton had walked home with Tom and Simon.

The clock chimed 3am. Branna was kneeling over Finn's unresponsive body in the conservatory. He had been stripped down to his underpants in order to assess the damage Cillian had inflicted.

'I have no idea where all these bruises have come from,' she said, taking the welcome mug of tea and sipping it. 'That's lovely, thanks Serina.'

'I thought Camomile would be more relaxing, it's been a long day. What about that burn?' Serina asked, staring at the remnant of the enchanted necklace on his neck.

'I'm going to tackle that next,' she said. 'Finn's head must have hit something hard, his skull appears to be fractured.'

'It's a good job you're here,' Bastian said, rubbing his eyes. 'Did I fall asleep?'

'You did,' Serina said, sitting next to him on the edge of the chair, ruffling his curly hair and giving him a hug. 'Look, there's something happening in the garden.'

A bright illumination announced the arrival of two familiar spirits who flew into the conservatory.

'Joe, Ellie ... what happened?' Serina asked. 'Did you find him?'

Joe: *We need to get physical first, see you in a minute, Honey.*

Both spirits raced off to find their bodies. Literally a minute later Joe and Ellie, somewhat exhausted, joined them in the glass room.

'What happened to you guys?' Jerry asked.

'We ran into Finn's mother Phoebe, she was searching with a lone Sentry,' Joe said. 'Good job we went out. Fortunately he was attracted to Ellie and it was easy in the end. They have Finn's soul and will be here soon. I've never seen anything like it.'

'That's good news, Joe,' Branna said.

Ellie was shocked by Finn's physical condition and couldn't take her eyes off his body. His eyes were sunken and his skin was pale grey. 'Don't worry, Darling ... they're coming,' she whispered.

'I've fixed some of the minor injuries but his body's switched off – want for a better description – nothing's gelling. I won't know if I've healed anything until he wakes up. If he gets the soul light back, it could heal him but he has to learn how to master it first. Nothing's binding right.'

Ellie held tightly onto his cold hand. 'You've done all you can, Branna. Let's hope we can fight the fatigue long enough to see him wake up.'

Branna looked at her. Ellie's eyes were red with tears and she squeezed her other hand. Inside Ellie was breaking apart, not fully believing he would come back to life.

Branna: *I was with Finn at the end. Let me show you this, I'm sure it was intended for you.*

She rested her hand on Ellie's forehead and closed her eyes. The memory rose to the surface and played out in her mind of the moment Finn's spirit disappeared in the Parsonage garden. His eyes conveyed a message for her, that he would always love her no matter what.

'I arrived too late to save him, I'll never know if I could've made a difference.'

'It wasn't your fault,' Ellie said. 'Thank you for showing me. All we can do now is wait.'

Above the barn's conservatory, the spirits of Marcio and Phoebe floated in the darkness.

Marcio: *The mortals are so optimistic it will work. I have never encountered so much love for one person. Our kind finds this love diminishing in the world. This gives me hope that my brother Guilar did not perish in vain.*

Phoebe: *How is Finn's soul?*

Marcio: *It is fusing slowly but there is something I must explain. We must fly to Etherea because I am not able to resurrect him to his body. The procedure is beyond any power I possess, or any soul in Etherea for that matter. There is a way but it requires serious commitment. The only way to bring him back will be as a Sentry.*

Phoebe: *You said you would help him, not turn him into a Sentry.*

Marcio: *I will help him but you are not aware of the first trial of training to become a Sentry and what it involves.*

Phoebe: *What are you suggesting?*

Marcio: *The first trial is to carry out a mission from within a mortal body.*

Phoebe: *How is this possible?*

Marcio: *We will go to Etherea and present this course of action. If approved then Finn could be returned intact to his body. To reanimate his body will require a power from outside our system; it exists light years from here on our ancestors' spiritual home. Only with their blessing can the first trial take place. You must understand that this is the only way your son can be mortal again. Without this course of action, I fear nothing can be done to return him to a mortal life.*

Phoebe: *I guess we'd better go to Etherea.*

Marcio: *When we get there, one of the elders will split the soul light within you and decide what is best for you. I expect you will be recommended for Sentry training.*

Phoebe: *How will this affect Finn, if it works?*

Marcio: *Either way, he will never be the same. Once the process begins, he will learn the knowledge and secrets of our universe. He will see how we really look because he will become a Sentry himself. Our ghoulish appearance is merely a guise to fool mortals. However returning to a mortal life might be too much for him to bear. Our knowledge is incredible. The first trial normally lasts a few days at most, but this is different. We are discussing him coming back to life. The pull of the spirit is overwhelming. It is possible the council will allow him to live a normal life if it succeeds, then complete training after his body dies. At this stage I do not have all the answers.*

Phoebe: *I am certain Finn would want to try.*

Marcio gently took Phoebe's hand and they flew away in the direction of the Lizard.

17

eyes wide open

In a world without magic, Phoebe Milton would have lived a longer life with her husband Finlay. They would have shared a happy marriage with possibly more children. She would have survived childbirth and watched her son grow into a healthy, contented man. Finn would have never lost his childhood to a curse. It would have been a totally different life with laughter and long days but because of the actions of a jealous witch she had been denied that life and those memories. Her broken and bereft soul had been split apart following her premature death and forced to roam the surface for years. In the few hours since her rebirth, she could hardly believe what she had learnt from Marcio about her son's spiritual adventures.

Time held no meaning in *Etherea*.

The sealed chamber had milky opaque walls. Lying on the floor of the cell was her son. His spirit was beginning to wake from his fatigue-laden slumber. Consciousness was returning as though waking from a long sleep. His spirit was white, long and transparent, simply clothed in loose trousers and a long sleeved top. She had been watching him the whole time since they had been placed inside.

Finn opened his eyes. He lifted his head and looked at the youthful female spirit with disbelief. Instantly he recognised her.

All his life he had wanted to know her and there they were, alone in each other's company for the first time.

Finn: *Is it really you this time or am I dreaming?*

Phoebe: *I'm your mother and you are not dreaming, Finn.*

Finn: *You look so young. I can't believe it.*

Phoebe: *How are you feeling?*

Finn: *Like I've been beaten to a pulp by a nasty hangover.*

Phoebe: *It will get better. Give it time.*

Finn: *Are we in Etherea? This place looks so familiar.*

Phoebe: *You have been here before, only this time ...*

Finn: *I hope they don't keep me here too long; I need to get back to my body.*

Phoebe: *It's different this time.*

Finn: *What do you mean?*

Phoebe: *When Cillian removed all of your soul light, it killed you. He was too strong and overwhelmed you. Ellie found your broken spirit and a Sentry brought us here. You're not going to fade like you think you will.*

Finn could hardly take the words in: *I'm dead? What happened to me? I don't remember anything.*

Phoebe: *Soul light fused itself to your soul. Having it removed tore your soul apart.*

He stared at her for a long moment. She was the real deal. His mother Phoebe was floating right beside him, talking to him as though they were mortals. His emotions were running wild.

Finn: *What happened to Cillian?*

Phoebe: *He's dead.*

Finn: *You helped to kill that sociopath. How?*

Phoebe: *A Sentry called Guilar sacrificed himself to help me. He distracted Cillian and threw my broken spirit at him. I disappeared inside him and found part of my lost soul then I was able to draw back all the soul light. As a consequence, Cillian's spirit was broken and the Sentries were able to destroy him.*

Finn: *Guilar has gone? He helped me on more than one occasion. What a shame. Cillian was waiting for me to return from Etherea. I destroyed his talisman but he caused me so much pain. He was determined to kill me and he succeeded.*

Phoebe: *I know but that time is over.*

Finn: *So what happens now?*

Phoebe: *We wait for Marcio to return with some positive news.*

Finn: *What kind of news?*

Phoebe: *Whether we qualify for Sentry training.*

Finn: *We? You have got to be joking. There is no way I am going to be a Sentry. This is what they wanted for me all along. I don't believe it. This wasn't supposed to happen.*

Phoebe: *Marcio will explain everything.*

Finn: *So, we don't have much time? Just when I find you we have to part again. We always seem to play a bad hand.*

Phoebe: *There was many a time I would have traded anything to spend five minutes with you, Finn. Don't think of it as a life of servitude yet. Marcio is campaigning to have your soul placed back into your body. I'll have to remain here but there is a chance that your mortal life can be saved.*

Finn: *I wish I had known you, Mum. Is it okay I call you that?*

Phoebe smiled and touched his arm. Soul light seeped into him and poured out of her like a torrent. The iridescent light coursed through his soul paralysing him. Their spirits were locked together in a massive colourful stream of light.

Finn: *Let go of it.*

Phoebe: *I can't, it's too powerful.*

Her spirit weakened when the last of it disappeared into him. She gasped when part of her spirit broke away with the soul light. A split second passed that seemed to last forever. A lone Sentry entered the chamber and forced his hand inside Finn's spiritual body to find the tiny speck of light that belonged to his mother. Finn was reeling with the spiritual changes as soul light spread throughout him.

It burned and fused itself making his spirit shudder involuntarily.

The Sentry held onto Phoebe with his other hand, charging her with energy. Her body shape became very defined. Her spirit was trembling and Finn could see almost every hair on her head. The Sentry placed the single speck of light inside Phoebe and her erratic behaviour ceased. Her spirit calmed and the being let go of her.

Sentry: *That was a textbook transference and went exactly as expected. You will be pleased to hear that the council has approved you both for Sentry training. Say your farewells. You won't be seeing each other for a long time.*

The Sentry left as quickly as he arrived. Finn felt the soul light within him settle and his whole spirit glowed. He felt himself growing in strength and colour as it adjusted.

Phoebe: *They knew if they left us together the soul light would take its natural host and it was you, Finn. It was always you. I can see it clearly now. It glows so white inside you like it's a part of you. You can use it for so many things. It can destroy or create. It's alive and made of so many souls all linked together in a long helix.*

Finn: *Souls?*

Phoebe: *Your great-grandfather Kingsley told me it came from the stars. It's made of lost souls, some of them were very powerful and they became one entity. It remained unbroken as it passed from sentient being to sentient being, gaining in size every time it found a new soul. You have become its lifeboat. In return it will bestow abilities on you that can change the world. It's governed by your own imagination and command. Once you understand it you can use it to help others. Maybe even heal them by touch alone.*

Finn: *I knew, I always knew. The visions were always about this but I never understood them.*

Phoebe: *When I was mortal I had vivid dreams of events that had not even taken place. They were visions of the future only they made no sense to me either, at the time. I knew all of this was going to happen when I was alive because of the visions. Etherea wants to keep the soul light organism intact. We cannot share it or split it. You have become many things, my son and I'm very proud of you. The path ahead of you is just the beginning. Do not be afraid. You will live again.*

He didn't know how to respond.

Marcio entered and their moment alone had passed: *You explained soul light to him.*

Phoebe: *He needs to know the truth so he can heal himself.*

Marcio: *Do you feel alright?*

Finn: *I think so.*

Marcio: *Good. You will know far more once you start the training. Everything will make sense. I'm looking forward to our future conversations and getting to know you better. Come with me Finn Milton and we will see what you're really made of.*

He tentatively touched his mother's hand and they exchanged an unspoken truth. They would see each other again. A moment later he was outside the chamber and being pulled behind the Sentry down darkened tunnels and along gaseous tubes at breakneck speed. He closed his eyes trying not to let the idea of his death consume him. He hadn't allowed himself the luxury of thinking about Ellie and Sam; it was too much to bear. The hopeless concept of possibly never seeing them again would eat him alive. If he allowed himself that liberty, he knew he'd not be able to contain it.

When he opened his eyes he was standing beside Marcio in what looked like a cave.

The cave was semi-circular and dark save for small blue orbs which floated in the air. On one side was an opening, and when he floated closer he found himself on the edge of a cliff. Above him were the stars of the night sky, or so he thought. It was like standing on the edge of the world on a stone platform jutting out into space.

Finn: *What is this place?*

Marcio: *It is called Janua and it is where you start your training.*

Finn: *Are those real stars?*

Marcio: *This is the portal to Alpha Centauri.*

Finn: *Isn't that on the other side of our galaxy?*

Marcio: *Yes but this isn't what you think. Once you commit to the torrent, you'll begin your journey. The elders are setting up the energy flow. It's time. We will see it as it travels back to Earth and makes contact with your human body.*

There was no sound in the cave but he could hear what he thought were tiny droplets of water dripping. Icy particles floated in the air. Reality seemed distorted as though it was a dream. The floor began to vibrate and like a narrow compressed waterfall, a massive stream of energy appeared beyond the platform. It gushed down and remained constant.

He approached the edge and looked over. Below, the stream of energy appeared to direct itself towards what looked like Earth. It was at this point he realised they were no longer on the planet he had become accustomed to. He was somewhere else altogether. The beam travelled equally back in the other direction, its source coming from one of the millions of stars in the black space.

Marcio: *You are correct in determining that this is not Earth, Finn. Many truths are about to come your way. If this works I'll see you when you wake up down there. Fear is no longer an option for you. You must embrace it and jump into the stream. It cannot kill you. All the Sentries have walked this path, including myself. The elders are waiting on the other side. Soon you will know more and it will make sense, I promise.*

Finn: *What about my body on Earth?*

Marcio: *A locator beacon will be placed on your physical body by one of us. Once you have passed the Alpha test and acquired the knowledge your soul will be forced back into your reanimated body on Earth. Unfortunately your friend Branna has been unable to heal your wounds. When you wake you must use soul light to heal yourself or you will die from your injuries.*

Finn: *What happens if it doesn't work?*

Marcio: *You'll return to Etherea and a new trial will be formulated. This is a one shot deal. There are no guarantees.*

Finn: *What will happen to my mother?*

Marcio: *Her path is different to yours. In time you will understand. Now you must leave before the torrent closes.*

He stared forward at the flowing energy stream and stepped onto the stone platform. Below, it seemed to drop off forever, as though they were floating on a large asteroid in space. He determined to not look back at the Sentry and threw himself forward into the torrent.

When he made contact, everything turned eerily silent. It was like being in the lull of a storm. The next moment all control was lost. His spirit was pushed higher, travelling through space at great speed. He closed his eyes and had no sense of where he was or what was happening. The wormhole tossed him like a feather to the other side of the galaxy and he resigned himself to the stream. Part of him was excited, the other fighting off the terror of what would come next. His spirit was glowing bright with colourful soul light and he could feel the fierce heat emanating from the energy source.

The next conscious thought he possessed was glimpsing a landscape made up of dusty orange canyons, peppered with tiny yellow lights and dense citadels. The terrain was rugged and untended. As he was forced to travel on further, he could feel the torrent as though it was a part of him. An enormous building emerged through the mist and reminded him of *Etherea* with its grand ostentatious glass appearance.

He stepped on to a solid transparent platform, high above a valley glistening with dew and blue coloured trees. Above him were millions of stars and impressive planets of varying sizes and colour.

The world seemed to have little atmosphere. A few metres away, a white fuzzy shape was approaching him. The being appeared to be extending its hand before everything went black.

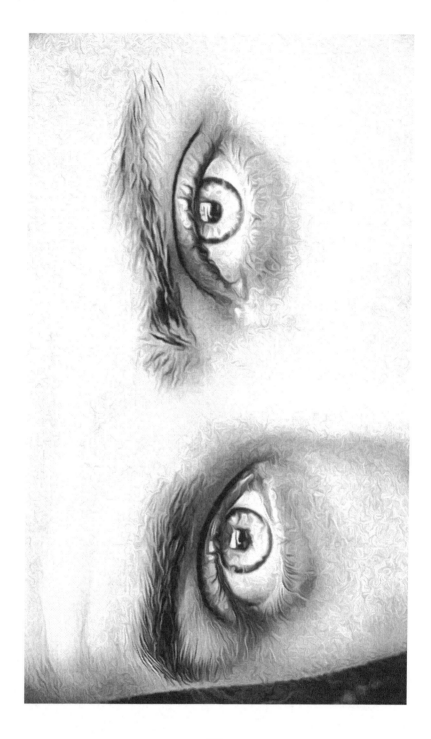

18

⤳

koru (new beginning)

St Ives, Cornwall

'Bastian, wake up.' Branna nudged him gently.

He was slouching in a chair when he rubbed his eyes and stared at her. 'What is it, Branna?'

'It's Finn,' she said. 'A red light appeared on his chest and then *that* happened.'

Finn's inert body was lying on its back on a large sofa by the conservatory door. From his chest to the window and spiralling up into the sky was a thin beam of light, which seemed to vanish into infinity.

She said. 'I've never seen anything like it before.'

'Is Ellie still asleep?'

'Joe and Ellie are both fatigued. I don't think we'll get much sense out of them tonight.'

'You're right,' he said. 'Let's hope something positive is happening to Finn, wherever he is.'

'What's that?' Jerry appeared from grabbing a nap in the round lounge.

'We don't know,' she said.

'It's started,' Serina spoke from the mezzanine level bedroom. 'That light beam woke me up.'

'Me too,' Joo added.

'That's nuts,' Jerry said, looking up at the night sky. 'It goes right up into space.'

'If it's coming from space,' Joo said standing behind him, 'then we'd better not touch it, Jerry.'

Above the conservatory two Sentries were watching and waiting. Moments later Marcio joined them, his clock billowing in the wind.

Flacus: *Did he reach Centauri?*

Marcio: *Yes and he should be here any time. The Centaurians are efficient with their methods. If Finn survives the download, that is. It will be a lot for him to process. Time behaves differently there.*

Qarii: *I remember my first trial but resurrecting a soul to its own dead body is controversial.*

Marcio: *He won't be dead if it works, Qarii. It was successful once, many years ago and it could work again. He's only been dead for a few hours. Soul light will repair him.*

Flacus: *How did you persuade the powers to agree? Can we trust this mortal with our secrets? The world is changing so quickly with technology, if they know what is really going on, it could cause civil war.*

Marcio: *Finn has no choice but to obey the code. He will understand. The Centaurians are interested in soul light; they like to preserve this kind of entity, because it is rare. To find it in the universe is unusual after all this time. They are going to monitor his progress. Look, something is coming through.*

Qarii: *The humans are witnessing this. They must not learn the truth.*

Marcio: *Make them sleep.*

The invisible Sentries entered the conservatory and one by one approached the mortals, tapping each one in turn. Bastian fell asleep first. When Joo fainted, Jerry knelt down to check on her. 'Hey Joo, are you alright?'

'We're not alone.' Serina whispered, closing her eyes.

'Sentries.' Branna said and passed out next to Bastian.

'No way,' Jerry said, falling asleep with his hands resting on Joo's shoulders.

A slight bulge in the white torrent rushed down into the glass room. The room illuminated completely with a bright colourful light explosion when it hit the body. The white beam dissipated and Marcio looked upon his two comrades. While Flacus and Qarii stood watch, the Sentry floated across. He placed a hand over his heart and gave it an electrical jolt. Finn's body juddered and rose up from the sofa.

Marcio: *This is it. Wake up, Finn.*

Finn slowly opened his eyes and saw the ghostly outline of a Roman man of around forty years, standing above him. He took a sharp intake of air and tried sitting up but his head was crashing with a shrill and heavy pain. His back and neck throbbed with abandon.

Marcio: *Finn, use soul light to heal yourself.*

He sensed the others sleeping, he could hear them breathing. Being conscious brought many thoughts rushing into his brain. His hearing had changed. It was far more attuned than it was before. He had no idea where he was but the new information and knowledge from the intergalactic journey was overloading his senses. He remembered everything from diving into the torrent to visiting Centauri and meeting nine spiritual alien god-like beings. There was so much information it was like a cosmic filing system.

Marcio: *Finn, soul light… Heal yourself now or you will die!*

He thought about the injuries. Instantly soul light flooded through his body touching all of his wounds. For several minutes his body shook and he cried out in agonising pain as it healed. He sighed when the aches grew less frequent and flexed his arms. The pain was slowly melting away. He could hardly believe how swiftly soul light had healed him.

'I can see you,' he spoke softly. 'I can't believe it healed me.'

Marcio: *Use your telepathy, Finn. We cannot make sound like a mortal.*

Finn: *You are a Roman centurion. You were human.*

Marcio: *A long time ago.*

Finn: *Does this mean I won't see the cloaks and spears anymore?*

Marcio: *You can now see how we used to look, before we became Sentries. I bet you never saw that one coming.*

Finn: *Originally our species were seeded from the elders of Centauri. There's too much information, I don't know how to process it. What have you done to my friends?*

Marcio: *Your friends are in a state of sleep but you must tell them nothing about what happened to you. It will get easier in time and I will mentor you. I will always be checking on your progress. For now you're doing remarkably well. You are alive.*

Flacus: *He seems to have survived the process well.*

Finn: *I have met you before, Flacus.*

Flacus: *Your mind reading is good, Finn.*

Finn: *How come you were all Romans?*

Flacus: *There are times in history when there were more mortals with abilities than at others. Many Sentries were once Roman citizens. We were comrades in another life.*

Finn: *That makes you all very old compared to me.*

Qarii: *Indeed it does. We are the older Sentries of Centauri but we were born on Earth. You are young and have much to learn.*

Marcio: *For now you must understand your position. Use your soul light in future to heal your own mortal wounds. Only when you die will your spirit return permanently to Etherea. Only then will you complete your Sentry training. Our leader, Clinthia, spoke with the Centaurians and you have been granted a reprieve due to your service to our code. She will be delighted by your successful resurrection.*

Finn: *The Sentries of Centauri. I had no idea there was any life outside Earth. Etherea is one small part of it. It's only an outpost for Earth. The colony is vast.*

Marcio: *There is so much life out there. Humans consider life should relate directly to them. Of all the species in the universe they are the most self-absorbed, hubris and narcissistic. They cannot see it or are even allowed to comprehend it due to their own destructive and selfish nature. You must never talk of what you know, for it will only lead mortals into confusion but you did very well... for a mortal. You will see the world in a different light now you have changed.*

Even colours will seem different. You are unique and remember you must keep this part of you concealed. I will visit again and help you through the first stages. You will never be alone, Finn.

Finn watched as Marcio, Qarii and Flacus flew through the glass roof and disappeared. They would treat him differently because he was now one of them. Seconds later the barn fell eerily silent. He checked on Bastian who was sleeping beside Serina in a wide armchair. He touched his forehead and read his mind. On planting a memory he began to stir but it took a moment for him to comprehend.

'Finn? Bloody hell,' he blurted in shock and instantly stood up. 'It worked. I don't believe it.'

'Yes, it did.' Finn was standing naked aside from a pair of light blue boxer shorts. 'They made you fall asleep. I'll wake the others.'

'Are you hurt?'

'Not anymore, I feel quite different.'

'You look the same,' Bastian said. It defied everything he understood about medicine. 'I'll get your clothes.'

One by one they woke up when he placed an older memory in their minds. They all stared at him. He knew they were unable to believe he had come back from the dead. Even though there was a slim chance it would work, not one of them truly believed it would, least of all Branna.

He burst into a wide grin. 'Why the long serious faces? *Etherea* fixed me, I thought you'd be happy about it.' He was feeling remarkably well. 'I need a new shirt.' There was dried blood on the front.

'You were dead for hours,' Bastian said. 'Your hair is half white.'

He checked his reflection in the glass. 'At this rate it might be better if I shave it all off.'

'Do you think you'll end up with completely white hair if you continue with this line of work?' Jerry asked.

'You're funny, Jerry.' He said.

'I'm surprised your hair hasn't fallen out completely.' Branna had tears falling down her face when she hugged him. 'I thought we'd lost you for good. You gave us all a nasty scare, including your dad.'

Joo wrapped her arms around him, tears falling down her face. 'Ellie and Joe are asleep. You scared us all rigid today. Don't you ever do that again!'

'I know, I'm sorry,' he said. 'I was ambushed by Cillian.'

'How do you feel now?' Branna asked.

'I feel good.' It felt as though he had been away for weeks not hours. Where there was no fatigue, he felt invigorated and hungry. 'I'm starving.' He touched his chest and felt where the enchanted necklace had been hours before.

'It left you with a strange tattoo.' Branna said. 'Are you in any pain?'

'Strangely, no. The soul light healed me.'

He could feel soul light glowing inside him. The colours in the room seemed to dance around, brighter and more defined than before, as though there was more colour. He approached his cousin who seemed rooted to the spot in shock and put his arm around him. 'Bastian, I'm back and I feel great, don't worry.'

'You seem different to before,' he said.

'I *am* different but I'm still me.'

'You have no memories of last night,' Serina said, attempting to read his mind. 'No memory of dying or coming back to life, or where you've been for the last few hours.'

'Maybe that's for the best.' He embraced her and was pleased the new Sentry technique for mind blocking was working. There was a whole section of his brain that was closed off to everyone except him.

'Cillian Connelly is dead.' Serina said.

'I know.' He was finding his bearings in the barn and walked into the kitchen. 'I could murder a cup of tea though.'

'I'll make you one,' she said. 'You are welcome to stay, Ellie's asleep.'

'Thanks Serina, I was hoping you were going to say that.'

Bastian pulled on his jacket. 'I'm heading home. I need some decent sleep.'

'I'll catch up with you soon, Finn,' Branna gave him a kiss on the cheek. 'By the way, Ellie's asleep in the ground floor guest room, the last door on the left.'

I can hear her breathing. 'Bastian, thanks for keeping my body safe, I wouldn't be alive if you hadn't made that call.' *I have so many of you to thank, I don't know where to start.*

'It was your mother,' Branna said. 'She was the one who believed she could find you. She was the one who made all of this happen.'

My mother. He thought about the young blonde haired woman who had saved his life. They were both Sentries in training now. The knowledge would always be a part of him. *I will see you again.*

Bastian was standing at the door. 'Let's catch up soon.'

'Sounds good to me.'

'Take care, Finn,' Jerry followed Branna and Bastian outside into the early morning light.

Joo decided to stay the rest of the night and climbed back under her blanket in the lounge. Serina made Finn a ham sandwich and a mug of tea, before heading back to bed and her sleeping husband Joe.

Finlay Milton tapped his pipe into an ashtray and looked at the clock in his sitting room. It was almost 5am. He drank down the last of his whisky and stared at the phone when it began to ring. The professor commanded the handset to fly into his hand. 'Hello?'

'Dad, it's me, Finn. I'm back. I'm alive.'

Tears were falling onto the biggest smile he had ever made. 'You never fail to astonish me, Son. Are you alright?'

'Yes and I have soul light again. My mother gave it back to me in *Etherea*. Her soul is whole again. There's so much I wish I could share with you. I have seen amazing things but I wouldn't be here without my mother, she came back for me, she always knew she would.'

'She always had the strangest visions,' he said. 'Some were about you as an adult and you hadn't even been born. I can't tell you how happy this makes me that it's all worked out. I can sleep easier knowing you're safe. It's been the worst few hours of my life thinking I had lost you.'

'I'm sorry for putting everyone through this. I always try to do the right thing but I must learn to have more empathy for others. I spent a little time with Mum. She remembers everything and wants you to start your life again. She wants you to be happy.'

'She was at the Parsonage when it happened, wasn't she?'

'Yes and she stopped Cillian.'

'I feel so guilty I wasn't there for you, Finn. I've been going over and over it in my mind. I should've listened to you more, been more supportive. It won't happen again.'

'I wasn't alone. The Sentries helped me. One of them sacrificed his life to save Mum and me. I know how to control soul light now. I can heal myself. You don't have to worry about me anymore.'

'Finn, I'll always worry about you, that's the deal of being a parent. It never stops. I thank my lucky stars you are back in one piece. It's the best news I could've ever hoped for.'

Dawn was stretching its light arm across the coast where the clouds were turning from purple to pale grey. Seagulls cawed in the distance and the smell of the sea hung tightly in the bracing air. A handful of locals were quietly walking their dogs. There was debris, sand bags and rubbish strewn everywhere from the previous night's storm. A few palm trees had fallen down in gardens. People had begun to clean up what looked like an enormous job. Bastian,

Branna and Jerry were walking down the hill into town and their respective homes.

'That was a flipping weird night,' Bastian said. 'I can't believe Finn came back to life as though he'd been sleeping. He was so dead.'

'There are many strange things out there,' she said. 'Things we'll never understand.'

'You're telling me,' Jerry added. 'At one point something knocked us out. It was weird.'

'That was the Sentries,' Bastian said. 'They don't want us to see everything.'

She turned to Jerry and touched his arm. 'You need to pluck up some courage and ask her out.'

Jerry stammered. 'What?'

'What are you waiting for?'

'Branna, stop reading my mind,' he said, visibly nonplussed. 'It's my personal business. No one else's.'

'You should at least tell her.'

'Who's this, Jerry?' Bastian asked, a smile crossing his face.

She slipped her arm through Jerry's. 'Let's say this guy needs some honesty at this juncture in his life before he misses his chance.'

'Honesty? Branna! That's enough.' He pulled away shaking his head. 'It's none of your business. I'm going home, you can be so interfering at times, Mrs Smith. There's such a thing as tact, you know.'

'Did I touch a nerve, Mr Nancarrow?'

Jerry grumbled them a terse goodbye and approached the door of his house.

'You have a talent for pushing buttons,' Bastian remarked after.

'Jerry *is* an idiot. Considering how intelligent he is, he has no common sense at all.'

'Who the hell is he hung up on? Come on spill the beans, you can't leave me with nothing.'

'I did say I wouldn't tell anyone,' she said. 'Time will out him, you'll see.'

'It's me, you can tell me. Jerry's been single for two years. It isn't like him to be like this. He's the only eligible one left.'

'Sorry Bastian, but I can't spill any of Jerry's beans. He gave me a get out of jail free card.'

'What a night, I forget sometimes what normal is. I'm not sure if that's a good thing or not.'

'I tried reading Finn's mind but something was blocking me,' she said. 'I could sense a Sentry in the conservatory with him while we were asleep. There is also something strange about his soul, it's different. It's as though he isn't quite human anymore.'

'Now you're letting your imagination run away with you, how is that possible?'

'Bastian, how is *any* of this possible? Finn died. He was brain dead. I couldn't even heal him. He was so calm when he woke up, so self-assured. This is Finn we are talking about. He could even be a zombie. We may never know the truth. He might not be allowed to talk about it. Sentries have strict codes.'

She hooked her arm through his when they approached the top of Porthmeor Hill and were presented with a wide view of the Atlantic Ocean.

'When I get the Parsonage, I am thinking of levelling it. Half of it's been reduced to rubble and I never want to live there again.'

'Completely demolished?'

'It could be a park donated to the people of St Ives in memory of my grandmother. It will never make up for the damage my father caused but it could be a start towards something better.'

'Duana Park, I like the sound of that.' He smiled. 'It's something to look forward to. I hope this is the end of all this madness, with Cillian gone at least we can rest safer.'

'It's hard to believe it only happened last night,' she said. 'I wonder where Finn's been.'

Bastian looked up at the sky. A few stars were twinkling in the pink and blue sky when they stopped on the brow.

'Maybe we'll never know. Are you alright from here?'

She merely smiled and turned towards Barnoon Hill. Bastian headed down the steep hill towards Porthmeor beach and shook his head wearing a welcome smile on his face.

Finn found Ellie sleeping. He pulled off his shirt and slipped out of his jeans before climbing under the duvet next to her. He could smell her and wanted nothing more than to hold her in his arms but held back.

He was content to watch her sleep and for the next two hours he couldn't close his eyes. He was surprised to find he wasn't from suffering from planing fatigue.

The new intense knowledge from Centauri consumed him. The truth was incredible. So much of what he had learnt made sense. The Sentries, *Etherea*, Centauri, soul light … all of it. He'd have to bury the knowledge and get back into the flow of his old life. The one thing he was absolutely certain of was that the fear factor had gone completely. He was a different man.

She opened her eyes and screamed aloud.

'Finn! When did you get back?'

'A few hours ago.'

'I thought you were a ghost.'

'It worked, whatever the Sentries did to me … I can't remember anything.'

'I don't care, hold me,' she demanded.

He stretched out his arms and cradled her tightly, kissing her. Listening to her heartbeat he closed his eyes. Nothing else mattered in that moment.

'Promise me this is over,' she whispered.

'It's over,' he said. 'I have a strange memory of finding you on the beach.'

'You found me.' She looked into his grey eyes and stroked his hair, which was half-white and half-copper. 'Every time something happens to you, your hair changes colour.'

'It must be the shock.' He kissed her for several minutes before they made love. 'I love you so much, Mrs Milton. Can we get married now?'

'You want to talk about getting married?'

'I don't want to wait a minute longer. Marry me Ellie.'

'I will marry you even though you keep putting me through the mill with all this paranormal stuff,' she sighed.

'It's not going to be a problem anymore.'

'Good.'

'We are going to be alright,' he said. 'I promise you.'

'Our lives will never be normal but I do love you Mr Milton and I'm so glad you're back.'

19

~

wave goodbye, say hello

The service of remembrance for Duana Connelly was held a week later on a very wet and rainy afternoon. There was a welcome break in the clouds when everyone filed into the church to take their seats. The atmosphere was still and serene. Everyone present was suited and booted.

Pallbearers Finn, Bastian, Jerry and Joe slowly carried the tiny coffin into The Parish Church of St. Ia, virgin & martyr. Murray and Branna walked behind them with Heather Pengelly and her son-in-law Professor Finlay Milton. Ellie and Sam were sitting on a pew beside Rose, Caron and Cara. Joo was perched next to Simon, his wife Chloe and their young son Toby. Serina, her brother Tom and his family sat behind them. It was an intimate funeral, for only those present, including the gifted vicar, Reverend Harry Thomas, knew the real story of Duana Connelly.

Half way through the service, Finn approached the pulpit and addressed the small gathering with a new air of confidence. His half-white hair was trimmed very short. Standing clean-shaven before them, he was wearing new contact lenses and a dark suit, white shirt and tie. He placed his hand on the small oak coffin embellished with a carved dove. Looking at the small gathering he composed himself. Branna was seated in the front row next to her husband, Murray and she was looking at him keenly.

'I didn't know Ana very long,' he caught Heather's eye and smiled. 'But I will never forget her. She was a brave and beautiful soul and she died before her time. Her courage helped me to overcome diversity in a time when I had more questions than answers. Her life was cut short in the worst possible way, but her soul and memory will live on because of the people she touched. Without her assistance and wisdom, I would not be standing here today talking to you. The impact on never knowing Ana would have left me with no choices and no future to look forward to.' He glanced at Ellie and smiled.

'I have a quote from the Dalai Lama which I would like to share with you all. 'There are only two days in the year when nothing can be done. One is called *yesterday* and the other is called *tomorrow*, so today is the right day to love, believe, do and mostly live.'

'I would like to adopt this attitude. I cherish the gift of life that I have been given and intend to live more in the moment. Life is a gift, no matter how you dress it up. I want to offer Ana my gratitude, on behalf of everyone here today. This is nothing less than she deserves. She was one of those rare beings, one of the unsung heroes of our time but please understand that she is in a far better place now. I owe her my life and trust she will always rest in peace, wherever she is.'

He took a deep breath and began to sing *Amazing Grace*. His friends and family listened as he breathed new meaning and poignancy into the words without any musical accompaniment. The interior of the church was silent as he sang the hymn pitch perfect.

After the service, the group reconvened at The Lifeboat Inn on Wharf Road. It was the first time they had seen each other since Finn's bizarre resurrection. He was surprised by the turn out having organised a small wake in memory of Ana's short life. Outside the rain poured down in sheets and the skies turned darker.

The Reverend Harry Thomas approached him with a smile on his face. 'That was a beautiful tribute, Finn. Can I get you a drink?'

'A single malt with ice would be good, thanks Harry.'

'My pleasure, it won't be long before your big day.' Harry said, glancing at Ellie who was holding their son Sam. 'Let's hope you have better weather.'

'Indeed,' Finn said, noticing his cousin approach Jerry.

Even through the mixed din of everyone talking, he could hear the conversation clearly. He had known about the issue for some time, having read both parties, and was amused by the new development.

'Thanks Bast, but I'm on the wagon today,' Jerry responded after he offered him a drink.

'I know what she means to you, but if you don't do something about it, she'll assume you're not interested in her.'

'What are you talking about?'

'Oh come on Jerry, everyone knows about it except Joo.'

'That's far too personal, Bastian.' Jerry looked across at Joo, who was fussing over Sam and talking to Ellie. 'Not today.'

'Man up and ask her out.'

'I will ... when I find the right moment,' Jerry responded. 'I don't think a wake is the best place for chatting someone up.'

'It's hardly a wake, Ana died fifty years ago.'

'Look, just get off my back. You're as bad as Branna.' Jerry was more irritated.

Bastian grimaced and approached his wife.

'Is he going to ask her?' Caron asked.

Bastian exchanged a glance with Jerry. 'At this rate it might be easier if I told Joo myself.'

'I've seen the way she looks at him, it's hardly a secret,' she said. 'Those two are hopeless.'

'I might have a word with Ellie later,' he said. 'Maybe she can tell her.'

Jerry frowned openly at Bastian then approached Joo and asked if he could have a private word with her.

Joo sighed to Ellie. 'It's probably another wind-up.'

'You look beautiful today, Joo,' Jerry said after he prized her away from the bar. He was wearing his usual charming smile and his shaggy brown hair was tied into a neat tail at back of his neck.

The heat was visibly rising in her cheeks. 'Why Jerry Nancarrow, I believe you're making me blush.' She left his gaze and turned away. 'Either that or it's getting hot in here.'

'About time, Miss Williams,' he said under his breath.

'What do you want, Jerry?'

He was developing a cold sweat. 'It's about time you found yourself a man.'

She rolled her eyes. 'Am I having problems with being single? Are you for real? Honestly, Jerry, I suppose you have all the answers.' She brushed past him, shaking her head and sat down next to Ellie at the bar.

'How did it go?' Simon asked his brother. 'Did she say yes?'

Joo was only a few feet away but he could hardly keep his eyes off her. 'I blew it, like I always do. I can never figure women out. They're like a whole different species. I'm out of here.' He grabbed his suit jacket hanging up beside the bar and promptly left.

On the way back to the house, the rain stopped and the sun poked through the clouds. Everything seemed fresh and new. The women walked ahead, not registering that Finn could hear their conversation clearly.

'What a lovely afternoon,' Ellie said. 'It was good seeing everyone.'

'It was.'

'I've got to ask you this before it drives me mad: what do you think of Jerry Nancarrow?'

'That's a random question.' Joo laughed.

'Why?'

'Well, he's Jerry for starters,' she replied.

'But you like him? I mean, *really* like him?'

'In *that* way?' Joo asked.

'Yes, in *that* way.'

She didn't answer straight away. Having known Jerry for years Joo had always felt uncomfortable when he was in a relationship with someone else. When they were alone together he was different, verging on clumsy. Either way she had always secretly liked him.

'Jeremy Nancarrow has always been out of my league, what with his PhD and his job. He's very cute not to mention fit and he has this cheeky grin when his eyes light up. Any girl would go out with him, he's a handsome guy. He's on the gig team and those guys are all popular. But seriously, there's no way he'd go for someone like me, Ellie, not in a million years. I am no way fit enough for him.'

'Jerry *likes* you.'

'What are you saying? Now you're being ridiculous,' she laughed.

'He's been single for the last two years because he's hung up on you. When you were missing it was Jerry who was jumping up and down, wanting to go round to the Parsonage to rescue you, all guns blazing.'

'Has he told you this? This is unbelievable.'

'He admitted it to Bastian,' she added. 'In fact, the others know but haven't said anything. He's been keeping quiet about it because he didn't want to lose you as a friend, but he's got it bad for you.'

Joo laughed again. 'In that case I'm going to the bank tomorrow morning to confront him.'

'Really?'

'I'm not going to let this one get away. It certainly explains that strange behaviour at the pub. It explains a lot. Thanks Ellie.'

'I didn't think you'd believe me. What with all these wedding whispers going on, I was wondering, will you be my bridesmaid?'

'Of course,' Joo said. 'You don't have to ask.'

'Since it's imminent, I'm going to need some help.'

'I did have a short chat with Serina about it, she has some ideas. She suggested we all go round there one evening and start organising it. You're going to need a dress. Rose is going to make the cake. It's all logistics if we all pitch in.'

'Oh thanks, Joo. Finn's got a gorgeous tuxedo, he's not going to need anything,' Ellie said.

'Unless he wants a new suit, you know what he's like. It wouldn't surprise me if he went to London to buy one. Besides it gives us an excuse to go shopping. I'll see when I can get a day off.'

'What are you going to wear tomorrow?' Ellie asked.

'I have a rather nice little blue number,' Joo said when they arrived at the house.

'I'm getting a take-away, do you girls want anything?' Finn placed Sam in his high chair in the kitchen. 'I'm going to the Indian. Beige sandwiches do not make the man, I'm afraid.'

'I could murder a tandoori.' Joo replied.

'Ellie?'

'Chicken Jalfrezi please.'

'I'll be back soon,' he said.

'Oh Finn?' Ellie asked.

He came back pulling on his brown coat. 'What, Sweetheart?'

'Just make sure you do come back,' she smirked and he merely smiled back.

He felt a real sense of freedom strolling into town and could almost taste the normality of the situation. It felt strange but welcoming. He wished he had spent more time with his mother but knew she had always been close to him. It gave him comfort.

He was itching to discuss it in more detail with his father but had already said too much. The burdening reality of his soul being a Sentry had caused him undue stress.

He could block off sectors of his mind to stop anyone learning the truth, which was his issue to bear alone, but the act had been noticed. The infinite knowledge and power at his fingertips was blowing his mind.

To deal with this, he spent an hour or two every day by himself meditating. He knew in time, Marcio would join him, counselling him in coping with the new overload of information. He would walk for several miles along the coastal path to be alone. For the time being he remained attentive.

He ordered the takeaway and lent against the wall outside, waiting for his number to come up. Looking idly around he watched people going about their business oblivious to the averted apocalypse that took place the week before. He thought how ironic it was that no one would know the truth of how truly close it came to being catastrophic. He glanced at the cinema and was reminded of Ana's plight when bullets were spraying all around. There was so much history everywhere, most of which had been forgotten.

He knew their wedding was being planned. Their friends' excited attempts at secrecy were dire since he had read all their minds at the wake. But he kept the charade going. He had considered going to London to buy a new suit and wondered if he ought to be less predictable in future. He smiled at the satisfaction of being financially set up and was glad he'd had no previous interest in money. It could have so easily been squandered.

'Pigging out already?'

He snapped out of his thoughts and saw Bastian approaching.

'Hey, how are you doing?' Finn caught his extended hand and embraced him.

'I'm doing well but we're dragging you out tomorrow night, so we can talk about what happened at the Parsonage. I'm working tomorrow so we'll be round at seven.'

'So what you're saying is, I don't have a choice?'

'That's the rule,' Bastian said.

'Just one rule?'

'To make sure you get back to normal. Most of us aren't working the day after so expect to get a bit messy,' he grinned.

'It's been strange this time.'

'It would be good to hear what happened in detail.'

'Don't worry, I'm sure I can think of something. Bast, will you be my best man?'

Bastian grinned. 'Of course, I'd be gutted if you asked someone else.'

Finn watched him walk away and read his mind: he was happy and relieved he was alive. On hearing his number being called, he grabbed the food and walked home. The smell was driving him crazy. It was heavenly. At the house they all dived in and he ate denoting his pleasure vocally.

'It hasn't been that long since you've had a curry, surely?' Joo asked.

'It's amazing, it tastes way better than I remember,' he said. 'I can't tell you how happy it makes me that we have a great curry house right here in town.'

Ellie smiled and kissed him. 'I'm so tired, sorry guys but I'm grabbing an early one, it's been a long day and Sam was awake most of last night.'

'Night Ellie.' Joo said.

'Night, Darling. I'll take care of our boy.' He looked at his blond haired son sitting in front of him, sucking his thumb. 'So what have you two been talking about?'

'Wedding attire mostly,' she replied.

'Oh right.' He caught her eye. 'You do know I can read your mind.'

'I can see the wedding being in about a week's time. I can tell you needed some warning. We should know more tomorrow when we meet at the barn to talk about it.'

'A week? No way,' he pretended to choke on a king prawn.

'Have you thought about what you're going to wear?'

'I have as it goes,' he was thinking of teasing her a little. 'I'm going to London.'

She dropped her fork and began to chuckle with annoyance. 'I knew it.'

'Knew what?'

'You have a perfectly good tuxedo.'

'I can't wear it, not to our wedding. Joo, don't be ridiculous. It's Armani.'

'And your point is?'

'I don't want to outshine Ellie.'

'Oh you're too much sometimes, Finn Milton. Ellie had the right idea.'

'What are you talking about? Joo? I was joking. Where are you going?'

'To bed. You can do the dishes. Good night, Finn.'

Smiling to himself, he decided to finish the curry. He wasn't going to London to buy an expensive suit. He pushed the empty plate into the middle of the already crowded table and walked into the studio. He left the lights off because Sam was falling asleep, slowly closing his eyes. The boy lay calmly relaxed in his arms without a care in the world. He kissed his son's forehead and rocked him gently in the moonlight.

He could see the stars in the sky and felt at peace. He hoped his fragile life with Ellie would work out and that they would be free of any more conflict.

The constellation of Centauri was way below the horizon and only visible much further south, but he could visualise its strange landscapes and found comfort knowing they were out there and he was now a part of something much bigger than anything he had imagined before.

He was thinking about everything that had happened since they had returned from New York. Slipping Sam into his crib, and lifting a blanket over him, he glanced at Ellie dozing in bed. An ache began to spread through him and he couldn't get her out of his mind. He undressed and moved closer to the bed. It was dark and the curtains were slightly open. He lifted the duvet and reached his arm around her.

He lent close until he was almost touching her mouth. He was staring into her face when she opened her eyes. She lifted her hand to his face and reached for his lips. For a moment she was bathed in light as though her whole being was submerged in it. A glow of bright sparkling colours radiated from him all around her. He stopped kissing her and she was gazing at him with awe.

'What happened to you Finn? You're so different.'

'I'm not sure. If I'm fixed maybe this is how I'm meant to be. I've been muddled for so long, it feels like everything's right this time. I haven't been the same since I passed out in the Parsonage garden.'

'It feels good. A bit too good.'

'It's *me*, remember?' He began to laugh.

'Too much, Finn.'

'Never too much. There is something. I want to show you some of my work.'

'I read what you were working on in New York,' she said.

'No, not that work. The work I did in my twenties. I'm not sure I can write like that anymore.'

'You can do anything you put your mind to. You never know, once everything settles you might get it back.'

His eyes brightened. 'That's true.'

'Why don't you give yourself a break? It's not important right now. We have Sam and a wedding to plan.'

'It's good to hear you say that.' He kissed her again. 'I can't wait to get married to you, Mrs Milton and then we can make more babies.'

'You're funny,' she whispered.

He rose early leaving her to sleep and began working on the storeroom. It was full of clutter and the perfect size for a small person's bedroom. Half an hour earlier, Sam woke him up with gurgles and laughing. He changed his son's nappy and fed him, before placing some toys in his tray and positioning the highchair next to him at the kitchen table. He made a large pot of coffee and started making notes on which materials to use and sketched out some designs. He was immersed in the project when Joo came out of the shower.

'You're up early.' She yawned, reaching for a mug to make some coffee.

'I'm going to get this sorted so that Sam can have his own room.'

'Blimey, you're keen,' she said.

He noted her sarcasm. 'I know I should've done it months ago. Joo, can I ask you a favour?'

'Go for it.'

'When Ellie decides on her dress, can you get me a sample of the material?'

'I could, why?'

'I'm not going to London, I was only teasing you last night. I'm sure I can find a suit in Truro but it would be nice to get something similar.'

'Ivory would look nice,' she said. 'I thought you'd be splashing out on some expensive designer garb.'

'Not this time,' he replied. 'I don't want to wear the tux.'

'I'll see what I can do. My lips are sealed.' She smiled.

'I think a window in Sam's room would be nice, what do you think?'

'I would get some advice. If you can get rid of that scorch mark it would be a start.'

She was referring to a mark on the kitchen wall. The burn hole travelled through to the storeroom. It was the consequence of a brutal altercation, when he had a violent fight with Branna's twin brother Jared the previous summer.

'I need to plaster that up,' he said. 'Are you working today?'

'No, but I need to go into town.'

'Time to make the missus some breakfast in bed.' He stopped what he was doing and dived into the fridge. 'I'll get some groceries today. I need to take the Porsche out for a spin, but I need to fit a new alternator first.'

'Are you out with the boys later?'

'It rather looks that way,' he said.

'I've made some arrangements for later,' she said. 'Us girls have a lot of planning and scheming to do.'

'It looks like I have a lot of alcohol in my future,' he replied.

'Right, I'm getting dressed,' Joo said in her red and white spotty pyjamas.

By the time he filled a tray with boiled eggs, toast and a pot of tea, Joo was fully dressed and ready to go. Finn thought she had gone to a lot of effort for first thing in the morning. He read her mind and smiled. She was off to see Jerry. She gave him wink and hurried out the door.

He carried the tray into the bedroom as Ellie was beginning to wake up. 'Morning sleepyhead, I thought you might like breakfast in bed.' He placed the tray in front of her and gave her a kiss. 'Joo has gone out dressed to the nines to impress Jerry.'

'I hope they can sort it out. It's easy when you want the same thing.' She stared at the tray of appetising breakfast fare. 'How did you find so much food? I thought we were out of everything.'

'I have my ways,' he said. 'I'm going to get Sam.'

'Now you're spoiling me.'

He reappeared with Sam on his shoulders and they sat on the bed. 'I'm going to look after you and Sam and I'm not going anywhere without you again. Apart from being forcibly dragged out tonight by the posse.'

'I knew the time would come.'

'It'll do me some good,' he said.

'Joo and I are going to Serina's for a girls night. Only one boy allowed but Sam will be a distraction more than anything. I'm so looking forward to having a normal life with you.'

'I know but we need more baby things,' he said. 'I'm going to get the car started later.'

'Definitely, Mr Domestic.' She smiled and he kissed her again. 'I like you like this.'

'I love you just the way you are. Don't ever change.'

Joo walked up the high street and stopped briefly outside the bank to check her reflection in the window. Wearing heels was not something she was accustomed to. Bravely she pushed the door, went inside and approached one of the tellers. 'Can I see the bank manager please? Mr. Nancarrow.'

'Give me a moment, do you have an appointment?' The teller demanded.

'No.'

'Your name please?'

'Juliet Williams.'

'I'll be right back.' She disappeared through a door.

Joo waited for several minutes before Jerry appeared with the teller. His blue eyes gazed at her through the glass. He opened the security door and shook his hands because they were beginning to sweat.

'Come up to my office, Miss Williams.' He said in an intense tone, mainly for the benefit of his female staff. The last thing he wanted them to know was how well he knew her.

They were all staring at the impressive thirty year old man like they hadn't eaten in a week and he was their last meal. His long hair was expertly tied back from his face. He was wearing a crisp tailored pin stripe dark blue suit, pale blue shirt and navy tie. Shiny black shoes adorned his feet. He looked and smelt immaculate. She followed him up two flights of stairs to the top floor trying to remain calm. His full name was printed in gold letters on the glass door of his office, which intimidated her even more.

Jeremy P. Nancarrow, PhD, Bank Manager.

He opened the door and let her enter the office before him. She was feeling nervous. 'Your office is so organised. Blimey Jerry, you've even got a surf board in here.'

'It has to be like this. It's a serious business, banking. So what can I do for you, Miss Williams?'

She could see he had his serious work-head on. He was leaning casually against an enormous oak desk. There was the hint of a smile in his eyes.

Behind him the window offered a sliced view of the bay in the distance. To his left, an enormous bookcase was filled with immaculately bound volumes.

'I just want to know one thing and then I'll leave you alone.' She half smiled. 'Are you interested in me? I can't believe I just asked you that. You must think I'm mad. I'd better go.'

Jerry grabbed her hand as she turned towards the door and pulled her back to his side. He parted the blonde hair from her eyes, sweeping it to the side. She could feel his fingers wrapped around hers.

'I will show you,' he said.

Before she could say anything, he was kissing her. She hadn't been prepared and the kiss seemed to last forever. His eyes were closed as though he was in deep meditation. He opened them, smiled at her and then gently kissed her hand. 'Better. That's so much better.'

'Wow,' she said.

'I've wanted to do that for ages.'

'Really?'

'Are you doing anything tomorrow night? I could cook up some dinner if you fancy it? I'm all out to get messy with the lads tonight.'

'You're offering to cook dinner for me?'

'I'm a dab hand with Cordon Bleu. I promise to impress you. I've been on a course because I love my food too much.' His blue eyes seemed to reflect the light as he stared at her.

'It sounds like something I would like to try.'

'Come round at seven, unless you want me to walk you round.'

'I think I can manage to find your place,' Joo said, in danger of turning into a jelly.

'Did they tell you about me?'

'Ellie told me,' she replied. 'I had no idea.'

'I've fancied you for ages. I can't deny it. I was just too scared to make a move. I've been such an idiot. There were so many times I could've asked you out. I'm making you blush again but I'm so glad you came to see me, Joo.'

'I had to know or I would've been left wondering whether it was true or not. I'd better let you get back to work.'

'What about lunch today?' He suggested suddenly. 'I'm free for an hour from one.'

'I can meet you here if you like.' The words tumbled out before she had even thought about it.

'Deal. Wait a minute.' He stepped towards her. Raising one hand to her cheek, he kissed her again. 'Yep, definitely.' He grinned and opened the door, leaving her pink faced.

'See you later, Mr Nancarrow. Thank you for your help. It was very constructive.' She winked at him.

Jerry's female staff were all but shadowing her until she walked out of the bank. Feeling flushed, she held it together until stepping on the pavement outside where she jumped and punched the air.

'Yes!'

Jerry phoned Bastian at work immediately.

'I can't talk for long Jerry, is it important?'

'I'm taking Joo out for lunch today.'

'You could've asked her out ages ago, you only have yourself to blame for procrastinating, Nancarrow.'

'I know but you don't have to rub it in my face.'

'Still it's a result and pretty cool even by your standards.'

'Thanks for the vote of confidence, Pengelly. You really should add matchmaking to your repertoire. You can get the drinks in later.'

'See you at Finn's at seven.'

'Cool, later dude.' He hung up smiling.

It was late afternoon and Finn was totally immersed in the Porsche engine, covered in grease and oil as he tried to get the car started. He jumped into the driver's seat and tried starting her up again. A loud pop and a large flume of smoke left the exhaust and the car started.

Keeping her running, he climbed out to find Branna mildly amused by his efforts.

'How long have you been standing there?'

'Not very long,' she said. 'You look pretty good considering you're covered in oil.'

He had a smudge of oil down his face and his hands were black. Slamming down the engine cover at the back he turned her off.

'I'm lucky to be alive.' He wiped the dirt off the bodywork onto a rag. 'I'd give you a hug but I'm very oily.'

She smiled warmly at him. 'We haven't had a chance to talk about what happened to you. Do you remember anything from the night you came back to life?'

'I remember passing out in the garden with you and waking up at Joe's place but everything else is sketchy.'

'When I got there you were already dying. There was this strange mist and the Sentries were lighting up the place like daylight. It caused quite a commotion, there were police and reporters everywhere.'

'I vaguely remember it now.'

'One minute it was daylight and then the Sentries disappeared. Cillian was lying dead on the path with a broken back,' she said. 'He fell out of the sky.'

'I had no idea how he died.'

'You have your soul light back,' she pressed him. 'I wonder how that happened since Cillian removed all of it. There's a missing part to this puzzle, Finn.'

'I don't know.' He thought quickly. 'My mother was a troubled spirit. Taking soul light from Cillian must have regenerated her spirit. Part of your soul breaks off when it's extracted. It happened to my mother and it happened to me. It must have something to do with Cillian's death.'

'Serina said you've changed. It's hard to believe you're the same person. You're blocking your mind with an intensity. I know you died the other night. There's more, isn't there?'

'I appreciate your concern but a lot happened to me that I cannot discuss with anyone. *Etherea* has a code. Ellie's inside if you want to catch up with her.'

'It's funny how you can read me clearly now and I can't read you. You couldn't before. There is something I want to ask Ellie. I am happy you are still alive. I wasn't sure how you were going to pull yourself out of this one and I still have no idea how it happened.'

'That makes two of us,' he said, trying desperately to change the subject. 'Right, I'm going to take her out for a test drive. Can you tell Ellie for me? It was good seeing you, Branna.'

He lent over and kissed her cheek. He was curious but just smiled not accepting her invitation. 'I'm giving this mind reading thing a break for a while. My head's done in enough and I have things to do. I want to keep busy, it helps me feel normal.'

'Another time then.' She showed some disappointment. 'Take care of yourself.'

She went inside and found Ellie sorting out some finished canvases in the studio.

There was cardboard and bubble wrap as far as the eye could see. 'Branna, how are you?' She smiled.

'Good, here let me help you.' She lifted the canvas from the packing and let it float to the floor.

'Thanks,' Ellie said. 'I'm exhausted, it's been a crazy time lately.'

Sam was sitting upright on a thick rug on the floor, sucking on a plastic toy and staring at Branna.

'He's psychic, I can feel it and he's growing like mad. He'll be walking next.'

'I guess it's to be expected,' Ellie said. 'Our children are bound to be gifted. Sam is part of the mystic gene pool.'

'I came to ask if you needed anything for the wedding?'

'We're going to Serina's tonight, why don't you join us? Just us girls though, the lads are hitting the town,' she explained. 'I can see what the hot topic's going to be.'

'Finn isn't going to explain what really happened to him,' Branna said.

'Do you think he knows?'

'Yes I do,' she said. 'Before he came back to life, there was this energy beam which went into space.'

Ellie rested a friendly hand on her shoulder. 'Maybe we aren't supposed to know.'

'But don't you want to know? Aren't you the least bit curious to where his spirit went for so many hours?'

'Finn came back to me and that's all that matters. I know he's changed, everyone can see that.'

'Okay, I'll drop it,' she said. 'What time are you meeting tonight?'

'Around six. Serina's making a Thai curry.'

'It sounds like fun. Finn's got the car working and he's taken it out for a spin.'

'He's been at it for hours.' Ellie rolled her eyes.

Branna smiled and made her way out promising to catch up later. She sat down in the studio with Sam and picked up the phone to phone her father. Jeremy Morgan had been living in Hong Kong since she was six years old. He was a corporal in the army.

It had been over a year since they had last spoken.

'Ellie, is that you?' Jeremy asked with a gravelly tone.

'I know it's been ages, Dad, and I'm sorry. I thought it was high time I told you my news.'

'News? Are you okay? Has something happened?'

'I'm fine,' she said smiling at Sam. 'I was wondering if you might be free in the next week or so.'

'Free? I'm on the other side of the world,' he replied. 'I would have to check, why?'

'We don't have an actual date yet, but I was wondering if you would like to give me away.'

'Give you away? Are you getting married? Hell Ellie, I didn't even know you were serious about Finn.'

'It's a long story, but yes, we are very serious. I'm also staring at our gorgeous baby son as we talk – you're a grand father.'

'I need to sit down. Why didn't you tell me any of this? I mean for God's sake Ellie, I didn't even know you were pregnant!'

'I wanted to tell you but everything's been nuts for so long, there was never a right time.'

'Are you alright? He isn't putting any pressure on you, is he?'

'No Dad, it's nothing like that. Finn's great and we can't wait to get married. He's going to make a good husband and father.'

'I can't believe you're actually marrying Finlay and Phoebe Milton's son. We used to all hang out together as teenagers. I even went to their wedding. It's strange to comprehend but of course I'll be there. Call me with the date and I'll book a flight. I can't believe this is happening and I haven't even met Finn. Of course I'd love to give you away. You know what you want, you always have done. You don't need me to tell you that.'

'Thanks, Dad.'

'So you have a boy, what did you call him?'

'Samuel Bastian Milton.'

'I'm a grandfather,' he said. 'I wish your mother was still around to hear this. She would love it.'

'You're going to like Finn and it's going to be so good to see you.'

'Alright Ellie, I have to go. It's late here, take care and I'll speak to you in the next day or so. I'm sure I can organise some leave. Give my love to Rose when you see her.'

'I will, bye Dad.'

Serina had fixed a date and announced it when Ellie and Joo arrived at the barn. She had left Finn at home busy plastering the wall in the kitchen. Branna arrived at the same time as Tom and Simon's wives, Winter and Chloe.

'You have a week, it's next Friday at the church.' Serina said. 'It's booked with Reverend Harry at midday. He was legendary booking it in at such short notice but he does have a soft spot for you guys, which isn't surprising.'

'A week? Golly, there's so much to do.' Ellie replied. 'I'm getting married.'

'Not after it's broken down.' Branna said. 'Come on, let's make some lists.'

Serina began to make notes as Chloe uncorked the sparkling wine. 'Fizz, ladies?'

Joo was grinning at Ellie. 'So this is it, Morgan. Single no more.'

'I called my dad, he's giving me away,' she said.

'No way. He's coming over?' Joo asked.

'I haven't seen him for years. He hasn't even met Finn.'

'That will be interesting.' Branna said. 'What are you going to wear?'

'Your dress Ellie, what do you fancy?' Serina asked.

'Something simple and understated.' She laughed. 'I don't know, I like the Celtic ones.'

Serina opened a plastic bag and tipped out half a dozen wedding magazines and they all took one.

'If you see anything you like, I'm a dab hand with a needle.' Branna said. 'I could've been Mary Poppins in another life.'

'Really?' Ellie was surprised and they laughed together. 'Right, I'd better make up my mind, ladies, and quickly.'

The time flew by as Finn filled in another hole on the kitchen wall. His hands were covered in plaster when he stepped off the stepladder. The doorbell was ringing off its mount when he glanced at the clock. It was seven already. *Nuts, how could I forget about the time again?* He went to answer the door and stood before them totally under-dressed and caked in drying plaster. The six men were dressed up and ready to go. He invited them in explaining it would only take him ten minutes.

'I can't believe you forgot. Not good enough, Finn. This is why we agreed to start here so you wouldn't back out of it,' Simon said. 'I can see you've been busy. State of this place, honestly. I guess that's what happens when you have a fight in your house with Jared Connelly using telekinesis.'

There were scorch marks on the floor and ceiling. 'It was only once and I've been trying to get it finished ever since.' Finn responded from the bedroom. 'I've had too many crazy distractions.'

'It's a good job you're getting married, you could do with a new house.' Jerry remarked finding it all rather amusing. 'At least Joe helped with the kitchen.'

'It's going to look great when it's done,' he said.

'You're doing it?' Jerry raised his eyes brows. 'This I would pay to see.'

He dived into the bathroom and changed into some dark jeans and a white shirt. He played with his hair in the mirror and could hardly believe how much white hair there was. The 'tattoo' around his neck resembled a perfect necklace and he shuddered. There was a matching one on his wrist. *What mementos.*

'I suppose you scrub up well in ten minutes.' Joe said. 'Serina's fixed your hitch date.'

'When is it?' He asked.

'Next Friday.'

'That was quick.' The reality of it shook him momentarily when his cousin slapped him hard on the back.

'Which means Thursday's your stag night, cousin!' Bastian's eyes lit up. 'Prepare to get well messy.'

'Since you're going to be my best man, it's your job to organise that.' He ruffled his hair.

'I can always step up to a challenge,' Bastian replied.

'Who else would I ask, you idiot?' He smirked. 'You *are* my best man.'

'Let's go.' Jerry said. 'I need a pint, it's been mental today. I can't believe you expect Joo to cope in this place, Milton.'

'She came to see you?'

Jerry stopped and stared at him. 'You can read my mind. We had our first date today.'

Jerry: *We don't normally have secrets from each other, believe me it's so much easier.*

Finn: *It's going to take a bit of getting used to. It's kind of new to me, all this openness. I've spent my whole life hiding from it by getting drunk.*

'You can still get drunk Finn; but you don't need to hide it anymore.' Tom added. 'Not with us.'

He smiled knowing his secret was firmly locked away in his mind. It felt good to feel a part of something other than himself and his family. The evening was about having friends and knowing their trust. Seeing Bastian with them gave him their trust unconditionally. It would be awkward to block them but he had no choice.

Although part of him would always be concealed, including his spirit's appearance, there was a certain Sentry code to abide by. He found their combined sense of honesty amusing and most welcome.

'The objective, Finn, was to get you out of the house.' Joe said. 'What you do with your mind is your business. Be yourself, we'll put up with you anyway. You're one of us. Now where's this pub? I'm literally dying for a pint.'

20

~~

bond

The sun peaked out from behind the thick white cloud and for a moment, Finn felt the warmth on his face. His suit was made of crisp ivory linen, topped off with a white shirt and ivory tie. Standing beside him and decked out in a dark blue wool suit, was his best man and cousin, Bastian. Both of them were wearing dark shades. Having grabbed only a few hours sleep and nursing unmentionable hangovers, Finn could hardly believe he had made it there at all after the crazy stag night he had just experienced.

Tom's wife, Willow Rose, was armed and poised with a couple of cameras outside the church. Joe and Serina arrived with her brother Tom and his two children, Winter and Charlie.

Jerry was dressed to the nines in a new suit and his hair was arranged in a neat tail. Willow Rose winked at them as she snapped away. All the men were wearing dark sunglasses to conceal their jaded condition.

'Almost time, Finn,' Reverend Harry said with a smile. 'It's best you come into the church now.'

Finn gazed at the church gate and could feel butterflies in his stomach. Soon Ellie would be arriving with her father. She would walk with him through the wrought iron gate and into the church. The anticipation was making him feel light-headed. After everything he had been through, he could hardly believe it was happening for real.

'This is it, Finn. Any last requests before you sign your life away?' Bastian asked. 'It's now or never.'

'For as long as I can remember, Ellie has been everything I've ever wanted but I really should've stopped drinking well before that last bottle last night.'

'Did you truly expect to get off lightly?' Bastian asked. 'You're only doing this once.'

The church was packed with family and friends. Flowers lined the ends of the pews with ribbon and soft organ music was playing in the background. Near the front he nodded at his father who was sitting beside Rose. On her lap sat his son Sam who was oblivious to all the fuss. Finn smiled at them hardly concealing his excitement, he couldn't have felt more proud. They walked to the end of the aisle and took their places to the right at the front, before the small choir and beaming vicar.

Jeremy Morgan had not seen his daughter for three years. Dressed in army uniform, and boasting an array of medals, he was tall with peppery grey short hair. Ellie's lace sleeved dress was light ivory, with a chiffon skirt, pulled in to emphasise her tiny waist. On her feet were ivory heels and when she stepped up next to him, she almost matched his height. She wore light make up which only enhanced her features more. Her copper hair was raised up and gathered at the back, dotted with small crystal clips. Small ringlets fell down her face.

Cara was dressed similarly and carried a small basket of flowers. Joo was wearing a cream coloured dress with matching heels and a smile as wide as the sun. In her hands was a smaller bouquet. Caron passed Ellie a trailing bouquet of white roses and carnations.

'Ellie, you look so beautiful,' he said. 'Are you ready?'

'I think so, Dad.' She replied with a mixture of excitement and nerves. She smiled at Cara and Joo. 'It's only a short walk. Shall we go? I don't want to be too late. He's waited long enough for me.'

Joo held her hand and together they walked towards town. Passers-by smiled at the small wedding party en-route to the church. Everything had been planned to the smallest detail during the previous week, sometimes late into the night. There had been no room for stress, only fun as Ellie had insisted. Evenings were spent making notes, invitations, colour schemes, clothes, music, drinks and food choices. Everyone had pitched in. The reception was prepared and ready to go inside a large marquee on Joe and Serina's lawn.

When the church was in sight, Jeremy withdrew a small velvet box from his pocket.

'Your mother would have wanted you to have this, Ellie. She used to wear it all the time and it's a lovely memento for something old.'

She opened the tiny blue velvet box and found a small gold locket and chain. There was a tiny photo tucked inside. She was a young girl of no more than four years old, sat between her mother and father. Tears formed in her eyes as she stared at the image of her mother immortalised in the photograph.

'I know she'd be so proud of you today, Darling,' he said unclasping it and placing it around her neck. 'Don't cry, love, your mascara will run and we can't have that.'

'Thanks, Dad. It's beautiful.'

The Reverend Harry met the group outside the church and Ellie pulled the ivory lace veil over her face. 'How are you feeling, Ellie?'

'Nervous,' she smiled.

'That's a good sign. Don't worry, everyone is here. Just remember to breathe and you'll be fine.'

Harry walked ahead of the small party and made his way to the altar where Finn was waiting anxiously with Bastian. Cara stepped out into the first stage of the aisle where she waited for Ellie. Caron made her way swiftly to her seat near the front, next to Bastian's parents, Rob and Sophie, and Rob's mother, Heather. Behind them sat Branna and Murray, Tom and his two children, Simon and his wife Chloe and son Toby, Jerry, Serina and Joe.

Jeremy lifted his arm and Ellie accepted it, taking the first steps into the church. A Celtic wedding tune began on the organ. At this point the whole congregation turned to look to the entrance.

With her father, Ellie made her glamorous way down the aisle with Joo closely behind, holding on to her long lacy train. In her hands, she carried the trailing bouquet of flowers.

Finn stared at his fiancée and his heart leapt into his mouth with awe. His hands glowed white. Cara walked ahead of the bride dropping white rose petals on the carpet. Moments later, she was standing beside him, with her veil down, grinning a wide smile. They faced each other and when the music stopped he found her hands. Their eyes met and he was glowing all over.

'We are gathered here today to witness the marriage of two remarkable people.' Harry began, noticing the strange change in Finn's physical appearance. He winked at Harry, which prompted him to continue. 'I'm not the first to say miracles can happen and we will all gladly witness this new found happiness from the simple union of Finn Milton and Ellen Morgan.'

Sam's cry could be heard briefly from the congregation followed by a few ripples of laughter.

'I think one of our youngest approves of this union,' Harry said to everyone, then quietly to Finn. 'Are you okay, Finn?'

'I'm excited,' he whispered. 'I'm not going to explode or anything. Soul light makes me glow when I'm happy.'

'Are you ready to get married?'

They nodded and smiled. After half an hour of exchanging vows and rings, Harry announced their marriage. There were cheers and clapping from their family and friends when they kissed.

They walked out of the church and the sun was shining. He kissed his new bride under swathes of confetti, rose petals and smiles. 'I love you, Ellie Milton, *my forever girl.*' He said into her ear.

'I love you too, Finn Milton, my husband.'

Another hour passed taking photographs and the party moved across town to a marquee tent on Joe and Serina's lawn. Finn had thrown money into the pot to cover private caterers, a live blue grass band and a fully stocked bar. At one end was a small stage for music. One large dressed table dominated the space, decorated with flowers, balloons and more rose petals.

Rose had poured all her love into creating a tall elaborate fruit cake, decorated with ivory icing and sugar flowers. Real flowers and greenery decorated the tent making it feel more homely, romantic and intimate. Tea lights and lanterns sparkled everywhere. An acoustic guitarist began to play light background music.

As the guests took their seats, Milton approached his son and new bride and embraced them both. Slyly he passed his son a large brown envelope. 'I finally have a daughter. Open it later, it's a surprise.'

'You know I don't like surprises, Dad,' he replied.

'Believe me, it's a good one. Enjoy it, both of you.'

'Thanks, Dad.' He scrutinised his father's face but he wasn't giving anything away.

As the drinks and party began to flow, he found a private moment with Ellie to open the envelope. He withdrew the paperwork and examined it closely.

'What is it?' She asked.

'It looks like the deeds of a house. Wait a minute, there's a picture.' He looked at the image of a rundown Art Deco house, overgrown gardens and views of the sea. At the top in an old italic typeface were the words *Quillet Cove, built by Kingsley Pengelly.*

'Quillet Cove,' she said. 'Is that what it's called?'

'It's been in my family for years and now it's yours.' Heather overheard their conversation and came up behind them with a wide smile.

'It's far too much, Gran,' he said.

'On the contrary, it's just what you need. Jessie and Kingsley had many happy years there. My Samuel was born there. It just needs some tender loving care and *you* are the people to provide it. Your father approves. It was his idea after all. When your mother died, he couldn't bring himself to live there and he couldn't sell it either, so he saved it for you.'

Ellie threw her arms around Heather in an instant. 'Thank you so much, Heather. You're far too generous.'

'Where is it?' He asked.

'Near Portheras, right by the beach,' Milton added.

'No way,' Ellie said. 'It's so close as well.'

'Enjoy it, both of you deserve to be happy,' Milton said. 'It's all I've ever wanted for you. A unique family home.' He hugged his father and a few tears were falling down his face. 'And besides, you need a home of your own, it just needs some work.'

'I don't know what to say,' he said.

'You don't need to say anything, Finn,' Heather said. 'Now let's enjoy this party. You have some fine friends and I need a top up.'

After Milton and Heather left them alone, he put his arm around his new wife. 'Can you believe it? A new home and a brand new start.' He kissed her. 'It's been the best day of my life.'

'And mine, Finn.'

After the wedding breakfast, a band set up and began to play. One of the players had a double bass. A space had been cleared for dancing as the light faded outside. Tea lights sparkled in the twilight. Finn and Ellie stepped forward for the first dance and the band performed a blue grass version of *How long will I love you* by the Waterboys. There wasn't a dry eye in the tent. After it finished the tempo was raised and everyone piled onto the floor. He swayed with his arms around his new bride and kissed her.

He glanced to the opening of the tent and could see Marcio standing there watching in the half-light. Visible only to his eyes, the Sentry nodded his approval and disappeared.

'What are you looking at?' She asked.

'Nothing, I was just thinking how wonderful everything has been today. Look at everyone. I can't believe we've done it.'

'I know, have you seen your dad dancing with Rose? They make a good couple, don't they?'

He scoured the floor and spied them, smiling and laughing together. Milton's hand held onto Rose's and they were dancing. He couldn't remember ever seeing his father look so happy.

'It's time for us to dance-mingle, my darling wife,' he said when Bastian approached, asking for Ellie's hand to dance. Bastian whisked her away and Finn approached his father and Rose.

'May I have this dance?' He asked his father and took Rose as his partner. 'You look lovely, Rose.'

'Don't be so daft, Finn.' She replied with a smile.

He read her mind and touched her soul while they danced. Without her being aware, soul light penetrated her very briefly while he held her hands.

Finn: *You have my approval.*

There was an absolute calm emanating from him. He smiled and moved on to Branna, who was dancing with Murray.

'This is the most romantic wedding I have ever been to,' she said. 'You guys had me in tears in the church.'

'You and Murray are happy.'

It was more like a statement as he read her mind. Some soul light entered her as he touched her hands. It filtered through her body with such subtlety she never noticed. Satisfied with the outcome, he spied Jerry dancing with Joo.

Aware that by touch alone he was ever so slightly changing the physiology of his friends and family, he happily passed Branna to her father for a dance. He moved towards Joo with his hands outstretched and peeled her away from Jerry. Ellie stepped in to dance with Jerry and they all grinned at each other, laughing while they danced.

As the evening wore on Finn found time to smoke a cigar with Jerry, Bastian and Joe in the garden.

'What a beautiful wedding,' Joe said. 'Well done, guys.'

'Wouldn't it be funny if in a years time there were more of us,' he said, seemingly out of nowhere.

'More of us? What are you talking about?' Jerry asked with a modicum of confusion.

'Children,' he said.

'Finn? What have you been up to?' Bastian asked.

'Me? I haven't done anything.' He replied sounding more innocent than he intended. 'I'm feeling broody, don't mind me.'

'It's a shame Serina can't conceive. She's never been able to have children. It's something we came to terms with a long time ago. It broke her mother's heart. Serina borrows children now to make up for it.'

'I don't think Caron wants anymore,' Bastian said.

'It's a bit too soon for Joo and I to be making such plans, although in the future, I can't see why not. Hey Finn, is that your dad? He's kissing Rose.' Jerry was flabbergasted as were the others.

'There's always room for magic,' he said. 'It would be good for them to get together.'

'What have you been up to?' Joe asked enquiringly.

'Nothing,' he said. 'I've done nothing.'

Jerry, Joe and Bastian all stared at him for a moment.

'I think there should be more of us,' he said. 'A new generation of gifted children. The world would be a better place with more of us. The future isn't written and we can all be a part of it, even you and Serina.'

'I'm a realist, Finn and it isn't going to happen to us,' Joe grunted. 'Not without a miracle.'

Marcio was watching and listening and staring directly at him. No one else could see the tall Roman Centurion's ghost except Finn.

Marcio: *What have you been doing, Finn?*

Finn: *Only some home improvements. The rest is up to them. You gave me these powers and I'm going to prove good on them.*

Marcio: *I have created a monster.*

Finn: *No Marcio, you've helped me create a new beginning.*

Marcio: *It isn't in our code to make pathfinders like you.*

Finn: *Maybe not but it is in mine.*

Marcio: *There will be consequences. The Empress will not be pleased.*

Finn: *This is my party Marcio and it's time you were leaving. I thought you weren't allowed to commune with mortals.*

Marcio smiled at his dry comment before disappearing: *You have so much to learn for a young Sentry. I command respect and I will keep a closer eye on you.*

Bastian lent in close to him. 'Are you and Ellie going anywhere special after the party?'

'Jeremy gave us a honeymoon on the Scillies as a wedding gift. We're flying out tomorrow to Tresco for a week at the Island Hotel. Rose is looking after Sam while we're gone.' He replied. 'We're going on the helicopter from Penzance.'

'Man, that place is amazing,' Jerry said. 'You're going to love it there, Green Beach is one of my favourite places ever.'

'I've never been,' he replied. 'But I've always wanted to visit.'

Milton came out to join them with Rose. They were holding hands and behaving like teenagers. 'We're leaving. See you tomorrow morning to collect Sam. Have a lovely time tonight.'

Milton looked lovingly at Rose and they left together, leaving blank faces on everyone except Finn.

'I never saw that one coming,' Ellie said.

'Neither did any of us,' Bastian said. 'What a sly dog your father is. Who would've thought that he and Rose would get together.'

'It's been too long for both of them, they deserve to be happy,' he said. 'Rose has held a torch for my dad since we were kids.'

'I'm very happy about it,' Ellie smiled.

'What are you guys doing out here?' Joo appeared. 'Come on Jerry, I want to dance.' Jerry subsequently followed her back into the marquee holding on to her hand.

'Love's young dream,' Joe said, looking at Joo and Jerry together. 'It took them long enough.'

'Next year is going to be a good year,' Finn announced. 'I'll put money on it.'

'I'll drink to that,' Joe said.

Bastian and Joe went back inside leaving Ellie alone with him in the darkness. The light seeped from the marquee and they were alone in each other's company.

'It went well, didn't it?' She sighed leaning into her husband as he brought his arms around her.

'In more ways than one, Darling,' he replied, kissing her.

'Let's head home and relieve the babysitter.'

'Right now?'

'Don't you want to consummate our union, Mr Milton?'

'Oh Ellie, I thought you'd never ask.'

Finn and Ellie returned from their honeymoon refreshed and invigorated. They were about to head out to visit Quillet Cove, and the house generously gifted by Milton as a wedding present.

Ellie had placed Sam in his car seat on the kitchen table, ready to go when she had extreme nausea and rushed to the bathroom where she promptly vomited her breakfast down the toilet.

'Ellie, are you alright?'

He looked around the door to find her hugging the bowl.

'I feel rough,' she said.

He put his hand on her brow and it felt warm. 'You're not running a temperature.'

He concentrated and let his hand drop to her belly, where he focused on her womb.

A moment later a smile crept across his face.

'You're not sick, you're pregnant. We're going to be parents again.'

'So soon? Oh goodness, I thought there was a bug going round. Everyone has it.'

'Who is everyone?'

'Joo has been sick two mornings in a row, and there's Serina. She's crook. I saw Branna yesterday, she isn't well either and Caron and Willow Rose are down with something too.'

'Maybe it's a coincidence,' he said.

'Rose has a bug too.'

'Rose too? Blimey, I didn't expect it at her age.'

'Finn, are you suggesting that we're *all* pregnant?'

'Would it be so awful?' He was wearing a mischievous grin.

'What is it you're not telling me?' She demanded.

'Me? I had nothing to do with it. I mean, how could I?' He looked on inquisitively. 'I can't make people have babies.'

'We'll know soon enough. Rose is 45. It would make the child your half sibling, and my half cousin, no, that's too weird. We can't all be pregnant. Serina can't conceive, she had endometriosis when she was twenty. None of this makes sense.'

He changed the subject.

'Do you still want to go out and see this house?'

'I suppose, maybe it's my imagination but I have a funny feeling you had something to do with this bug.'

Finn said nothing as they piled into the Porsche. He started her up first time and they drove off towards Sennen.

The sun was shining but it was a bitterly cold winters day. Dressed in a thick jumper and jeans, Ellie rested her hand on his, and squeezed it.

She touched her belly and found a small smile.

Sam was belted into the back seat, staring forward and chewing on a plastic toy.

'What do you know about this place?' She asked.

'My great grandfather Kingsley built it for Jessica as a wedding present, back in the twenties. They lived there until he died in the mid-sixties. Since then, it's been slowly turning back to nature. No one wanted to live there after what followed. I hope it's in better shape than what I've been told.'

'Quillet Cove is a strange name, I've never heard of it before.'

'Quillet means stretch of land.'

'I can't wait to see it,' Ellie said.

'Me too – it could be a new start for us.'

END OF BOOK TWO

THE FLAME
& THE MOTH

VOLUME TWO ETHEREA

appendix

maps

character connections

locations

family trees

about the author

United Kingdom & Ireland

Meath
Dublin
Southern Ireland

United Kingdom

London

Cornwall

Cornwall

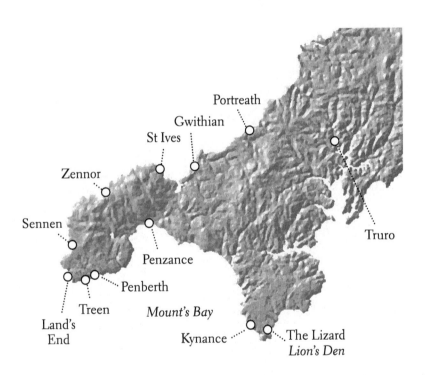

Portreath

Gwithian

St Ives

Zennor

Sennen

Penzance

Penberth

Treen

Land's
End

Mount's Bay

Kynance

The Lizard
Lion's Den

Truro

THE FLAME & THE MOTH

VOLUME TWO ETHEREA

character connections

Pengelly

Milton

Tremaen

Morgan

Connelly

Posse

Pengelly & Milton ~ Cornwall

The Pengelly family have lived in St Ives, West Cornwall for many generations. Born in 1900, Kingsley Pengelly became a wealthy land owner and farm proprietor. His bloodline share supernatural abilities from telekinesis, astral planing, telepathy, mind reading to heightened senses and physical strength. He passed on a strange and powerful entity known as soul light to his granddaughter shortly before he passed away.

KINGLSEY PENGELLY [1900-1952]
wife: JESSICA THOMAS [1904-1996]
child: SAMUEL PENGELLY [1923-1966]

JESSICA THOMAS [1904-1996]
husband: KINGLSEY PENGELLY [1900-1952]
child: SAMUEL PENGELLY [1923-1966]

SAMUEL PENGELLY [1923-1966]
wife: HEATHER TREVASKAS [1925 -]
children: DR ROBERT PENGELLY [1943 -]
& PHOEBE PENGELLY [1945-1966]

HEATHER TREVASKAS [1925 -]
husband: SAMUEL PENGELLY [1923-1966]

DR ROBERT PENGELLY [1943 -]
wife: SOPHIE REED [1944 -]
child: DR BASTIAN PENGELLY [1967 -]

DR BASTIAN PENGELLY [1967 -]
wife: CARON (EVANS) PENGELLY [1968 -]
child: CARA PENGELLY [1990 -]
cousin: FINN MILTON [1966 -]

PHOEBE (PENGELLY) MILTON [1945-1966]
husband: PROFESSOR FINLAY MILTON [1943 -]
child: FINN MILTON [1966 -]

FINN MILTON [1966 -]
wife: ELLIE MORGAN [1966 -]
child: SAMUEL BASTIAN MILTON [1997 -]
cousin: DR BASTIAN PENGELLY [1967 -]

Tremaen & Morgan ~ Cornwall

The Tremaen family are from Penberth in West Cornwall. David Tremaen
was a farm tenant. The Tremaen bloodline share supernatural abilities from
astral planing, telepathy to heightened senses.

DAVID TREMAEN [1923-1969]
wife: MARTHA TREVENEN [1925-1970]
children: VIVIAN TREMAEN [1945-1972]
and ROSE TREMAEN [1951 -]

VIVIAN (TREMAEN) MORGAN [1945-1972]
husband: JEREMY MORGAN [1944 -]
child: ELLIE MORGAN [1966 -]
sister: ROSE TREMAEN [1951 -]

ROSE TREMAEN [1951 -]
sister: VIVIAN (TREMAEN) MORGAN [1945-1972]
niece: ELLIE (MORGAN) MILTON [1966 -]

ELLIE (MORGAN) MILTON [1966 -]
husband: FINN MILTON [1966 -]
child: SAMUEL MILTON [1997 -]
father: JEREMY MORGAN [1944 -]
aunt: ROSE TREMAEN [1951 -]
father-in-law: PROFESSOR FINLAY MILTON [1943 -]
best friend: JULIET "JOO" WILLIAMS [1966 -]

Connelly ~ Cornwall

The Connelly family are split into two clans. Their origins are Meath, Southern Ireland. Liam Connelly was a pastor and relocated to Cornwall in 1900 where his descendants live to this day. Their bloodline share inherited supernatural abilities from healing, telepathy, telekinesis, mind reading and spell-casting.

REVEREND LIAM CONNELLY [1878-1918]
wife: SHARA DALY [1882-1923]
child: SHANNON CONNELLY [1901-1966]
brother: PAUL CONNELLY [1876-1939]

SHANNON CONNELLY [1901-1966]
lover: TREVELYAN KEAN [1903-1983]
child: DUANA CONNELLY [1923-1943]

DUANA CONNELLY [1923-1943]
husband: JAMES CONNELLY [1897-1943]
child: LOGAN CONNELLY [1943-1996]
best friend: HEATHER (TREVASKAS) PENGELLY [1925 -]

LOGAN CONNELLY [1943-1996]
wife: MELANDRA POOLEY [1948-1967]
children: JARED CONNELLY [1967-1996]
and BRANNA (CONNELLY) SMITH [1967 -]

BRANNA (CONNELLY) SMITH [1967 -]
husband: MURRAY SMITH [1965 -]

Connelly ~ Ireland

The Connelly family who currently live in Meath, Southern Ireland.
Paul Connelly was the older brother of Liam Connelly. The bloodline
shares inherited supernatural abilities from telepathy, telekinesis, mind
reading, spell-casting to heightened senses.

PAUL CONNELLY [1876-1939]
wife: MOONA BURKE [1878-1938]
children: JAMES CONNELLY [1897-1943]
and LORNA CONNELLY [1897-1897]
brother: REV. LIAM CONNELLY [1878-1918]

JAMES CONNELLY I [1897-1943]
1st wife: CAREN FLYNN [1903-1940]
children: JAMES CONNELLY II [1923-1943],
ART CONNELLY [1925-1964]
and LARA CONNELLY [1927-1965]
2nd wife: DUANA CONNELLY [1923-1943]
child: LOGAN CONNELLY [1943-1996]

JAMES CONNELLY II [1923-1943]
wife: MARY REGAN [1924-1960]
child: LIAM CONNELLY [1942 -]

LIAM CONNELLY [1942 -]
wife: GAEL MULLAN [1950 -]
children: DESMOND CONNELLY [1968 -]
and NIALL CONNELLY [1970 -]

ART CONNELLY [1925-1964]
wife: MARA HAYES [1926-1968]
child: MICHAEL CONNELLY [1946-1997]

MICHAEL CONNELLY [1946-1997]
wife: CIARAN KING [1948 -]
children: CILLIAN CONNELLY [1967-1997],
JARLATH CONNELLY [1969-1997]
and KAITLIN CONNELLY [1971

Posse

~~

The Posse are predominantly a group of old school friends who come together to help Finn Milton to defeat the evil forces threatening his life. They share a range of supernatural abilities from astral planing, telekinesis, healing, telepathy, mind reading to heightened senses and shape-shifting.

DR BASTIAN PENGELLY [1967 -]
wife: CARON (EVANS) PENGELLY [1968 -]
child: CARA PENGELLY [1990 -]

JOE PRAED [1966 -]
wife: SERINA (ELLERY) PRAED [1967 -]
brother-in-law: TOM ELLERY [1965 -]

SERINA (ELLERY) PRAED [1967 -]
husband: JOE PRAED [1966 -]
brother: TOM ELLERY [1965 -]

TOM ELLERY [1965 -]
wife: WILLOW ROSE [1966 -]
children: WINTER ROSE ELLERY [1990 -]
and CHARLIE ELLERY [1992 -]

DR SIMON NANCARROW [1965 -]
wife: CHLOE THOMAS [1966 -]
child: TOBY NANCARROW [1992 -]
brother: JEREMY "JERRY" NANCARROW PhD [1967 -]

JEREMY "JERRY" NANCARROW PhD [1967 -]
brother: DR SIMON NANCARROW [1965 -]

FINN MILTON [1966 -]
wife: ELLIE (MORGAN) MILTON [1966 -]
child: SAMUEL "SAM" MILTON [1997 -]
cousin: BASTIAN PENGELLY [1967 -]

BRANNA (CONNELLY) SMITH [1967 -]
husband: MURRAY SMITH [1965 -]

Ellie's family tree

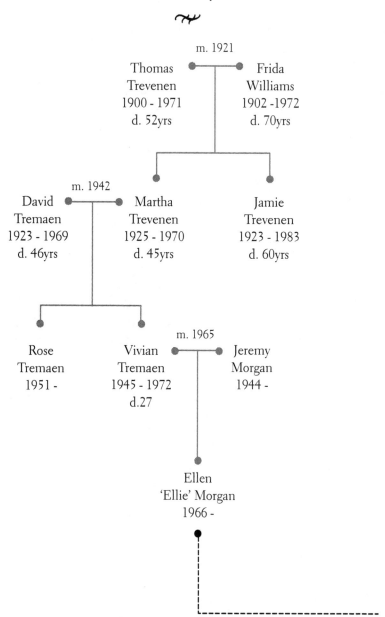

Finn's family tree

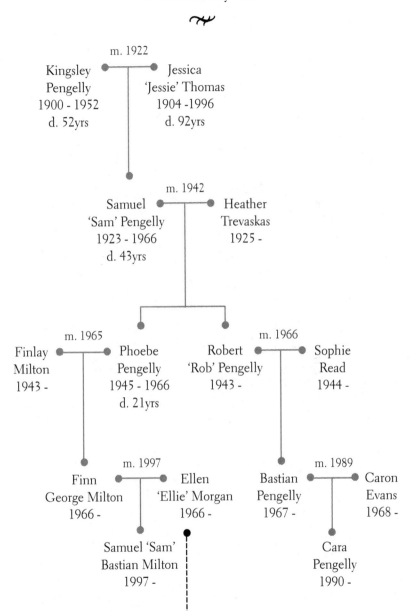

The Irsh Conelly family tree

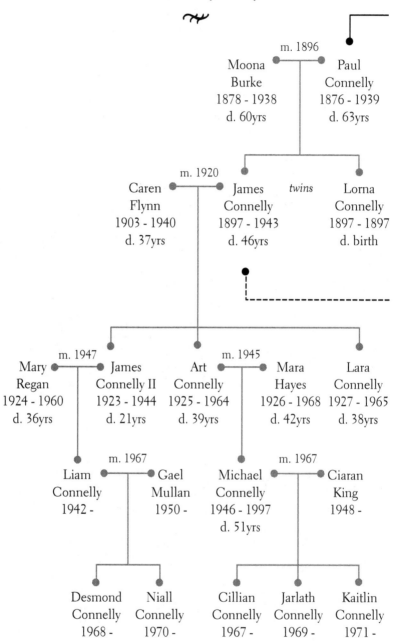

The Cornish Conelly family tree

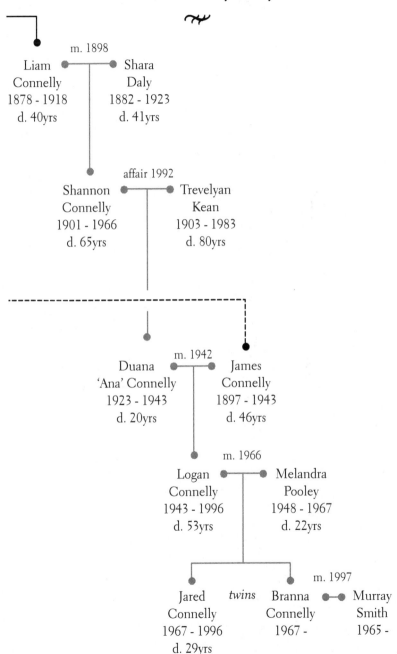

m. 1898

Liam
Connelly
1878 - 1918
d. 40yrs

Shara
Daly
1882 - 1923
d. 41yrs

affair 1992

Shannon
Connelly
1901 - 1966
d. 65yrs

Trevelyan
Kean
1903 - 1983
d. 80yrs

m. 1942

Duana
'Ana' Connelly
1923 - 1943
d. 20yrs

James
Connelly
1897 - 1943
d. 46yrs

m. 1966

Logan
Connelly
1943 - 1996
d. 53yrs

Melandra
Pooley
1948 - 1967
d. 22yrs

m. 1997

Jared
Connelly
1967 - 1996
d. 29yrs

twins

Branna
Connelly
1967 -

Murray
Smith
1965 -

.

about the author

Vivian Mayne was born and raised in Cornwall. She has travelled to London, France, South Africa, Belgium, Germany and Holland during her 30 year graphic design career.

She lives in West Penwith with her husband and works by day in a branding agency in St Ives. Inspired by unrequited love she began to write her first novel *The Curse of Finn Milton*, the first part of a trilogy called Etherea.

The sequel is called *The Flame and The Moth*. Both titles are available in paperback and ebook.

Part three called *The Sentry of Quillet Cove* is in progress and will be available soon.

All titles are published by Koru Designs in Cornwall.
Contact: korudesignsuk@gmail.com

Read the first one

GHOSTS OF THE TALISMAN

To save the love of his life, a spirited and eccentric loner teams
up with a shapeshifting raven to lift an ancient curse from
a corrupt and tyrannical family.

Two families are at war and the feud goes back years.

The year is 1996. Finn Milton has been living a strange double
life, denying his true calling. He has been inexplicably in love
with Ellie Morgan for nearly twenty years – only she cannot
see, hear or remember him. He is also dealing with strange
supernatural powers he has little control over.

An emerging writer, he is trying to escape his darker past but
can no longer ignore it. She is an aspiring artist but already a
victim of their past and forced to live a life like no other.

The Connellys have a history of unexplainable power.
They are victims to no one. Unpredictable, not even their
own kin are safe from their ruthless appetite to
dominate and intimidate others.

© Vivian Mayne 2016 | Koru Designs

GHOSTS OF
THE TALISMAN

VOLUME ONE ÆTHEREA

VIVIAN MAYNE

63957818R00220

Made in the USA
Charleston, SC
17 November 2016